CRITICAL ACCLAIM FOR JOHN LANGAN'S *THE FISHERMAN*

"*The Fisherman* is an epic, yet intimate, horror novel. Langan channels M. R. James, Robert E. Howard, and Norman Maclean. What you get is *A River Runs Through It*…Straight to hell."

—Laird Barron, author of *X's for Eyes*

"Stories within stories, folk tales becoming modern legends, all spinning into a fisherman's tale about the one he *wishes* had gotten away. Langan's latest is at turns epic and personal, dense yet compulsively readable, frightening but endearing. Already among the year's very best dark fiction releases."

—Adam Cesare, author of *The Con Season* and *Zero Lives Remaining*

"In this painful, intimate portrait of loss, two damaged men take steps toward redemption, until the discovery of an obscure legend suggests a dangerous alternative. Can men so broken resist the temptation to veer away into strange, unfamiliar geographies? *The Fisherman* is a masterful, chilling tale, aching with desire and longing for the impossible."

—Michael Griffin, author of *The Lure of Devouring Light*

"Reading this, your mouth fills with worms. Just let them wriggle and crawl as they will, though—don't swallow. John Langan is fishing for your sleep, for your soul. I fear he's already got mine."

—Stephen Graham Jones, author of *Mongrels*

"John Langan's *The Fisherman* isn't about fishing at all. Yes, there's fishing in it, but it's really about friendship, loss, and bone-deep horror. What starts as a slow, melancholy tale gains momentum and drops you head first into a churning nightmare from which you might escape, but you'll never forget, and the memory of what you saw will change you forever."

—Richard Kadrey, ⸱ ⸱ ⸱ ⸱ *The Everything Box*

"Whenever John Langan publishes a book I am going to devour that book. That's because he's one of the finest practitioners of the moody tale working today. *The Fisherman* is a treasure, the kind of book you just want to snuggle up and shiver through. I can't say enough good things about the confidence, the patience, the satisfying cumulative power of this book. It was a pleasure to read from the first page to the last."

—Victor LaValle, author of *The Ballad of Black Tom*

"A haunting novel about loss and friendship, *The Fisherman* is a monstrous catch in the sea of weird fiction."

—Cameron Pierce, author of *Our Love Will Go the Way of the Salmon*

"For some fishing is a therapeutic, a way to clear one's head, to chase away the noise of a busy world and focus on one single thing. On good days it can heal the worst pains, even help develop a sense of solace. John Langan's *The Fisherman* isn't about the good day fishing, it isn't even about a bad day fishing, it's about the day that you shouldn't have even left the house, let alone waded chest deep into a swollen stream of churning water. Langan tells you that up front, warns you this isn't going to be that story, but you ignore the signs, lured in by the faint smell of masculine adventure, hooked by tragedy and the chance of redemption, and reeled in by a nesting tale of ever growing horrors. By the time you realize what has happened it's already too late, you're caught in an unavoidable net of terror that can end in only one way. It doesn't matter how strong you are or how prepared, John Langan has you hook, line and sinker, and he doesn't let go until the very last page."

—Pete Rawlik, author of *Reanimatrix*

"John Langan's *The Fisherman* is literary horror at its sharpest and most imaginative. It's at turns a quiet and powerfully melancholy story about loss and grief; the impossibility of going on in the same manner as you had before. It's also a rollicking, kick-ass, white-knuckle charge into the winding, wild, raging river of redemption. Illusory, frightening, and deeply moving, *The Fisherman* is a modern horror epic. And it's simply a must read."

—Paul Tremblay, author of *A Head Full of Ghosts* and *Disappearance at Devil's Rock.*

THE
FISHERMAN

Other Books by John Langan

Novels
House of Windows

Collections
Sefira and Other Betrayals
The Wide, Carnivorous Sky and Other Monstrous Geographies
Mr. Gaunt and Other Uneasy Encounters

THE
FISHERMAN

JOHN LANGAN

WORD HORDE

PETALUMA, CA

First Edition

ISBN: 978-1-939905-21-5

A Word Horde Book
http://www.WordHorde.com

For Fiona

Is it that by its indefiniteness it shadows forth the heartless voids and immensities of the universe, and thus stabs us from behind with the thought of annihilation, when beholding the white depths of the milky way? ...

— the palsied universe lies before us a leper; and like willful travelers in Lapland, who refuse to wear colored and coloring glasses upon their eyes, so the wretched infidel gazes himself blind at the monumental white shroud that wraps all the prospect around him. And of all these things the Albino whale was the symbol. Wonder ye then at the fiery hunt?

—Herman Melville, *Moby Dick*

PART 1:

MEN WITHOUT WOMEN

I

HOW FISHING SAVED MY LIFE

Don't call me Abraham: call me Abe. Though it's what my ma named me, I've never liked Abraham. It's a name that sounds so full of itself, so Biblical, so...I believe patriarchal is the word I'm after. One thing I am not, nor do I want to be, is a patriarch. There was a time I thought I'd like at least one child, but these days, the sight of them makes my skin crawl.

Some years ago, never mind how many, I started to fish. I've been fishing for a long time, now, and as you might guess, I know a story or two. That's what fishermen are, right? Storytellers. Some I've lived; some I've had from the mouths of others. Most of them are funny; they bring a smile to your face and sometimes a laugh, which are no small things. A bit of laughter can be the bridge that lets you cross out of a bad time, believe you me. Some of my stories are what I'd call strange. I know only a few of these, but they make you scratch your head and maybe give you a little shiver, which can be a pleasure in its own way.

But there's one story—well, it's downright awful, almost too much to be spoken. It happened going on ten years ago, on the first Saturday in June, and by the time night had fallen, I'd lost a good friend, most of my sanity, and damn near my life. I'd come whisker-close to losing more than all that,

1

too. It stopped me fishing for the better part of a decade, and although I've returned to it once again, there's no power on earth, or under it, could bring me back to the Catskill Mountains, to Dutchman's Creek, the place a man I should have listened to called *"Der Platz das Fischer."*

You can find the creek on your map if you look closely. Go to the eastern tip of the Ashokan Reservoir, up by Woodstock, and backtrack along the south shore. It may take you a couple of tries. You'll see a blue thread snaking its way from near the Reservoir over to the Hudson, running north of Wiltwyck. That was where it all happened, though what it all was I still can't wrap my head around. I can tell you only what I heard, and what I saw. I know Dutchman's Creek runs deep, much deeper than it could or should, and I don't like to think what it's full of. I've walked the woods around it to a place you won't find on your map, on any map you'd buy in the gas station or sporting-goods store. I've stood on the shore of an ocean whose waves were as black as the ink trailing from the tip of this pen. I've watched a woman with skin pale as moonlight open her mouth, and open it, and open it, into a cavern set with rows of serrated teeth that would have been at home in a shark's jaws. I've held an old knife out in front of me in one, madly trembling hand, while a trio of refugees from a nightmare drew ever-closer.

I'm running ahead of myself, though. There's other things you'll need to hear about first, like Dan Drescher, poor, poor Dan, who went with me up to the Catskills that morning. You'll need to hear Howard's story, which makes far more sense to me now than it did when first he delivered it to me in Herman's Diner. You'll need to hear about fishing, too. Everything'll have to be in its proper place. If there's one thing I can't abide, it's a poorly put-together story. A story doesn't have to be fitted like some kind of pre-fabricated house—no, it's got to go its own way—but it does have to flow. Even a tale as coal-black as this one has its course.

You may ask why I'm taking such care. Some things are so bad that just to have been near them taints you, leaves a spot of badness in your soul like a bare patch in the forest where nothing will grow. Do you suppose a story can carry away such badness? It seems a bit much to hope for, doesn't it? Maybe it's true for the little wrongs, you know, the kind of minor frustrations that you're able to turn into funny stories at parties. For what happened at the Creek, though, I doubt there's such a transformation waiting. There's only transmission.

THE FISHERMAN

And there's more to it than that. There's the tale Dan and I heard in Herman's Diner. Since Howard told what happened to Lottie Schmidt and her family, some ninety years past, I've been unable to shake it. You could say his words stuck with me, which would be the understatement of the year. I can recall that tale word for word, as could Howard from the minister who told it to him. Without a doubt, part of the reason for the vividness of my memory is the way that Howard's story seems to explain a good deal of what happened to Dan and me later that same day. That tale about the building of the Reservoir and who—and what—was covered by its waters, prowls my brain. Even had we heeded Howard's advice and avoided the creek that day—Hell, had we turned around and headed back home as fast as I could drive, which is what we should have done—I'm convinced what we heard would still have branded itself on my memory. Can a story haunt you? Possess you? There are times I think recounting the events of that Saturday in June is just an excuse for those more distant events to make their way out into the world once more.

Again, though, I'm running ahead of myself. There will be a time and a place for everything, including the story of Lottie Schmidt, her father, Rainer, and the man he called *Der Fischer*. Let's back it all up. Let's begin with a few words about my life's great passion—well, what I used to think of as my life's great passion: a few words about fishing.

It wasn't something I'd learned as a child. My pa took me once or twice, but he wasn't much good at it himself, so he concentrated on teaching me the things he knew, like baseball, and the guitar. One day, it must have been twenty-five, thirty years after pa and I had spent our final Saturday morning subjecting a bucketful of worms to protracted drowning, I woke up and thought, *I'd like to go fishing.* Scratch that. I woke up and thought, *I need to go fishing.* I needed it the deep-down way you need that tall glass of water with the ice cubes clinking around in it at three o'clock on a blistering July afternoon. Why I needed fishing, of all things, I don't know and can't say. Granted, I was at a bit of a rough patch. My wife had just died, and us married not two years, and I was living the clichés you watch in made-for-TV movies and listen to in country songs. Mostly, this meant drinking too much, and since pa wasn't much with the liquor, either, this meant drinking badly, half a bottle of Scotch followed by half a bottle of wine, followed by extended sessions of holding onto the toilet as the bathroom did a merry dance around me. My job had gone all to hell, too—I was a systems analyst over at IBM in Poughkeepsie—although I was fortunate in having a manager who put me in for extended sick leave, instead of firing my ass, which is what I deserved. This was back when IBM was a decent place to work. The company approved three months with pay, if you can believe it. Almost the entire first month I spent looking up out of the bottoms of more bottles than I could count. I ate when I thought about it, which wasn't too often, and my meals were basically a steady stream of peanut butter and jelly sandwiches interrupted by the occasional burger and fries. The second month was pretty much the same as the first, except for visits from my brother and my late wife's parents, none of which went well enough to bother relating. All of us were suffering. Marie had been something else, like no other girl. We felt her loss the way you'd feel it if someone reached into the back of your mouth with a pair of pliers and tore out one of your molars; it was an open wound that ached all the way through you. The same way you couldn't stop testing that spot where your tooth used to be, probing it with your tongue until you felt the jolt of pain, none of us could help poking around our memories until we made everything start hurting all over again. By the time the third month was half done, I was sitting in my underwear on the couch with the TV on, sipping from whatever was closest to hand. I had learned a little, you see.

I had these shoeboxes full of photos I'd never gotten around to placing in albums, and when the alcohol in my blood hit the right level, I would fetch those boxes from the bedroom closet and surround myself with the archive of my marriage. Here was Marie when I'd first met her—when I first talked to her, I should say, since we'd been introduced at work at the beginning of the summer, when she'd joined the company right out of college. We were connected to two of the same projects, so we saw each other in passing throughout July and August, though we didn't pass more than a couple of pleasantries back and forth at any one time. That September, there was a Labor Day party at someone's house—I want to say Tim Stoffel's—and we wound up sitting next to one another at one of the card tables set up around the yard. Marie had come with Jenny Barnett, but Jenny had disappeared with Steve Collins, and of the remaining party goers, I was the one she knew the best. She always denied it, but I'm reasonably sure that, when she asked me how I was doing, she was just killing time until she could finish her plate and make for home. You'd expect that conversation would be burned into my brain, but damned if I can remember much more than the pleasure of learning she was a fan of Hank Williams, Sr., too. Truth to tell, I was too busy trying not to pay too close attention to the bikini top she was wearing with a pair of cut-off shorts and tennis shoes. Typical guy, I know. We sat there talking until Tim was standing on the opposite side of the card table from us, telling us we didn't have to go home, but we couldn't stay here. We did go home—I mean, each of us went to our own home—but our time together had left me with a feeling—once we'd gone our separate ways, everything seemed a bit less bright than it had while we were sitting together.

Even so, an hour or two of pleasant talk does not guarantee anything, and I might never have come into possession of that photograph Jenny had taken of Marie, her hair done up in a single ponytail, her eyes and a good portion of the rest of her face concealed by a pair of enormous sunglasses, the yellow and white straps of that swimsuit top making her summer's tan look darker still. I had a good fifteen years on her, and that was sufficient distance to keep me cautious about what I thought I'd felt between us. I'd like to say my hesitation owed itself to not wanting to harass a woman young enough to be my niece, if not my daughter, but it had as much to do with my fear of looking the fool. "No fool worse'n' an old fool," my pa used to say, and although I hardly considered myself old, set next to Marie, I wasn't exactly what you'd call fresh off the rack.

Another photo, and I leapt ahead to the following spring. Marie and I were standing knee-deep in a stream—well, it was knee-deep for me; for her, it was more like thigh-high. One of her friends had invited us to spend the day in the Catskills, where said friend's brother had a weekend place that turned out to be nicer than I was expecting. It was located halfway up a tall, rolling hill, along a gravel road you had to ease your car over if you didn't want to tear out the undercarriage. From the outside, the place resembled an abbreviated barn, taller than it was long. Inside, new wooden surfaces, stainless steel appliances, and a stone fireplace gathered under a cathedral ceiling and a loft. Apparently, the place had been built by a Manhattan lawyer who'd had to divest himself of it shortly after its completion; whereupon Marie's friend's brother, who worked for the Post Office, had picked it up for the proverbial song, and not a terribly long one, at that. We arrived at lunchtime, and passed one of the more pleasant afternoons of my life wandering further up the gravel road with Marie's friend, whose name, I'm reasonably sure, was Karen. They had grown up beside one another. After maybe a mile, the road crossed a wide meadow, at the far side of which, a line of trees marked the course of a stream. It was a hot day, the air heavy with the sun, and the shade of the trees, the surprising cold of the water, were too much to resist. We tied our sneakers around our necks, and waded in. The stream bed was rocky, so you had to step carefully. Karen walked with both hands held up, as if she were expecting to fall at any moment. Marie stayed close enough to me that she could reach out to steady herself if necessary. I can't recall what we talked about. What I remember is staring at the water's surface, at those little bugs that skate across it—water-skimmers? Funny, I don't know their proper name. There were dozens of them, sliding over the stream in a way that made its top seem more solid than my legs pushing through it told me it was. In the murk beneath them, trout whose size would have beggared their insect imaginations flitted amongst the rocks. Every now and again, a plop and a spreading ripple of rings would show where a water-skimmer had found himself swallowed by a great black cavern. I don't suppose we waded more than a hundred yards downstream until we came in sight of a small dam. What we could see of it through the skin of water pouring over it showed it old, but there was nothing on the banks on either side of it to explain how or why it had come to be placed there. It seemed a reasonable spot to turn around, head back to the cookout Karen's brother was preparing, but before we did, Karen snapped a picture of Marie and me in the stream. Her hair's down in this one, and she's wearing an oversized tie-dye that she'd found in one of my drawers and that had struck her as about the funniest thing ever. ("Mr. George Jones and Merle Haggard in a tie-dye?" she'd said, laughing over my protest that I listened to the Grateful Dead, too.) In her hands, she's cradling the green bottle of Heineken that had accompanied us on our trek and would remain in her possession until we were ready to leave. She wasn't much of a drinker, but she'd learned that if she carried an open bottle of beer with her, she could appear social. To our right in the picture, sunlight streams down, lighting the water. To our left, darkness gathers in the trees.

Between that photo and the one before it, there was the better part of a better year—one of the best years. If I had searched the shoeboxes around me, I could have put my hands on pictures of most of its highlights, from the Christmas dinner I'd eaten with Marie's family to the Halloween party that had been our third date—and that we'd attended dressed as Kenny Rogers and Dolly Parton—to the early spring weekend we'd taken up in Burlington. I don't know if, deep down, all stories of falling in love are the same. Some days, it seems to me that, once you duck your head beneath the surface details, you find yourself in pretty much the same sequence of events. Other days, I think, *No, it's those details that are the point.* Either way—or both, even—that was what happened to us in the space between those pictures. We'd fallen in love, and shortly after that second photo was taken, I was down on one knee, asking her if she'd marry me.

There was another year and a half from that picture to the next one. In that time, the darkness that had thickened the spaces among the trees in that second photo had gathered about us, swallowed us the way those trout had consumed the water-skimmers. The week after we returned from our honeymoon in Bermuda, Marie found a lump in her left breast. From the start, things were bad. The cancer was pretty well-advanced, already storming her lymph nodes, and it resisted the radiation and the chemo like some kind of unstoppable beast in a low-grade horror film. I'm not sure when we knew that Marie wasn't going to survive this, or when we accepted it. Maybe a month before the end, a change came over her. In a way it's hard for me to describe, she became calm; I don't know if I'd say peaceful so much as *still.* It was as if she'd moved into the lobby of the long, dark house she was heading towards. She wasn't morbid, or listless—if anything, she relaxed, laughed more than she had in months. I didn't see what was happening. I thought the difference in her might be a sign that things were turning around, that she was finally getting the upper hand on the creature that had rampaged through her system. I went so far as to float this idea past her, one Saturday afternoon. I'd driven her down to the Hudson, to a little park she liked a few miles south of Wiltwyck. We'd found it one of our first weekends together, when we'd gone for a drive just to have another way to spend time together. This day, there was a breeze off the river, which made it too cold for her to leave the car, so we sat watching the water and I ventured that maybe her recent improvement was an indication that things were looking up. Did I sound as desperate as I fear I must have? Marie didn't answer; instead, she took my right hand in her left, lifted it to her lips, and kissed it. I told myself she was too overcome with emotion to reply, which I guess she was, just not the one I thought.

The third picture was taken right around that time. In it, Marie's leaning forward on the kitchen table, looking up and to her right, where I'm standing with the camera, telling her to smile, which she is, but there's a year and half's struggle behind that smile, a deep weariness eighteen months in the making. She's wearing a kerchief around her head, dark blue with white flecks. She was never happy with the wigs they provided her. Her skin has pulled tight against the bones of her face, her arms; it's as if she's aged at an accelerated pace, as if I'm getting to see what she would have looked like had we seen our thirtieth anniversary. Behind her, the morning sun is spilling through the windows over the sink, outlining her in gold.

Two weeks after that photo, she was gone. In a matter of two days, the bottom fell out from beneath us; there was barely enough time to rush her to the hospital bed she died in. What followed: the endless phone calls to tell people she'd passed, the visit to the funeral home (which we'd both put off), the wake, the funeral, the reception at the house afterwards, all of it was like some strange play I'd been cast in, but for which no one had provided me the script. I guess I did all right; however you judge such things. And when everything was over, the door shut on the last guest's departure, there was the liquor cabinet, freshly stocked by a number of the friends and family who'd come to see Marie off. That cabinet, with its rows of bottles, and more shoeboxes full of more pictures than I'd expected.

So there I was, in, I don't mind saying, a bad place, my wife gone and me doing what I could to join her. It was, you might say, a cold February in my soul. And then one morning my eyes pop open and waiting for me is this thought, *I need to go fishing.* I wish I could make you understand how powerful it was. I lay there for a while, waiting for it to go away. I lay there for a good long while, and when it was still there, glaring in my mind like a big neon sign, I decided I would give in to it. What the hell, right? I found a shirt and pants that weren't too dirty, fished my car keys out of the toilet (don't ask), and set off in search of fishing gear.

As you may have guessed, I had no idea what I was doing. From my house out towards Frenchman's Mountain, I drove into town, to Huguenot Hardware, because I had this notion that a hardware store would be the place to go for your fishing tackle. I'd like to blame it on the booze, but it was just ignorance. Fortunately for me, the sales clerk there was kind enough not to send me on a wild goose chase, and pointed me across Main Street to what was then Caldor's. For less than twenty dollars (I can't remember exactly how much I spent; I want to say twelve fifty, but I'm not sure that's right—wasn't a lot, anyway), I was able to set myself up with a rod, reel, line, tacklebox, and net. Hat, too. When I told her I was planning a day of fishing, the checkout girl insisted I run back to men's clothing and fetch a hat. She didn't specify what kind of hat, just said that after having grown up with a father who was a fisherman, and an older brother who was a fisherman, and knowing a bit about fishing herself, she could say with confidence that if there was one thing I didn't want to be caught without, it was a hat. Her advice sounded good, so I hurried to the men's department and grabbed a Yankees cap that I still wear.

The same checkout girl told me I needed to see the Town Clerk for a fishing license, and suggested a spot off to the side of Springvale Road where she and her family had fished the Svartkil River on occasion. I thanked her for her good advice, and hurried out to take it. Springvale's a narrow road that runs parallel to 32, the main north-south route in and out of town. For the first part of its length, the road hugs the west shore of the Svartkil, which is only about fifty yards across there, and fringed with maples and birch that hang out over the water. The checkout girl's spot was a steep bank across the road from a horse farm and across the river from the town golf course. What a sight I must have made, a couple of hours later, sitting by the side of the river in my dirty slacks, wrinkled white shirt, and baseball cap, holding my new fishing rod like it was a strange tool I hadn't the faintest idea how to use. I suppose it was. I'd broken open the tacklebox and taken hold of the first lure I laid my eyes on, a red and black number with a double set of triple hooks whose barbed points seemed as likely to snag a fish as anything. Cast after cast, I sent out that same lure, with nothing to show for it. It wasn't until I'd been fishing for a good two weeks—and catching the handful of bluegill I'd pulled wriggling up from the water through as much dumb luck as anything—that an old man with a long gray ponytail who'd been fishing beside me passed me a plastic cup full of fat, muddy worms as he was leaving and suggested I might find one of these of more use.

Yes, I'd gone back. Even though that first day had been fruitless, not even a ghost of a nibble, just five hours of sitting on the riverbank watching the slow current carry my line past me, as well as of tangling my line in the trees overhanging the river a half dozen times; even though all I had for my efforts was a slightly stiff neck, I went back the next day. And the day after that. And the third day. And so on. Each day, I pulled into the spot on Springvale Road a little earlier, left it a little later, until my entire day was taken up with fishing. When I was done, which was to say when the last trace of daylight had seeped out of the sky, I packed up my gear and drove not home but into town, where I stopped at Pete's Corner Pub for a burger and fries and a beer. I quickly became enough of a regular at Pete's that the waitresses knew both me and my order, and, instead of wasting time bringing me a menu, brought me my beer—Heineken, in a tall glass—and checked that I was having the usual, which they'd already called into the kitchen. After I started back at work, I discovered I could still squeeze in a couple hours of fishing at the end of the day if I were organized and brought my rod and reel with me in the car. As I say, it was around that time that I switched from my lure to worms, and all of a sudden, my line was singing. The Svartkil, I learned, was full of fish: besides the bluegill, there were pumpkinseed sunfish, smallmouth bass, bullhead catfish, even a monster walleye that snapped my line before I could bring him all the way on shore. Since I didn't know anything about cleaning and cooking fish, I threw back everything I caught, but that didn't matter.

I realize all of this must sound like some kind of inspirational story, "How Fishing Saved My Life," or the like, and I don't mean it to. For a long time after that first day at the river, especially once fishing season was over that fall, there were more than enough nights I rode to sleep on a wave of Scotch. The house stayed a mess, and my meals at Pete's, which remained a daily habit, were the best I ate. Sitting on the couch or lying in bed thinking of Marie, I felt as bad as I ever had, maybe worse, because each day that passed was another reminder of how far away I was from her. Fishing was no miracle cure.

When I was at the river, though, if I didn't feel any better, at least I didn't feel any worse. Perched on the bank, I was visited by feelings that had been keeping their distance since Marie breathed her last—since she first found the lump in her breast, really. There was satisfaction, which came with a good cast, with watching the hook arc out overhead, listening to the reel unspooling, finding the spot where the line plunked through the water. There was joy, which came but rarely and never stayed long, at pulling back on the rod and watching the green length of a smallmouth break the river's skin, twisting as it hit the air. Mostly, there was calm—I might even call it peace—which came from sitting watching the brown water slide by, on its way from a lake down in the mountains of western New Jersey up to its destination in the Hudson. Those hours on the Svartkil were breathing room, if you see what I mean, and it's hard for me to say what would have been my fate if I hadn't had them. Maybe I'd have been all right, anyway. But when I was fishing, I usually didn't drink as much at night, since, after having stopped at Pete's, it was already pretty late and I was already pretty tired by the time I pulled in the driveway. And although, as I said, the house stayed a mess, I found that if I kept it a little less so, I could locate things like my shoes more easily, which let me get to fishing all the more quickly. My nightly burger and beer were the highlight of my day, culinarily speaking, but after the second day of fishing I started stopping at different delis in town for a sandwich, bag of chips, and a soda. The sandwiches were things like baloney and American cheese on white with extra mayo, or salami and provolone with mustard and onion; the chips left a shiny layer of grease on my fingers; and the soda coated my teeth with sugar; but it was a meal, and it was more regular eating than I'd been used to.

So fishing was no miracle cure but, on balance, I guess it did save my life. I'll let you in on a secret: for the longest time, I thought I had been, well, *led* to fishing, if you know what I mean. It was the only explanation I could come up with for why this activity so far outside my everyday routine had caught me up. I didn't think so at first. At first, I just thought it was dumb luck, chance, something I hadn't remembered watching on TV that had snagged on my brain. The more time passed, however, the less that explanation convinced me. Fishing felt too right; the fit was too close, which I discovered the second year I fished, after a winter of trying to find something to fill that space fishing had occupied for me. I won't say I tried every sport and hobby known to man and woman—I never made it as far as fencing—but I went through a good many of them, and none hit the mark. It wasn't until I was back at my spot on the side of Springvale, Yankees cap on my head, rod in my hands, trying something new, a green and white jitterbug lure, that I felt myself unclench, like a fist you've been making so long your fingers have forgotten they ever knew how to stretch, and then, all at once, your hand opens. From talking to people at work, comparing notes, I've learned that not many men or women feel this way, this passion so strong you can completely relax in it, about much of anything. To say that I'd stumbled into it by accident seemed, the more I reflected on it, harder to believe than that something, or someone, had brought me to it, someone who knew me well enough to know that this would be perfect for me.

Of course I mean Marie. In the months after her death, I hadn't had any of those experiences you hear people babble on about on the afternoon talk shows. I hadn't felt her touch, hadn't heard her voice, hadn't seen her. She'd been in my dreams, every one I could remember, but I thought that was no more than what you'd expect. I hadn't sensed her, so to speak, in any way; although when her sister stopped in to visit one afternoon, she told me she was positive she'd heard Marie's voice singing a song they'd sung as children outside the kitchen window. When she ran outside to look, the yard was empty. I didn't feel especially bad that I hadn't seen or heard Marie. She'd suffered much, too much, and I didn't begrudge her her rest. I'm not really much in terms of religion. I was baptized Catholic, and went to C.C.D. until my confirmation, but neither of my parents was all that religious. It was more something they felt they had to do to me until I was a certain age, when they could stop. They stopped, I stopped, and that was that. I never gave much thought to God, heaven, or any of that stuff. Marie and I were married in a church, but that was because it was important to her. For the same reason, I made sure she had a funeral mass, with her favorite priest on the altar. When she was dying, when she was gone, all sorts of folks, from close family to fellows I barely knew at work, talked to me about religion, about faith. They told me that I needed it, that a creed would be a help to me. I suppose it might've been. I just didn't seem to have it in me, if you know what I mean.

This one night, my cousin, John, who's a priest, a Jesuit, stopped by with the intent, it's safe to say, of making a convert, or whatever it is they call it when you go back to the Church. At one point, I remember him talking about death, asking didn't I find it terrible to think about ending, about just dying and that was that. Didn't I think it was terrible that Marie had died and it was all over, that she'd gone and I'd never see her again? I told John it didn't bother me, which was the truth. She'd been sick a long time, all our marriage, and she'd put up a good fight, and I was the last one was going to deny her a little peace. Tell the truth, I liked the idea of her at peace, at rest. It seemed a lot nicer, a lot more charitable, when you came right down to it, than any busy heaven where she'd be flitting here and there like an oversized hummingbird.

During that second year of fishing, though, I did start to wonder a bit. Maybe it was all the stuff my cousin had said. Those Jesuits are supposed to be clever, aren't they? And he'd certainly given me the works. With each year that passed, I came to ask myself if Marie might not have gone out of this world so much as gone more deeply into it. From being wrapped up in earth, maybe she'd made her way out into it, into the soil, the water, until she was part of things. Maybe she'd found a way to lead me back to her.

As time flowed on, I refined my gear, moved from a spincast reel to a spinning reel (I never could master a baitcaster), learned how to use a lure to bring in my fish. I searched out other rivers, other streams, to fish. Although it was close, about twenty minutes' car ride, I never was much for the Hudson. For one thing, for the longest time, you couldn't eat most of what you caught, and that was a treat a fellow at work had introduced me to that I was reluctant to surrender: not so much bass, but catfish, walleye, and especially trout. For another thing, love the river though I do, and I do, the Hudson's just too damn big. I prefer a smaller river, one that's more intimate. I can't do without moving water, either. I've fished lakes, and while I agree it is pleasant to while away a couple of hours floating around in a boat, I prefer being able to stand up and stretch my legs when I want to. So I tried out the Esopus, then the Rondout, and then I started driving up into the Catskills. I don't know much—anything, really—about my part of the Hudson Valley. Pa had his roots in Springfield, Kentucky—his family was Kentucky Melungeon—although he'd moved around quite a bit as a boy; and Ma came from Scotland: from St. Andrew's, where they have the golf courses. She stepped off the boat when she was eighteen, met and married Pa in Queens, and the two of them moved up to Poughkeepsie so Pa could take a job managing a bank there. Neither of them knew the area that well, and neither ever showed any inclination to make its acquaintance. Aside from that long-ago day Marie and I had spent at her friend's brother's, I'd never been to the mountains. This meant that, when I turned west onto

Route 28 heading out of Wiltwyck that first Saturday morning, I was striking out into uncharted territory.

Right from the beginning, I loved it up there. I don't know if you've spent time in the Catskills. From a distance, say, the parking lot of the old Caldor's (which became an Ames that became a Stop 'N' Shop) in Huguenot, they've always made me think of a herd of giant animals, all standing grazing on the horizon. Up close, when you're driving among them with the early morning light breaking over their round peaks, they seem incredibly present, more real than real, these huge solid heaps of rock that wear their trees like mile-long scarves. You glance at them, trying to keep your eyes on the road, which is already pretty busy with people driving up for a weekend getaway, and somehow you wouldn't be surprised if the mountain closest to you were to cast off its trees in one titanic shrug and start to lumber away, a vast, unimaginable beast. When you turn off onto whatever secondary road you need to take, and you're following its twists and turns back into the mountains, and the ground is steep to either side of you, opening every now and then on a meadow, or an old house, you think, *Here, there are secret places.*

Well, that's what I thought, anyway. I fished as far west as Oneonta, and as far north as Catskill, taking fish from most of the streams between these towns and Wiltwyck. And while I was standing streamside on a Saturday morning, sunlight bouncing on the water as it tumbled over a small waterfall into a broad pool I was sure held a trout or two, and so had cast the spinner with the tri-hook and was watching the lure descending into the water, waiting to reel it in as I tried to decide if that shadow beneath it was just a shadow or a fish come to see what was for breakfast—I say, moments like this a kind of silence seemed to fall over everything. I could still hear the water chuckling, and the birds having their morning conversation, and maybe a car, far away, but I could hear this other sound, too, this sound that wasn't one, that was quiet. It was like another space had opened up around me, and it was in that quiet, so to speak, that I came to believe I could hear Marie. She didn't say anything, didn't make any sound at all, but I could hear her just the same. I couldn't have said if she were happy or sad, because I had realized that the moving shadow wasn't a shadow but a trout, and a big one at that, and I had started winding the handle quickly, making that spinner leap forward through the water, my arms already tensed, waiting for the fish to strike and the struggle to begin. Maybe in another situation, another setting, I would have felt differently, the hair on my arms and neck might have stood straight up and my mouth gone dry. Holding on for that trout, though, whose mouth was about to close on the lure, there wasn't more I could do about that strange silence than know it was there. Later, after I had helped the fish and a few of his friends out onto the ground beside me and was treating myself to a chocolate bar, I would think about what had happened, about that deep, deep quiet.

Even then, I didn't feel especially scared. The world's always seemed a pretty big place to me, full of more things than any one body could know, and I'd be the last person to pretend to understand it all. After Marie died, I hadn't believed there was anything more, but could be I'd been mistaken. Hell, yes, I wanted to be wrong. Who wouldn't? Her watching me fish didn't seem threatening, and, really, why should it have? What time we'd had, we'd had good, and maybe she missed me the same way I missed her and wanted to have a look and see how I was doing. I wouldn't claim I felt her there with me at every river and stream. I can't say she was always present when I sat at a particular spot, or came on a certain day. I felt her first and most often in the mountains. She was there once when I had worked my way from the Esopus up a little fast-moving stream whose name I meant to learn later but never did. She was there one afternoon when I returned to my spot on Springvale to discover I'd have to share it with two old women sitting on lawn chairs. I can't say I was haunted, exactly—that sounds a bit too regular for what happened to me. But I did have a visit or two.

II

RUNGS ON
THE LADDER OF LOSS

I reckon I could go on talking about this for the rest of today and tomorrow besides. You'll have to excuse me: when I think back to what fishing used to be to me, I can almost forget what it became, so I'm inclined to linger on the memory. It's a nice feeling to be able to look back on a time when I didn't spend most of my day at the river wondering what exactly might be swimming up to take my line, and when my memory wasn't full of images to offer as answers. A school of what might have been large tadpoles, except that each one ended in a single, outsized eye; a fish whose back boasted a tall fin like a dragon's wing and whose rubbery mouth was hedged with long fangs; a pale swimmer with webbed hands and feet and a face that wavered as you looked at it: all of these and more were ready to set my palms sweating and my heart racing. What's important right now is that you know the place fishing held in my life; it helps to explain why I started taking Dan Drescher with me.

I knew Dan from work. He was two offices down going towards the water cooler. *Tall fellow:* that was the first thing I thought when he was introduced to me, and I suppose my reaction was typical. Dan was six foot seven inches, thin as the proverbial beanpole. After his height, you noticed Dan's hair, which was bright orange and appeared never to have been introduced to the benefits of a comb. He kept it cut short, and I can't imagine what those sessions at the barber's must have been like. His face was sharp in a way that made you think of something struck from granite: sharp brow; big, sharp nose; round—but sharp—chin. He smiled a lot, and his eyes were kind, which diminished the sharpness some, but if you reflected on his appearance, you might have thought that his was a face made for fierceness.

At first, Dan and I didn't say much to each other, though what words we did pass were pleasant. There was nothing unusual in this. I was a good two decades his senior, a middle-aged widower whose favorite topics of conversation were fishing and baseball. He was a young man not that long out of M.I.T. who favored expensive suits and whose wife and twin sons were admired by everyone. Marie's passing had been long enough ago for me not to feel a pang at the family portraits and snapshots Dan displayed on his desk. I'd been on dates with a few women in the last few years, even had what I guess you would call a relationship with one of them. But I never could bring myself to marry anyone else—just didn't have it in me. A few months before we were married—this was when we were planning the reception—Marie turned to me and said, out of the blue, "Abraham Samuelson, you are the most romantic man I know." I don't remember what my answer was. Made a joke out of it, most likely. Maybe she was right, though, maybe there was more of the romantic in me than I thought. Whatever the case, I was alone and Dan had his family, and at the time that seemed to make an unbridgeable gap between us.

Then, one day, I believe it was a Tuesday, Dan didn't show up for work. In and of itself, this wasn't such a big deal, except that Dan hadn't called in sick, which struck anyone who heard it as unusual. Dan had earned a reputation as an especially conscientious worker. At his desk every morning by eight twenty at the latest, a good ten minutes ahead of the rest of us, he took no more than a fifteen-minute lunch—if he didn't work right through it—and when the rest of us left at four thirty, we waved to him on our way out, knowing that it would probably be another half-hour before he followed us. He was dedicated, and he was talented enough that his dedication counted. I assumed he had his sights set on early and rapid promotion, which, with those twins at home, I could appreciate. All of this is to say that, when Dan wasn't there and no one knew why, we were inclined to feel a bit more uneasy than we would have otherwise.

As we found out the following day, we'd had every right and reason for our concern. Some read it on the front page of *The Poughkeepsie Journal* with their morning coffee; others heard it on the radio as they drove to work; still others had it from Frank Block, who was a volunteer fireman and whose absence the previous day also had been noted, but not connected by anyone to Dan's. There had been an accident. Dan was an early riser, you see, as were the twins. Sometimes his wife, Sophie, took the opportunity to sleep in a little, but yesterday, for whatever reason, she had risen with the rest of them. It was early enough, just a little past six, that when Dan suggested the four of them nip into town for a quick bite of breakfast before he left for work, the idea seemed reasonable. So they bundled the babies into their car seats, and set off. Dan drove, and he failed to fasten his seatbelt, which Sophie noticed. Dan shrugged. It was no big deal, they were only going a short way. *It's your ticket*, Sophie said.

The Dreschers lived off South Morris Road, which intersects Route 299, the main road into Huguenot, about three miles east of town. 299's a fast road, has been for as long as I've lived on this side of the Hudson. There should have been a traffic light where Morris crossed it, instead of a pair of stop signs. Maybe the light wouldn't have made any difference. Maybe the fellow steering the big white eighteen-wheeler would've had it up around seventy anyway. Dan said he saw the truck approaching from his right as he turned left onto 299, but it didn't look to be moving as fast as it was. He pulled out, and that great white beast slammed into his Subaru like a thunderbolt. Dan was thrown through the windshield to, as it turned out, safety. Crushed together, car and truck skidded along the road, jagged bits of metal showering sparks as they went. Before they'd stopped moving, the car erupted in a fireball that was answered, a second later, by an explosion from the truck. By the time the first police car raced to the scene, it was too late. It had been too late, I suppose, from the moment Dan's foot pressed on the accelerator, the car swept out onto the road. Could be it'd been too late the moment the idiot driving that rig had glanced at his wristwatch, realized that, if his morning delivery was to arrive on schedule, he was going to have to make up some time, and stepped on the gas, shifting up as he did. The fire took his life, which I wish I could say I felt worse about, and it consumed Sophie and the twins. Two days later, the coroner told Dan that, in all likelihood, his wife and children had been killed in the impact, and most likely hadn't suffered much if at all. I guess the man thought that he was giving what consolation he could.

Dan was polite enough to that coroner, but I think he still was wrapped in the same daze a cop had found him stumbling around the side of the road in. His face was bright with blood, as was the sweatshirt he'd pulled on for going out. At first, the officer wasn't sure who this tall guy was. As he led Dan toward one of the ambulances that had arrived to find themselves useless, he assumed Dan was a bystander who'd been caught in the accident, an early-morning jogger hit by debris. It took a few minutes for him to sort out that this man had been the driver of the car that was so much fire and metal. When the lightbulb went off over his head, the cop tried to question Dan about the chain of events, but he couldn't get much coherent out of him. Eventually, one of the EMTs told the guy that Dan was most likely in shock, and in need of the hospital.

The fire took the better part of an hour and three fire companies to extinguish. Traffic coming into and out of Huguenot was delayed and diverted until early afternoon. Two weeks after the accident, a traffic light was hung at that intersection, which I reckon is what four lives is worth these days. Too late for the Dreschers, it became their memorial.

A full six weeks passed before any of us saw Dan again. There was a memorial service for Sophie and the twins at the Huguenot Methodist Church, but it was small, for immediate family. By the time I walked in one Monday morning and, despite myself, jumped at the sight of Dan, back at his desk, his losses had faded from my mind, I'm ashamed to admit. I'd like to say this was because I'd been so busy in the interval, or because my own private life had been very good or even very bad, but I'm afraid none of that would be true. Not much more than out of sight, out of mind, I fear. It's hard to hold onto any tragedies that aren't your own for very long. That's something I learned after Marie died. In the short term, folks can show compassion like you wouldn't believe; wait a couple of weeks, though, a couple of months at the outside, and see how well their sympathy holds.

Dan returned to work bearing the scar from his trip through his car's windshield. After his height, that scar became the thing about him that caught your notice. Threading out from among his red hair, which he kept longer now, the scar continued down the right side of his face, skirting the corner of his right eye, veering in at the corner of his mouth, winding down his neck to disappear beneath his shirt collar. You tried not to look, but of course you couldn't help yourself. It was as if Dan's face had been knitted together at that white line. I was reminded of the times my pa had taken me walking round the grounds at Penrose College, which he'd liked to do when I was a boy. Without fail, Pa would stop to point out to me a tree that had been struck by lightning. I don't mean a tree that had had a branch blown off; I mean one that had acted as a living lightning rod, drawing the spark in at its crown and passing it down the length of its trunk to its roots. The lightning's course had peeled and grooved out a line in the bark from top to bottom that Pa would stand and run his fingers over. "You know," he'd say every time, "the ancient Greeks used to bury anyone struck by lightning apart from the rest. They knew such people'd had a tremendous experience—a sacred experience—but they weren't sure if it was good or bad."

"How could something sacred be bad?" I'd ask, but the only answer I ever received was a shake of his head as he ran his fingers over the channel a river of white fire had rushed through.

Everyone did their best to welcome Dan back to work; even so, a good few months passed before I thought to invite him to come fishing with me. You might expect I would've been one of the first people into Dan's office to talk to him, but you'd be mistaken. If anything, I tended to avoid him. I know how that must sound: if not heartless, then at least weird. Who was in a better position to talk to him, to understand what he was going through and offer words of comfort? We'd both lost our wives, hadn't we?

Well, yes, we had. The way we'd lost them, though, made for all the difference in the world. All loss is not created equal, you see. Loss is—it's like a ladder you don't know you're standing at the top of and that reaches down, way down past the loss of your job, your possessions, your home; past the loss of your parents, your spouse, your children; down to the loss of your very life—and, I've since come to believe, past even that. In that awful hierarchy, what I had undergone, the slow slipping away of my wife over the span of almost two years, stood as far above what Dan had suffered, the disappearance of his wife and children in less time than it takes to tell it, as someone who hadn't lost anything at all stood above me. Marie and

THE FISHERMAN

I had had time, and if a lot of that time had been overshadowed by what was rushing toward us, ever-closer, at least we'd been able to make some use of those months, take a road trip out to Wyoming before she was too sick, draw some good out of the bad. You can imagine how much someone in Dan's position might envy me, might hate me for having what I had more fiercely than he might someone whose wife was happily alive. I could imagine that hatred, so kept what I intended as a respectful distance.

Besides, there didn't seem to be anything wrong with the guy. He didn't go to pieces the way that I had. Sure, there were days when the shirt he was wearing was the same one we'd seen him in yesterday, or his suit was wrinkled, or his tie stained, but there were enough single men at the office about whom you could notice the same or similar things for such details not to strike you as too serious. Aside from the scar and the slightly longer hair, the only change I saw in Dan lay in his eyes, which locked into a permanent stare. Not a blank stare, mind. It was a more intense look, the kind that suggests great concentration: the brow lowered ever-so-slightly, the eyes crinkled, as if the starer is trying to see right through what's in front of them. In that stare, something of the fierceness I'd seen dormant in his face came to the surface, and it could be a tad unsettling to have him focus it on you. Although his manner remained civil—he was always at least polite, frequently pleasant—under that gaze I felt a bit like a prisoner in one of those escape from Alcatraz movies the moment the spotlight catches him.

When I finally did ask Dan to fish with me, I acted on impulse, a spur-of-the-moment kind of thing. I was standing in the doorway of Frank Block's office, telling him about my struggle the previous weekend to land a trout. The trout hadn't been the biggest I'd ever caught, but he had been strong. My efforts had been complicated by the fact that, when the fish struck, I'd been away behind a clump of bushes, answering a call of nature brought on by a cup of extremely powerful coffee I'd drunk not an hour before. My line had been quiet prior to the moment I'd felt the uncontrollable urge to visit the bushes, so I thought it would be safe to leave the rod wedged in between my tacklebox and a log whilst I did what must be done. Naturally, this was the moment the fish chose to take the fly and run. When I heard the reel buzzing, I started looking around furiously for some leaves. Then, with a clatter and a crash, the fish pulled the rod over and began dragging it toward the river. There was no time for me to do anything but rush from my improvised toilet, pants still around my ankles, and dive for the rod, which I just managed to catch. I staggered to my feet, and spent the next ten minutes working that fish, giving him a little line, drawing him in, giving him a little line, drawing him in, naked from waist to ankles as the day the doctor took me from my ma. When at last I hauled the trout from the water and stood there holding him up to admire, I noticed movement on the other side of the river. Two young women were standing across from me, the one with a pair of binoculars, the other with a camera. Both were pointing in my direction and laughing. I don't like to think at what.

"What'd you do?" Frank asked, laughing himself.

"What else could I do?" I said. "I bowed to them both, turned around, and shuffled back up the bank."

"You fish?" Dan asked. He'd come up behind me as I was talking. I must have been aware of him, since I didn't jump ten feet in the air and shout, "Jesus!" I turned and said, "I do. I fish most days it isn't raining, and some when it is."

"I used to fish," Dan said. "My dad used to take me."

"Really?" I said. "What kind of fishing?"

"Nothing that exciting," he said. "Lakes and ponds, mostly."

"You ever catch anything?" Frank asked. He was one of those fellows who likes to talk fishing more than he does fish fishing.

"Some," Dan said. He shrugged. "Bass. A lot of sunnies. My dad caught a pike, once."

"No kidding," I said. "Pike's a tough fish to land."

"You can say that again," Frank said.

"It took us the whole afternoon," Dan said. "When we got him into the boat, he was almost three feet long. It was a record for that lake. This was in Maine. My dad gave the fish to Captain Pete—he was the guy who ran the bait and tackle shop on the lake. We bought our bait from him, soda, too. He had this big cooler full of cans of soda. Anyway, he was so impressed, he had that fish mounted—you know, gave it to a taxidermist—and hung it up on one of his shop's walls. He had my dad's name and the date the fish was caught carved on the mount."

"Wow," Frank said, whether at the story or at Dan's having told us it I couldn't say. As far as either of us knew, Dan's anecdote was the most he had said to anyone at work since the accident. I asked, "You fished since then, Dan?"

"Not for years," he replied. "Not since before the twins were born."

Frank looked down at his desk. I swallowed the lump that had formed in my throat and said, "Want to come with me?"

"Fishing," Dan said.

"Uh-huh."

"When?"

"How about this weekend? Say, Saturday morning? Unless you have plans, that is."

He scowled, and I realized Dan wasn't sure if I was mocking him. He said, "I don't know."

All at once, it was the most important thing in the world for Dan to come fishing with me. I can't say exactly why that should have been. Maybe I wanted to prove my sincerity to him. Maybe I thought that fishing would do for him what it'd done for me; although, as I've said, I had no evidence to suggest that Dan's life had collapsed the way mine had. Or maybe my motive was something less well-defined, something as simple as wanting to have another person to pass a few words with while I fished. I don't know. Until that moment, I'd always done well enough fishing on my own. What-ever the reason, I said, "Why don't you come along? I've got an extra rod if you need it, and more'n'enough tackle for the two of us. I was just planning on heading out to the Svartkil, so it won't be that far if you don't like it and want to leave. I go pretty early—this weather, I like to be set up and have my line in the water by sunrise—but you're welcome to come whenever you can make it there. What do you say?"

Dan's scowl wavered, then dissipated. "What the hell," he said. "Why not?"

And that was how Dan Drescher and I started fishing together. I told him where the spot on Springvale was, and he was there waiting for me when I drove up in the pre-dawn dark. He'd brought his own rod and tacklebox, and from the sheen and smell of both of them, I knew they'd entered his possession in the last day or so. That was okay. It reminded me of myself, those many years ago. He'd brought a hat, too, a kind of straw cowboy affair that I later learned he'd purchased on a vacation in Arizona with his wife. We chose and attached our lures, cast, and as the sun burst through the trees across from us, were sitting waiting to see who might be interested in the early breakfast we were serving.

That first morning—that first day, actually, since Dan stayed there with me until the sun had moved from our fronts to our backs and then left for the night—we didn't say much to one another. Nor was there a whole lot of conversation the next day, when (somewhat to my surprise, since he hadn't mentioned it the previous day, just thanked me as he was leaving) I pulled my car onto the side of the road and my headlights picked out Dan sitting on a tree stump, considering the contents of his tacklebox. He offered no explanation, nodding at me as I walked over and saying, "Morning. Weather report says there might be rain today."

"You can still catch 'em in the rain," I said.

He grunted, and that was pretty much that for the remainder of the day. The following weekend, we fished the Svartkil again and didn't do too badly for ourselves. On Sunday night, as we were packing our gear, I said, "I'm thinking of heading up the Esopus next Saturday. Not too far: about forty minutes' drive. You interested?"

"Yeah," he said.

"Good," I said, and meant it.

So we fished the Esopus the following weekend, and Frenchman's Creek the weekend after that, and then I took him up to the Catskills, to the Beaverkill, up by Mount Tremper. Sunday night, on our way home, we stopped at Winchell's, a burger place right on 28, just the other side of Woodstock. This was where I learned that Dan's family hailed from Phoenicia, a town in the thick of the mountains, and that he knew the area and its history fairly well. He'd never fished it, though. In fact, he said as he wiped the ketchup off his plate with his remaining fry, he hadn't been up here since before Sophie was pregnant, when he'd driven her out 28 so she could see where he'd grown up.

It's always tricky when someone who's lost what Dan had speaks about it, especially so soon after. You're never quite sure what to say, because you can't tell if the person's only offering a passing comment, or if they're looking to talk. I imagine this is how folks must've felt with me after Marie died. With Dan and me, there wasn't the kind of long friendship or deep family bond that would allow you to feel you could risk making a blunder, since you could count on the other person knowing you were trying your best. This wasn't the first such remark Dan had made in my hearing. It seemed he'd been voicing a few more of them each weekend; I suppose that was why

I decided to chance it and said, "So, what did she think?"

"Who?" he asked.

"Your wife," I said, already afraid I'd blown it, "Sophie. What did she think of Phoenicia?"

For the barest instant, long enough for it to be visible, a look swept across Dan's face that was equal parts disbelief and pain, as if I'd broken into the private vault of his recollections. Then, to my surprise, he grinned and said, "She told me she understood me and my redneck ways a whole hell of a lot better, now."

I grinned back, and the worst was past. For the rest of that summer, on into early fall, as we roamed the Catskills, fishing streams I'd fished on my own, trying some spots that were new to me, I learned a little about Dan's wife, and about his family, too. He never said much at any one time. I don't believe he'd ever been the kind of fellow to speak about himself for too long. As you may have noticed, that's a condition that's never afflicted me, and once I saw it was all right with Dan, I had no problem talking about my life, which I hadn't thought was all that interesting, just long enough for me to have seen and heard a bit. I talked about Marie, some, though not about her dying. If there was one topic that was off-limits, it was our respective bereavements. This complicated my conversation, since, as I've said, she was sick for really all of our short marriage. I solved that problem by speaking about the way things had been before we'd married, during our courtship. I talked about Marie, and I continued to feel her occasional visits, often when Dan was sitting only a few feet from me. I don't know that I ever got used to those moments—however regular they might become, I don't know that a body could—but I continued to take an odd sort of comfort from them.

Consciously or no, Dan followed my lead, by and large sticking to the beginning times, to events far enough removed you had an easier time convincing yourself the pain you felt in your chest was nostalgia, nothing more. He never spoke about the twins, Jason and Jonas, and, to be honest, I was grateful for that. Marie had wanted children in the worst way, and it had been one of her bitterest disappointments to have to leave this world without having had at least one. She and I had spoken about the matter a fair bit, up until the morning of the day she died, in fact, and after she was gone I found I had trouble being around children, seeing Marie's nieces and nephews at the family events I continued to be invited to. Seeing them, seeing any small child, reminded me of what Marie and I hadn't had the chance to have that we had wanted to have, and that focused my hurt the way a magnifying glass does sunlight. Over the years, those feelings had silted over. I found it easier to cope with the presence of children. But I guess they weren't as far off as I might've wanted. All it took was the strong wind of me talking, and there they were, a little dusty, but in one piece.

Still and all, I liked to believe that whatever slight discomfort I might've felt was worth it if our talking was helping Dan. In fact, when the fishing season was over that fall, I worried a little for him. I'd yet to find my winter substitute for fishing, you see—never have, to this day—so it wasn't as if I could say to Dan, "Well, now that fishing season's over, we'll have to start practicing our curling." After having fished and talked together as much as we had, we shouldn't have needed that kind of excuse, I know, but, lacking an activity like fishing, I felt strange saying to Dan, "Hey, let's get together this weekend and talk." Stupid, yes. In any event, Dan was expecting company that first fishing-less weekend, his brother and his family. The first anniversary of the accident was rearing its hideous head, and his and Sophie's families had decided that he shouldn't be alone for the weeks to either side of it. He was busy well into the New Year.

Although I saw Dan every day at work, passed a few words with him here and there, it wasn't until late February of that next year that I finally had him over for dinner. Despite its abbreviated length, February's always struck me as an especially bleak month, at least in these parts. I know it's not the darkest month, and I know it's not the coldest or the snowiest month, but February is gray in a way I can't explain. In February, all the big, happy holidays are gone, and it's weeks and weeks—months, even—until Easter and spring. I suppose that's why whoever decides these things stuck Valentine's Day smack dab in the middle of the month, to help lighten its load. To be honest, though, even when I had a reason to celebrate the fourteenth, I still thought of the second month as a bleak time. I think this was part of the reason I invited Dan to join me in a meal, and why, when I opened the door that Sunday night and saw him standing there, unshaven and obviously unshowered, wearing an old track suit reeking of mothballs and mildew, I wasn't as surprised as I might have been, especially considering that, when I'd seen him on Friday, he'd been his usual tidy self. I looked at him standing in the doorway, his eyes red-rimmed and bloodshot, and thought, *Of course: it's February.*

They say that, for most people, the second year after you lose someone is harder than the first. During that first year, the theory goes, you're still in shock. You don't really believe what's happened to you has happened; you can't. During that second year, it starts to sink in that the person—or, in Dan's case, people—you've been pretending are away on a visit aren't coming back. This wasn't what happened to me, but I guess that was because I'd been losing Marie for a long time before she was gone, and so had been using a lot of those same tricks on myself most folks don't discover until much later. But the theory held true for Dan. He'd made a brave face of things through Thanksgiving, Christmas, New Year, had done his best to be a good host to his various visiting relatives, and once the last of them—a cousin from Ohio—had been gone for going on a week, with no promise of anyone else appearing in the immediate future, the knowledge of how alone he was had crushed him like a truckful of bricks. Until this point, he'd been doing all right sleeping—not great, mind you, but not bad—and he'd been able to distract himself watching old movies on the VCR, one of his passions. Now sleep had fled, chased away by the memory of that huge white truck rushing toward him, its grill like a great set of chrome teeth grinning at him as it prepared to take a bite out of his life from which he'd never recover. When he tried to watch TV, his copy of *Red River*, say, or one of the late-night talk shows, whatever was on the screen was replaced by Sophie's face, turning away from him to look at the roaring tractor-trailer, her expression sliding from early-morning fatigue to wide-eyed terror, her mouth opening to make a sound Dan never heard.

He told me this over the course of dinner, which was spaghetti and meatballs with garlic bread and salad, in answer to my asking, "So, Dan, how are you?" I didn't interrupt him, confining myself to making sympathetic grunts. This was the most he'd spoken to me at one time, and the most about the subject of his loss, and once he'd started I knew better than to derail him. He took most of dinner to unburden himself, during which time he ate little—some garlic bread was all—but managed four full glasses from the bottle of red wine I'd set on the table. This was sufficient to start him swaying ever-so-slightly, and to pull his eyelids lower. Once I thought he was finished talking, I said, "Now, don't take this the wrong way, but maybe you should talk to someone, you know, professional. Maybe that'd be a help to you."

His voice slurring, Dan said, "No offense taken, Abe—Abraham. You want to know what helps? I'll tell you. At about four in the morning, when I'm lying on my bed with my eyes wide open, staring at the ceiling, which is kind of like a movie screen hanging there above me, because it's white, and because I can see everything that happened played out there on it, again and again—when it gets to be four in the morning, and I think, *I'm going to get up in an hour and a half anyway, why not now?* I haul myself out of bed, throw on some clothes, doesn't matter what, make myself a cup of coffee to go—can't miss my morning cup of coffee—and I go, take the car and drive out to the corner of Morris Road and 299. Morris has a wide shoulder there, so it's no problem for me to pull off onto it and sit drinking my morning cup of coffee. There's a traffic light there now, did you know that? Did you?"

"Yeah," I said, "I did."

"Of course you did: who doesn't? It marks the spot where the Drescher family—where we—where the happy family of one Daniel Anthony Drescher was forever *reduced*. I sit at that spot—that historic spot, coffee in hand, and I look at that traffic light. I study it. I contemplate it. I watch its three glass eyes trade off commands. If it's warm enough, or if it isn't, I open my window and listen to it. Let's say the light starts off green. There's a buzzing, almost like an alarm clock, which is followed by a clunk, and the light is yellow. Another buzzing, another clunk, and it's red. It's like gates being opened and shut, like prison gates. The light stays red the longest, did you know that? I've timed it. This is looking at it from Morris. From 299, it stays green the longest. After red comes green, then yellow. Buzz, clunk. Buzz, clunk. Gates opening and shutting, Abe. Gates opening and shutting.

"I'll let you in on a little secret, too. Looking at the light doesn't help in the slightest. I don't think, *Well, at least some good has come out of this terrible tragedy.* The intersection's just another place to be. I can't escape it. I can't escape any of it. Myself am hell, right? So I might as well be at the spot where I took the plunge, so to speak, the place where I was cast out. I do feel calmer there. Strange, huh? I have the strangest thoughts lately. I swear I do. When I look at things—when I look at people—I think, None of it's real. It's all just a mask, like those papier-mâché masks we made for one of our school plays when I was a kid. What play was that? It seems like it must have been *Alice in Wonderland*, but I can't remember. I wish I could remember that play. I wish I could. All a mask, Abe, and the million-dollar question is, *What's underneath the mask?* If I could break through the mask, if I could make a fist and punch a hole in it," his hand slammed the table, rattling the dishes, "what would I find? Just flesh? Or would there be something more? Would I find those things the minister talked about at the funerals? You weren't there, were you? I guess we didn't know each other so well then. Beauty, the minister said, the three of them were in a place of beauty, beauty beyond our ability to know. Joy, too, it's a place of unending joy. If I could punch a hole through the mask, would I see beauty and joy? You would think, either it's got to be heaven, because that's what we're talking about, right? Or it's what it is, the mask is everything. But I'll tell you, when I'm sitting at that intersection, watching the light go through its cycles, I think of other—other possibilities. Maybe whoever, or whatever, is running the show isn't so nice. Maybe he's evil, or mad, or bored, disinterested. Maybe we've got everything completely wrong, everything, and if we could look through the mask, what we'd see would destroy us. You ever feel that way?"

"Not exactly," I said.

"That's all right," Dan said and, leaning back in his chair, promptly fell asleep.

Recalling Dan's words now, it's hard for me not to shudder, to wonder, *How did he know?* They say extreme states of mind can push you to—a visionary state, I guess you'd call it. Could be that's what happened to him. Then again, I have to remind myself that what transpired that day at Dutchman's Creek: what we heard; what we saw; God help me, what we touched; that all of that doesn't necessarily bear out Dan's words. It feels a lot like special pleading to say that, though. Actually, it feels more like flat-out, Pollyanna, pie-in-the-sky denial. But there are some things, no matter if they're true, you can't live with them. You have to refuse them. You turn your eyes away from whatever's squatting right there in front of you and not only pretend it isn't there now, but that you never saw it in the first place. You do so because your soul is a frail thing that can't stand the blast-furnace heat of revelation, and truth be damned. What else can a body do?

Since he wasn't in any shape to drive home, I gave Dan my bed and I took the couch. It was no fun trying to get him out of that chair, maneuver him through the living room and down the hall, and guide him into the bedroom. He kept wanting to stop and lie down, and it's no small task convincing a big man drunk on wine and exhaustion not to decamp in the middle of the hallway. Despite everything Dan had said, I had no trouble sleeping. Later that night—technically speaking, it must have been the next morning—I had a nightmare, the first since Marie died. As a rule, my dreams had been of the mundane, this-is-what-I-did-today variety. Seldom, if ever, did my mind conjure any strange, exotic dreams, any dream-like dreams. I've always been this way. Truth to tell, I used to sort of envy those folks who dreamed they were on great adventures, or having passionate love affairs, or dining with famous people. To me, those dreams seemed like starring in your own private movie. This dream was no happy Hollywood extravaganza. It was the kind of film you want to turn off but can't, because switching it off would mean standing up from the couch and crossing the living room, and you're literally too scared to do that. It seems like a tremendous risk. But that's not all, no. You're fascinated, too. So you sit there, unable to stop watching, knowing full well you'll regret your failure to change the channel later, when you've pulled the bedclothes up over your head and are praying that the creak you heard outside the bedroom door was the house settling, not a footstep.

In the dream, I was fishing. I want to say it started out normally enough, except that isn't true. I was standing beside this narrow, winding, fast-moving stream. When I say it was fast-moving, I mean the water was frothing, the way it does after a torrential storm. I couldn't see into it at all. To my left, the stream descended from a steep hill. To my right, it foamed on level for a dozen yards before dropping away. In front of me, across the stream, the other shore rose steeply to a dense line of evergreens. Behind me, the ground also sloped up to a heavy cluster of trees. Overhead, the sky was pure blue, the sun dazzling. Despite the sunlight, the trees across from me—not only the spaces between them, but the trees themselves—were dark, not simply in shadow, but truly dark, as if they'd been shaped out of night itself. Standing there at the edge of that raging stream, rod in hands, line cast, I could not take my eyes from those trees, those dark trees, even though looking at them gave me the most intense vertigo, as if in looking over at them I were looking down a great distance, into a deep chasm. What was worse, I could feel myself being watched, could feel the eyes of things at the edge of the trees, and of things much farther in, which I somehow knew were bigger, much bigger—I say I could feel those eyes, their gaze, like a swarm of insects crawling all over me. A scream was building in my throat. I was on the verge of tossing my gear and bolting, when something took my line.

The rod bowed with the force of it. Line started to run out, and run out fast, faster than I'd ever seen, making the furious sound you hear on one of those shows about deep-sea fishing, when a marlin or a swordfish takes the bait. It ran out fast, and it ran out long, as if the fish I'd hooked had decided to dive straight down, down much deeper than I thought a stream this size could be. Afraid to grab the handle in case the line snapped, (and wondering if that would be such a bad thing), I held the rod. My catch dove ever-deeper; the line sizzled out. Abruptly, whatever I'd hooked stopped dead. I hesitated, waiting to see if it was only pausing. Nothing. I started turning the handle. For what seemed like hours, I wound that line back in, drawing in more of it than I could have had. Even in the depths of the dream, I knew this. Apart from a brief tug, which immediately stilled my hand, until I'd determined I wasn't going to have a fight on my hands, and went back to winding the reel, my catch was limp, passive. For the life of me, I couldn't figure out what kind of fish I'd caught. I'm no expert, not by a long shot, but I'd never heard tell of a fish that took your line, dove straight down with it until, apparently, it exhausted itself, then allowed you to draw it in with no further struggle. For the matter, I'd no idea what stream this was, that let my mystery fish dive so deep. The landscape resembled the Catskills, but where in the mountains, I didn't recognize.

I can't say how exactly I knew what I'd hooked was drawing closer, since I couldn't see through the seething water, but know I did, and along with that knowledge came the sense that all those things in the trees around me were holding their collective breath, eager, anticipating what, I didn't know. As what was on the other end of my line broke the water's froth, time slowed. I saw something dark, swirling in the water like so many snakes. No, not snakes, more like some kind of plant, seaweed. No, not seaweed, more like hair, like a headful of hair. It was hair, thick and brown, soaking, hopelessly tangled. The hair parted to either side of a high, pale forehead, and long, narrow eyebrows arching over closed eyes. I knew, at that moment, even before I saw her high cheekbones, her sharp, almost pointed nose, her

31

mouth that was the only feature out of proportion on her face—two sizes too small, I'd teased her—her mouth, through whose upper lip the barbed hook of the fly had slid and from which my fishing line now dangled. There was no blood. Instead, black, viscous liquid smeared the wound. I stood there, looking at my wife, at my poor, dead Marie—I still knew she was gone from me—I stood on the side of that dream-stream holding onto that rod tightly, desperately, because I couldn't think what else to do. Half of me was so terrified I wanted to fling that rod away and run, no matter if it meant finding out what was waiting in those evergreens. Half of me was so heartbroke I wanted to fling myself into the stream and grab her, hold her before she could slip back to wherever she'd risen from. I might as well have lost her five minutes ago, the pain was that sharp. Hot tears poured down my face like there was no tomorrow.

Then she opened her eyes. I whimpered, that's the only word for it, this high-pitched noise that forced its way out of my mouth. Marie's eyes, her warm, brown eyes, which had held so much of passion and kindness, were gone, replaced by flat, yellow-gold disks, by the dull dead eyes of a fish. As she stared impassively up at me, I was suddenly seized by the conviction that, if I were to haul her out of the raging stream, I would find the rest of her similarly transformed, her lovely body given over to rows of slime-crusted scales and sharp fins. My arms and legs, and everything in between, were shaking so badly it was all I could do to keep standing where I was.

Her lips parted, and Marie spoke. When she did, it was faint, as if she were simultaneously calling to me from across a vast distance and whispering in my ear. "Abe," she said, in what I recognized straight away as her voice, but her voice with a difference, as if it were coming from a throat that wasn't used to it anymore.

I nodded to her, my tongue dumb in my mouth, and she went on in that same distant-close way. "He's a fisherman, too." Her words were slurred, from the hook piercing her lip.

Again, I nodded, unsure whom she was referring to. Dan?

"Some streams run deep," Marie said.

My lips trembling, I mumbled, "M-M-Marie?"

"Deep and dark," she said.

"Honey?" I said.

"He waits," she went on.

32

"Who?" I asked. "What do you mean?"

I couldn't understand her answer, a word the hook tugging her lip wouldn't let her get her mouth around. The word, or name, collapsed in the saying, a mess of syllables that I thought sounded German, or Dutch. "There fissure"? That was what it sounded like. Before I could ask her to repeat it, Marie said, "What's lost is lost, Abe."

"The who?" I said, still trying to piece together those syllables.

"What's lost is lost," Marie said. "What's lost is lost."

From the spot where my lure pierced her lip, a deep gash raced up her face into her hair, splitting her skin. As I watched, horrified, the edges of it peeled away from each other, revealing something shining and scaled underneath. I cried out, stumbling backwards, and without a backward glance Marie dove beneath the rushing white stream. The fishing line, locked in place, tightened, pulling me headlong toward the water, my hands unable to release their grip on the rod. A half-dozen lurching steps, and I was at the water's edge, which bubbled and danced like a thing alive. I knew, with dream-certainty, that under no circumstances did I want to venture any nearer that stream. I was dizzy with fear, of Marie, of whatever was in there with her, of the very water itself, which chuckled and laughed at my desperate struggle to avoid it. I fought furiously, digging my heels into the sand as I was dragged forward. For a moment, the line relaxed and, fool that I am, so did I. This meant that when the next big tug came, I flew headlong into the white water and open mouths full of white teeth, rows and rows of white teeth in white water, and beyond them—

Sitting bolt upright on the living room couch, I woke, mouth dry, heart pounding.

III

AT HERMAN'S DINER

With the benefit of hindsight, I find it difficult not to see that dream as an omen. To be honest, I can't see now how I could have taken it for anything else. That's the problem with telling stories, though, isn't it? After the dust has settled, when you sit down to piece together what happened, and maybe more importantly how it happened, so you might have some hope of knowing why it happened, there are moments, like the dream, that forecast subsequent events with such accuracy you wonder how you possibly could have been deaf to their message. Thing is, it's only once what they were anticipating has come to pass that you're able to recognize their significance. The morning after I'd had that dream, while the sight of that raging stream, Marie's face opening up, were more than fresh in my memory, if you'd asked me what I thought the dream signified, I imagine I would've said it was expressing my fear that I'd replaced my wife with fishing. I reckon we've all seen enough pop psychologists on this TV program or that for a lot of us to be able to offer convincing interpretations of their dreams. Had you asked me if I thought the dream a caution, a prophecy like you read about in the Bible, I'd most likely have given you one of the looks we give to characters we're pretty sure are pulling our legs and asked you what you'd been drinking. After all, even if I were the kind of person

34

who believes that dreams can tap into what's waiting for us down the road, what was there for me to fear in fishing?

On top of that, the dream never recurred, and isn't that what those psychic warnings are supposed to do, don't they repeat themselves to prove their seriousness? I suppose it remained sufficiently clear in my memory not to need repeating; if I pondered it at all, however, it was as a curiosity of my own psyche, a peculiarity my mind had thrown up from its depths. I'd been a bit lax in visiting Marie's grave that winter. I assumed the dream had more to do with that than any real place, or person. Nor, for what it's worth, did I connect my dream of Marie with her visits to me while I was fishing; the thought never even occurred to me.

Dan's appearance, his state of mind, that Sunday night were the first signs of a change that overtook him during the next couple of months. To this day, I'm not sure exactly what triggered it, but his grief, kept at bay so long, found a way to tunnel under Dan's defenses, and, while he was otherwise distracted, seized the moment and fell on him, burying its dirty teeth deep in his gut and refusing to let go. Dan wore the same suit and tie for days at a time. A scraggly beard surged and ebbed across his face. His hair, longer still, frequently jutted out in strange configurations. His hours at work became erratic, to say the least. Some mornings he wouldn't show up until nine or nine thirty; others, he'd be at his desk by quarter to seven. Even on those days he was in well ahead of the rest of us, he'd spend most of his time staring at the screen of the computer he hadn't switched on yet. His stare, that look that I had felt wanted to pierce through you, worsened to the point it was next to impossible to hold any kind of conversation with him. He didn't appear to be listening to anything you were saying, just boring into you with those eyes that had been turned all the way up, blowtorch bright. He never left work later than the rest of us, and it wasn't unusual to walk by his office at the end of the day and find it empty.

Before long, his job was in serious jeopardy. He'd been team leader on a pair of important projects, one of which demoted him, while the other dropped him outright. The company had changed. This was not, as management had started trumpeting, your father's IBM, which I guess meant it wasn't my IBM. The notion of a corporate family that took care of its own and in so doing earned their loyalty was on the way out, evicted by simple greed. What this meant practically speaking was that Dan could not be assured of the same understanding and indulgence I had received more than a decade prior. That he didn't much care if he kept his job or not at this moment didn't mean he wouldn't feel differently in the future, and I did my best to make him see this. He wasn't much interested in what I had to say. His grief had taken him far into a country whose borders are all most folks ever see, and from where he was, caught up in that dark land's customs and concerns, what I was worrying over sounded so foreign I might as well have been speaking another language.

If you'd asked me, after my second try at speaking to him, whether I thought Dan would be around when fishing season started that spring, I'd have told you flat-out, "No." Frank Block had been unceremoniously let go the previous month, escorted from the building by a pair of security goons when he started to yell that this wasn't right, he deserved better than this. My own manager, a young fellow whose chief qualification for his position must have been his smarminess, since it was the only quality he possessed in abundance—my manager had taken to dropping none-too-subtle hints that the company was offering exceedingly generous severance packages to those who were wise enough to take them. It wasn't just the night of the long knives. Up and down the corridors of our building, it was days and weeks and months of management given leave to slice down to the bone and keep going. And in the midst of this carnage, here was Dan, laying his head on the chopping block and holding out the axe for anyone who was interested. I'd have been wrong in my prediction, though. Somehow, Dan held onto his job. No matter what shape he was in, Dan was a bright guy—graduated near top of his class at M.I.T.—and I guess he must have contributed enough for it to have been worth more to keep him on board than it was to throw him to the sharks.

I wonder, sometimes, if we'd have gone fishing that spring if Dan and I hadn't been working together. He hadn't returned to my house since that night in February. I'd invited him over a few times, but he'd always claimed to be constrained by this or that obligation—though their visits had fallen off from what they had been, both his and Sophie's families still made sporadic attempts to visit him, which always seemed to coincide with my invitations to him. He never offered to have me over. I was pretty sure he was embarrassed about everything that had happened, yet I couldn't see a way to tell him he shouldn't be without stirring those memories up for him and making him uncomfortable all over again. My warnings to him about his job aside, I did my best to respect the distance he demanded.

With some measure of surprise, then, I returned from lunch one day about two weeks from the start of trout season to find Dan waiting in my office, perched on the edge of my desk like a big, skinny gargoyle. "Hi, Abe," he said.

"Hello, Dan," I said. "What can I do for you?"

"How long is it till trout season starts?"

"Thirteen days," I said. "If you give me a minute, I can tell you how many hours and minutes on top of that."

"Are you going?"

"Dan," I protested, "how could you ask such a question?"

He didn't smile. "Would you mind some company?"

"I'm counting on it," I said, which wasn't exactly true. I hadn't been sure Dan would be joining me this year. Given his embarrassment over February, combined with his general remove from everyone of late, I'd assumed there was a better than likely chance he'd want to do any fishing he had in mind on his own, and so hadn't raised the subject with him.

"That's good," Dan said. "Thank you."

"Don't mention it. Where would I be without my fishing buddy?"

"Can I tell you something?" he asked, shifting forward as he did.

"Sure."

"I've been dreaming about fishing," he said. "A lot."

"I dream about it, too," I said, "although most of my reverie occurs in the middle of meetings."

Dan's eyes, which had widened at the news of my dreaming, narrowed at my joke. "Right," he said, the slightest annoyance curdling his voice. He stood from the desk and asked, "Are you going to the Svartkil?"

I nodded. "It's where I kick off every season. Kind of a tradition, you know?"

"Fine, of course," he said. "And after that? Are you going back up the Catskills?"

"Indeed I am. There's a couple of new streams I'm looking forward to trying out."

"Good," he said. "I might want to suggest one myself—if that's all right with you."

"That would be great. Where did you have in mind?"

"Dutchman's Creek," he said. If this had been a movie, I guess this would have been the moment ominous music boomed on the soundtrack. As it was, there was only the din of people talking as they continued to make their way back from lunch. Dan continued, "Have you heard of it?"

"Can't say I have. Where is it?"

"Up around Woodstock. It runs out of the Reservoir to the Hudson."

"Sounds like a possibility, then. How'd you come across it?"

"In a book."

As a rule, I am one of the worst people I know when it comes to sniffing out a lie. Throughout my life, my family and friends have exploited this almost limitless gullibility by playing an almost endless number of practical jokes on me, some of which would make you shake your head in pity. Right then, however, I knew Dan was lying. I can't say how I knew, since it wasn't as if he rubbed his hands together and shifted his eyes from side to side, but I was sure enough to say, "Really?"

"Really," he said, frowning at my tone.

"Which book?" I asked, unable to figure why he would feel the need to lie about such a thing.

"Alf Evers's history of the Catskills," he said. "Do you know it?"

"No," I admitted, "can't say as I do." Although I was certain Dan was lying, equally certain he'd named Alf Evers's book because I'd told him I didn't read much, and what did pass beneath my gaze tended to split between spy thrillers and Louis L'Amours, I couldn't see how it made much difference where he'd found the name of this creek. Maybe he'd had it from a woman he met at a bar, and was ashamed to reveal such a source. As long as the stream was where he said it was and the fish were biting, what difference did it make? I said, "Well, then, we'll have to add Dutchman's Creek to our itinerary."

My decision, minor though it seemed to me, pleased Dan past all measure. His face brightened, and he shook his head up and down happily, saying, "Yes we will, Abe, yes we will." Our plans made, it was back to work. We agreed to meet at the usual spot on Springvale the Saturday after next. Dan volunteered to bring coffee and donuts.

That night, I sought out Dutchman's Creek in my Ulster County Atlas, which took me longer than it should have, since the creek had no listing in the book's index. This struck me as a little odd. In general, the Atlas is pretty detailed. I had to leaf through, find the pages mapping the Ashokan Reservoir, and search its borders. My finger passed over the spot where the creek flowed out of the Reservoir at least twice, but on the third try I found it. When I did, I couldn't believe I hadn't seen the creek right away. It was hard to miss, a blue thread winding its way from the Reservoir's south shore over to the Hudson, running well north of Wiltwyck, south of Saugerties. I traced its course with my index finger, something I like to do for a place I'm going to fish. Dutchman's Creek kinked and twisted, almost looping back on itself a couple of times. I figured this would provide the fish a host of spots to congregate. As my finger followed the creek's perambulations, I wondered where it drew its name from. All up and down the Hudson, from Manhattan to Albany, originally had been settled by the Dutch, and you still find a fair number of towns on both sides of the river whose names show it: Peekskill, Newburgh, Fishkill. I hadn't studied the matter, of course, but it seemed to me that, while you found a lot of places named by the Dutch, you didn't find many named for them. In fact, aside from this creek, I couldn't think of one. *Who was the Dutchman?* I wondered, closing the Atlas.

I had an answer to that question two months later, while Dan and I sat at the counter of Herman's Diner on Route 28, just west of Wiltwyck. Dan had wanted to stop there for a cup of coffee and breakfast on the way up to the creek, which he did from time to time. I prefer to eat before I leave the house or, if I'm hungry, to order my egg and cheese sandwich to go. On the occasions Dan wanted to stop for breakfast, he liked to sit down and study the menu, order a plate of something he hadn't had before, the Greek omelet, the walnut pancakes. Had he done so too often, I suspect it would have become an issue. However, his requests that we sacrifice a half-hour at this or that diner were few and far enough between for me to say to myself, *What the hell. It's been a while since I had any walnut pancakes, and maybe a side of sausage would be nice with them.* Besides, I guessed from my own history that Dan wasn't eating as well as he should have been, so I figured at least he'd have one decent meal today.

This morning, there was no rush for us to arrive streamside. For the better part of the last week, the sky had been crowded with gray clouds that dumped so much rain on us I swear you needed gills to walk around outside. The rain had tapered off late the night before, but the clouds had not yet departed the sky, and I reckoned any stream we wanted to fish was going to be swollen and fast-running, dim with mud and debris. There are those fishermen who'll tell you that, after the kind of downpour we'd had, you might as well wait a day or two till you cast your line, but I'm among the "a bad day of fishing is still better than a good day of just about anything else" crowd. I was then, anyway, which was why we had driven out west of Wiltwyck on Route 28 at the usual pre-dawn time, Dutchman's Creek our destination. On the way, we'd stopped at Herman's Diner.

Herman's was off to the right-hand side of the road, the last building in a sequence that included a combination gas station/car wash, a furniture warehouse, and an ice cream stand. The diner sat at the center of an otherwise empty lot, one of those silver boxcars that you associate with the nineteen-fifties. It's empty now, out of business for the last several years, which I can't understand, because, while Herman's was small, most times I went in, it was jumping. You never saw Herman. In fact, I'm not sure there was a Herman any more. There were Caitlin and Liz, who worked the counter and the single row of booths, and there was Howard, who did the lion's share of the cooking, helped out by a pair of Mexican cousins named Esteban and Pedro. What I like about the place, what had kept me coming back after I first discovered it the second summer I fished, even more than the food, was the décor. The diner's inside had been done up in early fisherman. There were rods and nets hung on the walls among what must have been thousands of snapshots of guys with fish. There were a few of those fish, too, stuffed and mounted in places of pride. As you walked in, a bulletin board tacked full of fishing cartoons greeted you, some of them freshly clipped from the paper, others yellow and brittle with age. The one I liked best was several years old, and showed a pair of man-sized cartoon salmon standing beside a stream, one smoking a cigar, the other holding a beer. Both fish have lines out and in the water, which is full of tiny people, dozens of them heading upstream, arms against their sides, faces pointed straight ahead. That was all: no witty caption, only that simple reversal that tickled my funny bone. Every time I strolled into that diner, I chuckled, and despite what happened later that day, thinking about that drawing now brings a smile to my face. Dan didn't find it especially amusing.

The strangest thing in the diner, and it's worth remarking if for no other reason than that I studied it each time I ate there, was a large oil painting that hung above and to the left of the order window as you sat at the counter. This painting was so old, so begrimed with the smoke of a thousand omelets and hamburgers, that only by diligent and careful study could you begin to develop an idea of its subject. The canvas was such a mess of masses of shades and shadows that I half-suspected it was some kind of giant Rorschach Test. Where it hung wasn't especially well-lit, which didn't help matters any. You could make out a long, curving, black blotch of something hovering in the middle of the picture over a pale patch, with a wavy white line in the upper right-hand corner. You might think I would've looked at the painting, seen that I couldn't make head or tail of it, and let that be that. But there was something about it, this quality, that I don't know if I have the words for. The picture fascinated me; I guess because it was so close to showing you what it was, so close to revealing its meaning. Maybe it was a big Rorschach Test. I saw a different scene each time I sat down at the counter. Once, it must have been the first time I stopped at Herman's, I saw a bird swooping down out of the sky, a crow, maybe. Another time, I thought it might be a bat. Then, since the rest of the diner was done up in fishing memorabilia, I decided the painting must be a fishing scene. Throughout these deliberations, I received absolutely no help from the diner's staff, who told me they weren't sure where the painting had come from. Howard had an idea it had been purchased from an inn somewhere in New England—out Mystic way, he seemed to recall—but didn't know any more than that, except that nobody could tell what the hell it showed. Liz and Caitlin refused to be drawn into discussing it, despite my best efforts.

That morning, when Dan and I sat down at the counter and ordered our coffees, with no help from anyone else I saw a fish in the black blotch at the painting's center, something long, serpentine, a pike, say. The fish had been hooked, and was twisting as it fought its fate. The more I looked at the painting as I sat there drinking my coffee, the more sure I was that, at long last and after much cogitation, I had solved its mystery. In my solution, I saw a good omen for the day of fishing ahead. I was seized by the momentary impulse to tell somebody my discovery, share my success, but Dan had just stood to visit the facilities, and the rest of the diner was empty. By the time Dan returned, the impulse had released me.

As I glanced around the diner, looking for someone to decode the painting to, I noticed the air outside, which had been lightening with the first traces of a weak dawn, dimming; the first drops of rain spattered the windows a moment later. I didn't groan, but I felt like it. I'll fish in the rain—Hell, I'd fish in the snow—but that doesn't mean I especially care to. I suppose a light drizzle isn't so bad, but the kind of rain that was crackling on the diner's roof, the hard, driving kind that soaks you through in under a minute and then keeps on going, that is not my idea of fun. Maybe it would turn out to be a passing squall. But by the time Liz set my corned beef hash and scrambled eggs down in front of me, if anything, the rain had strengthened into a wall of water.

While we were sitting over our breakfasts, Howard emerged from the kitchen to pour himself a cup of coffee and chat with us. I'd seen him do this from time to time: I'm pretty sure that he owned the diner, and I think this was his version of customer relations. I'd had a brief conversation with him two or three years prior, though I wasn't sure he remembered. We hadn't done more than exchange pleasantries about the weather, which was warm and sunny, and how the fish were biting, which they were. After that, he'd nodded whenever he saw me, but I noticed that he nodded at pretty much everyone who walked into the diner. He was a tall fellow, Howard, with long arms that ended in oversized hands. His face was what my ma would have called unhandsome. It wasn't that he was ugly, exactly, more sort of homely. He had a lantern jaw that made him look as if he were perpetually holding something in his mouth that was too hot to swallow. His skin was pale and had that worn look you see on someone who's been a steady smoker for most of their life. His voice was low and rumbling, and from conversations I'd overheard him having with other guys, I knew he was reasonably sharp, enough so for me to wonder what he was doing cooking in a diner. I never did find out the answer to that one.

Anyway, Howard stood there, the chunky white coffee cup swallowed in one of his enormous hands, the dingy white chef's hat he favored tilted back on his head, and wished us both a good morning. When we returned the greeting, he went on, "Some weather we've been having."

Dan grunted from his cup. I said, "You can say that again. Streams'll be running pretty high, I imagine."

"Lot of flooding," Howard said. "Pretty bad in places. You fellows planning on fishing?"

"We are," I said.

Howard grimaced. "Can't say it's the day for it. Where you headed?"

"Dutchman's Creek," I answered. On impulse, I added, "Ever hear of it?"

Probably, I could count on one hand the number of times something I've said has caused a person to turn pale. Most of those cases would hail from my childhood, when I told one or both of my folks a particularly worrisome piece of news: that I had stepped on a nail in the basement; that kind of thing. Well, add that Saturday morning in early June to the list. Howard's pale skin went paler, as if you'd poured a glass of milk over a bowl of oatmeal. His eyed widened, and his mouth opened, as if whatever he kept in there couldn't believe its ears, either. He raised his coffee cup to his mouth, finished its contents, and went for a refill. I looked at Dan, who was staring straight ahead as he chewed a mouthful of Belgian waffle, his face formed to an expression I couldn't get a purchase on.

Howard poured a generous helping of sugar into his refill, and, without stirring it, turned back to us. His voice calm, his face still pale, he said, "Dutchman's Creek, huh?"

"That's right," I said.

"Not many folks know about the creek anymore. How'd you hear about it?"

"My friend here read about it," I said.

"Is that so?" Howard asked Dan.

"Yeah," Dan said, chewing his waffle.

"Where would that have been?"

"Alf Evers's book on the Catskills." He did not look at Howard.

"That's a good book," Howard said, and I noticed Dan's back stiffen. "Good history. I don't recall anything about the creek in it."

"It's in the chapter on the Reservoir," Dan said.

"Ah—that's where it would be, wouldn't it? I must've forgot," Howard said, the tone of his voice telling us there was no way he'd done any such thing. "I'll have to have another read of old Alf's book. It's got some good stories in it. Since my memory obviously isn't what it used to be, maybe you can tell me what else Alf says about the creek. Does he tell how it got its name?"

"No," Dan said, finishing his waffle. "He doesn't mention that."

"What about the fellows who died there. Does he mention them?"

Dan's head jerked up. "No."

"Hmmm," Howard said, rubbing his jaw with his free hand. "I guess Alf Evers wasn't as thorough as I thought."

"Died?" I asked.

"Yes," Howard said. "Been a few folks met their maker up at the creek. Seems the banks are steeper than they look, and the soil's pretty loose. On top of that, the creek's deep and fast-moving. All of which means it's easier than you'd think to take a tumble into the water and not come up again."

"How many have drowned?" I asked.

"Half-dozen, seven or eight, easy," Howard said, "and I'm just talking about in the time I've been here," he gestured to the diner with his mug, "say, in the last twenty years or so. I don't know what the exact total is beyond that, but I understand from some of the old-timers that the creek's taken enough men to put much bigger streams to shame. Mostly out-of-towners, folks from down the City come up here for the weekend. The locals tend to know better than to try the creek, though every now and then some high school kid'll decide to prove how brave he is to his friends or some girl and go tempting the waters. When he does—well, the creek isn't all that discriminating. It'll take whatever's on the plate, if you know what I mean. The old-timers say the creek's hungry, and from what I've heard, I'd agree."

"How did it get its name?" Dan asked.

"Beg pardon?" Howard said.

"You asked if we knew how Dutchman's Creek got its name," Dan said, "so I assume you do. Right?"

"That's right," Howard said. "It's quite the story. Some'd call it local legend, but there's more to it than that. It is long...longer than you'd think."

"I'm curious," Dan said. "I'm sure Abe is, too. Aren't you?"

I was—curious enough, anyway. Howard's warning had made me wonder what all the fuss was about. I was curious as well about the currents I felt flowing between him and Dan. Not outright hostility, exactly: it was more like Dan was afraid Howard was going to reveal something he wanted kept hidden, and Howard was annoyed at Dan for whatever that secret was. At the same time, we had come up here to fish. A glance back over my shoulder, though, showed the rain continuing. I sighed. "I suppose so," I said. "I'm always happy to hear a good story, legend though it may be. But we don't want to keep you."

"I guess Esteban and Pedro can manage for a few more minutes. Besides, it's not as if we're all that busy." He nodded at the diner, but for us, still empty. Caitlin and Liz sat together at a booth, Caitlin smoking, Liz reading the paper. "Strange, for a Saturday. Even with the rain, there's usually some folks come in for breakfast." He shrugged. "Almost like I'm supposed to tell it to you fellows, isn't it?" The tone of his voice was casual, but I was suddenly aware of a tremendous, heavy urgency behind it, as if the story he had promised were heaving itself towards us. For a moment, I was possessed by the almost irresistible urge to flee him and his tale, to throw whatever money was in my pocket onto the counter and run out into the downpour. Then he said, "Understand, I can't vouch for any of this," and I was caught.

What Howard told us next took the better part of an hour, during which the diner was as still as a church, sealed off from the world beyond by the wall of water pouring from the sky. His story was long, certainly the longest I've had from one man at one time. While he was telling it, I couldn't believe how much he'd remembered, how many details of speech and act, of thought and intent, and a little voice inside my head kept whispering, "This is impossible. There's no way anyone could have a memory this accurate, this precise. He's inventing this. He has to be." And although I'd had some strange experiences myself, the events Howard related made the weirdest of them seem plain as a cup of coffee and a slice of apple pie.

Funny thing is, while he was telling his tale, I believed much more than I would have guessed likely. Only once his voice had stopped was I convinced I'd just been buried under the greatest load of horseshit anyone ever had shoveled. Yet even after Dan and I had paid for our meals and left the diner and were continuing our drive to the creek, it was as if I were still listening to Howard's voice, as if I were inside his story, looking out at everything, as the story uncoiled around me.

If I say there was more truth to Howard's tale than I first believed, I don't suppose it'll come as much surprise. What I find almost as remarkable is that I can recall pretty much everything Howard said, verbatim. Given what was to happen to Dan and me, maybe that isn't such a surprise. But I can recall everything Howard didn't say, as well:

Some months after all this, when the summer turned hot and dry, I sat down at the kitchen table, a pen in one hand, a pad of legal paper in front of me. Howard's story had been gnawing at me for weeks, and I had decided to write down what I could remember of it. I expected the task would take me an afternoon, maybe a little longer. How long could it take you to write down an hour's worth of talking, right? I've never been much of a writer, and I spent as much time lining things out as I did putting them down, but I wanted to copy down everything I could recall of what Howard had said, get all of it exactly right. By the time the first night had rolled around, my hand was still moving that pen across the paper. For the next four days, I wrote. I wrote and I wrote and I wrote, and I understood that the story had passed to me, that somehow, Howard had tucked it inside me.

In the process, it had brought details with it Howard hadn't included, enough that they would have stretched what he told us through the rest of the morning and right through the afternoon into the evening. All sorts of tangents about the figures whose stories he was relating, Lottie Schmidt and her father, Rainer, as well as stories about men and women he hadn't mentioned, at all, like Otto Schalken and Miller Jeffries, crowded the pages. And yet, at the same time, every last detail I wrote down seemed familiar. I had the maddening sense that, even though Howard hadn't related anything like the complete story to us, I had carried it with me out of the diner all the same, had known it—or maybe been known by it, folded into its embrace.

I offer that much longer version of the story here, when and where we were first introduced to its principle players. Doing so means stepping away from my own tale for a lot more time than I'd like. Without what I can't help calling Howard's story, however, everything that happened to Dan and me, all that badness that found us out and chased us down, makes far less sense than it does with it. Maybe that isn't saying so much. You might imagine Dan and me sitting somewhere off to the side of the drama that's about to debut, while Howard points out to us who's who and what's what. Or maybe you should imagine us walking the margins, watching the story unfold across the page.

This is what I received from Howard, whose last name I never did learn:

PART 2:

DER FISCHER:
A TALE OF TERROR

I

I had most of it [Howard said] from Reverend Mapple. He was minister at the Lutheran Church in Woodstock, and what you'd call a local history buff. After I heard the story I'm going to tell you, I did some rooting around in different books, histories, that kind of thing, so I think the Reverend was onto something. He used to come in here early on a Sunday morning, before his services, for his Sunday breakfast. Big fellow, barrel-chested, looked more like a circus strongman than a man of the cloth. He had this long fuzzy beard like something you see in the pictures of those guys from the Civil War, you know?

Anyway, the Reverend got curious about the Creek. I'm not sure how exactly. Something he overheard one of the older members of his congregation say, I think, that stirred up his interest. He asked me about it one Sunday morning, but I was new here myself, just come down from Providence, where I'd made a go at writing a novel no one wanted to publish. I told the Reverend I couldn't help him, but added that he was right, the locals were kind of funny when it came to that creek. I like to do a spot of fishing myself, in case you didn't notice, and the one time I'd mentioned trying out the creek, which I'd stumbled across on a map, a couple of customers had done their level best persuading me you couldn't pull anything worth eating out of it. They'd been emphatic, and the thing was, these guys weren't that old—you expect weird advice from old guys, right?—in fact, they were younger than I was, barely out of high school. They raised my curiosity, yes, but they spooked me, too. I tried to learn what more I could, asked some of the regulars, the older fellows, what they knew, but no one was talking.

Reverend Mapple had an idea. Part of his duties as minister included making the rounds to visit the sick members of the congregation. Some were in the hospital; some were shut in at home. Like me, he realized that, if anyone would know what the story behind the creek was, it would be the old people. He hadn't had any luck getting them talking when he saw them together at church or in town, try though he did. But he thought if he could talk to one of them alone, his chances would be better. Like I said, he was a big man, and his presence could be pretty imposing. Hell, he almost had me going to his church, and I was raised Catholic. I guess his plan makes him sound a bit cold-blooded, doesn't it? I suppose it was, at that.

Even speaking to people one-on-one, though, in the privacies of their own homes, he had the devil's own time learning anything. The most anyone wanted to say was a handful of words, and few said that much. He did learn that the stream had originally been called "Deutschman's Creek," as in German's Creek; it's like the Pennsylvania Dutch, you know? Same thing. One old lady said her daddy had made reference to it as *Der Platz das Fischer,"* but she wasn't sure what the words meant. When she asked her pa, he gave her about the only beating she ever had.

The Reverend looked the words up. As you might have guessed, they were German, too, and meant something like "the place of the fisherman."

[At the word "Fischer," I had the briefest sensation of *déjà vu*, as if I'd heard that word once before, as if I'd dreamed it, and hearing Howard pronounce it, it was as if my dreams and my waking life had momentarily overlapped. I shook my head.]

To make a long story short—well, to make this part of a long story short—the Reverend was asking questions for a good year before he found any answers. These came from an old woman. Her name was Lottie, Lottie Schmidt. He went to visit her down in Fishkill. Her family had put her in a nursing home down there; I think so she'd be close to them. Yeah—her son was a guard at Downstate Correctional. Reverend Mapple would go to visit her every other week, because she asked for him and because he was that kind of man. He'd asked her about the creek, of course, and like everyone else she hadn't had anything to say.

Until this one Saturday. Lottie'd been sliding downhill at a pretty brisk clip ever since she'd been put in the home. That kind of thing happens to a lot of old folks, doesn't it? Whether she had Alzheimer's, was going senile, or had just decided to give up the ghost, I can't say, but it wasn't too long before the Reverend found it a challenge to do much more than pray with her when he visited. Sometimes, after they were done praying, he'd talk to her, although from the blank look on her face he suspected it was mostly a case of him talking at her. Still, as he said to me once, "There may be someone in there, Howard, way deep down, and it's important to let them know they haven't been forgotten." So he'd ramble on about his life, tell her what he'd been up to since he'd been around last.

He got to talking about his researches into the creek, asking her did she remember him asking her about it and her not telling him anything? Well, he'd finally learned something: it wasn't much, but it was a start. He'd found out about *Deutschman's* Creek, he said, and *Der Platz das Fischer.*

The Reverend had turned away from Lottie while he was speaking. He was filling a paper cup from the sink in the corner of the room. When he turned back around, the cup held to his mouth, what he saw made him jump and spill his water all over himself. There was Lottie standing not two feet away, her eyes open and clear and fixed on him. Reverend Mapple was speechless. He hadn't heard her get out of bed, cross the floor to him, anything. Before he could say anything, Lottie said, "That is a bad place, Reverend. It is a bad place, and you should not be asking about it." Her voice—well, that only made everything that much stranger. Lottie's parents had been German and Lottie herself had been born over there. The family had moved when she was a girl; although her English was fine, she had never completely lost her accent. You'd hear reminders of it every once in a while. When she prayed the Lord's Prayer with the Reverend, "Father" was "Fadter," that kind of thing. Now, Lottie spoke as if English were a language she was still trying to master, as if her mouth were still full of German. That wasn't all. Lottie had what you might call a typical little-old-lady voice, kind of high-pitched and crackly, like your grandmother's. It had vanished, replaced with a strong, clear voice, the voice of someone six decades younger.

Thrown as he was by all of this, the Reverend managed to ask Lottie why *Deutschman's* Creek was such a bad place. His curiosity was that strong. At first, Lottie wouldn't say anything, just shook her head and refused to look at him. Finally, he said, "Now Lottie, you can't tell me the creek is bad and not say any more. That isn't fair. In fact," the Reverend said, "that kind of talk makes me think I should take a stroll out that way, see what all the fuss is about." Without exactly intending to, he'd lapsed into talking to Lottie as if she were a girl again.

When he threatened to visit the Creek, Lottie near lost her mind. She grabbed Reverend Mapple's hands and said he mustn't, he couldn't, it was too awful, it was terrible, and then a flood of German came pouring out of her, all of it, I'm sure, saying more of the same. She was truly agitated, the Reverend said, it was all he could do to keep her from collapsing into sobs. She kept asking him—begging him to promise he wouldn't go to the Creek. For sheer pity's sake he almost promised, too. But Lottie's agitation—well, it seemed like proof there must be one hell of a story connected to Dutchman's Creek. Suddenly, the Reverend was on the verge of finding out the answer to the question that had been obsessing him for the past twelve months, and you can appreciate how that feels. He told Lottie the only way he was going to know if he should avoid the Creek was if someone told him the truth about it, the whole story, and didn't hold anything back. Then, if he thought the reason was sound, he'd give Dutchman's Creek a wide berth.

Lottie still held out. Her father, she claimed, had sworn her to secrecy. At that, the Reverend lost his temper a little bit, and said, "Am I not a minister of the Lord? Are not all things disclosed to Almighty God? Is there anything that can be hidden from Him? And if the Lord God knows all, then should His minister not be trusted with a secret?" When he told me about this later, Reverend Mapple looked kind of sheepish. I guess ministers have their own temptations.

Wrong or not, his outburst convinced Lottie. She would tell him, she said, but he must promise not to judge the men in her story too harshly. Her father had been one of them, and whatever she thought of what he'd been part of, she loved him and would not have him thought poorly of because of any tale she might tell. Yes, yes, the Reverend promised, of course.

II

The story Lottie told began before her family had departed the old country. She didn't know much of what had occurred while she was still a child in Germany—before she or either of her parents were born. Reverend Mapple pieced most of that together after he had Lottie's story, from visiting local libraries and museums, digging through archives, reading old newspapers and letters. Where most of it took place is under three hundred feet of water now, out beneath the Reservoir. I'm sure you fellows know that the Reservoir dates back to the First World War. Before that, it was the Esopus river valley, with eleven and a half towns in it. From west to east, you had Boiceville, West Shokan, Shokan, Broadhead's Bridge, Olive City, Olive Bridge, Brown's Station, Olive, Olive Branch, Glenford, and West Hurley. West-northwest of West Hurley was a half-dozen houses some people called Hurley Station, others the Station. A lot of folks didn't call it anything, either because they didn't know it was there or because they assumed it was part of West Hurley. It wasn't, though. Near as the Reverend could figure, the Station had been there first, built a good few decades prior to the settlers who streamed into the area in the early seventeen-hundreds. When the town had been put up, the Catskills were still Indian country, and that's no exaggeration. Twice the tribes swept down from the mountains and burned Wiltwyck. The families who founded the Station were Dutch. I don't know what led them to that spot, except that the Dutch as a whole kept moving further north up the Hudson to get away from newer settlers. Why those families called their settlement the Station is something of a mystery as well, since the railroad was close enough to two centuries in the future when they started clearing the land for their stone houses. The name could have had to do with the spring they built the town around. Reverend Mapple guessed that traders and trappers might have used the place as a way station on their journeys up from Wiltwyck.

Anyway, as far as the record shows, the Indians left the Station alone. And for a long time, until the eighteen-forties, not much of interest happened there. The other towns in the Esopus valley grew up around it. The hemlock tanneries were established and became a thriving concern—that was the big business here, the tanneries. Then, one summer's day, this man comes riding out of the west, along the turnpike. He isn't much to look at. Even for the time, he's a little fellow, with black, stringy hair—kind of greasy—and a black, stringy beard that hangs down from his chin like a cheap disguise. His features are delicate, boyish, even, what you can see of them under the wide brim of his hat. He's dressed in a black suit that's been whitened by the dust of too many days on the road. This man comes riding on a one-horse cart, and there isn't much remarkable about either horse—a brown nag that's wearing the same thick coat of dust as the man's clothes—or the cart. Oh, except for the cart's wheels: apparently, their rims are twice as thick as they need to be, and covered in pictures. Actually, this is a little unclear. Some folks who see the man making his slow way along the turnpike say that the wheels are wrapped around with symbols like hieroglyphs, you know? While others declare that the wheels are decorated with pictures that look like writing but aren't. A language that looks like pictures, or pictures that look like language: whichever it is, everyone who studies the cart for any length of time agrees that whatever is on those broad wheels seems to move in a way that isn't quite in sync with their turning. When greeted, the stranger doesn't say much, doesn't volunteer his name, certainly. If you call out hello, he'll touch the brim of his hat to you. If you ask him where he's coming from, he'll answer, "The western mountains," and that's that, won't tell if he means Oneonta or Syracuse or what. His English isn't too clear, his speech refracted by a heavy accent that folks think sounds German, though there's debate about the matter. He rides up the turnpike for several days, meandering along at what is, by any standards, a snail's pace. A few kids from the various towns along the way who're ducking their chores try to spy on his cart from up in trees along the side of the road, but they're out of luck. Everything is in boxes and bags and under tarps, none of it marked except for one sizable crate covered with the same strange markings as the cart's wheels. One daring lad tries for the stranger's hat with an apple, but the branch he's standing on snaps just as he throws, and the missile flies wide. He breaks his arm for his trouble, that boy. The stranger, who's moving slowly enough to hear the boy's cries for a good long while, ignores them.

Finally, the fellow takes the turn off for Hurley Station. By now, most of the residents of the towns up and down the Esopus have heard about this man in his black suit. A good portion of them could describe him better than I can, regardless of whether they've seen him in the flesh. Something about the man sets people's interest boiling. When the stranger halts his horse at Cornelius Dort's front door, speculation, already at a brisk canter, runs riot. The Dorts are one of the six families who founded the Station. When the foundations were dug and the first stones laid, they were the wealthiest, and that's a condition time has only improved. The Dort estate, I guess you'd call it, is considerable, as are their holdings in and around the area. Cornelius is in charge of the lot; there was a younger brother, Henrick, but he left as a young man and didn't return—lost on a whaling ship, was the report. There's a portrait of Cornelius, a painting, hanging in City Hall in Wiltwyck today. Seems in his younger days he was quite friendly with one of the mayors, so much so that he gifted the man with an addition to his house. What Cornelius received in exchange for this I don't know; aside from his picture in City Hall, I mean. Maybe that was all, though I doubt it. The portrait's not that good. It makes Cornelius look just a little more mad than you think he would have wanted. His eyes are open too wide, and his eyebrows climb halfway up his forehead, which is saying something. I think the artist, whose name escapes me at the moment, meant Cornelius's mouth to look stern, but it wobbles at one end, so it's more like he's on the verge of laughing or crying. Honestly, the more you look at the thing, the more you wonder how Cornelius didn't have the man who painted it horsewhipped. Graves, that was the artist's name. Did I mention the hair? This great wave of red hair that looks as if it's rearing up to strike. I guess it's lucky for Mr. Graves Cornelius Dort wasn't much of an art critic.

Because he's that kind of man. He'll horsewhip you himself if he thinks you've wronged him, and his definition of what constitutes wronging him is pretty loose. No one cares for him much. No one ever has. He's stern and unfriendly, a shrewd businessman who's increased his family's fortune through a series of deals that have forced more than one family from their land. When the stranger climbs down from his cart and walks to Cornelius's front door—moving no more quickly by foot that he did by cart—you can be sure anyone watching—mostly kids, hiding in the trees—expects him to make a quick and painful acquaintance with the toe of Cornelius's boot.

When that doesn't happen, when the heavy door opens and admits the man and he doesn't come running out two minutes later, Cornelius close behind, yelling at him to peddle his wares elsewhere—well, there's a fair amount of head-scratching. Then someone snaps his or her fingers and says, "Beatrice," which is immediately picked up by everyone else. You can practically hear the fingers snapping in succession like a row of dominoes falling, the mouths saying the name, "Beatrice," as if, "Of course." Beatrice is Cornelius's young wife, a pretty girl a good twenty years his junior who accepted his proposal, popular legend has it, to forestall him taking her father's hotel over in Woodstock. It's a cliché to say she's the apple of everyone's eye, but there you have it. Spring past, she was pregnant with the couple's first child, an event that seemed to sand the ragged edges off Cornelius just the slightest. You saw her all over the place, a tall girl with pale, milky skin and black hair. She liked to ride. Story goes, that was how she first caught Cornelius's eye, riding up the road to his front door to plead her father's case. When she fell pregnant, she didn't stop riding, despite her doctor's warning to the contrary, and that was how disaster struck. While she was on her way to visit her sister in Hurley, her horse, which she'd raised from a foal, spooked and threw her into a tree. She lost the baby, and fell into a lingering sickness she's been unable to pull herself out of. After first hacking Bea's horse to death with one of the axes for the woodpile—his face calm, the stablehand said, icily calm—Cornelius went through every doctor in the area—not a few of whom have felt the toe of his boot—before bringing in the specialists from Albany. When they proved unable to help, he brought in men from New York, Boston, Philadelphia. A steady stream of doctors young and old has tramped up the path to Cornelius's front door and tramped back down it. No one has had anything to offer. Whatever is wrong with little Bea, as folks call her, it's beyond the scope of the medicine of the day. Beatrice has grown worse, and Cornelius has grown more desperate.

The newcomer moves in with the Dorts the same day he arrives. Theirs is a large house, and Cornelius pretty much gives the second storey of it to the man, so the maid says. What the stranger promises Cornelius in return, that maid can't say, since the door to the library, where they spoke, was very deliberately shut, but most assume it's little Bea's recovery.

That assumption is wrong. Two days after the stranger's arrival, Beatrice's struggle comes to an end. She's buried in the cemetery of the Dutch Reformed Church down in West Hurley; though it takes her two full weeks to get there. That's a long time, in the first half of the nineteenth century. I guess it still is, but there's no embalming like we have, you know? Especially in the hot summer—and this summer's a scorcher—you don't want to leave the dead out of the ground too long. After Bea's been gone about a week and no word yet of a funeral, folks start talking, amongst themselves, of course, since, even in his grief, Cornelius continues to inspire respect and fear. There's word that Beatrice's father plans to talk to Cornelius, demand he release his daughter back to him for burial with her family, but after a day that proves to be only rumor. In the afterlife, it seems, as in this life, little Bea's family have abandoned her to Cornelius. Finally, when the second week draws to a close, the minister at the West Hurley Reformed Church—Reverend Pied is the fellow's name—screws up his courage and rides to the Station to tell Cornelius what's what. No one's known Cornelius to offend against a man of the cloth, but that's what everyone who sees the minister, a tall fellow come all the way from Amsterdam, riding to the Dort house expects. To everyone's surprise, Cornelius agrees with the minister's request straight away, says that Bea can be buried tomorrow if Reverend Pied thinks he can be ready. The minister figures he'd best take advantage of his good fortune, so says yes, without a doubt, and that's the matter settled. The stranger is nowhere to be seen.

Those who attend little Bea's funeral, a surprising number, given the suddenness of it, report that Cornelius appears bored with the whole thing. He's never struck anyone as the most devout of men, unless money is the god in question, but he's always known the value of keeping up appearances. You may kick folks up and down your front walk; you may maneuver them out of their businesses, land, and homes; but if you show up in church and contribute generously to the collection plate, it helps to mollify public opinion some. Even today, if you search out that same church, which was moved lock, stock, and barrel during the construction of the Reservoir, you'll find a host of little brass plates on things ranging from pews to the lectern with the words "Gift of Cornelius Dort" on them.

The morning of his wife's funeral, though, Cornelius sits in the front pew with his arms and legs crossed, bobbing one foot up and down like a boy who's impatient for home. During the minister's sermon, he makes a sound that some take for a sob, others a laugh. When the service is finished, Cornelius strides out of the church ahead of everyone, mounts his horse, and rides for home. It's the last time he'll see the inside of a church. He doesn't wait to accompany Beatrice to her resting place in the Dort family plot. Some, watching him gallop away, contend that Cornelius is fixing to take his revenge on the stranger for not having saved his wife. Others disagree. If he hasn't by now, they say, he won't.

That second group is right. Cornelius's guest, as the man comes to be called—eventually the Guest for short—remains in place, Cornelius not showing the slightest inclination to dislodge the man from the second floor of his house. No one sees much of the stranger, just glimpses here and there. The Dort estate borders that spring I mentioned, the one the Station was built around, and once in a while you'll see the Guest walking by it, a length of string looped from one hand. Folks like to joke he's fishing, earning his keep. Occasionally you'll see him walking with Cornelius, strolling through one of the Dort apple orchards. The Guest appears to be talking, gesturing with his hands every now and again, making big, sweeping gestures as if he's conducting a symphony. Cornelius walks with his hands clasped behind his back, his head bowed, brow furrowed, obviously hanging on the Guest's every word. That the man has made an impression on Cornelius, no one will deny. What they discuss, no one can guess.

Which is not to say that folks don't try. Some adventurous child overheard the Guest mention the Leviathan during one of his and Cornelius's orchard walks, and that, combined with the fact that the man continues to dress all in black, gives folks the idea that the man's a preacher. What denomination claims him remains a mystery, but it makes a certain sense to think that Bea's death has driven Cornelius to God. That is, if you don't remember Cornelius's performance at her funeral. Then news comes from one of the tanneries about some hides Cornelius sent up to have tanned. Did I mention that used to be a big business in these parts, hemlock tanneries? Well, apparently the hides Cornelius wants treated are like nothing the fellows at this particular tannery have encountered. I'm not sure what made them so strange, but the tanners state flat out that they're more like the skins of devils from hell than any beast they've ever seen. Along with these hides, Cornelius sends very specific instructions for how they're to be handled, and pays three times the going rate to insure his instructions are followed to the letter. At first, no one can understand how Cornelius could have come by such hides, not to mention how he's become so expert in tanning. It doesn't take long, however, for suspicion to light on the Guest, with that cart full of boxes and bags.

III

The incident at the tannery—they did the work, by the way—marks a change in people's attitudes toward the stranger. While there had been some folks suspicious of him from the moment he appeared on the turnpike, most have been more curious than anything. Now, that curiosity has been mixed together with unease. I wouldn't go so far as to say folks are afraid of Cornelius's Guest as that they're ready to be, you know? Suddenly, everyone's noticing the strange goings-on at the Dort house. There are a lot more storms than there used to be, or so the old-timers say, lots more thunderstorms, and don't they linger over the Station? Haven't the Dort house's windows been seen shining with a weird, blue light late at night? Hasn't one of the local children reported seeing something in the local spring, something she couldn't stop crying long enough to identify? There are stories that Cornelius has been seen, during a fierce summer storm, the lightning falling almost as fast as the rain, walking through one of his orchards, accompanied by a figure in black—not his Guest, no, this figure is distinctly feminine, wearing a long dress and a long, black veil. No one can make out her features, but there's something about the way she walks that seems off, as if she isn't used to using her legs her way, or has forgotten how. Certainly, she'll haunt the dreams of one man who witnesses her stroll with Cornelius, a minor painter named Otto Schalken, who's up from Brooklyn visiting his brother Paul, the schoolmaster in West Hurley. Otto's caught out in the storm when he ignores Paul's warning to delay his daily constitutional. Needless to say, he finds the experience of being in the thick of a true Catskill thunderstorm a bit traumatic; though, when all is said and done, it's not half so bad as the sight of Cornelius and the woman in black. Like I said, she walks through his dreams. Otto, whose previous claim to fame was illustrating an edition of Coleridge's poems, achieves the only celebrity he'll know for a half-dozen canvases rendering that woman in the long black veil. He doesn't include Cornelius in the paintings, which show the woman wandering not in a Catskill apple orchard, but next to the sea. I've seen a couple of them in art books, and there's something about the sea—it's black and storming, and the way he painted the woman's dress and veil, it's like she's wearing that angry sea. No one's sure what Otto was up to—I mean, a few critics have taken educated guesses, but the man himself left no word aside from a packet of cryptic letters he wrote to his brother once he'd returned to his apartment in Brooklyn. He was pursued, Otto wrote, "by a very Geraldine, to whom my soul is no more than water to drink." The brother sent a reply asking him what he meant, but he never received an answer. After completing the final canvas in the series, Otto sat down in the bedroom, took his straight razor in hand, and slit his throat from ear to ear.

Nothing like a bit of melodrama, huh? Otto Schalken's story aside, if you look into most of the reports about Cornelius and his Guest, you find that they trace back to one person, who tends to have been less-than-reliable: a child, say, in trouble for staying out playing too late and blames his tardiness on what he saw over at the Dort house, which is passed on by his gullible parents. There are one or two things that a number of people agree on. During the summer of, I think it's eighteen forty-nine, might be eighteen fifty, an especially bad storm blows in and hangs over the Esopus valley for the better part of a day and half. There's rain, yes, but folks will remember this storm for its thunder and lightning. The thunder shakes houses like an earthquake—in fact, it's blamed for cracking the rear wall of one of the houses in the Station. As for the lightning, there's so much of it night practically turns into day. Several people living in or staying at the Station swear that the Dort house takes more than a dozen direct strikes. The house has a lightning rod, of course, and those who witness the lightning touching that rod say that it seems to hang in the air for an instant longer when it does, like a long, snarled thread being drawn from the sky. The other thing folks agree on is that, after the night of that storm, the Station's spring tastes different. Most say the spring has become sulfury, but a few insist that isn't it, that the water tastes burnt, somehow.

If things have been strange at the Dort house, they never become so strange that folks feel they have to do anything about them. After the night of that legendary storm, the Guest appears less and less, and he was never that visible in the first place. Other things occupy people's attention. The tanneries start to close. By the time the Civil War breaks out, they'll be a thing of the past. The whaling industry's pretty much belly-up, too. I bet you didn't know that the towns on the Hudson used to send out huge whaling fleets. What was it? At one point, Hudson—the town, I mean—had more ships than Manhattan. Big part of the local economy, then the bottom fell out of it. And in the background of all this were the debates about slavery and states' rights that were laying tracks to the Battle of Bull Run. As time goes on, Cornelius Dort and his Guest become the kind of bogeymen you use to keep your children in line, and less anyone's real concern.

Years pass—decades. The Guest rarely if ever shows his face, to the point that younger folks, the ones who had been the audience for those tales of the man in black, doubt his existence. There's no doubting Cornelius, though. While the march of time stamps the red out of his hair and wears deep lines in his face, he remains as full of vim-and-vigor—not to mention vinegar—as ever. People say it's because Death himself is afraid of the man. What's that saying, you know, "Heaven doesn't want me, and hell's afraid I'll take over." That fits Cornelius to a T. Investing in munitions, he makes a ton of money off the Civil War, to the point he's one of the richest men in the country. He never remarries—doesn't keep company with anyone, really. When he reaches eighty, he suffers a stroke, which only slows him up for as long as it takes him to master using a cane. When he reaches the century mark, there are articles on him in the local papers, even a piece in the *New York Times*. The *Times* reporter rides all the way up from the City to try to interview Cornelius. For his trouble, he receives a jab in the gut from Cornelius's cane and the front door slammed in his face. He still writes a decent story about the old man. Like everyone else, the *Times* has no desire to stir Cornelius to wrath. None of the local reporters attempts to approach Cornelius.

IV

ight around the time Cornelius starts counting his age in three digits is when plans are being drawn up for the Reservoir. New York City is living beyond its means, and someone has to make up the difference. Spoken like a true upstater, right? I assume you know the story. After some discussion, the powers-that-be in the City and State decide to dam the Esopus and turn the valley behind it into a lake. This doesn't go down so well with the people whose houses, land, and businesses are going to be at the bottom of said lake, and they do what they can to fight the plan. Cornelius is at the forefront of that struggle, spending no small part of his fortune hiring lawyers and buying politicians in an effort to convince the City that the water from the Adirondacks would taste much better. Initially, there are a few, hopeful signs, but that soon changes. In the thirst of all those people, Cornelius has finally encountered a force he can't overcome. The Reservoir is approved for the Esopus valley.

It's a massive undertaking. Eleven and a half towns have to be relocated to higher ground. In some cases, this means entire buildings, houses, churches, will be moved. Whatever isn't being moved has to be destroyed, burned if it can be, torn down and carted away if it can't. Every last piece of greenery, every tree, bush, and shrub, must be uprooted. Even the cemeteries have to be emptied. You've read Alf's book, so you know what I'm talking about. You can appreciate why the old-timers, the ones whose families were living here before the Reservoir, have less than kind feelings for the City, even now.

As you might imagine, the Reservoir's construction draws a host of work-ers to the area, which is how Lottie and her family enter the story. She, her mother Clara, and two younger sisters, Gretchen and Christina, come up from the Bronx with her father. Rainer Schmidt's an interesting fellow. In the old country, he was an educated man, a professor of philology—that's the study of languages, in case you didn't know. Apparently, the man could speak something like half a dozen languages, and read another three or four besides. He taught at the University of Heidelberg, and was quite the rising young star. In the university system over in Germany, it takes you a long time to become a full professor. Before that, you're a kind of glorified gofer. Rainer had made professor at the age of twenty-nine, which I gather was a real accomplishment. The essays he wrote were read and debated all over Europe; the book he was working on was eagerly anticipated.

He was a striking-looking fellow. Not especially tall, but he carried him-self as if he were, the residue of a boyhood spent in military schools. His face was long, the majority of it taken up by a nose that joined a pair of deep-set eyes to a full mustache. Together, he and Clara made quite the couple. She was nearly as tall as he was, and she wore her head of brown hair up. Her face was broader than his, her features more evenly proportioned. The three girls favored their mother; though Lottie's eyes had inherited something of her father's sharpness. A fine, upstanding young family, you would have said.

Then something happened. Lottie wasn't too clear on exactly what it was, but it concerned a book Rainer was studying. Whatever he did got him drummed out of his school and made it impossible for him to find work at any others. It must've been pretty spectacular, because Lottie told Reverend Mapple that she could remember people crossing to the other side of the street when she and her papa were out walking. Once the family had gone through what savings they had, and no sign of another job for Rainer any-where on the horizon, they decided a move was in order, to some place with new horizons, where no one had heard of whatever it was Rainer had done. Lottie's mother, Clara, had a sister who'd immigrated to the Bronx years ago, and now ran her own bakery and restaurant. She wrote to her, and the sister sent them the money for their passage.

Once they arrive in New York, they all go to work in the sister's establish-ment. Since she paid their way, I guess that's only fair. Rainer, who numbers

English among the languages he speaks, tutors the rest of the family in it each night. Things trundle along like this for a good two years, and then Rainer, who's moved up to working the counter in the bakery, hears from one of his customers that there's going to be a massive new construction project upstate and that they're looking for workers. A skilled laborer, the customer says, a stonemason or a machinist, can do quite well for himself and his family. Rainer finds out whom he needs to talk to, and goes to see the man the following morning. Somehow, he convinces the fellow who interviews him that he's a stonemason, highly skilled, one of the finest in Germany, who's done work on some of the most important buildings in Heidelberg. I guess being a professor helps you fake your way through all kinds of situations. After all, when was the last time you heard one of them say he didn't know something? The man asks Rainer if he and his family can be at the work camp within the next couple of weeks. Sure, sure, Rainer says, no problem. He leaves that office with a new job he has no idea how to perform and two weeks to learn, in a place whose location he isn't exactly sure of and which he's going to have to convince his family they need to leave for in that same two weeks.

Through some combination of skill and luck, Rainer succeeds in both tasks. How he does, I can't imagine. All I can say is, with powers of persuasion like that, I can't see how he ever lost his job in the first place. Three weeks to the day after the interview finds the Schmidt family living in one of the four room houses the company provides for its married workers. What they thought they could take with them, they have. Only, they overestimated the size of their lodgings, which means that things are a bit cramped. You have to step carefully to avoid knocking over a pile of books or breaking this or that box of dishes. Lottie's aunt wasn't happy to have them all up and moving so quickly, but she agreed to store whatever they couldn't bring until they send for it. Clara isn't too happy, nor are Lottie, Gretchen, and Christina, with their new accommodations. When he described the place they'd be moving into, Rainer promised little less than a mansion. What they found was little more than a roughly built shack with no running water and no toilet. Compared to her husband and daughters, Clara's English isn't especially good—she spent most of her time in her sister's bakery in the kitchen, helping with the baking—and here she's living next to other women whose English isn't especially good. A few are German, a few Austrian, but most are from places like Italy, Russia, and Sweden. One of their next door neighbors is from Hungary. For the better part of the first month they're at the camp, Lottie lies awake at night, listening to her parents arguing.

V

I t's about this time—I'm talking the fall of 1907, when the first construction on the Reservoir is starting—that Cornelius Dort finally gives up the ghost. He's not yet surrendered the idea of halting the Reservoir's construction, and to that end has summoned a team of lawyers to his house to discuss possible strategies for doing so. As he walks down the front walk to meet them, Cornelius stops where he was, shudders, and looks down at the ground beneath his feet. His face twists into a look—one of the lawyers who sees it describes it as "the look of a man striding across a frozen river who realizes with sudden horror that the ice he has been traversing has become too thin to support his weight." Cornelius shudders again, drops to the ground, and in the time it takes the lawyers to rush up to him, is gone. Story is that final expression, eyes starting from their sockets, lips curled back, remains on his face all the way to the grave.

Cornelius's passing puts the axe to any lingering hopes folks in the valley might have been nursing that the Reservoir, not them, will be moved. To tell the truth, from everything I've read, once those fellows down in the City set their sights on having their water from the Catskills, it was only a matter of time before the valley was underwater. At the end of his life, though, for pretty much the first and only time in it, Cornelius Dort became something like a hero to folks. His meanness, his cunning, his ruthlessness, all those qualities that earned people's abiding hate, when they were turned against a common foe, were transformed into virtues, into almost heroic assets.

67

There's a considerable turnout for his funeral, which, interestingly enough, takes place over in Woodstock. This is a good couple of years before the valley's cemeteries start being dug up and their inhabitants moved to dryer beds. It seems that, despite the efforts he was making, Cornelius had seen the handwriting on the wall. Turns out he'd already had little Bea's body exhumed and transferred to the Woodstock cemetery almost a year earlier. No one could recall it having happened, but with all the fuss over the Reservoir, who can keep track of such things? A few people remark that, in death, Cornelius is admitting defeat in a way he never did in life, but what more is there to say?

With Cornelius gone, everyone assumes that the Dort estate will go to the nearest relative, a cousin living up in Phonecia. You can appreciate that young man's surprise, not to mention everyone else's, when who should reappear but Cornelius's long-ago Guest, claiming the estate for his own. He must be well into his eighties, if not older, but the years have been kind to the man. Kind, they've been positively generous. Some say it's as if the man hasn't aged at all. Obviously, this can't be the case. But he must dye his hair and beard, because they're as black as the day he first came riding out of the west, and his face shows none of the lines you'd expect the decades to have carved onto it. The Guest declares that he has a copy of Cornelius's will to support his claim, which, when the inevitable pack of lawyers descends on the situation, turns out to be the case. There is a will, and it's legitimate. The cousin is outraged. While there'd certainly been no love lost between him and Cornelius, neither has he had any reason to suspect the old man was plotting a slap in the face like this. There's a story that, once the lawyers have departed and the Guest retreated to his new property, the cousin sneaks into the house and takes everything he can lay his hands on, but, if that's true, no charges are ever filed.

It's going on twenty years since Cornelius's Guest was last glimpsed by anyone. For younger folks, it's as if a character from a storybook stepped off the page. For older folks, it's as if someone you haven't seen in years stepped from the last time you saw them to now, skipping all the years in between. With his return comes a change in the stranger's behavior. No longer furtive, the man begins appearing all over the place, as if inheriting Cornelius's fortune has given him substance he formerly lacked. He spends most of his time at the spring, conducting experiments that consist, so far as anyone can tell, of lowering different lengths of rope and chain into the water. Those who observe this activity assume the Guest is measuring the spring's depth. But why he should be so concerned with such matters, when the spring is going to be at the bottom of the Reservoir, no one can guess. People assume he's a scientist, or maybe a crack-pot inventor. He does the same thing at spots up and down the Esopus, casting the end of a length of rope or chain out into the water, waiting a couple of minutes, then hauling it back in. There are markings on the ropes and chains, which no one is close enough to read but which seem like units of measurement. A few folks say the man mumbles to himself all the while he's doing whatever it is he's doing. Keeping time, could be. If he notices anyone watching him, he tips his hat to them, then returns to his work. That gesture, that tip of the hat, bothers whoever's on the receiving end of it. There's mockery in the touch of hand to hat, not enough to be insulting, but more than enough to make a person self-conscious. There's a kind of warning to it, too, as if the man is saying, "Okay, you've seen me: now run along." There are few who see it who don't leave off their viewing and go straight home.

Pretty soon, the Guest is once again the center of rumor. What with everything, people in the valley are under a lot of stress, so any behavior like the stranger's is bound to set their imaginations, not to mention their tongues, running. More than one person claims they've seen the Guest walking around the spring late on a moonlit night with a tall, white-haired man they swear was Cornelius Dort. Old Otto Schalken's brother, Paul, out for a walk one afternoon, sees the Guest strolling the Dort orchards, accompanied by a woman wearing a black dress and a long, black veil. The sight of her inspires such a rush of fear in Paul that he bolts for home, running all the way to his front door as if the very devil himself were after him. As far as anyone knows, the stranger is the sole inhabitant of the Dort house, the last of the servants having been dismissed once the lawyers upheld the man's claim to the estate. There are nights, however, when every window in the house, from top to bottom and all around the sides, is ablaze with light that frames the silhouettes of men and women behind them. Voices drift across the open air. Though no one can make out what they're saying, a few folks claim to hear Cornelius's tones mixed in with them. Most likely, the fellow was just hosting a party or two, but no one sees the guests coming or going.

VI

eanwhile, at long last, Lottie Schmidt's family has started to settle into life at the camp. Rainer gets on well as a stonemason. Most of the other masons are Italian, some brought over from Italy expressly for this job, and Rainer speaks Italian with sufficient fluency to make a good impression on his co-workers—management, too, who appreciate his ability to translate. Clara decides what can't be cured must be endured, and finds herself a job in the camp's bakery. Lottie goes with her. Her sisters, Gretchen and Christina, attend the camp school. Rainer is making good money. A stonemason could bring home about three dollars a day; I don't know what the modern equivalent of that is, but, apparently, for a man with a wife and three daughters to take care of, it's all right. Between both parents' jobs, the Schmidts are able to repay Clara's sister, and then begin putting something away for the house they want to buy. Clara has dreams of returning to the City, to be close to her sister, while Rainer's thinking that Wiltwyck might be nice to settle in. I doubt it's the life either of them expected when they married, but they're doing well at it.

Working on the Reservoir is not risk-free. Basically, the laborers are building a pair of enormous walls: the dam to hold back and contain the Esopus, and the weir that will divide the Reservoir into east and west basins. Once they're done, and the valley floods, they'll have constructed a lake roughly twelve miles long by three miles wide. There are a lot of unskilled men on the job. There's a lot of machinery. Let's face it, even skilled workers make mistakes.

70

THE FISHERMAN

There are accidents. Men are hurt and killed. Medicine at this time isn't like medicine, now. Say your arm is crushed by a block of stone: amputation's going to be the procedure of choice. It's the remedy to a wide range of problems. If you manage to avoid injury, you still have disease to worry about. The flu alone is a significant cause of death. I don't think we really appreciate the difference a drug like penicillin's made. There's a hospital at the camp, but its facilities are limited. If you're seriously hurt, or sick, you're going to need to seek care in Wiltwyck—and you're going to need to survive the trip there. And, of course, all this goes for the workers' families as well. You might say that folks in general live much closer to death than do we.

When Lottie and her family have been at the camp about a year and a half, the woman who lives next to them is killed, trampled. There's a mule barn at the camp, mules being the animal of choice for hauling the wagons used to transport pretty much everything. There are three mules hitched to a wagon, and they're a pretty common sight. Every day at five, when the quitting whistle blows, the drivers of the wagons stage an impromptu race up the road leading to the mule barn. All the kids in the camp gather at the side of the road to watch the wagons roar by, the drivers standing up, one hand holding the reins, the other cracking the long whips they used, the mules' legs churning. On the day of this particular tragedy, Lottie isn't present—she's finishing up at the bakery with Clara—but Gretchen and Christina are. Later, they'll tell the rest of the family how, right as the teams were thundering down the final stretch of road before the barns, this woman, their neighbor, the Hungarian woman who never spoke to anyone, strode out in front of them. Her hair was unbound; she was wearing a plain blouse with the sleeves rolled up and a long skirt. It was as if she'd just stepped out of her kitchen. There was nothing any of the drivers could do. The wagons bore her down and crushed her. One of the drivers managed to turn his team around and race back to the spot where she lay broken and bloody. He leapt down from his seat, carried the woman to the back of his wagon, and made for the camp hospital like Mercury himself. The mule drivers are black, you see, and the woman they've run down is white. You can imagine what's going through the fellow's head.

Incredibly, the woman actually survives for half a day, long enough for her husband to appear at her side and collapse in sobs. I suppose it goes without saying that there's nothing the camp doctor, or any other doctor, for the matter, can do for her. Asked the reason for her act, the woman refuses

71

to say, but there have been stories circulating about her husband and another woman, one of Lottie and Clara's co-workers at the bakery, a Swedish girl. The husband's hardly what you'd call handsome, his hair thin, his face square, his body bony, but strange are the ways of desire. So far as anyone hears, the woman doesn't speak a single word, just lies there gritting her teeth as she sees the bitter task she started through to its end. Her husband weeps freely and often, and, once the final breath has passed his wife's ruined lips, and the nurse reaches down to close her eyes, throws himself across her body, howling his grief. It's a couple of days before she's buried. She's a suicide, remember, and at this time that's still a sin in the popular understanding. Finally, the Catholic church in Woodstock agrees to take her; although they insist that she be placed outside the cemetery proper. At Clara's request, Lottie attends the funeral. While it's a Catholic service, and the Schmidts have always been good Lutherans who keep a safe distance from the errors of popery, Clara is surprisingly insistent. "Those things don't matter in this place," she says, much to her pious daughter's shock. At the funeral, the husband is in worse shape than the day before. There's no helping the man, in part because no one speaks Hungarian and his English isn't that good. Ironically, it's at the woman's funeral that Lottie first learns her name, Helen, and that of her husband, George.

After Helen is committed to the ground, George retreats to their house and doesn't come out for a week. If he needs anything, he sends one of his children for it. The oldest child, a girl named Maria, tells Lottie that all her father does is sit in his bedroom in the dark. Once in a while, he laughs, or shouts something. Maria doesn't say her father's drunk pretty much all that time. She doesn't have to. She's doing what she can to keep him and the other children fed, but it isn't easy, without their mother. She's worried, and she's right to be. Every day her father stays home from work is one day closer to him being fired. This is the days before labor unions, before compassionate leave and all that kind of thing. A man who's newly lost his wife can expect a certain amount of sympathy, some leeway, but people's memories are short for any sorrow that isn't theirs, and his job has to be done. Over the course of those seven days, a number of people, including Rainer, try to talk to the man, with no success. Wherever he is in his dark room, he's unreachable.

VII

As I said, a week passes, with everyone growing more uneasy as the wait for the axe to fall. Then, one night, Maria shows up at the Schmidts' front door, her siblings in tow. She's fairly agitated, and when Clara asks, "What's the matter?" answers, "My father left the house this morning, and he didn't say where he was going or when he'd be back. We haven't seen him since. I don't know what to do." Clara takes them in, says, "He's probably just gone out for a walk and forgotten the time. I'm sure he'll be back very soon. You can sleep here tonight with my girls." All the while, she's thinking that there are thirteen bars between the camp and Stone Ridge alone, not to mention I don't know how many whorehouses—more than sufficient opportunity for a man out of his head with grief to heighten the agony.

Clara is mistaken, however; George returns in the wee small hours of the morning and, looking for his daughters, comes chapping at the Schmidts' door, himself. Rainer answers it. Later Lottie overhears her pa say that he nearly jumped out of his skin when he saw the look on the man's face. He was grinning, Rainer says, but it was no happy smile. It was the smile of a man who knows that he's committed a terrible act but is trying with all his might to convince himself that that isn't the case. He figures if he keeps on smiling, he'll be able to convince everyone else that everything is fine, and then maybe they'll be able to convince him. He's come for his children, George says. "It's the middle of the night," Rainer says, "they're asleep."

The man doesn't care. "Wake them up," he says. Then he adds, "I have something wonderful for them to see. There has been a miracle."

To say Rainer feels nervous is an understatement. It's obvious that George is laboring under a heavy load, one or maybe two steps away from being crushed beneath it. Rainer can't decide if the children will help the man shoulder his burden, or if they'll be the extra weight necessary to break him. George keeps insisting that he has something wonderful for his children, which Rainer doesn't like the sound of. Eventually, though, Rainer gives in to the man's request and goes through to wake the children. As he tells Clara, he's sure the kids will be happier knowing their father has returned, and he judges it better to give the fellow what he's asking for than to deny him. If there's any trouble—not that he can say what that trouble might be, but the thought crosses his mind—Rainer figures he's only a house away. He's right about the children. They're happy and relieved to see their father's returned, and rush to embrace him. For his part, George doesn't seem any better. That grin modulates only slightly. But the children clutching his pants and shirt don't appear to drive him any closer to the edge. Thanking Rainer profusely, his neighbor leaves, the children in tow.

Maybe five, maybe ten minutes after George's departure, just enough time for Rainer to have climbed into bed, closed his eyes, and felt sleep waiting for him, the screaming starts. High-pitched and loud, there's a lot of it. Rainer sits up; so does Clara. The screaming continues, hysterical, terrified. "That's the children," Clara says, meaning their neighbor's, but Rainer's already out of bed and heading for the door, cursing himself for a fool. He doesn't bother stopping to put on his boots, but hauls open the front door and runs across to the neighbor's house. All the while, the screaming keeps up. "Stupid, stupid, stupid," Rainer's muttering to himself. Other folks are at their front doors as Rainer lowers his shoulder and smashes into the neighbor's. His blood is up. He's ready for a fight. What he sees inside the house stops him in his tracks.

Directly in front of him, the children are gathered in a screaming knot around Maria, their faces full of tears and horror. To the other side of them stands their father, bent over slightly, his hands out to either side of him, as if he's apologizing for something. He's doing all he can to maintain that grin, though his face shakes with the effort. To his right, sitting on a chair, is his late wife.

THE FISHERMAN

When Rainer sees the woman there, his first thought is that George sought out her grave, dug it up, and carried the body back to the house. Then she raises her head and looks at him, and Rainer's heart stops. He takes a step forward. Strange as it sounds, he actually moves closer to her. George is babbling on about miracle this and miracle that, but Rainer isn't paying any attention to him. He's studying the woman—Helen's—eyes, which are different, somehow. Hard as it is to see in the light of the single lantern burning, Rainer is sure Helen's eyes are gold, entirely gold, with tiny black pupils dotting their centers. He can't remember what the woman's eyes looked like before, but he's sure it wasn't this.

In the meantime, more folks have shown up at the front door. When they see what's inside, some turn around and march straight back home. Others join the children in screaming. Still others start praying in whatever language they reserve for talking to God. One man, an Italian, Italo, who's a stonemason with Rainer, runs into the house and hustles the children outside. When he's seen them safely to his own house, a few streets over, he walks rapidly back to the house where Rainer is still gazing into Helen's gold eyes. "Rainer," he says, "what in the devil is this?"

The sound of his voice calls Rainer back from wherever the woman's eyes have taken him. He shakes his head, then looks at Italo. His voice hoarse, he says, "This is bad business."

Together the men turn to George, who's jammed his hands in his pockets, for all the world like a little boy caught misbehaving. "How did this happen?" Rainer asks. George doesn't answer him, just starts up again about what a miracle this is, how lucky they are to be here to see it, yes how lucky to see such a miracle. Italo crosses the floor to him, and slaps him. Rainer's colleague is a small man, his bald crown making him appear older than he is, but George's head swings with the force of the blow. His grin remains. Before he can pick up the thread of his babble, Italo slaps him again, and a third time. All the while, everyone's doing their level best not to look at what's sitting in the chair to George's right. Helen had been pretty badly beaten-up by the mule-carts, most of the bones in her body broken, and she still looks, well, jagged, misshapen.

Finally, George, his lips and nose bleeding from Italo's blows, drops the talk of miracles and says something about a man. "What man?" Rainer asks him. "The man in the house," George says, "the man in the big house."

75

Neither Rainer nor Italo has the faintest idea what George is talking about, but he goes on. "He understands," George says, that bloody grin making him look like a nightmarish clown. "The man understands what it is to *lose*—what it is to lose. He listens. He understands. He doesn't see why a man should suffer for what he didn't mean to do in the first place. Things happened, that was all. He doesn't ask for what you don't have. Strength—to add your strength to his. He gives you his cup. Not compassionate—no, he's not compassionate; he's interested, interested, yes. He will help you if you will help him. Things happened. Why not? Your strength. All he asks is that you drink from his cup. His task is almost done. Why not? He will help you if you will help him." He repeats those words a half-dozen more times, until Italo slaps him. "He's a fisherman," George says, and something about that statement strikes him as so funny he starts to giggle, then to chuckle, then to laugh, then to howl. It doesn't matter how many more slaps Italo gives him, he won't stop laughing. When he looks at his wife, still sitting calmly in the chair, his eyes start and he laughs even harder. Rainer and Italo exchange looks, and leave the cabin, shutting the door behind them. You can still hear the fellow laughing. All the camp hears it. "This is bad business," Rainer says again, and Italo agrees, it is.

There's a crowd gathered outside the house, composed of maybe a third of the men and not a few of the women in the camp. Every one of them has a dozen whispered questions for Rainer and Italo. Yes, they all speak in whispers. Most of their questions the men can't answer. Nor, it seems, can anyone answer Rainer's only question: Who is the man in the big house, the fisherman?

By now, the sun is on its way up, and, hard as it is to believe after a night like this one, soon it'll be time to start work. No matter what happens, your job is always waiting for you, right? The crowd breaks up. A couple of men ask Rainer and Italo to let them know when they learn anything. Inside the house, George's laughter has worn itself down to a low moaning. Thinking that he should check on George one last time, Rainer steps toward the door. Italo catches his arm. "Not until we know," Italo says, "not until we know what's sitting in that chair."

"But the man," Rainer says.

"He's made his choice," Italo says. "It's none of ours."

Rainer isn't happy, but he doesn't try to go in, either. He manages to convince Italo that they need to find out who the man in the big house, the fisherman, is; though I get the impression that Italo would've been happy to walk away from that house and never give it a second thought. What they're going to do once they discover who's behind the night's events, Rainer doesn't say, not to Italo and not to Clara when she asks him a short time later, when he's done relating the night's events to her. Lottie and her sisters listen to their father's story with a combination of wonder and terror as they prepare for their various days. When he's finished, Gretchen stops loading her schoolbag and asks Rainer if this is like in the Gospels, the time Jesus raised Lazarus from the dead. At that question, Clara flies into a rage, grabbing Gretchen with one hand and beating her about the head with the other, shouting, "How dare you? How dare you listen to your father and me?" Lottie and Christina are shocked. They've never seen their mother like this before, ever. Rainer leaps up and catches Clara's hand, and the look she gives him says that, were she stronger, she'd do for him, too. "Let's go, girls," Rainer says, and the sisters are out of that house one-two-three.

VIII

I t'll take Rainer two days to learn the identity of the man in the big house. As it so happens, it's actually Clara who figures it out. Late on the second afternoon after Helen's return from the grave, Clara hears a trio of women at the bakery discussing the Dort estate and the queer character who inhabits it. Right on the spot, she knows she's found what they're looking for. She sidles up to the women, asking if they're talking about one of the houses up in the mountains. "No, no," the first woman says, "the Dort estate's right here." In about ten minutes, they sketch out for Clara what it's taken me much longer to tell you. When Rainer walks in the front door later that night, he's greeted by Clara, who says, "I know what you're looking for."

Really, it isn't a moment too soon. In that same two days, things in the house next door have plummeted from bad to worse. Italo's wife, you may recall, is looking after Helen and George's children. About noon of that first day, Helen—or what was Helen—decides she wants those children back. How she knows where Italo has taken them, I can't say, but know she does. She stands from her chair, leaves her husband where he's still lying moaning on the floor, and sets out for Italo's place. Those who see her making her way over to Italo's say she doesn't walk right. She moves the way you'd expect a person trying to use a pair of shattered legs and a broken spine would. And if that isn't strange enough, the footprints she leaves are wet, as if she's newly out of her bath and not bothered toweling off. She lurches

78

her way to Italo's, folks stopping when they see her and hurrying away in the opposite direction. She ignores them. When she reaches her destination, she stands in front of it, swaying from side to side, before stumbling forward and knocking on the door.

You have to give Italo's wife, Regina, a lot of credit, because, although she sees Helen shuffling up the street toward her house, she hauls open the front door and stands there with her hands on her hips, facing this woman with the gold eyes. Regina's an inch or two taller than her husband, whom she probably outweighs by a good twenty or thirty pounds, too. She isn't stupid. She's already sent the children, her own and Helen's, into the back bedroom and told them not to open the door for love or money. (She'd kept them all home from school that day: Helen's children because of the shock of the night before; her children to keep them company. Her views on education were flexible, you might say.) Regina doesn't say a word to Helen. Later, she tells Italo and Rainer she was too afraid to speak. Why she opened the door in the first place, Regina wasn't sure, but I think I know. Have you ever been so scared of something you move toward it, try to touch it, that kind of thing? It's strange, isn't it? I don't know what the name for that reaction is, but I'm pretty sure it's what drove Regina to confront this woman knocking on her door. Helen, the dead woman, the woman who was dead and isn't any longer, is standing there on her ruined legs, looks at Regina, then looks at the room she's guarding. She says, "The children."

The sound of her voice is something awful. It's hard, raspy, as if it hasn't been used in a while, which I guess it hasn't. It's kind of liquidy, too, as if Helen's speaking from underwater. There's something else, a quality to the woman's voice Regina will have a hard time putting her finger on when she relates Helen's visit to her husband and his friend. She has an accent, Regina will say at last, but who doesn't have an accent in this place? It's not the accent the woman had when she was alive, no, not like what any of them has, moving from one tongue to another. This accent is what you'd imagine if an animal learned how to speak, something that wasn't trying to master your particular language, but the idea of language itself. It's not the way you'd think a dog or cat would speak, either. It's the voice you'd give a lizard, or an eel. Although she's the first to hear Helen speak—aside from George, presumably—she's far from the last, and the consensus is that her description hits the nail right on the head. When she hears Helen, the hairs on the back of Regina's neck stand straight up, and she has all she can do to keep where she is and shake her head no.

According to Regina, Helen doesn't so much look at her as through her. Apparently she sees her shake her head, however, because she repeats her request, those same two words, "The children." Regina repeats her answer, too, shaking her head so hard she's afraid it might fly off.

It isn't until Helen states her demand a third time, stepping closer to the door as she does, that Regina finally finds her voice. "They're not yours anymore," she says. "Go away."

The woman doesn't. Instead, she takes another, lurching step forward. Regina backs away, grabbing for the door with one hand. "Go away," she says, "go back where you belong. Get back in the ground."

When Helen makes to cross the threshold into the house, Regina swings the door shut. Not quite fast enough—before it's shut, Helen thrusts her arm inside and starts grabbing at Regina, who, panicking, throws herself against the door, pushing with all her strength against the woman on the other side. The arm catches at her hair, her ear, and Regina slaps it away. Helen's skin is stone cold, Regina will report, and damp. She pushes, and Helen pushes back, and the woman's strength is terrible. If not for the fact that her body is full of broken bones, Helen would have the door open and those children in no time. Regina can hear the sound of the woman's bones grinding against each other as she heaves herself against the door. Despite Regina's best efforts—which I gather were nothing to sneeze at; she was a strong woman—Helen is slowly gaining on her, inching the door open. Sweat pouring down her forehead, Regina calls on God and the saints for help and, when none of them inclines to answer, lets loose every curse she knows in English and Italian on the woman. None of it makes any difference. If she's thought to exorcise Helen by calling on the Almighty, it appears the woman isn't afraid of him; if she's thought to shock her by cursing, it appears Helen has heard worse. She continues pushing the door open, and Regina knows it isn't going to be long until the muscles in her arms and legs, already trembling with the fight, give out. She screams her frustration, slapping away that cold, grasping hand, and that scream is what does the trick. It summons the children, her own and Helen's, who pour out of the back room in a tide. Without stopping to figure out what's what, they rush to the door and pile against it. Their strength isn't much, but it's enough.

Now Regina is gaining, heaving the door shut. Helen flaps her arm at them, and the children, shrieking, scratch and claw it, one of them breaking her cold skin. Black blood—literally black blood—splatters the floor. The arm jerks back. The door slams shut. Regina's oldest throws the bolt.

Now comes Helen's turn to scream, and scream she does. Bad as her voice is, her scream is a thousand times worse. Like a devil burning in hell, is how Regina will describe it. Years later, I understand, each of the children will still be waking from nightmares of it. Regina braces herself against the door, ready for Helen to make another try at it. She doesn't. While the echoes of her scream are ringing in everyone's ears, she leans close to the door and whispers to Regina through it. Whatever she says is more than two words, yet the children either can't hear or can't understand her. They see the blood drain from Regina's face. They see her squeeze her eyes closed and suck in her breath a little, as if she's felt a pain. But they don't know the reason for any of it. Helen waits around for a moment after delivering her message, as if she's listening to its effect on Regina. The children hear her on the other side of the door, breathing heavily from her efforts. Maria, Helen's oldest, will tell Lottie's sister Gretchen that the breathing sounded like her grandfather's in the months before his death, hoarse and harsh, and something else, wet, like the way you breathe when you're congested. Slowly, Helen retreats from the door, shuffling back to what was her house and husband.

Regina tells no one except Italo about Helen's message to her. When he returns from work later that day, she sends the kids out to play—she's kept them inside and close around her since Helen's appearance, and even when she tells them to go outside, she insists they not go far—and she and her husband have a long talk about the day's events. One of the children—Italo and Regina's son Giovanni—hangs close to the house to try to spy on his mom and dad's conversation. Only natural, I suppose, given that Regina hasn't explained any of what happened earlier, just given abundant hugs to him, his brothers and sister, and the other children, and told them all to pray the rosary. The next day, Giovanni will tell Christina, the youngest of the Schmidt girls, about what he overheard. At first, he says, his dad was furious, ready to storm right over to the dead woman's house and put her back in the ground. He was on his way to do that very thing when his mom told him that the woman had whispered something to him. Her voice dropped as she told his dad what it was, and Giovanni couldn't hear.

Whatever her words, they stopped his dad in his tracks. "What?" he says and Regina answers, "You heard me." "Impossible," he says. "Not," says she. There was a lot of back-and-forth. The boy reports that Italo kept asking Regina, Was she sure? and, How could this woman know such a thing? his voice becoming more uncertain and quavery with each repetition. In return, Regina's voice gained strength as she said again and again that she didn't know how this woman could know, though the damned and devils in hell were supposed to know all manner of secrets, weren't they? But that yes, so far as she could tell right then and there, the woman was correct. In fact, it explained a number of things. By the conversation's end, Italo was in tears, sobbing, "What are we going to do?" over and over; Regina saying she didn't know, but that they still had a little bit of time. Understandably, young Giovanni was upset at listening to all this. When he took up his position to eavesdrop, he hadn't bargained on listening in on his dad sobbing. Finally, he couldn't stand it anymore, and ran inside to join his parents, weeping himself. For which consideration he received a clout upside the head from Regina for spying, and a teary embrace from Italo. He watched Regina tell Italo he must consult his German friend about this matter. He was an educated man, the German—more importantly, he struck Regina as owning a measure of wisdom, and wisdom was always a precious commodity, especially at a time like this. She thought the German stood a better chance than most of them of knowing what to do about this woman who should be lying in the ground but was up and walking around. Because dealt with she had to be. There was no arguing the matter. Still wiping the tears from his eyes, Italo agreed. He would talk to his friend.

Which is how, later the night of that same first day, Italo appears at the Schmidts' door, calling on Rainer. When Rainer greets him and invites him in, Italo wastes no time in saying what he's come to say: "This woman, your neighbor—the one who has left her grave—something must be done about her." "What do you mean?" Rainer asks. "We have to kill her," Italo says, "we have to put her back where she belongs." While Rainer asks him what's wrong, Clara sends Lottie, who's still up reading, off to bed. She starts to complain, but the flash of her mother's eyes tells her to do as she's told. Once the door to her room is safely shut, Rainer repeats his question, "What's wrong?" Italo summarizes the afternoon's events, refusing only to repeat Helen's message to Regina. "It doesn't bear being spoken out loud," he declares. He verifies, however, that what she whispered is true, a truth there's no way she could have learned. "The woman," he says, "is no longer human. You," he points at Rainer, "have seen her eyes. What happened today leaves no room for doubt." "What is she, then?" Clara asks. "I don't know," Italo says. "A devil? Something else? I work with stone. This is not my profession. I cannot say what she is, only what she is not. She is not human."

He's agitated. He's come inside and accepted the glass of iced tea Clara sets on the kitchen table for him, but he sits perched on the edge of his chair as if ready to jump and flee the house at any moment, maybe to seek out the neighbor's. He keeps running his hands through his hair, and rubbing them together when he isn't. Lottie, who has opened her bedroom door ever-so-slightly during the last part of Italo's conversation with her parents, thinks he looks as if the secret he's keeping is eating him alive, chewing its way out from where he tried to cage it deep down inside himself. To Lottie's surprise, her father appears to be agreeing with Italo. Although Rainer's favorite quotation is that Shakespeare one, you know, about there being more things in heaven and earth, he is, as a rule, the family's resident skeptic, champion of what he refers to as "clear thinking." Now here he is, nodding to Italo's wildest speculations, going along with the man's assertions that the woman has to be done away with, that she's no longer a creature of this earth. It's not so much that Lottie herself disagrees with Italo's assessment— she thinks there's more truth than not to what he's saying—so much as that she can't believe her father isn't arguing with his friend, offering rational alternatives to Italo's wild speculations. The two men sit up like this until well after midnight, long after Clara goes off to bed, Italo swaying from side to side as fatigue overtakes him, Rainer with his hands clasped together, his gaze on the floor. When Italo has run down, Rainer sends him home with a promise that they'll attend to what needs attending to. Rainer stands in the doorway watching his friend walk up the street, and Lottie, who's kept awake at her spot at the bedroom door, opens it and walks into the kitchen. Without turning around, Rainer says, "How much did you hear, Lottie?" When Lottie protests that she's just up for a glass of water, Rainer cuts her off. "You want to know how much of what Mr. Oliveri said is true," he says, which is close enough to the actual question plaguing Lottie—"How much of it do you believe, Papa?"—for her to claim it as her own. Rainer faces her, and Lottie is shocked to see the look written on his features: fear, fear so intense it has him on the brink of tears, his lip trembling. "What is it, Papa?" Lottie asks, "What's wrong?" But Rainer only shakes his head and says, "It's time for bed." So thrown is Lottie by that expression that she forgets to ask her father for the answer he promised, and hurries off to join her sisters in their bed.

IX

As I've said, it isn't until the following evening that Clara reveals the identity of the man in the big house to Rainer, so setting in motion the final chain of events in this drama. In the meantime, things at the house next door continue their downward spiral. Helen's husband, George, keeps more or less quiet all that first day. Folks hear him moaning from time to time, but that's about it. At dawn the morning after Italo's visit, George starts screaming and yelling to beat the band. Once again, Rainer runs over to see what the matter is. He finds the front door to the house wide open, George writhing on the floor like a man having a fit, and Helen nowhere to be found. Rainer rushes to the man and tries to grab him, to stop him thrashing around, but George throws him across the room like he's a rag doll. Knocks the breath right out of him. While Rainer's sitting rubbing the back of his head from where he struck it on the wall, a few more neighbors arrive, all of whom have the same idea as Rainer, and none of whom has any better luck restraining George. It's as if the man's in the grip of a great power: "like a river of lightning was pouring through him," is how Rainer will put it to Clara. As Rainer pushes himself to his feet, he realizes that the man's screams aren't just noise. They're words. Hard as it is to believe, the man convulsing on the floor, his eyes rolling back in his head, his mouth bloody from where he's bitten his tongue, is speaking. Rainer can't make out all the words, but he's reasonably sure of a few, and they make the scene in front of him even stranger. The man shuddering in front of him is speaking a hodgepodge of languages: English, and what Rainer is pretty sure is Hungarian, and German, French, Italian, and Spanish, as well as a few more that Rainer isn't too sure of but thinks are Russian and Greek, plus a couple that Rainer's never heard before, guttural barks and snarls that don't resemble any tongue he knows or knows of. He's skipping from language to language, George, but all his speech seems to be circling around the same two or three sentences.

When Lottie, who listens to this story alongside her mother, asks her father what the man was saying, Rainer will ignore her and try to proceed with his story, until Clara picks up her daughter's question and echoes it, insisting. "It was something about water," Rainer says, "something to do with black water." The answer will satisfy Clara, but not Lottie, who knows, from the way her father looks up at the ceiling as he delivers it, that he's not telling the whole truth. They're observant, your children. There's more to what the man was saying than her father's letting on, and for reasons Lottie doesn't yet know but that trail nervous shudders up her spine, her father doesn't want to tell his family everything he's learned.

Nor will Lottie be able to ask George what he was saying, because, about five minutes after Rainer's arrival, in the middle of his stream of languages, George's back arches, quivering, and he vomits a torrent of brackish water, a geyser that goes on and on and on, fountaining over his face, his clothes, the floor, the men standing closest to him, who leap back, cursing. More water pours from that man than you would think one body could hold, and Rainer's sure he sees it running out George's nose, ear, even from the corners of his eyes.

There's something else, too, something that Rainer flat-out refuses to tell, despite the threats and imprecations of his wife and daughter. Lottie will have to wait until later that same day, when she'll hear the story from one of the girls at work, whose older brother was among the other men who went to George's house. Splashed by the water the man vomited for his trouble, the brother said that the water was full of tadpoles. Only, they were such tadpoles as no one among them had ever seen before, black strips of flesh one or two inches long, every one capped by a single, bulbous blue eye, so it seemed as if the fellow who'd thrown them up had swallowed a bucketful of eyeballs. They flopped around on the floor, the things, as if they were trying to get a better look at the men standing horrified around them. For a moment, the men stood paralyzed as the things twitched about the floor, and then one of them flipped itself onto a man's bare foot. He cried out, and all the men responded in a fury of stomping, crushing whatever the things were under the feet and boots as if there were no tomorrow, splashing the foul water all over the place. Long after they'd crushed the tadpole-things beyond recognition, the men kept stomping, as if they were trying to stamp out the very memory of what they'd seen. By the time they got hold of themselves and stopped, panting, and thought to look to George, he was dead.

Sounds a bit much, doesn't it? Not that the whole story doesn't sound more and more fantastic—walking dead woman and all. It's just those tadpoles, they're—well, they push the tale that much closer to outright fantasy, don't they? (That's assuming, of course, you don't think it's already there.) Myself, I'd be inclined to believe that George had quenched his thirst at one of the local ponds after a bout of drinking, swallowing a school of tadpoles—plain, ordinary tadpoles—in the process. When he throws up, out come the tadpoles, which, to be sure, would be a pretty disturbing sight in and of itself. The monster-tadpoles I'd chalk up to the overheated imagination of the girl who told Lottie the story. Problem is, I'm not as sure as I'd like to be. You see, the same night that Lottie hears this story, after Clara has revealed what she's learned about the man in the big house, and Rainer is chewing over the information at the kitchen table, rubbing his jaw the way he does when he's thinking, Lottie comes right out and asks him if the story she was told is true. She's that kind of girl.

Rainer jumps up from his chair as if he's been stung. At first, he looks surprised, as if he can't believe how his daughter heard such a story. Then the anger comes, such anger as Lottie hasn't seen on his face in a long time, maybe ever. She can see his right arm twitching, and she's sure he's going to hit her—for the truth or the lie of her question, she doesn't know. Lottie tenses herself for the slap, and that's when Clara, who's been standing to the side watching, steps in front of her. Lottie can't see her mother's face, but whatever's in it washes the anger clear from Rainer's. His arm relaxes, his head slumps, and Lottie realizes that underlying the anger she's been the focus of is fear, a terror deep and profound. She thinks of the other night, what she saw in her father's eyes after Italo left. All of a sudden, she has one of those moments you have growing up, when you see your parents as people, as something like older versions of you and your friends. From head of the household, Rainer becomes a man whose heavily lined face and thinning hair are the badges of too much care and worry. Lottie understands that the fear she's found in him is not a new thing, that it's been part of her father for a while now. If not originally part of his fundamental architecture, then it's infiltrated him the way termites will devour the frame of a house, leaving only the brick exterior in place. And from mother, Clara becomes a woman whose worn hands mark the effort she's put into holding together not only the family she and Rainer have made, but Rainer himself. Lottie sees that Clara knows all about Rainer's fear, that if her mother has been unable to exterminate what's wormed its way into her husband, she's at least done her best to support him where she can. A burst of sympathy, of pity compounded by love, takes hold of Lottie, and she wants to throw her arms around her parents and comfort them. She doesn't, though, because she also wants to protect them from her revelation.

"This is bad business," Rainer says at last.

This isn't exactly the revelation of the year. Before Lottie can ask Rainer what the bad business is, Clara does. "Enough riddles," she says. "We know bad things are happening. What do you know about them? Who is the man in the big house?"

"I don't know," Rainer says, "I don't know who he is."

Lottie sees her mother's shoulders straighten, a sure sign she's ready to yell, so she steps in with her own question: "What is he, Papa?"

Rainer's face falls; he didn't expect that one. It's as if he's decided he won't lie to his family. He simply won't tell them any truth he doesn't have to. "I'm not sure what he is," he says.

But Lottie's started to figure out the rules to his game. "What do you think he is?" she asks.

When she was a child growing up in Germany, she played a game like this with Rainer, a game whose object was to find not only the correct question, but the correct phrasing of it. Lottie was good at that game, which she thinks about now. Maybe Rainer remembers it, too, because as she re-words her question into a form he can't evade, the faintest of smiles crosses his lips. "All right," he says, "all right. I'll tell you what I think. I think—I am afraid the man in the big house might be *ein Schwarzkunstler.*"

He uses the German, even though they're all speaking English, a house rule Rainer himself has insisted on. Lottie knows the word, which translates "black artist" and means something like "black magician" or "sorcerer." It's a word Lottie associates with childhood stories from the old country, not real life in a construction camp in upstate New York. For a moment, she thinks Rainer is having her and Clara on, then she sees that he's crossed his arms, something he only does when he's presenting an uncomfortable truth. He did it when he told the family that he thought the only recourse left them was to leave their home and go far away, maybe to America, and again when he described the fine job he'd taken in the beautiful country north of the City. Her skeptical father is telling Lottie and her mother that an evil magician is behind the strange goings-on next door and expecting them to believe it. *"Ein Schwarzkunstler?"* Lottie says. "Like in the storybooks?" The tone of her voice shows her opinion of her father's theory.

"Not exactly," Rainer says. "More a kind of," he waves his hands, "scholar, or surgeon, or—or a strongman, at the circus."

"A surgeon?" Lottie asks. "A strongman?"

"Someone who slices into the surface of things and peels it away to discover what is underneath," Rainer says. "Someone who wrestles with powerful forces." This doesn't help Lottie in the least, which Rainer sees. He says, "The result would be the same as in the books."

Clara, meanwhile, is slowly nodding her head. When Rainer has finished speaking, she says, "It explains all of this, doesn't it? God help us." Then, to Rainer, "What are you doing about it?"

"Me?" Rainer says.

"You," Clara says.

"Why should I do anything?"

"Because who else knows about these things?" Clara says.

"I'm hardly an expert," Rainer says.

"You're what's at hand," Clara says. "Besides, you've done well enough in the past."

"I don't think Wilhelm would agree with you," Rainer says. There it is, suddenly: that name. Lottie's never heard it said out loud before, only caught it in whispers from Rainer and Clara.

But if Rainer thinks bringing up this name will stop the conversation, he's mistaken. Clara steams ahead: "Wilhelm understood what he was doing."

"I don't think so," Rainer says, "I don't think either of us did."

"That's the past," Clara says. "Let the dead bury the dead. You have the living to worry about. Are you telling me that, since that woman appeared, you've been doing nothing?"

Rainer resembles the little boy caught with his hand in the cookie jar. "I have been looking at the books," he says. "After everyone's gone to bed."

"I knew it," Clara says.

"It's not as simple as all that," Rainer says. "It's not like looking up the dictionary for '*Schwarzkunstler*.' The books are difficult to read. The meanings are hard to follow—it's like they're written in code. The words keep shifting themselves. They don't want to give up their secrets. It's like an oyster with a pearl."

"You can make an oyster surrender its pearl," Clara says. "All you need is persistence and a sharp enough knife."

Lottie cannot believe what she's hearing. It isn't that she herself is especially rational. Of all the family, she's the most religious, and she has no trouble with the miracles found in the Old and New Testaments. Nor does she have any problems accepting the prophecies in the Book of Revelation. Manna in the desert, Jesus raising Lazarus from the dead, the coming of this and that evil beast, those are fine with her. If you ask her, she'd say that she believes in God's hand shaping events in the world, and in the Devil's efforts to frustrate that design. She isn't sure about guardian angels or personal demons. That may be veering too much towards popery; it depends on her mood, though. The Bible, however, is the past, except for Revelation, which is the future. As for the present, you have to look carefully for the supernatural in it. It's a matter for study and interpretation. God and the Devil, good and evil, are active, but their actions are subtle. All this—broken woman returning from the grave and threatening their children, men vomiting monsters, sorcerers—it's so blatant, so vulgar.

That isn't the only thing. There are her parents. I guess you could say that, as regards Rainer and Clara, this night is one of surprises for Lottie. First there's her insight into their humanity, which is disconcerting enough. Then it's capped by talk of magic. While Rainer and Clara attend church services with Lottie and her sisters, neither of them has ever appeared all that devout. Rainer, of course, is the skeptic. Clara prides herself on her common sense. In fact, one of Clara's favorite activities is teasing her husband about this or that example of his lack of common sense. Now, in a matter of minutes, both Lottie's parents have abandoned their hard-headedness for mysticism, and not a particularly Christian-sounding one at that. It's as if, up until this evening, Rainer and Clara have been acting, playing roles they're only too happy to set aside. For a second, Lottie's parents seem stranger to her than any woman with gold eyes and a weird voice.

Rainer notices this. He sees his daughter squeezing her eyes shut against the vertigo of the situation and crosses the room to her. Catching Lottie by the shoulders, he says, "I know. I know you're thinking, 'Who are these crazy people, and what have they done with my mama and papa?' It is difficult to hear us talking like this, isn't it? Here we are, your parents, who yell at you for too much day-dreaming, and we're saying there could be *ein Schwarzkunstler* making dead people get up and walk around. What's next? A witch in a gingerbread house? A handsome prince who's been changed into a beast? A little mermaid who wants to be a real girl? It is like a story-book. It is like you've fallen into one of the stories we used to read you when you were a child. You don't understand everything, but you understand enough, and that knowledge, it twists things, doesn't it? Maybe you are afraid this is madness?" Lottie nods. He's pretty much hit the nail on the head. Rainer goes on, "I thought the same thing, the first time I—I thought the same thing, once. I thought I could feel my sanity slipping away, the way water does when you try to hold it in your hands. I wasn't insane, though. I wasn't, and you aren't. This doesn't make a lie out of everything else. It complicates it, yes, but it's not a lie. Do you understand?"

Lottie doesn't, not as much as she thinks she wants to, but she nods anyway, because she isn't sure she can keep listening to this man who looks so much like her beloved father, yet talks like someone else entirely. She wants to flee the scene, run away to her bed and hide herself in sleep, and after Rainer hugs her tightly and releases her, she makes a beeline for her bedroom. She hasn't taken two steps before Clara catches her by the arm. "You wanted to know," Clara says. There's something in her mother's voice, a kind of quaver like, that the instant Lottie hears it makes her realize that, once upon a time, her mother went through what's happening to her now. She thinks back to those late night conversations—arguments, really—between her parents while the scandal was breaking around her father at the University. She remembers her mother walking around the house during the day in a daze. It was this, Lottie understands. Her father had been forced to tell her mother about it. Her mother had demanded and he had told her in such a way that she had no choice but to accept. "You wanted to know," Clara says again, jerking Lottie out of her own thoughts. "So. You know. You will live with this. Do you understand? You will live with this." Clara might be talking to herself. She says, "What is happening will be seen to. Your father will find out what needs to be done, and he will do it. He is right. This is bad business. It must be seen to. You heard about today?"

"Yes," Lottie says.

"That is what we can expect," Clara says, "that and worse. That foolish man started what will get worse." Without further ado, no reassuring hug, Clara releases her, and Lottie retreats to the safety of her bedroom. As you might guess, sleep, when at last it comes, is not the cozy sanctuary she hoped for. She never said what her dreams were, but I imagine at least some of them have to do with the events of that afternoon, what Clara asked Lottie if she'd heard about and Lottie said she had. Seemed most of the camp knew about it five minutes after it happened. Helen reappeared, you see, though that was only part of the story, and not the one that set everyone's tongue wagging.

X

I suppose we have to backtrack to Rainer and his fellows standing around George's corpse. Once the men have determined that George has indeed shuffled off his mortal coil, most of them flee the scene. No doubt some were terrified by what they'd been part of, but likely the majority wanted out of there before anyone in authority, namely the police, shows up. The camp has its own police force, and while I don't know that they're much worse than any other police force at the time, I haven't heard that they were any better. These fellows are all immigrants, besides, and the last thing they want is to be associated with a strange death. Their jobs are the best some of them have held since coming to this country, and they aren't going to do anything to jeopardize that.

So it falls to Rainer to walk to the police station and inform them that his neighbor has passed on. As a stonemason, one of the skilled workers, he's in a better position to convey such information, and the fact that his English is better than most doesn't hurt. He decides to say that, as far as he can tell, George died of a fit, which is close enough to the truth for him to be able to stick to it. And stick to it he does, even though the cop he tells stares at him for an uncomfortably long time after he's finished speaking, as if he thinks he can stare a confession out of Rainer. When the officer gets up from his chair and accompanies Rainer back to George's, somewhat to Rainer's surprise the officer agrees that Rainer's assessment appears to be correct. He'll have to send over to Woodstock for the undertaker, the cop says, Rainer's free to go. He thanks the cop, and takes his leave.

No one person witnesses all of what happens next. Lottie pieces most of it together from the combined gossip of a dozen different people that day and the next. The substance of it is simple. The undertaker's assistant, a young fellow by the name of Miller Jeffries, who's sent by his boss to collect George's body, upon his return to Woodstock shotguns his boss, then drives back to the camp to shoot his sweetheart and himself. The consensus among the camp's population is that Jeffries lost his mind, which is what the residents of the camp tell the newspaper reporters who show up to cover the crime. I know: not the most earth-shattering of explanations. No one breathes a word about the reason for Jeffries's insanity, although a good portion of the camp traces it to the trip he took to fetch that body. A smaller number of people know that he met Helen, the dead man's dead wife, who was waiting in the house for him when he arrived. About an hour before Jeffries shows up, folks see her walking up the street to her house. One moment, the street is empty. The next, she's in it, as if she turned a corner in the air and appeared. She makes her muddy way to the house, and takes a seat next to her husband's corpse. Maybe she's expecting the undertaker himself. He's otherwise engaged, though, so it's Jeffries who's taken the black horse and wagon over from Woodstock. He's a bit strange-looking, is Miller. The papers describe him as short, with bow-legs and long arms. Word is, he isn't the brightest candle in the box, either. Lottie, who met him a couple of times in passing, said his face looked like he was trying to solve a difficult math problem that was beyond him. He climbs down from his wagon, enters the house, and meets what's waiting for him.

A neighbor passing by the house a few minutes later glances in a window and sees Jeffries standing with his head bowed, Helen seated in front of him. The neighbor doesn't hear Helen saying anything to Jeffries, but he's in a hurry to get someplace and doesn't pay much attention. Whatever Miller Jeffries learns in the ten minutes he spends inside that house sends him out of it with more determination in his stride than anyone could recall him ever having shown. The corpse that occasioned his trip he leaves lying. He rides back to Woodstock, to the undertaker's, where he has a small room at the back, as well as a shotgun no one knows about tucked under the mattress of his bed. He finds his boss bending over a body he's almost done preparing for burial. As far as anyone can tell later on, there's no dramatic confrontation, no melodramatic scene. Jeffries simply lifts the shotgun and blows a hole in the undertaker's back. The impact bounces the man off the coffin he's leaning over. As he lies there, Jeffries walks over to him and empties the shotgun's remaining barrel into his groin. He reloads, and shoots the undertaker twice more, a second time in the groin, and once in the face. When he's finished, he takes the horse and cart and returns to the camp, to the hospital, where his sweetheart is a nurse. He finds her talking to a patient, a man recovering from the flu, raises the shotgun, and shoots her through the heart. She collapses onto her patient's bed, and that fellow will tell the reporters he was sure he was next, but Jeffries only looked at him with dull eyes, said, "She told me everything," and turned the shotgun on himself.

It's a pretty sensational event. The Catskills have seen their fair share of murders over the years—more, probably, than most folks realize—but this one causes a stir far and wide. There's even a song written about it, "She Told Him Everything." For a short time later that year, it enjoys a measure of success. Pete Seeger used to sing it once in a while. I think he recorded it, too. The song's written from the point of view of Jeffries's sweetheart, and portrays her as torn between two men, Jeffries, who's cast as a kind of schoolgirl crush, and the undertaker, who's presented as the girl's true love. She wants to do right by Jeffries, but she can't deny her feelings. Finally, she tells him, tells him everything, as the title says, and that's that. Tragedy.

Obviously, there was something going on between Jeffries's sweetheart and his boss. Well, he thought there was, at least. What the song misses is the source of Jeffries's information. From his final words, the songwriter, following the newspapers, assumes that Jeffries learned of his sweetheart's betrayal from her lips, that she confessed the whole thing to him. No one told the songwriter about Jeffries's meeting with Helen. If they had, he might have penned a different song.

Lottie knows about that meeting, as do Clara and Rainer. For Lottie's parents, there's no doubting what happened. Helen told Miller Jeffries his sweetheart's secret, and, in so doing, signed the death warrants for the girl and both her lovers. If they required any further proof of the urgency of the situation, this is it, in spades.

As it so happens, they're going to receive still more evidence, whether they want it or not. While Rainer pores over his books late into the night, sleeping an hour, the dead woman continues her mischief. She isn't around when the second undertaker comes from Wiltwyck for her husband's body. I guess she had her fill of morticians. George's mortal remains are carted off to Wiltwyck. I don't know what becomes of him. Buried in a pauper's grave, most likely. I think he'd drunk what little savings the family had. The children, though—whom I guess you'd have to call orphans, despite the fact that their mother was up and moving around—they receive another visit from Helen. The kids've stayed on at Italo and Regina's, which is where their late mother finds them later the same day Miller Jeffries sends himself to his eternal reward. The day is just getting on to dusk. Italo is on his way home from work when he sees Helen ahead, lurching towards his house. Right away, he knows what she's after, and, as he'll tell Rainer the following morning, he's simultaneously furious and afraid. Furious, because here's the woman—the thing—that threatened his wife and children, not to mention the orphans, whom he's already thinking of as his own. Afraid, because of the secret words she's whispered through the door to Regina. He speeds up his pace, rushing past Helen to his house. Once inside, he doesn't waste any time. He bolts the door and begins piling objects in front of it, the kitchen table, a trunk, a couple of chairs. The children he sends into the back room. Regina refuses to accompany them. I think she wants another crack at Helen.

They wait there behind Italo's makeshift barricade, him clutching a hammer and chisel, Regina a cast-iron pan. His heart is pounding so hard he's dizzy, Italo will report, and no doubt Regina felt the same. They wait there, and as the minutes drag by, they look at one another, confused. Granted, Helen moves slowly, but she should have been knocking on the door by now, uttering her request. Unless Italo was mistaken about her destination, which seems impossible. You know that line from the movies: "It's quiet. Too quiet." That's how they feel. They wait, their nerves screaming with the strain. When they hear the crack at the back of the house, and the children shrieking, it's almost a relief.

She went around the house, Helen, until she was outside the room where the children are huddled. She felt along the wall, and found a board that was loose and weak. While Italo and Regina stood ready at the front door, Helen worked her fingers under that loose board, gained a decent grip on it. She was quiet. None of the children noticed her fingers sliding steadily across the wood. None of them heard her easing the board back. It isn't until she tears the board free, all at once, thrusting her arm inside and catching one of the children, Giovanni, by the hair, that the children are aware of their danger. Helen jerks her arm back, smashing Giovanni against the wall. She releases him, and he falls to the floor, motionless. She swipes at one of her own children, who dances away from her grip, and then she starts pressing on the board to the right of the one she ripped away. She's coming in.

Before she can pry off that second board, however, Italo and Regina are in the room. The sight of their son lying in a heap on the floor tears a pair of wails from them, and they rush at the place where Helen has broken through, knocking over several of the children in their haste. Helen tries to withdraw her arm, but she isn't fast enough, and hammer and pan blows rain down on it. More bones splinter and crack, one of them puncturing her white skin and spilling black blood. Italo stops his attack to grab Giovanni by his shirt and drag him out of harm's reach, but Regina continues to pound Helen's arm. When Italo relates these events to Rainer the following morning, Rainer will think that the sight of his wife's fury unnerved his friend. By the time Regina pauses her assault long enough for Helen to draw her arm out, it isn't so much an arm anymore as more of a flipper. Regina strikes the wall once, twice, screaming, "What words do you have for me now?" Helen doesn't answer. Regina hits the wall a third time and throws the pan clattering down. She turns to tend Giovanni, who's unconscious but alive, while Italo goes to check outside. He can think of few things he's less inclined to, but he doesn't know what else to do. Helen is gone. Italo follows the trail of her strange blood and muddy footprints out into the street, where it ceases, as if she's walked off the earth.

Italo's too exhausted from the evening's events to seek out Rainer. That, and he doesn't want to leave his family alone, unguarded. He can't understand why the dead woman is so interested in these children, but this is the second attempt she's made on them, and that suggests the possibility of a third. He waits out the night in a chair set outside the children's room, his hammer in one hand. The following morning, he doesn't leave for work until the children are all off for school. He's exhausted and afraid, and that's a bad combination for a stonemason. Twice, he almost injures himself. He sees Rainer, but it isn't until lunch that he can unburden himself to his friend. Rainer's guessed something happened from the look on Italo's face. While they eat their packed lunches, he listens attentively to Italo recount the events of the previous night. When the story is finished, Rainer says, "That was bravely done."

Italo shrugs. "The woman is still out there. She will return." Rainer looks away, and Italo asks, "Why the children? What does such a creature want with children?"

"I am not sure," Rainer says. "Maybe she wants to regain the life she cast away."

"Do you believe that?" Italo asks.

"No," Rainer admits. "I'm not sure. I'm not sure what I think, but I believe you should continue to defend those children."

"Of course," Italo says.

"You know," Rainer says, "I have books that may be of help to us. Last night, I read something that may be of help to us. We shall see."

Italo starts to ask him what he learned, but it's time to go back to work. If he thinks he'll ask Rainer on the walk home, he's mistaken, because, when the whistle blows, Rainer's daughter Gretchen is waiting for him. Italo hears her say something to her father about Lottie, and then Rainer is off, running flat-out for home. Italo catches Gretchen's arm before she can follow him. "What is it?" he asks.

"I don't know," she says. "Something happened to my sister. My mother says she met the dead woman. Now she's asleep and she won't wake up."

XI

ndeed, Lottie had encountered Helen. The meeting occurred while she was at work, at the camp bakery. Lottie had been having a tough time at her job recently, the direct result of all the weirdness swirling around her. As a rule, she liked working in the bakery. It wasn't much in the department of intellectual stimulation, but that was part of its appeal. Instead of sitting at a desk all day, poring over old volumes in search of the answers to obscure questions, as her father loved to do, Lottie was engaged in a much more immediate enterprise. You mixed the necessary ingredients, heated them in the oven, and in an hour or two you had your result, to be enjoyed by men on their way home from work. There's a particular satisfaction comes with such things. It's like what you feel cooking at a diner. On the good days, at least.

There's more than the pleasure of this work, for Lottie. There's the pleasure of work itself, of having a job. This is a time, remember, when girls, especially girls from genteel families, are supposed to stay at home and learn piano. Had the Schmidts stayed in Germany, that's more than likely what Lottie would have done, ornamented her parents' drawing room, until she was ready to ornament some young fellow's arm. Had she insisted on working, Rainer would have found her something appropriate to the daughter of a professor. He'd have made her his assistant, given her enough money to foster the illusion she was helping him.

Needless to say, coming to America changed everything. Lottie worked in her aunt's bakery in the Bronx because her mother's sister demanded it, and Rainer and Clara were too much in need of the extra money she could earn to fight that demand. Once she had that experience, and since the family had not yet climbed back to their old social station, Lottie had a much easier time convincing Rainer and Clara she'd do much more good working at the camp bakery than she would sitting at the camp school. Rainer wasn't happy, but neither could he argue the economics of the thing. Clara kept her own counsel, though Lottie thought her mother pleased in a way she did her best to keep secret. They worked at the camp bakery together, Lottie and Clara, and Lottie enjoyed it in a way she'd never enjoyed working with her mother at her aunt's. There, under the watchful eye of her older sister, Clara had been constantly tense, waiting for the reproval her sister sprinkled as liberally as the powdered sugar on her donuts. If she could correct Lottie before her sister did, Clara jumped at the opportunity, with a sharpness that made Lottie flinch.

Since they moved to the camp, though, Clara's behavior has undergone a sea-change. Outside her sister's radius, Clara is relaxed, forgiving, and even funny. To Lottie's surprise and embarrassment, she's learned that her mother has a great talent and memory for dirty jokes, which she never fails to indulge while they're making long breads and pastries. It's won her popularity with most of her fellow workers, male and female, with whom Lottie has been shocked to see her mother enjoying the occasional cigarette. "You don't tell your father," Clara said to her when she first spied her puffing away. The thought hadn't even crossed Lottie's mind, since she was sure Rainer would never believe her. She wouldn't dream of imitating her mother's behavior. She's pretty sure that Clara's new-found liberalism doesn't extend to her oldest daughter. But once her initial surprise has faded a bit, Lottie has found that she likes this Clara better than the one who made her time working at her aunt's an exercise in extended misery. She still misses her old mother, the one she had in Germany, who sang bits from Mozart operas in a high, ringing voice as she went about the house, but she's come to seem more and more distant to Lottie, a pleasant ghost.

As I said, Lottie likes working in the bakery. The last few days, though, have not been among her better ones. She's done all the things she did when she first started working for her aunt, made all the same stupid mistakes all over again. She's mixed batter wrong. She's spilled batter on the floor. She's left things in the oven too long. She's taken things from the oven too soon. She's broken more bowls than she thought possible. Her co-workers have covered for her when and where they could—they don't like her quite as much as they do her mother, but they still like her well-enough. Even so, she's gone from being one of the favorite employees to someone whose job is increasingly uncertain. Clara has watched this happen, and I'm pretty sure she knows its cause. She knows that Lottie has gone from thinking the world is flat to learning it's round, so to speak, and pretty much all at once. For the last few days, her mother has done what she can to keep Lottie out of sight, sending her on as many errands as she reasonably can.

It's on one of these errands that Lottie has her encounter. Clara's sent her back to one of the storage closets to fetch some slivered almonds for the danishes. This closet is at the rear of the bakery, next to one of the back doors, and is used to keep whatever there isn't room for in the main closets. Already narrow and shallow, it's made more so by the supplies crowded into it. The closet has no light and no window, so Lottie leaves the door open as she searches for the slivered almonds. Later, she'll say that she heard the back door to the bakery squeak open, but didn't give it a second thought, since she was busy trying to shift a heavy bag of flour to see what was concealed beneath it. Sure enough, there are the almonds. Lottie heaves the bag of flour the rest of the way off the almonds, listening to the footsteps dragging across the floor behind her. An alarm bell starts ringing in her head, but at that moment she isn't sure why. I know, I know: with all that she's learned the past few days, how could she not have known what's sliding ever-closer? You know yourselves, though, that it's one thing to hear something in a story, another to meet it in real life. Lottie's busy trying to ensure the bag of flour isn't going to topple over, even as she grabs the bag of almonds. Her mission accomplished, she turns to leave and finds Helen standing in the doorway.

Lottie doesn't scream. She doesn't drop the almonds, either. It's funny, she later says the first thought to barge into her head was, *Don't drop the almonds.* She clutches the bag to her chest. Helen lurches forward, tugging the door closed behind her and plunging the little space into blackness. Lottie breathes in sharply and retreats a step. *The almonds,* she's thinking, *the almonds.* Helen stays where she is. Lottie can hear her breathing, a slow, labored inhale and a wet, bubbling exhale, what you might expect to hear from a fish dying on the shore, drowning in air. Lottie stands in the darkness, so afraid she can't breathe. *Dead*, she thinks, *I must be dead.* Before Helen closed the door, Lottie had a quick look at her, at those yellow eyes, those blank, pitiless eyes, which she's sure can see her plain as day. She can smell the woman, can smell her death, a reek of rotten flowers and spoiled flesh that rapidly fills the air in the closet. Lottie gags, momentarily feeling her breakfast churning at the back of her throat. At the sound of Lottie choking, Helen chuckles, a liquid wheeze that sends goosebumps chasing each other across Lottie's skin. She swallows hard, forcing her legs to take two trembling steps back, until she's pressed up against the closet's rear wall. Her left hand pressing that bag of almonds to her chest as if it's a bag of diamonds, her right hand flails out in the darkness, searching for anything with which she might defend herself. She tries to remember what she saw in this part of the closet and can't. All she can feel are the ends of bags of salt, stacked one on top of the other and immovable as a heap of bricks. She digs her fingers into one of the bags of salt, waiting for the dead woman's advance.

Helen chuckles again, that liquid wheeze. Her laugh goes on and on, filling the closet the way her awful smell has. She laughs and she laughs, and Lottie suddenly understands that the woman isn't laughing, she's speaking. What Lottie took for one continuous chuckle is actually sentences. They're in no language she's ever heard, and between Rainer and living in the camp, she's encountered a few, living and dead. The words seem little more than phlegmy coughs, grunts, and clicks of the tongue. For the briefest of moments, Lottie wonders if this is Helen's original language, what she spoke prior to coming to America, but she rejects that idea immediately. She knows, in the way you just know some things, that this is speech Helen has brought back with her from the grave. It is a death-tongue, the tongue you learn once you leave this life for lands uncharted, and Lottie realizes she understands what Helen is saying.

It isn't so much that Lottie is able to translate Helen's words as it is that she sees what the woman is saying. More than sees: for a moment, she's there. One second, she's standing in a dark closet full of the reek of death. The next, she's looking out at a vast, black ocean. Great, foaming waves rear and collapse as far as the eye can see, while overhead churning clouds flicker with lightning. When Lottie and her family crossed the Atlantic, they passed through a storm, and she well remembers gazing out at the waves bursting themselves against and over their ship's prow and deck. Boarding that ship, Lottie had thought it the most enormous thing she'd ever seen; but as it slid up and down the heaving ocean like a toy in a bathtub, its hull sounding the successive booms of the waves' relentless pounding, she knew that she'd been wrong, that here was true enormity. Now, faced with the black ocean, she confronts a vastness that makes the Atlantic seem little more than a pond. As she watches, huge backs slide up out of and back under the waves; Lottie's reasonably sure they aren't whales, since no whale she knows of sports a row of spikes down its spine. She has the sense of more, and bigger, beasts waiting beneath the water's surface, forms as immense as a nightmare. The ocean is everywhere. Not only does it stretch to the horizon in all directions, it's under everything as well. I don't mean underground, I mean—it's fundamental, you might say. If what's around us is a picture, then this is what it's drawn on. Reverend Mapple had a word for it, the *subjectile*. Lottie said it was like, if you could cut a hole in the air, black water would come pouring out of it.

Helen keeps talking. Lottie hears her there a few feet away from her, but also from across a long distance, as if she isn't just looking at the black ocean, she's there. From where Lottie is, which is kind of floating above the scene, a little bit beyond the reach of the highest waves, like she's in a hot-air balloon, she can see that the surface of the water is crowded, full of floating objects. There are thousands, tens of thousands, hundreds of thousands. She can't tell how many there are. They cover the ocean in all directions. As she peers at them, she realizes that they're heads, the heads of people submerged in the water up to their necks. It's as if the biggest shipwreck in history has occurred, and here are the survivors. Only, they aren't thrashing about and screaming, the way you'd expect people in fear of their lives to do. Lottie thinks they might be dead already, that this might be a sea of corpses. She focuses on one in particular, a girl, and it's like looking through a telescope. Suddenly, she can see the girl's face up-close. It's frozen, the eyes open wide and unblinking, a strand of oily seaweed tangled in her matted hair. Her skin is alabaster-white, her lips blue, but her mouth is moving. She's speaking, in a low monotone. If Lottie concentrates, she can pick out the girl's words.

It isn't very pretty. She's joined a monologue about a man, one of the girl's father's friends. Using the kind of language that would earn Lottie a smack upside the head from Clara and a night in her room without supper, the girl is describing the most pornographic of fantasies about this fellow. Lottie wouldn't repeat what she'd heard, and I don't see any need to improvise, but the girl's inventions made her cheeks burn. Nor is that the worst. From lust, the girl moves to anger. When she's finished describing what she'd do with the older man, she starts in on her sisters. They're younger, and has the girl ever stopped loathing them? From the first moment her mother had announced her pregnancy, there was that much less of her and the girl's father for her. The birth of her first sister made a bad situation intolerable. Her second sister's appearance, the following year, poured salt in a gaping wound. She, who had had nothing to do with these babies' creation, no say in the decision to bring them into the world, was expected to act as their third parent, to surrender her life to her sisters. She never lost the sensation she'd experienced holding them when they were infants, the maddening awareness of their delicacy, their fragility. Their paper-thin skulls, the soft-spots gently throbbing, had offered her an almost unbearable temptation, kissing-cousin to what she felt handling her mother's fine china, that urge to hurl the teacups against the wall, smash the saucers to the floor, watch it all burst into fine shards and powder. It was that same feeling, but magnified, intensified to the tenth power. Cradling her sisters in her arms, she sensed herself standing at the edge of a precipice, one step away from a lunge that would ever end. That sensation, that awareness of the violence trembling at the edge of her fingertips, was delicious. It was like drawing your nails slowly over a patch of skin that was itching, so that you felt it in the back of your mouth. There was the same mixture of pleasure and agony. As her sisters grew, so did the possibilities for harm. How often had she let her hands linger on their necks, trailing over their soft, downy skin, imagining what it would be like to slide her fingers around them and squeeze? How often, when she was drying the dishes, had she tested the heft of one of the sharp knives, imagining what it would be like to press the point against their throats, watch the skin dimple around it, then push until it slid all the way in? How often, playing with them, had she shoved a little too hard, pinched a little too fiercely, passed off as accident what was purest intention? How often had she stood at that precipice, one foot raised, balancing, feeling the emptiness in front of her beckoning, calling her as intimately as any lover?

The Fisherman

All it would take to send her plummeting was a sudden breeze, and how she prayed that breeze would come.

With a shock, Lottie realizes that the girl she's been listening to is herself. That's her mouth saying those horrible things. That's Gretchen and Christina whose lives are being threatened. That's Italo playing lead in that x-rated fantasy. Glancing about, she sees that she—the other one, I mean—is surrounded by her family, Clara, Rainer, and her sisters forming a tight circle around her, her aunts, uncles, cousins, and grandparents encircling them. Everyone's face is frozen in the same, blank stare, and everyone is carrying on their own monologue. None is any nicer than what Lottie hears her other-self saying. Quite a few are worse. Here's Clara, regretting that she never brought that tinker who came around the house every other week up to her bedroom. He was tall, and his hands and feet were big, not to mention that nose. Maybe he'd have been able to satisfy her. Here's Rainer, bemoaning the idiots who surround him, the buffoons he's forced to spend his days beside and who wouldn't understand the least of his thoughts, who understand only the satisfaction of their animal urges. Although, to be honest, none of his wretched family is as smart as even the dumbest of his co-workers, but what can you expect, with a house full of women? Here's Gretchen, wishing she were strong enough to hold the pillow over Christina's face until she could be the youngest again. Here's Christina, wondering what it would be like to set fire to that dog that scares her with its barking every time she walks past it—and while she's at it, why not set fire to the old woman who owns the dog and laughs at her fright? And so and so on out from there, everyone uttering their most secret depravities.

Lottie feels her skin crawling, as if the words she's heard are ants scrambling across it. Her head spins. She claps her hands over her ears, but it's too late. Those ants have already found their way into her head and are running madly round and round her brain. She pulls away from the scene, lowers the telescope, so to speak, until she's back above the highest waves. The roar of the ocean, she understands, is the accumulated voices of this multitude, of who knows how many monologues of rage, pain, and frustration. She hangs in space, still listening to Helen speaking in the darkness, and the sea begins to churn beneath her. When the Schmidts crossed the Atlantic, Lottie had stood at the railing on the front deck watching the sea froth as the ship sliced through it. Now the water below bubbles and foams in much the same way, as if it's a giant pot under which the gas has been turned to high. The people floating there are tossed in all directions; despite which, as far as Lottie can tell, they continue talking. Something is coming. Lottie can feel it rising beneath her, shouldering the ocean aside as it ascends from unimaginable depths. Something is coming. Lottie hears Helen's voice rising, feels the bag of slivered almonds pressed against her breast. Something is coming. Lottie can see its outline forming in the water, a rounded shape larger than any object she's ever seen, larger than the ship that brought her to America, larger than Brooklyn Bridge, larger than the dam her father is helping to build. It's drawing closer, increasing in size as it comes, until it breaks the ocean's surface and Lottie sees that it's a mouth, a titanic maw ringed with jagged teeth the size of houses. It continues to rise toward her, waterfalls streaming down its sides, waves crashing against it, hundreds of people sliding down into its cavernous gullet. It's like the mouth of an inconceivably huge snake, one of those monsters you read about in ancient myths, so big it wraps around the earth and holds its own tail in its mouth. Lottie sees that it's closing, that its edges are rising to meet one another, and that when they do she'll be caught within them, dragged down to wherever it is this thing calls home. Lottie tries to withdraw further, to raise herself to a safer distance, but it's no use. She's as high as she can go. Helen is shouting, the enormous jaws climbing with each guttural cough and grunt. Lottie feels herself overwhelmed. The sheer size of this thing—it's as if the immensity alone threatens to extinguish her, blow her out the way a strong wind would a candle. Faced with that mouth, that throat leading down to endless depths, Lottie feels herself flicker. She tenses, pushing the bag of almonds into herself so fiercely it actually hurts, and in that momentary flare of pain she's saved. Without really thinking about it, she clutches the bag, wheels back her arm, and throws the bag as hard as she can at the sound of Helen's voice. The jaws are scaling the sky to either side of her, each one taller than any building, when the bag of slivered almonds strikes Helen full in the face.

With a squawk, she breaks off her speech. Instantly, the enormous jaws, the black ocean, the crowds of people, vanish, and Lottie's in the darkened closet. All strength gone from her legs, she slumps against the wall. It's as if she can breathe again. She sucks in lungfuls of air, not caring that it's rich with Helen's stench, while her heart throbs so hard it makes her nauseated.

The closet spins around her, which squeezing her eyes closed helps only a little. She hears Helen shuffling toward her and does what she should have in the first place: she screams, as long and loud as she can. When Helen grabs her mouth with one cold, damp hand, Lottie lashes out, punching and kicking. The dead woman responds in kind, slamming Lottie's head with her other hand. Fireworks flash behind Lottie's eyes, and she swings out into unconsciousness and back. Someone is pounding on the closet door, shouting for whoever's inside to open up. That voice rapidly becomes a chorus. Helen hisses, no word in her death-tongue, just a sign of frustration. She heaves Lottie into the air and pivots around. Frantic, Lottie tears at Helen's fingers, trying to pry them loose. She can hear her mother's voice among those at the door. She kicks furiously, connecting with her captor's legs. Helen staggers, but maintains her grip. "He waits, girl," she says. "He will always be waiting for you."

Then Lottie's flying through the air. One instant, she's hanging suspended in space. The next, she's colliding with the closet door. She falls to the floor, and the door springs open, spilling the crowd outside it in. Lottie's co-workers pour into the closet so fast they don't notice her lying in front of them, and they trip and fall over her. All at once, she's at the bottom of a pile of men and women swearing furiously at one another as they try to regain their footing. Lottie's voice, knocked out of her by the crash into the door, returns, and she screams for help, screams for her mother to help her. Clara hears her above the din and starts hauling bodies off her, yelling at them to get up, that's her daughter they're crushing under their fat asses. A pair of hands catches Lottie beneath the arms, and she scrambles to her feet and into Clara's embrace. Lottie wraps herself around her mother, hugs her in that self-abandoned way she had as a child. "What?" Clara says, "All this over a bag of almonds?"

That's it. At her mother's joke, Lottie bursts into tears, sobbing as if her heart had broken. She continues to cry as Clara leads her out of the closet and out of the bakery. She cries all the way home, and after Clara has undressed her and put her to bed. She cries herself to uneasy sleep, and later, Clara will tell her that, even then, she continued crying.

As for Helen, she's gone, disappeared from the closet as if she opened a door in the darkness and stepped through it. Traces of her remain. Her smell, which sickens half a dozen people to the point of vomiting, lingers in the air, while her muddy trail dirties its floor. Seeing the dirty footprints, Clara knew what had happened, which is why she removes Lottie to the safety of their home. Why Helen threatened her daughter Clara isn't sure, but she guesses it's connected to whatever it is that kept Rainer at his books for most of last night.

XII

ainer runs in the door. As he's drawn closer to home, the conviction has been growing in him that whatever has happened to Lottie is the direct result of his experiments the previous night, what he had hinted at to Italo. The look on Clara's face as he stops, panting, in the kitchen, is confirmation that his recent activity has not gone unnoticed. On hearing that Helen has visited his daughter, Rainer is distraught. Despite Clara's assertion that the girl has been through enough excitement for one day, and she needs her rest, Rainer insists on seeing her. He swears he'll be quiet, but when he sees her lying in her bed, still faintly sobbing, a kind of strangled noise forces its way out of his mouth. Clara whispering, "Come back!" he crosses to the bed Lottie usually shares with her sisters and sits down on the edge of it. His daughter does not waken. Rainer places his hand on Lottie's forehead, and snatches it back, as if he's been burned. He looks down at the floor, his shoulders sagging, and mutters something Clara can't hear from her position at the door. Lottie inhales sharply, sniffles, sobs once, twice, and falls quiet. Rainer stands and walks quickly out of the room.

"What is it?" Clara asks when they've closed the door. "What's wrong with her?"

"She's sick," Rainer answers. "That woman—that thing has done something to her."

"What?"

"I don't know," Rainer says, "but she has been poisoned."

"Poisoned?" Clara says.

"Yes," Rainer says. "Her soul is sick, very sick."

Clara glares at him, trying to control her frustration. "Her soul," she says. "So has she really been poisoned, or are you speaking in metaphors?"

"Both," Rainer says. "That woman has done violence to a part of Lottie we cannot see or touch. But it is a crucial part of her all the same, and the wound to it has sickened the Lottie we can see and touch."

"Can she be cured?" Clara asks.

"I have given her a blessing," Rainer says, "which will help a little."

"Should we send for Reverend Gross?"

"The minister?" Rainer snorts the word. "What does a minister know about any of this? They spend all their days worrying about who might be thinking impure thoughts—who might be thinking at all. You might as well ask Gretchen or Christina for help."

"Who, then?" Clara asks, "Who is going to help our daughter?" Before Rainer can answer, she adds, "Surely the books say something about this kind of thing? It's all connected, isn't it? This maybe-*Schwarzkunstler*, the dead woman, Lottie's sickness, they're like links in the same chain. Understand the one and you will understand the others."

"It's not that simple."

"Why not?" Clara says.

"Because it isn't like links on a chain," Rainer says. "The relations among these things are more subtle, more complex. It's like the relations of the sun and the planets, the planets and their moons—it's like the relations of those moons to the sun."

"You're saying it's beyond you," Clara says.

Rainer stiffens. "I didn't say that. I'm among the few men alive who understands even a fraction of it."

"But not enough," Clara snaps. "Not enough to put that woman back where she belongs, and not enough to help your daughter."

"It's complex," Rainer says. "Half of what the books tell makes no sense, and the other half is close to madness."

"Mad as a woman who should be dead poisoning your child?"

"Worse," Rainer says, "far worse."

"I don't care," Clara says. "If the books can help Lottie, you will find out how and do what has to be done. No excuses. I don't want you wasting time worrying if this word means 'a' or 'one.' You should have done this by now, and then none of this would have happened. No more waiting. You act now."

Although ten years will elapse before Clara relates this conversation to Lottie, she'll still remember the fury she sees raging in her husband's eyes. There isn't much Rainer is proud about any more. In coming to America, he's had to eat a tableful of humble pie, and he's learned it goes down best with a smile. He's accepted his sister-in-law's snide reproofs in her bakery. He's accepted his co-workers criticisms of his masonry. He's even accepted his children's corrections of his English. Throughout it all, he's treasured his scholarship as the one place no one dares intrude, the kingdom in which he still reigns. Prior to the start of this mad affair, he managed to steal a few minutes every night with one book or another. Clara pretended not to see his lips moving soundlessly, his finger leaping from word to word, as he delivered an imaginary lecture. Though he's never voiced any such hope to her, Clara knows that he secretly dreams of finding a position at an American university, re-establishing the career he was forced to abandon. For her to attack him here, the last bastion of his pride and self-respect, is the kind of betrayal of which only someone you love is capable. It's thin ice to be skating onto, and Clara is aware of her danger. As Rainer struggles to find a reply, she says, "I have sent Gretchen and Christina to stay with the Oliveris. I'm going over to help them. That poor woman already has all she can do with her own children and those others. Help your daughter," she says, and leaves.

XIII

Since Clara isn't there to see what Rainer does, and since Lottie is unconscious, I can only speculate as to what happens next. No doubt Rainer thought of the perfect reply to Clara's accusations the second the door closed behind her. You know how that is. Maybe he walked around the kitchen, trying to bring his anger under control. Eventually, though, he fetched his books from wherever he concealed them and spread them out onto the kitchen table. Years ago, when they were in Germany, just before the storm broke over Rainer, Lottie saw one of the books. At the time, she didn't know what she was looking at. It was only in talking to Reverend Mapple that she stumbled across the memory and finally understood its significance. She was spying on her father, peering through the keyhole in his study door for no other reason than that he'd strictly forbidden her and her sisters to disturb him while he was in it with the door shut. Lottie observed him unlock one of his glass-doored bookcases with a key strung on his watch chain. From the bookcase's highest shelf, he reached down a tall, narrow volume. Bound between plain gray covers, it was secured with a lock, which Rainer opened with a second key on his watch chain. He sat down at his desk, turning back the book's cover. Lottie swore the room darkened, as if the air in her father's study had filled with particles of minute blackness, making it difficult for her to distinguish Rainer. Because of this, she couldn't say for sure if what she saw next was accurate, but the pages of the book appeared to be giving off a black light,

112

dimming her father's face. Lottie bolted, ran from what she seemed to be seeing, heedless of Rainer hearing her. For the better part of the week that followed, she kept as much distance between herself and Rainer as reasonably possible. When there was no escape, when she had to embrace him, she had all she could do keeping herself from shuddering at the tiny flakes of blackness she could see clinging to his cheek, like the flecks of shaving foam he missed. For years after, she woke gasping from nightmares in which her father looked up from his desk to show her no face, only a black emptiness.

So I imagine Rainer bathing his eyes in the black light that spills off the pages of those books and clots the very air. A few streets over, Clara makes small talk with Italo and Regina, the three of them doing their combined best to talk around the strangeness squatting in their midst like an enormous toad. Lottie tries to escape from the black ocean, where her dreams have returned her. There's no giant mouth rising to devour her. There's only the face of her other-self and that unceasing monologue. Sometimes the speech returns to familiar ground—fantasies of her father's friend, loathing of her sisters—other times, it ranges over new territory—fantasies of her father himself, loathing of her mother. Lottie has never heard anything like this, but it isn't the shock of the language her other-self spits out that's so disturbing. It isn't even the sheer strangeness of confronting another her. What is truly bad, in a way that pumps fresh meaning into that deflated word, returning to it all the force it possessed when her parents used it on her when she was a child—what is bad is that each vile chapter in the other-Lottie's fantasy of degradation evokes a response in her beyond simple revulsion. Every ugly assertion makes a part of Lottie jump with recognition. She's no liar, this blank face. She's telling the truth, giving voice to impulses Lottie hasn't wanted to be aware she has. She's tried to make of her soul a garden, so to speak, but the other-her's words dig into the soil and overturn it, exposing what is wet and wriggling there to the light of day.

Maybe all this sounds kind of naïve to us, kind of dated. We're much more used to the idea that we're full of all manner of unpleasant impulses, aren't we? What Lottie is experiencing, however, is more than just a pious, sheltered girl realizing her own impure thoughts. She's undergoing a recognition—a recognition of intent so intense it's for all practical purposes equivalent to having committed the acts themselves. The ground has fallen out from underneath her. She realizes that the words her other-self is saying are coming from her mouth, too. Her mind is becoming brittle, freezing over the way a pond does, her thoughts becoming sluggish, struggling through an increasingly icy medium. Only the horror gripping her seems capable of surviving the cold, moving freely within her. It trundles along like some kind of small, polar beast, tireless, persistent, heedless of the plummeting temperature. Once the process is complete and her mind has frozen, only that small beast will be left, only the horror.

Clara stays away from the house the entire night, refusing Italo and Regina's offer of their bed in favor of sitting up at their kitchen table when everyone else has turned in for the night, smoking away the hours. From what little I've heard of her, she strikes me as a woman prone neither to regret nor worry, but on this night I suspect she must taste a little of both. She must think about the house she was mistress of in the old country, in the days before everything went wrong for her husband. She must think about that old life, and the distance between it and this new one. Does she remember the first time Lottie was sick, truly sick, and she sat up with her? How could she not?

XIV

Returning home with Gretchen and Christina the next morning, Clara is met at the door by Rainer. His face is drawn with exhaustion, but his eyes are alive with a light his wife has not seen in them previously. This light doesn't seem to radiate from within his eyes so much as to be reflected upon them, as if Rainer is gazing at a source of illumination invisible to everyone else. Clara doesn't like the look of this light. It isn't the warm glow of the sun; it's the cold glare of lightning. Over the course of their marriage, Clara has been afraid of Rainer on one or two occasions, instances when his temper flared so bright she was sure it would push him to violence. In all that time, she's never been afraid for him, not once, not when he told about his secret studies and the terrible cost they took, not when he walked out the door to begin the work as a stonemason he had absolutely no training or, so far as she could see, no real inclination for. She has faith in her husband, in his fundamental ability, despite a persistent absent-mindedness, to take care of himself. It's one of Rainer's qualities she likes the best, the way he encourages confidence in himself. Now, seeing that dead light playing on his eyes, she pictures Rainer as a man promenading in the middle of a thunderstorm, carrying a long metal pole high in his hands as lightning shatters trees around him. The hairs on the back of her neck stand up as Clara trembles at what she may have pushed him to. She might lose not only her daughter, she realizes, she might lose her husband as well. But what else is there to be done? Putting on a brave face, she hustles the girls into the house past their father, telling them to hurry, they're almost late for school. When they're inside, she looks into Rainer's strange eyes and says, "Well? You've succeeded?"

"We'll see," is his answer. He walks past her, towards George and Helen's house. In his right hand, he's carrying one of the good dinner knives, the silver ones, that Clara packed away in the trunk at the foot of their bed. The girls, who have reappeared with their school things, stare at her. Usually their father is full of hugs and kisses for them. Who, their faces ask, is this? Clara shoos them on their way. She sees them glance back as they go, watching her watching Rainer.

He strides up to the front door of the house next door. He raises his right hand, and begins to score the door with the good dinner knife, his arm moving in long arcs and slashes. Clara can hear the metal tearing wood, but because the houses are positioned the same way, can't see the marks he's making. After watching him for a moment, she guesses that he's writing something. His arm drops to his side. He says something Clara can't hear. Then he moves to his left, around to the side of the house hidden from Clara's view. She notices that he carries the knife in close to his chest, point-down. Wishing she hadn't smoked her last cigarette at Italo and Regina's, she watches the back of the neighboring house, where she assumes Rainer will appear once he's completed whatever he has to do on the far wall. Sure enough, a minute or two later, here is Rainer, the knife held to his chest point-up. He marks the house's rear wall, says something else that Clara can't hear but that, from the way his lips move, she thinks is different from what he said at the front door, and proceeds to the last remaining wall. His back to his wife, Rainer sweeps the knife over the wall in the overblown gestures of a circus ringmaster. Clara's assumption is correct. He's writing, letters or maybe words in an alphabet she doesn't recognize, swirling arabesques that spin and loop and fall back on themselves, so that she can't tell where they begin or end. She stares at them, and they move, writhing on the wood in a movement she feels on her eyes. Crying out, Clara jerks her head back, rubbing furiously at her eyes, where she can still fell those shapes squirming under her lids. All at once, the sensation stops, and when she removes her hands from her face Rainer is back in front of their neighbor's house, the knife held high overhead. The picture Clara had of him holding a metal pole up into a thunderstorm flickers across her mind's eye. Rainer snaps his arm down, hurling the knife into the ground at his feet, where it sticks vibrating, the light racing up and down its sides.

That is that. Leaving the good dinner knife stuck in the dirt, Rainer walks back to Clara standing in the doorway. For all that he's just performed what looks to his wife very much like sorcery, there's a spring in his step she hasn't seen there for a length of years, and not ever in this country. He used to walk this way coming home from the University, sometimes. Clara would catch sight of him from the parlor windows and know he'd accomplished something significant that day, solved a particularly difficult problem, won an especially challenging argument. There's a kind of bounce to that step that's equal parts joy and confidence, with a sprinkle of arrogance. Witnessing it here and now fills Clara with sudden nostalgia, nostalgia tinged with unease. As Rainer draws closer, so Clara's nervousness grows. The unearthly light has spread, widening its glow to encompass his cheeks and forehead. The more she sees of it, the less she likes it.

When Rainer has walked past her into the house, Clara asks him, "What did you do?"

"I made a box," Rainer says, almost grinning as he does.

"Don't speak in riddles," Clara snaps. "What did you do?"

That half-grin refuses to leave his mouth. "I trapped her," he says.

"The woman? Helen?"

Rainer nods. "She's not a woman, anymore."

"I know that," Clara says. "I don't care what she is, as long as this helps Lottie. Will it?"

"It will prevent her from becoming worse," Rainer says. "Lottie has been enchanted—"

"I thought you said she was poisoned," Clara says.

"Another way of saying the same thing," Rainer says. "I have a better understanding of what afflicts her, now. She is staring into a mirror from which she cannot look away. What I have done is like throwing a cloth over the mirror. She still has felt the mirror's effects, though; she still is under its spell. It is like the Snow White story we used to read her when she was a girl. Even after the poisoned apple has fallen from Snow White's hand, there is the piece of it stuck in her throat. She needs the prince to loosen it.

"Sadly," Rainer says with a grin, "we do not have a handsome prince at our disposal to ride in and save our daughter. We have only her father and his books. Those books tell me that to break the spell Lottie is under is a dangerous thing. I must step carefully, or Lottie will fall into the mirror and be lost. So we must go ahead slowly. Trapping that woman is the first step."

"And the second?" Clara asks.

"We leave her there," Rainer says. When he sees the panic flash across Clara's face, he adds, "Not for long. A few hours should do. She must be weakened."

"So you can destroy her."

"Eventually, yes, I will destroy her," Rainer says. "But first I must make her answer questions."

"Questions?" Clara says.

"Yes," Rainer says. "Bad as she is, the woman is not the true source of what has befallen Lottie. That is—"

"The man in the big house," Clara says.

"Exactly," Rainer says. "He may not be the true source, but I do not think I need to go any further. I think I can stop all this if I can deal with him. The problem facing me is, I don't know anything about him. This is why I must question the woman. Once I have learned what I can from her, I will be more ready to meet her creator."

"What about him?" Clara asks.

"What about him?" Rainer answers. "I told you, I don't know anything—"

"I heard you," Clara says, "and I'm wondering, if you don't know anything about him, how you are so sure you can destroy him, too? For the matter, how do you know you can destroy the woman?"

"Ach, her, she is a water-thing. As for her master…" Rainer frowns. "I don't know if I can overcome him, not for sure. If the man is a dabbler, someone playing with fancy toys—someone like me—then I will settle with him and settle quickly. If he is more serious—if he is a true *Schwarzkunstler,* then—let us say there is room for doubt. I believe I have learned a way to—compromise him, you could say—so much that he will no longer be of concern to us. I could be mistaken, of course."

"Whoever this man is," Clara says, "surely he must be what you call a dabbler. What would an actual *Schwarzkunstler* want with this place?"

Rainer shrugs. "Who can say? In the books, such men's motives are often unclear, mysterious. They appear in strange places, in little, out-of-the-way villages, or in the middle of forests, or on the tops of mountains. Remember the fairy tales, all the witches and wizards with their houses in the woods. Maybe they want privacy for their work. Maybe there is something about the places they choose to live. Maybe the world is thinner there. Maybe they can hear the sounds they are listening for more clearly."

"You think this is one of those spots?" Clara says, waving her hand at the camp, taking it in and dismissing it with the same gesture.

"There are stories about this part of the country," Rainer says. "There is Irving and his *Sketch Book*, with old Rip Van Winkle meeting the strange little men in the mountains."

"That tripe?" Clara says. "The man stole those stories from German sources. They have nothing to do with this place."

"The same stories may hold true for different places," Rainer says, "or different times. It does not matter. What matters is that the water-thing has been contained and will not be able to work any more of her mischief. Lottie has been removed from immediate danger. When I return from work, we see this bad business through to its end."

Clara believes her husband, but she's less than happy at having to wait until the later afternoon for him to resolve this situation. Of course she isn't going to the bakery today. Even if she were willing to leave Lottie alone in such a state, with the dead woman in the house across the street—trapped, Rainer says, but who can be sure?—she figures her place is here. So after he's gone, his face still lit by that strange light, she pulls a chair up to Lottie's bedside, and settles in to wait.

It would be a lie to say the time passes quickly. It never does, when you want it to. Lottie does not awaken, but her sleep appears to be more restful. It is. For Lottie, it's as if a curtain has been drawn over her vision of the black ocean, the other her. She's in a dim place, surrounded by a kind of heavy fog. On the other side of it, she can sense the black ocean's heave and fall, but the fog insulates her from its worst effects. Though far from happy, she is calm.

XV

When Rainer walks up the street to his house later that day, he's accompanied by a small group of men. There's Italo, naturally, and a pair of brothers, Angelo and Andrea—also Italian, obviously— and a fellow named Jacob Schmidt. That's right, same as Lottie's family. No relation, though. Jacob's Austrian, a tall fellow with thick brown hair and a big round chin; his eyes set too close to a short nose that was broken at some point in the past and that sits above a mustache which droops down either side of his mouth. Because of a bad stutter, he mostly keeps to himself. He's sweet on Lottie, always waits to be served by her at the bakery. Clara's noted his interest, teased her daughter about it. In response, Lottie's turned scarlet and told her mother to hush. Once Rainer learned what was going on, he declared that he hadn't left his home and crossed the ocean to have his child marry a damned Austrian. I don't know what Rainer had against the Austrians. Whatever it was, it didn't stop him from accepting Jacob's offer to join his little company.

It will be from Jacob Schmidt that Lottie will learn the events of that afternoon and evening; although it will take her the better part of two decades to hear all of it. Neither her father nor her mother nor Italo will say anything about what happens first at the house across the street, and then up at the Dort house. To say that Lottie will accept Jacob's proposal in a few years' time so that she can finally find out what took place while she lingered in that gray space would not be fair to the man. He's a hard worker, a kind man who will do everything in his power to ensure that she and their eventual children do not want for anything. It is fair to say, however, that Jacob's conduct that afternoon and evening will help ensure that, when he goes to Rainer to ask for his daughter's hand, the older man will put aside his distaste for Austrians and give Jacob his consent.

By the time Lottie's husband forces the last words of his account past his quivering lips, her father will have been dead five years, taken by what's at the time called senility. Most likely, it was Alzheimer's of a particularly aggressive stripe, hacking away great slabs of Rainer's personality in a few months, until there was nothing left but an empty shell the disease would claim soon thereafter. Clara will have relocated south to Beacon, to live with her youngest, Christina, and her family. When she at last has the story complete, Lottie will be near the age her parents were as its events were unfolding, and I'd be surprised if she doesn't reflect on that fact. What happens in those few days looms over the rest of her life like a mountain in whose shadow she's been fated to dwell. How strange to think that the people in the thick of it, the man and woman whose decisions set her beside that peak, might be herself, Jacob, their neighbors in Woodstock.

XVI

At quitting time, Rainer and his group don't waste any time. They march up the street to the house formerly occupied by George, Helen, and their children, now covered in marks it makes your eyes ache to look at. They're carrying axes they've borrowed from work—as you might suppose, not the kind of activity the company favors, or allows, for the matter, but the clerk from whom Rainer asked for them raised no objection, nor did any of the other men milling around. Everyone knows about what's been happening, and about Rainer's increasing involvement with it, and if he and the quartet of men with him are on their way to do something about it, then no one will notice if a few axes are misplaced for a night. Rainer halts the group outside the front door to the dead woman's house, where the silver knife he flung into the dirt has continued to vibrate, ever-so-slightly, throughout the day. The men can feel whatever it is is causing the knife to shiver, a wrongness in the air that floods their mouths with the taste of metal, twists their stomachs like spoiled milk. They grimace, spit. Rainer asks Italo for his clasp knife, which Italo fishes from his trouser pocket, opens, and passes to him. Gripping his axe midway down the shaft, Rainer uses the knife to cut three marks into the wood just below the blade. Without being asked, Italo holds his axe out for the same treatment, and the others follow suit. The symbol Rainer cuts into each shaft resembles a cross, or an x, a pair of lines bisecting one another—except for the third line, which loops around the other two in an arabesque that looks too elaborate

122

for the casual flick of the wrist Rainer uses to produce it. It's hard to tell where this line begins and where it ends. The more Jacob studies it, the more of it there is to study. He can hear Rainer speaking, giving them some sort of command, but he can't yoke the words together into any kind of sense. That third line seems to pass behind the other two; there seems to be a tremendous depth concealed there, and Jacob is aware of himself floating over this depth, high, high over it—

Italo shoves him and says, "Pay attention. He said not to look at it."

Jacob shakes his head, which is spinning.

"All right?" Italo asks.

Blushing, Jacob nods.

The last axe marked, Rainer folds the clasp knife and returns it to Italo, who takes it with his thumb and forefinger, as if it's been dipped in some toxic substance. Having learned his lesson, Jacob is doing his level best not to stare at the plain door to the house, on which the figure Rainer cut this morning is writhing, crawling all over itself like a mess of snakes. Instead, Jacob keeps his eyes on the ground, where the knife Rainer left there is shimmering at the edges, like butter starting to melt on a hot skillet. He watches Rainer bend to tug the knife free, and sees how it stretches as he does so. For an instant, it's on the verge of losing its form altogether, and then it's a dinner knife Rainer's slipping into the front pocket of his pants. Jacob's already feeling like maybe he's in a bit over his head, and what Rainer says next doesn't help his nervousness. Addressing himself to the newer members of the group, Rainer says, "You have heard about this woman, this Helen, yes? She used to be dead and now she isn't. Now she walks around, telling people things they shouldn't know and attacking our families. No more. We are here to put a stop to it. For all of today, I have trapped her in this place. I have changed it, so that it will draw off the power that sustains her, make her weak. But although her strength is less, she is still dangerous. She may say all manner of things to you, tell you terrible things about yourself, or the ones closest to you. It is the last weapon left to her, and she will use it to whatever advantage she can. You must ignore her. It is not easy, but it is the only way." Before any of them can reply, much less decide that this is more than any one of them signed up for and run, Rainer walks to the front door and pushes it in. Jacob has the impression that the symbol on the door hangs in the air, wrapping itself around Rainer as he passes through it. With a deep breath, Jacob follows him.

123

Inside, the air is clogged with the smell of damp earth and must, a combination that forces its way up Jacob's nose, into his mouth, down his throat. It's like trying to breathe through dirt. His body responds with a fit of coughing and sneezing. His eyes, his nose, stream; his chest convulses. Dimly, he can hear the other men hacking and wheezing. After what feels like hours, his lungs succeed in clearing enough of what's invaded them for Jacob to breathe. They aren't easy breaths he takes in, but for the moment, they're sweet as honey. He wipes his eyes clear, and the cause of the air's thickness is revealed. The walls, ceiling, floor, all of the room he's entered is dark, furred with dense, black mold. It's impossible to tell where the windows are. The room is full of gray, diffuse light. Mold envelopes what must have been a steamer trunk. It joins a trio of chairs along the opposite wall. It transforms a small table into an enormous toadstool. The only thing in the room clear of mold is the woman standing in the middle of it, at the center of a large puddle of dark water.

Jacob knows he shouldn't look at the woman, at Helen. But she's been on the lips of everyone in the camp for the last several days, first for her death, then for her return from it, and then for her assorted activities after that. More people claim to have seen her than is likely possible. Their reports have assembled a hodgepodge monster in Jacob's imagination, a hunchback whose right arm is the tentacle of a cuttlefish, whose skirts rustle and shift in odd ways, whose shadow doesn't stay in place, but ranges around her like a dog on a long leash. It would be remarkable if he didn't lift his eyes to her.

What he sees might be considered a lesson in the difference between rumor and reality. Helen's right arm hangs at her side, no sea-beast's limb, the odd dips and bulges in its pale skin mementos of the beatings inflicted on it by Italo's hammer and Regina's frying pan. Her dress is like a drape thrown over a pile of rocks, but that's due to the injuries that took her from this life. As for her shadow, though it's difficult to see in the gloom, Jacob's reasonably sure it isn't moving. What catches his attention is the fact that the woman is soaked, from head to foot, as if she'd been doused with a barrel of water the second before Rainer stepped through the front door. Her hair, her dress, are sopping. Her skin shines. It almost looks as if the water is flowing out of Helen, but that's probably a trick of the light. The rumors are correct in one detail, the woman's eyes, which are dull gold, the pupils black holes. Should those eyes turn in his direction, Jacob is ready to drop his gaze, but Helen is fixed on the man standing closest to her, Rainer.

There's something about his posture, a certain formality, that calls to mind the professor in front of a lecture hall, the lawyer in front a witness, the priest in front of the altar. Rainer's work clothes, his rough shirt and trousers, laden with the dust of his day's labors, seem almost comically inappropriate. He should be wearing a suit, or the robes of a scholar or clergyman. The dead woman opens her mouth, and what sounds to Jacob for all the world like a low, throaty chuckle emerges. Jacob shifts from foot to foot. The laugh continues, spools out of the dead woman like thread snarling off a loom. It's almost tangible. Jacob can practically feel it winding around him. There's something inside it, a message for him and him alone. The message is extremely important. It concerns Lottie, Lottie and him. If he concentrates harder, lets the laughter tighten its coils about him, he's sure he'll be able to hear what it's trying to say to him.

"Silence," Rainer says.

The laugh stops. Helen frowns. Jacob shakes his head, as do the rest of the men.

"Who is your master?" Rainer says.

Helen answers in a voice like rocks cutting the surface of a stream. Jacob feels his bowels shudder. The others step back. She says, "His name is not for you."

"Who is your master?" Rainer says.

"Ask Wilhelm Vanderwort," Helen says.

That name sends a jolt through Rainer. He starts to speak, stops, and says a third time, "Who is your master?"

"The Fisherman," Helen says.

Rainer nods. "Why has he come here?"

"To fish," Helen says, her mouth twisting in a sly smile.

"Why is he fishing here?"

"The water runs deep."

"For what does he cast his line?"

"No thing."

There's a pause, then Rainer says, "Not whom, surely?"

"Surely," Helen says.

"Who?" Rainer says.

"You are not fit to hear the name," Helen says.

"Who?"

"You could not stand the sound of it."

"Who?" Rainer says again. Jacob has the sense of a ritual being observed in the exchanges between Rainer and Helen. She is under no obligation to answer his question's first asking, or its second, but if he persists, she is obligated, he's not sure how, to surrender the information he demands. Rainer is on the verge of delivering his request a fourth time when Helen utters a word that Jacob has never heard before. It might be "Apep," but she says it too quickly for him to be sure.

Rainer appears to recognize the name. He says, "Nonsense. He would not dare."

"You have asked," Helen says, "and I have answered. Would you prefer another name? Tiamat? Jormungand? Leviathan?"

"The truth!" Rainer shouts. "The Compacts—"

"I heed the Compacts," Helen says. "Do not blame me for what you cannot accept."

"He does not have the power," Rainer says.

Helen shrugs. "That is his concern."

"The consequence—"

"Does not matter to me."

"How much work is left him?"

"Not much."

"He has woven the ropes?"

"From the hairs of ten thousand dead men."

"He has forged the hooks?"

"From the swords of a hundred dead kings."

"He has set the lines?"

"Why do you continue with these questions?"

"Has he set the lines?"

"If you run home, you will have time to kiss your wife farewell."

"Has he set the lines?"

"The near ones," Helen says.

Rainer turns to the others, something like relief written on his face. He says, "We must leave, now."

"What about her?" Italo asks.

Without looking at Helen, Rainer motions with his left hand, what might be a throwaway gesture except that his fingers bend, rise and fall as if he were playing a complicated tune on a trumpet. Helen's form dims, then dissolves in a fall of water whose slap on the floor makes the men shout and jump back. For an instant, Jacob sees her shadow still in place, twisting like a thing in agony. He can hear a scream coming from somewhere, and it's as if it's that sound that carries him through the front door. Outside, he's a little surprised to discover that the scream isn't his, it's Andrea's. The man stands with his hands at his side, his eyes bulging, his mouth in an O from which a shrill noise rises into the evening air. Jacob thinks he should go to Andrea, try to calm him, but he's too busy inhaling huge gasps of that same air into his lungs. It's as if a boulder has been rolled off his chest. He sways, half-staggers as the oxygen washes through him. Never has it occurred to Jacob that breathing might be such a pleasurable, such a satisfying act. It's left to Rainer to take Andrea by the shoulders and say something to him that calms his screaming.

A small crowd has gathered near the cabin. Several of the men carry hefty sticks, improvised clubs, while a number of the women have repurposed items from their kitchens—pans, knives—as weapons. Rainer walks towards them. As he does, they close ranks, raise their makeshift arms. He halts a safe distance from them and addresses one of the men, a tall Swede named Gunnar. He says, "She is gone."

Gunnar nods. "For good?"

"For good."

The crowd releases its collective breath. Their weapons dip. Inclining his head to Jacob and the others, Rainer says, "These men and I are going to see to the one who is responsible for this. It would be wise to gather your families and stay inside, tonight. I would not answer the door, no matter who seems to be knocking on it."

"What about this place?" Gunnar says, pointing to Helen and George's cabin.

"This is not a fit place for anyone, anymore," Rainer says. "If it is burned to the ground, it will not be a bad thing. In the morning, though," he adds. "Tonight, leave it be."

Shortly after dawn the next morning, Helen and George's former home bursts into flames. The camp has its own fire brigade, which is usually the model of efficiency, but on this morning, they take their time showing up, and when at last they do arrive, they're noticeably short of the proper equipment. In fact, all they bring are sledge hammers to knock down any timbers left standing, buckets of sand for the embers, and shovels to spread the sand. For the length of time it takes the blaze to devour the house, the firemen stand with the group of people who have come to watch the conflagration. The smoke that pours off the fire is heavy, almost viscous. Several observers are sickened by its smell, and one boy who stands too close to the plume will be deathly ill by sunset, his skin riddled with what look like toadstools pushing their way out of it. He's the last fatality of this whole strange affair.

XVII

It's doubtful any of the company who embarked from the house the night before hears about the boy's death, or the fire that led to it, for another day or two. Around the time the flames have fully enveloped the house, Rainer, Italo, Jacob, and Andrea are stumbling into their homes, offering mumbled words of reassurance to their wives or bunkmates, and falling into their beds, from which they will not rise again for the next twenty-four to forty-eight hours. Their boots and clothes are sodden, streaked with reddish mud whose color and consistency no one recognized, as no one could identify the dark green leaves whose serrated edges had caught in the men's clothing. To a one, they moaned and cried out in their sleep, but none of their wives or bunkmates could rouse them. Those wives and bunkmates made excuses for the four to their bosses, despite which, Andrea loses his job. Once they've climbed out of their slumbers, the men offer little in the way of explanation, answering most questions with at best a shake of the head. Rainer and Italo both reassure their wives that the worst is over, the danger past, and Clara and Regina set about spreading the word. Free to depart the camp whenever he wishes, Andrea wastes no time in so doing: he packs his bags and leaves right away. If he has a destination in mind, he doesn't share it with anyone.

As for Angelo, the story that circulates is that he's run off, taken a handful of axes and lit out for parts unknown. It's an explanation that's so patently false, even the folks who know next to nothing about what's been going

129

on suspect it. Which is not to say that any of them challenges it, makes an effort to ascertain the man's actual fate. Now that the camp has returned to something like normal, there's no one in a hurry to disturb that.

What those folks would say if they heard what really became of Angelo, I don't know. Most likely, they wouldn't believe it. They'd refuse to believe it. Maybe they'd treat it as an elaborate joke, the shaggiest of shaggy-dog stories. Maybe they'd grow angry, the way people do, sometimes, when they're confronted with the marvelous, the fantastic, as if they're upset at the universe for springing this on them.

XVIII

With the exception of Rainer, I don't imagine any of the men who set out from the camp anticipates what lies ahead of them. Maybe Italo has an inkling of what they're headed towards, but there's nothing in Jacob's experience to prepare him for the night's imminent events, and I expect the same holds true for Angelo and Andrea. Nor, for the first part of their journey, is there any hint of anything out of the ordinary. It's a warm night, the air around them beginning to fill with mosquitoes on the hunt for a meal, the air above flapping with bats doing the same with those mosquitoes. The moon's on the wane, but gives enough light for them to follow the road to the Station, and the Dort house. To either side of them, the Esopus valley is a study in systematic destruction. While the five of them have been at work on the dam and weir, other parts of the project have been moving ahead, as well. Every piece of ground that's to be flooded has to be cleared of anything that might contaminate the water. That means houses, barns, shops, schools, churches, all have to go, either taken down and relocated, if someone can afford it, or burned to ash and carted away. Same thing with vegetation, from the tallest tree to the smallest weed, it has to be cleared and, in the case of the trees, the roots have to be dug up, as well. Every last grave must be opened, and its occupant removed, repackaged in a new pine coffin, and reburied somewhere else. The only thing that's allowed to stay is rock, the foundations of some of the houses. I don't know if you've seen photos of the First World War, those

131

battlefields in France and Belgium, but that's what it reminds me of, that same, almost lunar terrain. If there's a difference, it's that the devastation in the war pictures is more chaotic: in the midst of a cratered field, there'll be a single, untouched apple tree, its branches drooping with fruit. What happens in the valley is methodical, relentless.

It's possible for the men to judge how far they've walked from the camp by the state of their surroundings, the stage of the clearing. By Jacob's estimate, they're about halfway on their journey when Italo says, "So."

There's no mistaking whom he's addressing. Rainer says, "So."

"When the dead woman said her master was the Fisherman, you didn't ask her any more about him."

Rainer doesn't answer.

"Does this mean," Italo says, "you know him?"

"No," Rainer says.

"But you know of him," Italo says.

"Yes," Rainer says. "Not much, but yes."

Italo does not ask the obvious question. Rainer goes on, "You have heard of Hamburg, yes? In the north of Germany. It is a port city, to which all manner of people come. It has been for a thousand years. In the later years of the sixteenth century, a man named Heinrich Khunrath lives there. He is a scholar—"

"He is the Fisherman, this professor?" Italo says.

"No," Rainer says. "Khunrath is interested in alchemy, in magic. He wants to find out whether a man can practice magic and be a good Christian. He is looking for those places where magic and faith meet. In the process of his research, he assembles a remarkable library. It is full of rare books, many of them from distant lands—one of the advantages to residing in an active seaport. I do not think the titles of these books would mean much to you, but there is one, *The Secret Words of Osiris,* that is the prize of the collection. It is very old.

"One day, a man presents himself at Khunrath's door. He is young-looking except for his eyes, which are old, older than any Khunrath has met. This young man with the old eyes says he has come to study with Khunrath. Khunrath says he is not interested in taking on any more students. He is too busy as it is. The young man insists. He has heard of Khunrath's investigation of magic, and he has a great deal to share with him. Eventually,

Khunrath agrees to let the young man study with him. Maybe he showed Khunrath a magic the scholar had not seen before. Or maybe Khunrath worried the young man might tell his neighbors the subject of his study. Hamburg prides herself on her sophistication, but there are limits to her tolerance. Always, there are boundaries, borders beyond which a man of learning is not to pass. If he does, the consequences can be…severe."

"Yes, yes," Italo says. "This boy with the funny eyes, he is the Fisherman. Does he have a name?"

"No," Rainer says. "Khunrath does not write it down. In his letters, he refers to him as his young friend. Once, Khunrath calls him his young Hungarian."

"Hungarian?" Italo says.

Rainer nods. "He was from Buda, which was then under the control of the Turks. He lived there with his wife and children. At the end of the fifteen-hundreds, the Hungarians fought a war with the Turks to drive them out of the country. This young man and his family were caught up in it. His wife was a Turk, you see, the daughter of a merchant who had followed the Turkish army to Buda. The young man thought that, if they did not draw any notice to themselves, he and his family would be left in peace. He was wrong. Khunrath did not know the exact circumstances, only that the man's wife and children were put to the sword by Hungarian soldiers. Those soldiers stabbed the young man, too, but he survived. After he buried his family, he fled west, to Vienna. From Vienna, he went north, first to Prague, then to the Elbe, which he followed through Dresden, through Magdeburg, through Wittenberg, to Hamburg. At every city on his route, and some towns in between, he sought the men like Khunrath."

"Magicians," Italo says.

"Scholars," Rainer says, "with similar interests."

"Why is he called the Fisherman?" Jacob says.

"Yes, why?" Angelo and Andrea chime in.

Rainer scowls. He doesn't like having his story rushed. He says, "Because the man wants to catch one of the Great Powers."

"What Great Power?" Italo says. "Do you mean a devil?"

"No," Rainer says. "This is something else. The old Egyptians spoke about it as a great serpent with a head of flint, a thing of darkness and chaos." Seeing the looks the other men give him, Rainer sighs and says, "It is what Scripture calls Leviathan."

"I thought that was a devil," Andrea says.

"It is not a devil," Rainer says. "You remember how God makes the earth? There is water over everything, and God brings forth the land from it, yes? Leviathan is swimming in that water."

"What is it?" Andrea says. "Is it another god?" Angelo crosses himself.

"It's closer to a god than it is to a devil," Rainer says. "It's like that first ocean, but it is not the ocean."

"This is blasphemy," Angelo says.

"A dead woman walking around," Rainer says, "that is blasphemy. This is knowledge, very ancient knowledge."

"Like what was in the book the scholar had," Italo says. "What did you say the name was? *The Secret Words—*"

"*Of Osiris,*" Rainer says. "Yes, that book talks about Leviathan; although it calls him a different name."

"That is why the young man came to the scholar," Andrea says.

"Khunrath," Rainer says. "Yes, that is so. He took advantage of Khunrath's hospitality for almost a year, and when he left, he took *The Secret Words of Osiris* with him."

"He stole it," Italo says.

"He won it," Rainer says. "How is unclear. The night before he left Hamburg, the sky over the city was full of strange lights, and there was a noise like many men shouting."

"So the young man fishes for Leviathan," Andrea says, "and this book tells him how. Why? What does he expect if he catches it?" Almost at the same time, Italo says, "Where does he go to find such a beast? What ocean is deep enough?"

"Power," Rainer says, nodding to Andrea. "If he could set his hook in Leviathan's jaw, he could bend its strength to his purpose. He could have his wife and children back. Who knows what else he wants? What would any of us ask for?" Before anyone can answer, Rainer says to Italo, "The ocean that is Leviathan's home lies *underneath*, below everything."

"Under the ground?" Andrea says.

"In hell," Angelo says.

"It is as it is underground," Rainer says, "as if the world is as flat as men once believed it to be and it is floating on the dark ocean. In places, the earth is thinner, the distance to the ocean not so great."

THE FISHERMAN

"This is one of those places?" Italo says, the tone of his voice indicating his opinion of such a claim.

"If the Fisherman is here," Rainer says, "it must be."

"How are we supposed to defeat such a man?" Angelo says.

"Ask the dead woman," Italo says.

"The Fisherman is not without his strengths," Rainer says, "but he is not a full *Schwarzkunstler.*"

"A what?" Italo says.

"Uno strégone," Rainer says.

"Ah," Italo says.

"We should have a priest with us," Angelo says.

"There is no time," Rainer says. "Your devotion will have to do for us."

XIX

ooner after this than Jacob would have expected, the men reach the outskirts of the Station. Here, the wide-scale clearing has yet to begin. Trees run right up to the road. The handful of houses that comprise the village proper are still standing, empty but undisturbed. To look at them, you'd never know that, within a year, all of this will be gone, scraped away. Night has pitched its tent over them. Shadow lies heavy on the houses, their yards, fills up the spaces between the trees. As they pass out of the Station and off onto the driveway up to the Dort house, Jacob sees movement out of the corner of his eye. In amongst the trees to his right, what he thinks might be a deer, except that it's too fast, and it doesn't bound away, it kind of flicks away, with a fluidity unlike that of any forest creature Jacob knows. Thinking it's probably nothing, a bird disturbed by their passing and made strange by his anxiety over the coming confrontation, he shakes his head and dismisses it.

When he notices the movement again, this time on the trees to his left, it's harder to discount, and with the third incident, also on the left, Jacob stops and stares into the woods. They've walked no more than a hundred yards up the drive, but the trees have drawn in closer together. The darkness among them is denser, almost tangible. Jacob strains his vision to distinguish whatever has been making that weird, liquid motion. You know how it is trying to see at night. Your eyes pick out all kinds of shapes in the shadows, even where you're sure there's nothing. Jacob stares into the blackness, unable to decide if the pale forms that appear to be dancing somewhere deep in the trees are actually there. He considers calling out to the others, who have not picked up on his absence and are already leaving him behind, but, wary of looking the fool, he hesitates.

With a sudden motion, one of the white shapes is at the edge of the tree line, startling Jacob so much he trips backwards and sits down, hard. He loses hold of his axe, which clatters musically on the rocky drive. Eyes bulging from the sockets, heart pounding at the base of his throat, Jacob gapes at the thing in front of him. No nightingale, it regards him from gold eyes that shine in the moonlight. Dark hair floats around its head, coiling and uncoiling as if with a life of its own. Its arms stretch to either side of it, slowly waving up and down, the light sliding back and forth along them. They're covered in scales, Jacob sees, the dull nickel of old coins—all of its skin is. Not just its arms, but its entire body is moving, bobbing up and down ever-so-slightly, as if suspended in water. When he sees its feet hovering a good two feet above the ground, Jacob realizes that the thing is floating, that, impossibly, the space between the trees is full of water. Jacob is swept by the sensation that he's looking not across but *down*, that instead of sitting firmly on the ground, he's perched precariously on the side of a cliff. His hands scramble for purchase amidst the dirt and stones beneath him, but find nothing to forestall the feeling that he's about to tip headlong into the water that shouldn't be there, that can't be there.

The fingertips of his right hand brush something smooth, polished—the handle of his axe. Jacob grabs it, drags the tool to himself. With a sickening lurch, the ground is the ground, again; although the water between the trees remains where it is. As he struggles to his feet, he feels hands under his arms, on his back, hears voices asking if he's all right. It's Rainer and Angelo, run back to see what happened to him. Afraid that the nausea that hasn't subsided will find its way out of his mouth if he opens it, Jacob gestures at the trees.

When Rainer sees the thing floating amidst the trees, he grunts. Angelo crosses himself repeatedly and unleashes a stream of what Jacob assumes are Latin prayers. He's surprised at his relief that the others see this thing, too. The symbol he carved on it faced out, Rainer raises his axe. The creature's eyes widen, and it darts away, farther back into the water. Rainer continues to hold his axe outstretched. Jacob waits for the water to vanish. From

Rainer's bearing, Jacob has the impression that he's expecting the same result. It doesn't happen. Rainer maintains his pose for a good minute or so, before lowering his axe with a sigh, an expression on his face Jacob doesn't like in the least, puzzlement, mixed with unease.

Angelo notices it, too. "What?" he says. "What's wrong?"

"It is nothing," Rainer says, which the three of them know is a lie but which neither Jacob nor Angelo disputes.

As they walk the remaining distance to the Dort house, the water lapping the nearest trees flows over them—Jacob thinks that it's rising, except that that's the wrong word, the wrong direction. It's more as if the five of them are passing between walls of water that are sliding steadily closer to them. By the time the Dort house is in view, the treeline is barely visible beneath ten feet of water that is oddly dark. The men glance to either side of themselves nervously. Even Rainer spares the nearing water a look. Not far enough away for comfort, several of the white things Jacob saw keep pace with them. There isn't one of the men who doesn't want to say something, but it's Italo who finally says, "Rainer. What the devil is this?"

"The dark ocean," Rainer says. "Here, it is leaking through."

"What the hell does that mean?" Italo says.

"It means our friend is further along than I had hoped," Rainer says.

Jacob is desperate to ask about the white things shadowing them. It's the face of the one he confronted that bothers him the most—not its inhumanity, the eyes, the scales, but the maddening suggestion of the human, its proximity to any, to all, of them. If he could shape his unease into a question, he would force it out of his trembling lips.

In front of them, the Dort house sits lightless. It's the kind of structure you encounter throughout this part of the state, its lower storey constructed of round stones of a variety of sizes cemented together, its upper storey and attic wood. The house isn't especially tall, but it is wide, at least twice as much as any of the Station's other houses. Both ends of the house are difficult to make out clearly, because the walls of water that flank the men extend across the distance to it, where they intersect it seamlessly, leaving only the central portion dry. Jacob is reminded of a tunnel, and the similarity does nothing for the nervousness that's made every square inch of his skin feel supersensitive, responsive to stimulus too subtle for him to notice otherwise. As ever, Rainer leads the way, but Jacob is gratified—and guesses the others must be, too—to catch the slight hesitation before he steps forward.

"Like Moses at the Red Sea," Angelo says. The allusion hadn't occurred to Jacob, but he supposes it's a fair one. There are no trees visible at all in the recesses of the water, only the white creatures, maintaining their distance. Odd as it might sound, the absence of trees makes the walls of water loom with added menace. As long as there were trees at or close to the water's surface, Jacob could convince himself that their trunks and branches were helping to restrain the dark water. Without them, the great blocks of water appear that much more tremulous. There's nothing Jacob would love better right now than to cross the remaining yards to the house's wide front door as fast as his legs would carry him, but he's certain with a kind of dream-logic that, the second he started to run, the water would crash down on him. So he controls himself and does his best not to look at the white things, which are darting back and forth amongst themselves with what appears to be ever-growing excitement. And when something much larger than the group of them combined darkens the distance behind them, swimming with the lazy back-and-forth of a turtle riding the current, Jacob tells himself that he didn't see anything. The door to the house can't be ten feet away from him. It's plain, made of heavy planks of dark wood bound together with strips of metal dull with neglect. In the center of the door, a large ring hangs from the mouth of a creature Jacob can't identify. It might be a snake, except its mouth is closed in a very human grin around the top of the ring. Rainer's pace has picked up, these last few feet. He has both hands on his axe, all the way at the end of it. Without breaking stride, he heaves the axe up over his shoulder and brings it crashing down into the middle of that smiling snake face. As axe meets knocker, Rainer shouts a word Jacob doesn't understand.

There's a flash of light—only, Jacob will tell Lottie, it was black light, momentary dark instead of momentary bright. The effect on their vision is the same. They can't see anything; they keep blinking and rubbing their eyes until the black spots in front of them have faded enough for them to make out the door, split apart and forced in as if by a small explosion. Jacob wouldn't be surprised to smell gunpowder. Instead, the air reeks with scorched metal. Whatever the knocker was supposed to represent, it's so many smoking pieces.

Emboldened by this show of force, Italo goes to climb through the door's wreckage, the others following close behind. Rainer holds up his left hand, and they stop. The weird radiance that Clara first saw on her husband's face, as if someone were focusing a white light on it, and which each of his companions has remarked, has grown stronger. It doesn't shed any light of its own. All it does is overwhelm Rainer's features, make them harder to distinguish. Without speaking, Rainer picks his way between the door's planks. His right hand holds the axe up, the symbol he engraved on its haft facing out. His left hand forms a gesture, the thumb touching the middle finger, the other fingers curled into the palm, making a rough oval that he positions in line with his heart. It's the way you or I might hold a flashlight. Once he's crossed the threshold he says, "Come. Keep close."

XX

Jacob is prepared for the interior of the house to be dark. He isn't prepared for it to be full of trees, evergreens, from the feel of their branches. It's as if he and the others have walked into a thicket. The sharp odor of pine threads the air. Needles tickle his cheeks and neck. Branches rustle as he follows the others through them. *Who plants a forest inside his front door?* he thinks, and the question strikes him as so ridiculous, he laughs out loud, a high-pitched whinny that rings on the tree trunks. It isn't happy laughter. It's the sound of someone who's watched a woman who should've been dead days ago collapse into a pool of foul water, of someone who's stared at a white creature whose gold eyes hold too much of knowledge, of someone who's passed slowly between rippling walls of water. Rainer's, "Steady," quiets Jacob's laughter, but it's still there at the base of his throat, ready to geyser out.

A dim light whose source Jacob cannot locate renders the trees visible. The evergreens extend far back into the house. Although he couldn't see how deep the house was, Jacob is fairly certain he and the others must be a good part of the way into it. Overhead, the trees are so high and so dense he can't see the roof. Nor is the floor visible, though it feels more like dirt, rather than wood or stone, underfoot. Jacob supposes it makes sense. If you wanted to fill your house with a forest, you would need soil to plant it in. *My God*, he thinks, *I'm reasoning like a crazy person.*

The dirt floor angles down, gradually, at first, then more sharply. The trees appear to be thinning, drawing apart enough for Jacob to see Andrea in front of him, Angelo in front of him. To his left, Jacob hears a dull roar, like a storm blowing through a wood. The trees around him are still. If anything, the ground seems to be responding to the noise, shuddering slightly. As the trees yield to a small clearing, Jacob identifies the source of the roar. It's a small stream foaming through a narrow ravine running roughly parallel to the course the five of them have been descending. White, the water gallops down the ravine as if it's in flood. Rainer waits on the far side of the clearing, observing his companions.

Almost immediately, Jacob's first thought—*This man has a stream inside his house, too?*—is replaced by another—*We are not in the house, anymore*—and a third—*We never were.* A look the way they came shows only evergreens ascending the slope. Above, the sky glows with the same dim light that's disclosed their way. Beyond where Rainer stands observing them, the ground drops more dramatically—still passable, Jacob estimates, but with need of the trees that continue down it to help keep their descent manageable. Past that, his vision will not reach.

He is nervous, but not as much as he was walking the last few yards between those walls of water. To be frank, he would rather Rainer had not brought him wherever he is, but he assumes that, if Rainer has led them here, then Rainer will be able to lead them out of here. (He understands that this is not necessarily the case, but does not dwell on it.) Neither Italo nor Angelo appears particularly delighted, either, but they appear to be managing their emotions. Andrea is not doing as well. He passes his axe from his right hand to his left hand and back again. Whatever hand is not occupied with the tool steals to his face, where it rubs his jaw as if there's a weighty problem he's deliberating. Jacob supposes there is. The cast of the man's features suggests his deliberations have stuck, if they ever got moving in the first place.

Rainer's noticed Andrea, too, and is walking towards him. His lips are moving, but he's speaking too softly for Jacob to pick out his words over the stream's roaring. No doubt, he's offering Andrea some form of reassurance. Andrea's features relax. His hand leaves his jaw. Whatever Rainer's saying to him, Jacob hopes he'll repeat it for the rest of them. Rainer's standing next to Andrea. He puts his left hand on the younger man's shoulder, and that's when Andrea bolts. Knocking Rainer over, he sprints straight downhill.

For a moment, Jacob, Italo, and Angelo stare at one another, open-mouthed. Then they're at Rainer's side, helping him to his feet. "What did you say to him?" Italo says.

"Never mind that," Rainer says. "We must—" He waves after Andrea.

Angelo plunges after him, and before he can think better of it, so does Jacob. Past the clearing, the ground slants so sharply he finds himself in more of a controlled fall than a downhill run. He tries to dig his heels in, slow himself, but that almost tumbles him face-forward, so he's forced to let gravity pull him along, his arms out for balance, his legs kicking up behind him, almost snagging on an exposed root and tripping him. To his left, the stream is practically a waterfall. To his right and in front of him, the trees have spread even further. He's too busy keeping himself upright to devote much attention to it, but he's reasonably sure the trees aren't evergreens, anymore. No expert, Jacob doesn't recognize the type at all. These trees are tall, slender, their branches and leaves clustered at their crowns. It's another detail to put to the side, like the ground, which has lost its carpet of pine needles and is a dark, brownish-red. Already, the muscles up and down Jacob's legs are protesting, and there's at least half the slope left to go. Ahead and to the right, Angelo twists, trying to avoid the trunk directly in his path. He almost succeeds, but at the last second, his left shoulder connects with it, spinning him around and off his feet, into a roll. Jacob would stop to help him, if he could figure a way to do so that wouldn't send him flying ass-over-teakettle. Besides, he's sighted Andrea, almost at the foot of this steep hill. So he pushes past Angelo, who's managed to throw himself onto his back and is sliding down feet-first, the leading edge of a plume of red dust. Beyond Andrea, Jacob can see something—he isn't certain what, because he'd have to hold his head up to look for longer than he's willing to risk running at this speed. Trees whip past him. To his left, the stream leaps and foams. To his right, in the middle distance, the reddish ground climbs to a ridge stationed with trees. His legs are on the verge of moving too fast for him. Andrea has reached the bottom of the slope, where, Jacob is relieved to see, he has come to a halt. Through the tops of the trees in front of and below him, Jacob glimpses something vast, something in motion. Andrea sees it, too; the sight of it seems to have fixed him to the spot. Jacob's lungs are burning in his chest, his pulse drumming in his ears. His feet kick up sprays of dirt as they carry him down the hill. The axe threatens to fly from his grasp. Andrea has not moved from his place. Jacob is almost upon him.

And then the ground levels, and he's running towards Andrea. He tries to bring himself to a stop, but it's as if there's a weight hung from his neck, pulling him on. On legs at their very limit, legs like taffy, he stumbles past Andrea, one, two, three steps, when the weight around his neck pulls him to his knees. Hand still on his axe, Jacob leans forward. Andrea—he has to see to Andrea. If only his heart wouldn't beat so fast. It seems to be taking all his strength into itself. Muscles trembling, he tries to stand, cannot. There is a noise in front of him, a sound his brain is telling him he should know. He raises his head and what he beholds chases all thought of his discomfort—all thought—from his mind.

XXI

aybe fifty yards away, an ocean crashes its waves against a rocky shore. Jacob has seen the ocean, before—he had to cross one to travel to America—but that in no way prepared him for this one. This is an ocean whose water is dark, as if Jacob is seeing it at night, as if it's made of night. It's an ocean in storm. Even though the sky above is clear, the dark water lifts itself in frothing waves large as houses. Some of these burst on the jagged boulders that constitute the beach, shooting spray high into the air. Others smash into one another, larger waves sweeping over smaller ones, consuming them, rows of smaller waves angling into larger ones, collapsing them. It's as if this is a spot where a host of opposing currents converge. A few hundred yards from the stony beach—it's hard to estimate distances with any accuracy in this tumult, but much too close for comfort, let alone sanity—something enormous raises itself amidst the waves. For a moment, Jacob's mind insists that what arcs out of the water is an island, because there is no living creature that big in all of creation. Then it moves, first rising even higher, into a more severe arch, then subsiding, lifting itself from the waves at both ends while relaxing its middle into a gradual curve, the whole of its dull surface traversed by the ripples of what Jacob understands are great muscles flexing and releasing, and there's no doubt this is alive. Before now, if you had asked Jacob to name the largest thing he's ever seen, he might have answered with St. Stephen's cathedral, in Vienna. But the beast against whose scaly side the black water batters itself

145

dwarfs that structure. There is so much of it that its very presence presses on Jacob, as if mere proximity to it might be sufficient to snuff him out, like a candle in a hurricane.

Because of the creature, Jacob fails to notice any of what's closer to him until Angelo comes huffing behind him. His "Mother of God!" jolts Jacob out of the fog that's enveloped him. It requires a vigorous shaking to bring Andrea out of his reverie, but by the time Italo and Rainer have joined the three of them, Jacob has risen to his feet and is surveying the ground between the beach and himself. He sees the blood first. The soil bordering the beach is soaked in it. It collects in bright red puddles, winds its red way to the rocky shore. Its source is a trio of carcasses, two to the right, and one to the left. They're cattle—bulls, Jacob thinks—but of such a breed as might inhabit a child's fairy tale. Each animal is large as a small elephant, its hide a rich, sunset gold. Were it not for the beast filling the ocean, Jacob would be awed by the cattle's size; as it is, he is impressed by them. The bull to the left, and one of those to the right, have been decapitated, the heavy heads set between them, beside what seems to be an anchor; albeit, an anchor that might have held fast the ship that brought him across the Atlantic. Instead of splitting into a pair of arms, the thick shank divides into three upward-curving lengths of metal, all of them tipped with a barb longer than Jacob is tall. It's a hook, he understands, the bulls' heads the bait to be impaled on the points. There's no line tied to the eye, though there are plenty to choose from. The ground this side of the slaughtered cattle is full of rope, coils of it, stacks of it, heaps of it. There is coarse rope wide as a strong man's arm. There is smooth rope slender as a shoelace. There's rope smeared with what might be pitch. There's rope white as milk.

Some of the rope has already been put to use. Between where it's piled and Jacob and his fellows stand are what appear to be a half-dozen round, wooden tables, each of such a dimension as to suggest it's for the herders who raise the giant cattle. They're stumps, Jacob realizes, the stumps of trees that must have towered overhead like skyscrapers. None of them is higher than his chest, now. At varying distances from the ground, holes have been bored through the stumps. Rope has been threaded through the holes and out around the remnants of the trees, tied at irregular intervals into elaborate knots, secured to the wood at other spots with large metal staples. From the wrap around each abbreviated trunk, a length of rope runs out to the left of the dead bulls, into the ocean. Most of the ropes stretch taut into and under the waves. Jacob can see them thrumming, like guitar strings being tightened to the point of snapping. These lines are joined by a dozen or so from the left, on the far side of the stream that raced Jacob down the hill and surges to the ocean. These ropes, too, are held fast by a group of enormous tree stumps. Beyond them, the headless remains of more of the great cattle lie under a buzzing cloud of greenish flies.

"What?" a voice calls. "What is it you want?" The words are uttered in German, but it is a version of the tongue that is crusted with age. The man who asked the question is standing behind the one bull whose head has not been removed. The animal's bulk must have concealed him. He is wearing a rugged apron that appears to have been stitched together from a number of mismatched pieces of material, and that is spattered and caked with gore, as is the sizable knife in his right hand. Beneath the patchwork apron, he is dressed in a white shirt and black pants whose best days are long behind them. His hair is lank, greasy, his chin fringed by a stringy beard, the face between young, almost boyish. He must be Rainer's Fisherman, but if you told Jacob he was a junior butcher, he'd believe you.

"The ropes," Rainer says. "Go."

Italo advances to the closest of the stumps, circles the spot where the rope reaches to the ocean, and swings his axe at it. The rope isn't especially thick, but the axe rebounds from it with a crack and a shower of sparks. Italo steps back as if pulled by his axe's rebound. The rope has been cut only a little. Italo frowns, and strikes again.

"Hurry!" Rainer shouts at the others, who are still standing, watching Italo's efforts. Angelo runs to the next closest tree stump and commences chopping at its rope. His cheeks burning, Jacob follows suit. Rainer shoves Andrea forward, and he stumbles to the nearest stump.

The rope Jacob is faced with is stout, its rough surface shining with the fishhooks whose eyes have been braided into it. The majority of them are the size you would employ to lever a trout or bass out of a stream, but there are a few clearly fashioned for larger sport, including a hook as large as Jacob's hand that swings wildly from side to side when he strikes the rope. From its width, Jacob expects the rope will not be easily cut. What he does not expect is the sensation that runs up the axe when its blade bites the fibers. The shaft twists in his hands, as if the axe has connected to a source of tremendous power. Jacob has a vision of himself trying to sever a lightning bolt. There's a flat crack and the axe is flung back with such force it's almost torn form his grip. The scorch of burnt hair stings his nostrils. He's cut the rope, but just barely.

Around him, the air snaps with the crack of his companions' axes connecting with these strange ropes. A rapid-fire burst of Italian that's probably a prayer bursts from Angelo's lips as his axe flies up from the rope it's struck. The recoil flings Andrea's axe out of his hands, over his head, and onto the ground behind him. Only Italo succeeds in maintaining something like a regular rhythm, though the sweat already soaking the back of his shirt testifies to the effort it's costing him. Jacob adjusts his grip and raises his axe.

Throughout all this, which hasn't taken more than a minute or two, the Fisherman has remained in place, watching the five of them. When Jacob is three difficult strokes into his task, the Fisherman leaves his spot beside the great bull's carcass and walks toward the stream. He still has hold of that knife, though he carries it almost casually. Jacob doesn't care for the sight of him approaching the frothing water, doesn't like the deliberation with which the man kneels beside it and plunges the bloody knife down into it, but Rainer hasn't told him to stop chopping, so he delivers a fourth and a fifth blow to the rope. He is making progress. The dense strands that compose the rope are separating, however reluctantly. As each does, he's aware of something escaping from it, a force that eddies in the air around him, stirring the hairs on his arms, the back of his neck.

The Fisherman remains bent at the stream, the knife and the hand holding it underwater, for a long time, enough for Jacob to have cut almost halfway through his rope, Italo three-quarters of the way through his. Jacob has been expecting Rainer to approach the man, confront him, but it's only as he's rising from the stream and turning to them that Rainer strides past Jacob. From his efforts, Jacob is drenched in sweat. Sweat matts his hair to his head, streams down his forehead, runs into his eyes, blurring his vision. For this reason, he isn't sure whether, when he sees the water clinging to the Fisherman's arm, from his elbow to the tip of his knife, as if he's wearing it, his eyes are playing tricks on him. The Fisherman snaps his arm, as if he were cracking a whip, and the water rushes to the knife, gathering around it in a globe. Rainer breaks into a run, and it's this that convinces Jacob his eyesight is fine. A flick of the wrist, and the ball of water surrounding the

THE FISHERMAN

Fisherman's knife elongates, lancing at Italo, who's holding his axe above his head, ready for the next cut. Before the water-spear can reach him, Rainer's at his side, his right hand holding his axe marked side forward, his left making a sweeping motion outward. Like a snake sliding around a rock, the water curves away from Italo and Rainer. Instead, it targets Angelo.

Jacob is close enough to him to mark the exact location the water strikes, the hollow at the base of the throat, and to hear the sound it makes as it punctures the skin and streams into the wound, the whoosh of water descending a drain. Angelo goes rigid, his mouth gaping, his eyes bulging, while the water invades him. Andrea shouts, "Angelo!" Jacob knows he should do something, but it's as if his arms and legs have locked. Before movement has returned to them, the tail end of the water-spear has left the Fisherman's blade and vanished into the wound in Angelo's throat.

XXII

His axe gripped near the end with both hands, Rainer advances on the Fisherman, who half-crouches, as if weighing another plunge of his hand into the stream. Italo resumes chopping through his rope. Angelo turns to face Jacob. He moves stiffly, as if the water that's entered the hole in his throat has swollen his joints. A sheen of what appears to be sweat shines on Angelo's face, his hands—the Fisherman's water, Jacob realizes, seeping out Angelo's pores. As if he's crying uncontrollably, Angelo's eyes shimmer. Beneath the water, they're gold. Jacob groans, and as if in response to his displeasure, Angelo coughs. It's a rough, wet noise, the sound of a man trying to clear his lungs of the water that's drowning them. Little spouts of water splash from the wound in his throat as the cough goes on and on and on, bending Angelo over with its force.

Within each liquid bark, Jacob hears something else, what might almost be a word, words. There's a language forcing itself out of Angelo, a harsh assemblage of phlegmy coughs, grunts, and clicks of the tongue that Jacob nonetheless understands. It's not so much that he can translate individual words as it is that he can see their subject. More than see—for an instant, it's as if he's inside what's being described. One moment, he's hovering airplane-high in the air, so far up the coastline below him might be the kind of oversized map you sometimes encounter on the floors of museums. He doesn't recognize the contours of the shore, but he already knows the black ocean, as he knows that the humps rising from it, parallel to the coast, aren't islands, but more of the great beast he's watched shift its back in front of him, Rainer's Leviathan. And this might well be the Biblical personage, because it continues along the shore in both directions, to the limit of Jacob's view. From points up and down the coast, a lattice of fine lines stretches to the water, some of them ending at one of the enormous humps, others plunging beneath the waves. The Fisherman has done this, Jacob understands. Working over a length of time Jacob does not even want to consider, the man with the lank hair and scraggly beard has cast his lines and lodged his hooks into the bulk of this immensity with a patience that's equal measures mad and heroic. He has brought this monster, this god-beast, to the brink of complete capture, and while doing so must be a trespass of a fundamental order, Jacob cannot help himself from admiring the man.

With unnerving speed, the scene beneath begins to draw closer. Though he can feel his feet planted on the ground, Jacob has the sensation of dropping from a great height, like a bird who's lost the use of his wings. Wind pushes against him as the ground gains in definition. Through eyelids squinted almost shut, he sees that the ropes directly below him are also fastened to the remains of giant trees. His ears fill with roaring, the sound of the air he's plummeting through. It is absurd—his feet rest firmly on the red soil. He hears Angelo expelling the jagged language from a throat that must be raw from it. He is standing listening to Angelo, and he is dropping towards a tree stump the width of a field, and when he strikes that expanse of blond wood, Jacob knows he will fall over, dead. He closes his eyes, but it makes no difference. The tree stump fills his vision, a wooden plane. He sees that the rope tied around it has been painted with symbols, angular markings midway between pictures and letters. They appear to float above the fibers. What a peculiar detail, he thinks, to accompany him out of this life.

Somewhere in front of him, there's an explosion of sound, sounds, a train of them slamming one into the other. A drawn-out yell collides with the thud of one body crashing into another, which smashes into Angelo's weird speech, which breaks into random coughing. The tree stump Jacob's fifty feet away from meeting bursts as if it had been projected onto a giant soap-bubble. With it goes the impression of falling, the departure so sudden that Jacob staggers forward a couple of steps. This brings him to where Andrea and Angelo are wrestling in the red dirt, carried off their feet by the force of Andrea's charge. Angelo is on his back, Andrea half on top of him. Andrea's left forearm presses across Angelo's throat, his right arm raises his axe. Angelo's right hand is under Andrea's chin, forcing his head back, his left hand grips Andrea's elbow, holding his axe at bay. Andrea's eyes dart in Jacob's direction. Through teeth clenched shut, he hisses, "Come on!"

For a second, Jacob does not understand what Andrea is saying to him. Then the weight of the axe in his hand clarifies it. He hurries to Andrea's right, where more of Angelo's body is exposed. Angelo's gold eyes lock on Jacob standing there, both hands on his axe, and his lips draw back in a snarl. The water coating his face writhes. His legs kick, his hips buck, as he attempts to throw Andrea off. "Do it!" Andrea shouts.

Jacob wants to shout back that he's trying, but Angelo is twisting around so much, he keeps putting Andrea in the way. The axe over his head, Jacob shifts right, left, right again. "For Christ's sake!" Jacob bellows and, raising his foot, shoves Andrea out of the way. The move catches Angelo by surprise. He's been straining so hard to force Andrea up, that his efforts carry him almost to a sit. *Now*, Jacob thinks.

As he does—it's not so much that time slows down as it is that he's aware of everything happening around him. Rainer and the Fisherman are in the midst of a fight, of a kind of duel. Each grasps his weapon in his right hand, and knife and axe clash in a rain of sparks. The weapons are followed by their left hands, each of which centers a sphere of Jacob can't say exactly what, except that the Fisherman's shines like mercury, while Rainer's is dark as obsidian. When the spheres collide, the air around the men dims, and Jacob's teeth ache.

Italo, in the meantime, has reached his final stroke. The edge of his axe is dull, notched, as if he's done a year's worth of work in the last five minutes. Like Jacob's rope, Italo's is hung with all manner of fishhooks, which jangle as the rope spins, clockwise and counter-, against the forces that strain it. Italo's exhaustion is evident. His shirt is transparent with sweat. He sways from side to side as if drunk. Nonetheless, he musters the strength for one more heave of his axe. It cleaves the remaining strands of rope cleanly. A thunderclap knocks Italo off his feet, radiates outwards. The rope rears back like a wounded serpent, its rigid straightness released into loops and snarls. Hooks flaring, a length of the rope coils at Rainer. He's already started to turn his head, probably in response to Italo's axe slicing through the rope, so he sees the flashing hooks, the curving rope, and, with a speed Jacob would not have guessed he possessed, throws himself to the ground. One of the hooks catches the back of his shirt and as quickly rips free, following the rest of its fellows as the rope rolls above Rainer and into the Fisherman. Maybe he's been too focused on his contest with Rainer—maybe that black globe surrounding Rainer's left hand has affected his eyesight—either way, he doesn't react in time. The rope slaps up and down him, burying a host of the smaller and several of the larger fishhooks in him.

This is Jacob's moment. Pivoting his hips to give the blow its maximum force, he swings the axe down. In the quarter-second it takes for the blade to traverse the arc up, down, and into the base of Angelo's neck, where it joins the shoulder, Jacob watches Angelo's eyes darken from gold to brown, the water slide off his face. *STOP!* his brain screams, but it's too late. Already, the blade has reached Angelo's skin. It cuts deep, through the muscle and collar bone, down to the edge of his breastbone. Blood vents from severed arteries. With a cry, Jacob releases the axe and stumbles back. The handle of the axe protruding up like some awkward new limb, blood bubbling red onto his shirt, Angelo attempts to raise himself to his feet. All he manages is to bring his right arm around in front of him, to shift his legs underneath him. As soon as he has, he slumps over, supporting himself on his right arm. Blood pattering the soil, Angelo lurches into a half-crawl. Jacob can't imagine where he could be headed. Nor is it likely Angelo has much idea. He manages to place one madly trembling hand forward before his arm gives out, dropping his face into the dirt that's already damp with his blood. His mouth opens and closes, opens and closes, opens and remains open. Though he damns his cowardice, Jacob can't bear to approach him. It's left to Andrea to kneel beside their comrade and search his neck for the pulse both men know won't be there. Italo staggers to their sides, but there isn't anything he can do.

A scream jerks the men's attention from the crimson pool spreading under Angelo. It's the Fisherman. He's struggling against the rope that has stitched itself to him, crossing from his right hip to his left shoulder like a sash. Behind him, the rope has drawn taut, and is pulling him toward the rocky shore, and the dark waves beyond. Although blood streams down his apron from dozens of spots where the fishhooks have pushed through it into him, the Fisherman fights mightily to stay where he is. Grabbing the rope at a spot high on his chest, sucking in his breath as the hooks stab his palm, the Fisherman raises his knife to ease the tip between his skin and the rope. The rope yanks him back a step. He licks his lips, his brow furrowed, as he concentrates on sliding the knife under the rope.

Which is when Rainer steps in close to him, his axe swinging up. It clangs on the blade of the knife, spinning it out of the Fisherman's grasp. Rainer reverses his stroke, and sweeps the Fisherman's legs out from under him. The man sits down hard. To his rear, the rope sags, then straightens, slamming the Fisherman onto his back and dragging him in the direction of the beach. His one hand still hooked to the rope, the Fisherman slaps the ground with the other, searching for purchase. His fingers dig into the soil, carve trenches in the dirt as he's pulled across it. Blood spills and splashes from his apron. His breathing is loud, hoarse, a much larger sound than you would expect from so slight a man. Keeping a few steps behind, Rainer follows him as he's towed from the dirt onto the stony beach. Rocks clatter and click as he drags over them. Frantic, he tries to dig his heels in among the rocks, but they're scattered by the force drawing him on.

Maybe halfway down the beach, the Fisherman succeeds in wedging his left foot into a narrow fissure in a long table of a rock. He howls when the rope continues to pull at him, and the howl increases its volume as he pushes his way to his feet, crescendoing in a victory cry that's interrupted by Rainer hammering the blunt end of his axe head on the Fisherman's left knee. Bone cracks. Face blank with this new pain, the Fisherman pulls away from it, and in so doing, inclines in the very direction he's only just succeeded in resisting. When the rope yanks him down, his foot remains caught in the stone that has switched from brace to vise. With the snap of a dried branch, his ankle breaks. For much too long, his foot is caught in the rock as the rest of him is dragged towards the water. Further bones, ligaments, crack, pop. A high, keening sound leaks from the Fisherman's mouth, which is clamped shut. With his free hand, he pushes at his trapped leg; with his free leg, he kicks at it. At last, his heel slides loose and he's pulled off the long rock.

This is it. There's nothing of any size to prevent the Fisherman being drawn the rest of the way to the black ocean. He appears to know this, which is not to say that he accepts it. In his antique German, he lets fly a volley of curses at Rainer. "Go fuck your mother," Rainer says. The next volley of curses expands its targets to include Jacob, his companions, and their families. "Go fuck your father," Rainer says. What Jacob assumes is a further round of invective is delivered in a language he thinks is Hungarian. "Go fuck yourself," Rainer says.

Whatever the Fisherman is about to say next is interrupted by the furthest edge of a wave surging over his face and chest. Coughing, he shouts in German, "I turn my body from the sun! I turn my mind from the sun! I turn my spirit from the sun!" Another wave rolls over him. Rainer has halted his march just beyond the water's reach. When the wave has subsided from the Fisherman, he raises his head to look at Rainer. "From hell's heart," he shouts, "I stab at thee! For hate's sake, I spit my last breath at thee!" Rainer doesn't answer. The next wave that falls on the Fisherman is larger; it buoys him up, momentarily, delivering him to the following wave, and the wave after that. Jacob thinks that maybe the dark ocean has hold of him, now, but the water retreats, depositing the Fisherman on sand studded with rocks. He's pale to the point of white, as if the water has washed all the blood that was left out of him. Tilting his head to the sea, to the vast coil waiting for him, he shouts, "To thee I come, all-destroyer! To the last I grapple with thee! Let me then tow to pieces, tied to thee!"

A wall of water crashes down on him. Jacob loses sight of him in the resulting foam, and doesn't regain it until the Fisherman has been carried a dozen yards from shore. Amidst the rioting waves, it's difficult to distinguish much with any certainty, but Jacob could swear he sees the Fisherman grasped by a multitude of silvery arms; it's impossible for him to say if they're holding the man up, or dragging him under. Then he's gone, taken by the water.

XXIII

ainer doesn't waste any time marking his passing. While Jacob and the others are still squinting at the ocean, Rainer turns and starts up the beach. On the way, he stoops to retrieve the Fisherman's knife. As he comes closer, Jacob's eyes are drawn to his face. The white light that's been focused on his features has brightened to the point they're almost impossible to discern. He stops next to Angelo's corpse, and crouches beside it. Jacob—it isn't so much that he's forgotten about Angelo, slumped over in a pool of his own blood, as it is that his attention has been commanded by the spectacle of the Fisherman's undoing. Now that he's met whatever fate was awaiting him in the ocean, his hold on Jacob has ceased, leaving him to face the man he's killed.

Not murdered, mind you, but killed, though he doubts Angelo would appreciate such niceties. All at once, the contents of Jacob's stomach are boiling at the back of his throat. He bends over and empties them onto the ground in one long spasm that sends tears streaming from his eyes, snot spilling from his nose. *Angelo*, he thinks, *I killed Angelo*. The words don't have any of the weight you would expect from so momentous a declaration. They seem impossible, more fantastic than this place in which they're standing, the beast rising out of the waves. All the same, when he straightens, neither of his surviving companions is near him. Italo and Andrea have withdrawn, to allow Rainer to assess the scene and deliver whatever verdict on it he deems fit. Jacob is weak, feverish the way you are after you've

156

vomited. Though some sense of decorum suggests he should keep his gaze fixed straight ahead, he can't help himself. He stares at Rainer staring down at Angelo. The expression on his bright face is impossible to distinguish, let alone read. The Fisherman's knife dangles from Rainer's left hand. Up close, it's enormous, more a short sword than a knife. The blade is broad, curved, so sharp Jacob doubts you'd feel it cutting your throat. He knows he should be wracked with guilt over Angelo, should be on his knees weeping for mercy, but the only emotion he can manage is fear of a particularly paralyzing nature. When Rainer sighs and looks up at him, all Jacob can think is that he can't believe he's going to die for an act he can't believe he committed. He'll lie here beside Angelo, and no one will ever know what became of either of them. Rainer shakes his head, and dips first the knife, then his axe, into Angelo's blood. He nods at Jacob's axe, angling out of Angelo. "Take it," he says.

Jacob doesn't question him. He bends over, takes hold of the axe handle tacky with Angelo's blood, and pulls up. Angelo's body starts to rise with it until, with a wet noise, the axe slides free. The corpse falls face-first into its puddled blood.

Waving the bloody knife, Rainer calls Italo and Andrea over. He points at Angelo's blood. "Dip your axes in it," he says. The men exchange glances, but follow Rainer's command.

So it's to be the three of them, Jacob thinks. He supposes it makes sense. If all three men cut him down, then it's less likely any one of them will reveal his fate.

Rainer stands, holding the knife out. He opens his mouth to speak, and so prepared is Jacob for him to pronounce his doom that that's what he hears, Rainer saying, "Jacob Schmidt, for the death of this man, your life is required of you." Jacob closes his eyes, hoping that, when his companions strike, they'll be quick and accurate. He hopes that Rainer won't tell Lottie the truth about what happened to him; he wishes he'd requested that of the man. For a dozen rapid heartbeats, Jacob waits in his self-imposed darkness. When he can bear it no longer, he forces his eyes open, fully expecting to be greeted by the edge of an axe speeding into his face. Instead, Rainer is looking at him quizzically, while Italo and Andrea are watching Rainer. "The blood of the innocent," Rainer says, "has power. It will help us to finish our work." He's talking about the ropes, Jacob realizes. That was what Rainer said to them: "We have to cut the rest of the ropes."

Jacob's certain his confusion is written all over his face. "B-b-b-b-but Angelo," he manages.

"Do you mean to tell me," Rainer says, "that this was not an accident?"

Jacob shakes his head from side to side, furiously.

"So." Rainer nods at the ropes in front of them. "It would be best if we were not here much longer. But be careful. You saw what happened to the Fisherman." The men nod, and set to work.

XXIV

ven though the Fisherman is gone, the ropes still hum with energy. Jacob's fingers stick to his axe's handle as he shifts his hold on it. The air above the gap he cut in the rope bends and blurs; the hooks to either side of it pull horizontally, as if buffeted by invisible streams spilling out of it. Trying not to recall the expression that spread across Angelo's face in the instant before his death overtook him, Jacob raises his axe.

In a blow, the rope is cut. A great crack, the sound of a mountain halving, throws the rope high and shoves Jacob back half a dozen rapid steps. Torn loose by the force, a handful of fishhooks whiz in all directions; a smaller one spears Jacob's right cheek, just below the eye. He cries out and too late raises his hands in defense.

Around him, a series of booms and crashes breaks the air. The Fisherman's ropes rear up like living things. Rainer and the others stagger and stumble with the forces unleashed. As if it's being reeled in, one of the ropes streaks towards the waves. Another falls onto one of the great tree stumps and digs a handful of its hooks into the wood. The third rope flails from side to side like a thing in pain; Italo barely manages to duck its swipe. The fourth rope, Jacob's, lies flat on the ground, making its slow way to the beach. One last rope remains, off to the left, beside the raging stream. Rainer drops his axe as he approaches it and, taking the Fisherman's knife in both hands, cleaves it. Jacob flinches at the resulting boom. Cut free, the rope curls and loops amidst the stream's spray.

His ears ringing, Jacob joins Italo and Andrea to wait for Rainer. Neither man will look at him. As Rainer walks up to the them, Italo gestures with his axe across the stream, where the other set of ropes hooks the titanic beast to the land. "What about them?" he says, speaking too loudly, the way you do when your hearing's been dulled.

"By all means," Rainer says with something like good humor. "If you want to swim over there and tend to those ropes, none of us will stop you."

Italo frowns. It's clear he has no desire to try the stream and whatever might reside there, but if cutting the ropes on this side of it has been important enough to risk and sacrifice their lives over, then surely the ropes on the other side must be no less significant.

Rainer has returned to Angelo, whose shoulders he has taken hold of in order to ease him up and over onto his back. Angelo's eyes are open, full of the distance of his death. Rainer closes them, straightens Angelo's arms at his sides, and pulls his legs out from under him, speaking as he does. "You are right," he says, "it would be better to take care of those ropes, too. And if we could walk along this shore to the next set of ropes, and the one after that, it would be better still. Oh yes, our friend has been busy. He has spent many years at his labors, many, many years. To undo all he has done would also take a long time. Not as long as it took the Fisherman—always, it is quicker to tear down than it is to build up—but enough time that our children would be old men and women when we were finished." He shakes his head. "I will not speak for you, but for me, that is too much."

"But," Andrea says. He points at the vast gray curve rising out of the dark ocean.

"What we have done is enough," Rainer says. He considers the Fisherman's knife. "For that," he nods at the enormous beast, "to be bound requires a precise distribution of forces. Next to this, planning the dam we are building is child's play. If those forces are disturbed, then the whole thing comes undone." Rainer leans forward, raises the knife, and drives it into the ground above Angelo's head, improvising a cross. "I am sure," he says, "that our comrade would appreciate some prayers." He stands, bows his head and clasps his hands, and waits.

It's Andrea who answers Rainer's suggestion, crossing himself and speaking rapidly in Latin. Italo follows suit, and together they run through what seems like a Sunday service's worth of prayers. Jacob keeps his head bowed for the duration. Needless to say, he keeps his eyes from Angelo's face, not to mention the wound that insults the base of his neck. He focuses on Angelo's boots, which are the same, worn variety the rest of them are wearing. They're coated with the red dirt and dust of wherever this is Rainer's led them. The left foot sticks straight up; the right leans against it. When Angelo tugged these boots on this morning, tightened and tied the laces, he had no inkling they would be his funeral wear. This strikes Jacob as painfully sad.

Once Andrea and Italo have said "Amen," and crossed themselves again, Rainer unclasps his hands and turns to the hill they descended on their way here. Italo says, "Wait."

"What is it?" Rainer says.

"We aren't done burying him," Italo says.

"I have made a marker," Rainer says. "Prayers have been offered."

"He can't be left like this," Andrea says. "He needs a grave."

"How are we going to dig one?" Rainer says.

"The stones, then," Andrea says, pointing to the beach. "We can pile stones over him."

Rainer shakes his head. "I am sorry, but there isn't time."

"Why not?" Andrea says. "We don't need that long."

"I would guess that, while we speak, the Fisherman is drawing his strength back to himself. This means that we do not have very much time before the passage that took us here collapses."

"I thought this Fisherman was dead," Italo says, and the crease in his brow makes Jacob uneasy.

Rainer ignores it. "Who told you that?" he says.

"My eyes," Italo says. "I watched the man dragged into the water by one of his ropes."

"And you think that that is enough to kill the one who did all this?" Rainer flings his arm to take in the broad tree stumps, the heaps of rope, the slaughtered cattle, the monster in the ocean. Jacob recalls his aerial vision, and the nervousness Italo's glower provoked uncoils into fear deep and profound. What has led them to believe the figure who caught and was on his way to bending the power in front of them to his will could be slain by the likes of them, a threadbare professor and a handful of stoneworkers? Jacob's fear swiftly verges on panic, and it may be that Rainer notices this, or that he reads a similar change on Italo and Andrea's features. He says, "Make no mistake:

161

we have won a great victory, here. We have removed the threat to our families. We have disrupted the Fisherman's plans. And we have caught the Fisherman, himself, trapped him using his own tools. If we are lucky, then the great beast he is bound to will break free and swim into the ocean, taking him with it. If we are not so lucky, then he will find his way free before that. Even if such is the case, though, it will be the work of decades for him to escape the prison we have locked him into."

Anything else Rainer wants to say is interrupted by a succession of crashes. "The ocean," Italo says, but the rest of them are already turning toward it. For the second time since he arrived here, Jacob watches the vast arc of flesh offshore move. But where its previous movement was the tensing and relaxing of a creature shifting into a more comfortable position, this is something different. The beast—Jacob can't help continuing to think of it as the island—is swaying, the right side leaning closer as the left side leans away, then the left side leaning closer as the right side leans away. The motion disrupts the surrounding waves—the crashes that drew the men's attention. Still swaying, the creature raises itself, the dull, scaled mass of it growing from large hill to small mountain, from small mountain to bigger mountain. Jacob's mouth drops open—he can't help it—as yet more of the thing emerges from the ocean, bigger mountain growing to Alpine peak, water pouring off it in great rivers, Danubes and Hudsons falling down its side. The dark ocean seethes around it, thrashes against it.

Beyond terrified, beyond awestruck, Jacob is blank, his mind wiped clean by the enormity eclipsing the sky in front of him. When a pair of hands grabs his shoulders, spins him around, and pushes him in the direction of the hill backing the shore, his feet shuffle forward out of simple muscle memory. Not until he catches sight of Andrea sprinting ahead of him, and Italo running to catch up to him, does Jacob start to move his legs in earnest. Rainer is beside him, and despite the pale light washing his face, Jacob can sense the concern on the older man's features. His recognition of Rainer's emotion spurs him to pick up his pace, close the distance to Andrea and Italo. By the time he reaches the foot of the hill, Jacob is running all-out, his arms hammering, his legs pistoning. He powers up the slope, the muscles in his thighs, his calves protesting almost immediately. A quick check over his shoulder shows Rainer behind him, the vast bulk of the great beast continuing to rise in the distance. Ignoring his burning legs, his heaving lungs, Jacob maintains his pace. Around him, the strange trees peculiar to this place thicken on the hillside. His breathing thunders in his ears. Darkness crowds the edges of his vision, until he's watching Andrea and Italo crest the hill through a long, black tunnel. Something presses on the small of his back—Rainer's hand, urging him forward. In no time at all, it seems, Jacob's legs have become blocks of concrete, which grow heavier with each step he takes. He's still carrying his axe, hasn't lost hold of it this entire time. He might as well be hefting an oak. He would drop it, gladly, but his fingers have forgotten how to release it.

Once Jacob tops the hill, it takes him half a dozen strides to realize what he's done. He doesn't stop so much as slow, his legs momentarily unable to cease their motion. Like a runner who's completed the race of his life—which, in a sense, he has—Jacob walks in a circle, knuckles on his hips, head tilted back, eyes closed, mouth inhaling bucketfuls of air. Somewhere close, he hears Rainer's labored breathing. He should open his eyes, but Jacob can think of nothing he's less inclined to. He's gone straight through exhaustion to nausea, to this side of shuddering collapse. Weights fall on his shoulders. He opens his eyes to Rainer, grabbing him and bringing him to a halt. Jacob's already shaking his head, refusing Rainer's insistence that they must keep moving. He has nothing left. Jacob waves Rainer away, points him up the track they made on their way here, which Andrea and Italo have located and are on the way along.

If Jacob expects an argument from Rainer, he's disappointed. Having said what he had to say, the older man moves past Jacob, after Andrea and Italo. As he goes, however, he says, "And what about Lottie?"

Jacob's head jerks back as if he's been slapped. That name is maybe the one word capable of slicing through the torpor that's snared him. Questions crowd Jacob's tongue: Why did Rainer mention Lottie? Does this mean he no longer objects to Jacob's attention to her? How is that possible, since not only is Jacob still Austrian, but his hands are wet with another man's blood? Unsure what's going to emerge, he opens his mouth—but Rainer has set off after Andrea and Italo at a brisk pace. Perhaps Jacob spends a moment debating whether he can summon the strength to carry him to the door of the Dort house, but the argument is *pro forma*, its outcome already clear. For what he's reasonably sure is the promise implicit in Rainer's question, Jacob will find his way out of this place.

XXV

In years to come, when Jacob relates his and his companions' experiences that strange night to Lottie, that detail will remain her favorite part. No wonder at first, I suppose, but even after the romance has dimmed and their union settled into its predictable patterns, the image of Jacob trudging through the forest, those odd trees being joined by and then replaced by evergreens, the others far ahead of him, with only her face bright in his mind's eye to keep him putting one foot in front of the other, will stir something deep within her.

During his trek to the door, Jacob looks behind him once. By this time, the trees have gathered thick and tall about him—actually, he isn't that far from exiting this place—obscuring his view almost completely. Despite this, through the tops of the evergreens he can distinguish a vast, rounded edge—the great beast, the Fisherman's catch, this segment of it risen to a height Jacob does not want to estimate. As he watches, it begins to shift, tipping with the slow gravity of very large things towards the dark ocean. In an instant, it's gone, and Jacob can picture the enormous length of it smashing into the waves, thrusting a wall of black water up to the sky. He doesn't wait for the titanic crash; he runs for the spot in front of him where he can see his companions.

They're waiting for him; or, Rainer is forcing the others to wait for him. Rainer is holding open a heavy wooden door, which appears to be set within an especially dense cluster of trees. It shouldn't surprise Jacob that the door

164

Rainer is gripping by its thick edge is the same one that was sundered by the force of his earlier attack on it, but it does. Rainer is straining to keep the door from closing. As Jacob hurries near, Rainer nods, and first Italo, then Andrea, steps through the passageway. "Faster!" Rainer shouts at Jacob, who wants to shout back that he's hurrying as fast as he can, but doesn't have the breath to do so. Somewhere far behind him, noise is gathering itself, the roar of a mountain toppling into ruin. The weird light on Rainer's face has dulled enough for Jacob to see the sweat trickling down his forehead. He brushes Rainer as he runs past him and over the threshold.

XXVI

acob emerges into night, and cool air. Rainer follows close on his heels, slamming the door shut after him and staggering back against it. The metal ring that serves as its knocker clinks on the wood. For what feels like a long time, Jacob stands where he is, as do Italo and Andrea, the three of them staring at the front door to the Dort house. They're waiting—for exactly what, they can't say. A sign, maybe, that their adventure has concluded. All they hear, however, are the songs of the various birds anticipating the dawn; all they see is the sky overhead lightening from black to dark blue. It's Rainer who, pushing himself off the door, waves to either side of them and says, "Look."

The men glance around them. Jacob notices immediately: the walls of water that bordered the last leg of their journey to the house are gone; nor does the grass where they stood appear damp with anything other than the dew. As Italo and Andrea understand what no longer encloses them, Italo says, "We have succeeded." The expression on his face says it's meant to be a statement, but the tone of his voice makes it more of a question.

"It appears we have," Rainer says.

"What the hell does that mean?" Italo says.

"That apparently, we have been successful."

"Why 'apparently'?" Italo says.

"Because it is too soon to know for sure," Rainer says.

"How long will that take?" Italo says.

"When each of us dies in his own bed," Rainer says, "from whatever has been ordained to end his days on this earth, then he may say that his work tonight was a success. If, in however much time has passed, his family has gone unharmed by anything other than the typical calamities, then he may breathe his last breath with ease. Should he never again hear the under-speech—the speech of the Fisherman's creatures—then he may close his eyes for the last time in peace."

"And what if it's our children who must answer for what we've done?" Italo says. "Or our grandchildren?"

"We will be dead," Rainer says, "and beyond caring." Before Italo can add an objection to the frown this answer provokes, Rainer starts up the front walk, on his way back to the camp. First Andrea, then Jacob, and finally Italo follow him.

XXVII

None of them returns to the Dort house; although Jacob, Rainer, and Italo, the three who remain at the camp, keep their ears open for any mention of it. This will come several more months—almost a year later, when the crews clearing the valley reach the Station. As far as what you might call the general public knows, the Dort house is still the possession of the figure popularly referred to as Cornelius's Guest, or the Guest. No one can recall the last time the man was seen outside the house, or inside it, for the matter. No light has troubled any of the mansion's windows for a good while, since about the last time anyone caught a glimpse of the Guest. This has not stopped a steady stream of official-looking men from bustling up to the house's front door, sounding the knocker, waiting for a response, trying it again, waiting again, and tramping away. Sometimes, they've left official-looking envelopes on the doorstep. The more dedicated fellows have persisted in knocking on the door for approaching a half-hour, and one particularly enterprising young man circled the house, fighting his way through the vegetation that overgrew its yard, in search of some sign of life. For his troubles, he received a bad case of poison ivy and a pants leg full of thorns.

Each of these callers has been on a version of the same mission: to inform the Guest that his time in the house is at an end, that he has until this-and-such a date to depart the property and take with him whatever he doesn't want destroyed. The visitors are empowered to write the Guest a not-inconsiderable check for the value of the land and buildings that are being taken from him. Were he resident at the majority of other dwellings in the valley, the Sheriff would have been called upon to evict him long ago. But something of old Cornelius Dort's reputation adheres to his former estate, and when at last the Sheriff is summoned to clear the house of its inhabitant, it's the last of a long line of attempts at removing him. A local boy, the Sheriff has grown up hearing the rumors attached to the Guest, which may explain why he doesn't put in his appearance at the Dort house until the crews are a good portion of the way through their work on the Station proper. Nonetheless, he stands patiently awaiting an answer to his knock, and when it is clear that none is coming, orders the deputies he brought with him to break it open. This, they do, though not without some effort.

Inside, the house is a wreck. The sight that greets the Sheriff and his men is not the typical disorder of a dwelling-place abandoned, left for the traveler, the animal in search of a more secure dwelling. Every last piece of furniture in this house has been broken, shattered, as if flung against the walls. The Sheriff doesn't need to walk very far over the threshold to ascertain the extent of the damage, because the interior walls have been knocked down, the ceiling collapsed, leaving the Dort house a great shell. Black mold furs the ruined furnishings, scales the stone walls. What appears to be the largest pile of wreckage is heaped against the wall to the right of the doorway. Protruding from near the bottom of the pile is a limb—the Sheriff registers it as a hand and forearm. He steps towards it before one of the deputies catches him and recommends a second look at what's hanging in the air, there. Though he shakes off the deputy's hold, the Sheriff takes the man's advice. When he focuses on the hand dangling towards the floor, he sees the extra joint in the fingers, the webbing between them, their flattened tips, nails that curve into points.

Were the Sheriff a different kind of man, he might continue across the floor and clear away the debris until the rest of whatever this is lies exposed. But this is no champion of scientific inquiry, or even a reckless adventurer. This is a cautious man whose career has been a study in avoiding bold action. Ordering the deputies out of the house, he retreats after them, closing the broken door as best he can. The Sheriff is within his rights to declare the Dort house a public hazard, which he does, though the county attorney might question his subsequent order that the structure should be doused in whatever flammable liquids were close to hand, set alight, and, when the house was encased in flame, splashed with more gasoline, oil, anything to prolong the blaze. So hot does the fire burn that, while the stone walls remain standing, it is a full day before they're safe to touch with a bare hand. The entirety of the house's contents is reduced to ash, which the Sheriff makes certain is shoveled out and carted away—to where, exactly, isn't clear: maybe a junkyard in Wiltwyck, maybe the waters of the Hudson. After the exterior walls of the house are leveled, a similarly mysterious fate befalls the stones that composed them.

XXVIII

The Dort house seen to, the Sheriff is satisfied. He's already declared the estate abandoned, clearing the way for the crews to move in and begin working on the remainder of the property. Even with the dozens of men who report for duty at the end of the driveway, the task of removing all trace of the Dort estate from the earth is a daunting one. Not only are there a number of outbuildings, including a substantial barn, to be taken down, but the acres of Cornelius's old home grown thick with trees, from apple orchards whose long rows haven't been tended in too many years, to remnants of the forest the first European settlers cut their way through. There are rocks large and larger that have to be pried from the soil and carted away. Every last green thing, from bush to flower to weed to grass, must be uprooted, the socket it leaves behind filled in and smoothed over. It's during this phase of the work, when the Sheriff has left and word of what he and his men found in the Dort house has sprinted to the work camp and run up and down its streets, that one of the work crews unearths the other oddity that will be associated with the place.

They're in one of the orchards. After cutting down the trees, the men fire the stumps, chain them to teams of mules, and haul them out of the ground. By this point, the crew has this process down to a science, and it runs smoothly until they arrive at the second-to-last stump, which, despite its firing, resists the efforts of the first and second team of mules to be chained to it. This stump demands three sets of mules straining mightily

171

before it will move, shifting slightly and then tearing free of the earth all at once. When it does, it brings a good deal of its root system with it, far more than is usual. Later, at one of the local taverns, a couple members of the crew will compare the tangle of pale tendrils that rips out of the soil to the tentacles of a squid or octopus. Thicker than any of the branches from which the tree hung its fruit, the larger roots knot around a translucent stone the size of a man's head. Pale blue shot through with white, the stone appears to be some variety of gem; though none of the crew can identify it. Snake your fingers in amongst the pallid wood, and the gem is warm to the touch. What the crew can see of its surface is faceted, quartz-like. One of the pair at the bar claims to have stared into one of those facets and seen a distant, fiery eye looking back at him, but the man is well in his cups by the time he delivers this proclamation, and no one gives his words much weight. Though reluctant to leave their find out in the open, the crew doesn't have much choice. They've discovered it at the end of a work day, and excited as they are by its appearance, they're tired and can see that it will require a fair bit of careful sawing to free the gem from the roots. Not to mention, the crew boss, never one to miss a chance to curry favor with his bosses, has insisted on notifying those above him of the discovery, and ordered the crew to leave tree and gem where they are. Were any or all of the men more certain of the stone's classification, those instructions might be cheerfully ignored. However, since the gem may have no more value than the dirt it was drawn from, they go along with their boss's command. For his part, the boss assures the crew that, should the gem be worth anything, there's no doubt the company will reward them, a statement so blatantly absurd, not one of the men bothers arguing with it.

Generous or greedy, the company's actions will remain a subject of speculation and debate, since when their representative arrives at the orchard the next morning, the gem is gone. The tree lies where it was left, the clutch of roots that cradled the gem undisturbed. Of course suspicion falls on the members of the crew, whose protestations of innocence and alibis do nothing to stop the company summoning the police to search their various dwellings. (It doesn't help the members of the crew that they, like most of the other work crews, are black, while their superiors are white.) The gem unfound, the company turns is scrutiny on the crew boss, whose house likewise receives a visit from the police. Already, though, the higher-ups in the company are losing interest in what a few of them are starting to suspect was a case of misidentification. When one of the scientists on the company's payroll speculates that what the crew unearthed was a kind of mineral deposit that, as he puts it, "spontaneously sublimated," the rest of the higher-ups treat his suggestion as fact and let the matter drop.

Rumors about the vanished stone will spread and persist much farther and longer than those about the interior of the Dort house. The majority of them treat the gem's disappearance as theft, the responsibility for which is laid at the feet of those in power: the company, usually, whose men are imagined to have snuck out to the orchard in the middle of the night and made off with the stone. Some stories name the police as culprits; others blame more fanciful figures: agents of Henry Ford, John D. Rockefeller, even the Kaiser.

Jacob Schmidt, who has commenced his lengthy courtship of Lottie Schmidt, listens attentively to the descriptions of the interior of the Dort house, of the blue-white stone. If he closes his eyes, he pictures the foaming edge of a tide of black water rushing through the house, lifting chairs, tables, cabinets, and smashing them against the house's walls. Why the water doesn't burst through those walls, flooding the valley ahead of schedule, bothers Jacob enough for him to ask Rainer about it, but his future father-in-law answers only that the water went as far as it could go. Nor is Rainer much help when Jacob queries him about the enormous gem. "The Eye?" Rainer says. He waves his hand. "Someone else will worry about that."

XXIX

Jacob seeks out Italo's opinion on both matters, but in each case, the older man offers a shrug and a "How the devil should I know?" Jacob attributes Italo's shortness to the burdens of his expanded family. Since arriving at Italo and Regina's house, Helen and George's children haven't left. There's nowhere for them to go, no other relatives anyone knows of to claim them, and Regina grows livid should anyone mention the word "orphanage." Practically speaking, Italo and Regina have adopted these children, and their house, already tight with their own family, is straining at the seams. Not to mention, feeding those extra mouths has stretched Italo's pay thin. Once every three or four weeks, Clara will cook and send over a meal to them—nothing too extravagant, a pot roast, say, which one of her younger girls will deliver after school—and Lottie saves what extras she can from the bakery—to which she's long returned—for them, but Italo and Regina's act of charity has had its price.

Secretly, too, Jacob has wondered how much of Italo's gruffness with him has its roots in the memory of Angelo's sightless eyes, the mortal wound Jacob's axe had opened in his neck. There are moments Jacob can barely believe he struck Angelo down; the act feels as distant as Austria, a scene from a dream he had long ago. Other times, though, the shock of the axe chopping meat and bone echoes up his hands and arms as if it's just happened. Perhaps, he thinks, it's the same for Italo.

Truth to tell, most of the time, Jacob's presence appears barely to register on Italo. As the adage has it, the man has bigger fish to fry; despite what they went through the year before, Jacob can't muster the courage to ask him about whatever's in the skillet. As it turns out, he won't need to. A couple of months after the Dort house and its surroundings have been reduced to a foundation and bare ground, there's a morning Regina doesn't rise from bed. Italo sends his oldest boy, Giovanni, for the doctor, but by the time the man arrives, she's well on her way to her last breaths. Cancer, apparently of the uterus, which likely has spread to other places in her body, the doctor opines. Italo and the children sit with her as she completes the remainder of her journey out of this life. At the very end, Regina's eyes flutter, her lips move as if she's about to say something, utter a final instruction or bit of wisdom, but all she manages is, "The woman:" the rest is pulled down into death with her.

Everyone who knows them expects that, with Regina gone, Italo will collapse, crushed by the weight of his sorrow and the responsibility of so large a family. After work, Clara stops at their house to lend what assistance she can with the cooking and cleaning, as do Lottie and her sisters, but mother and daughters alike judge it only a matter of time before Helen and George's children finish their long-delayed trip to the orphanage, and take Italo and Regina's brood with them. While Italo hasn't retreated into the glassy depths of a bottle of alcohol, or mummified himself in layers of grief, the façade he shows to his family, to the rest of the camp, is riven with cracks. To Clara and her girls' surprise, however, Maria, the oldest of the adopted children, steps forward and seizes the reins of the situation. The general expectation is that she'll be no match for it, that it'll whipsaw her back and forth and fling her away broken. But the girl digs in her heels, braces her legs, and winds the reins around her arms and shoulders. It's neither easy nor smooth, but over a course of months, she settles what's become her family into a new kind of normal. Nobody leaves school; nobody loses their job—except for Maria, herself, who doesn't return to school and quits the part-time position she's had at the bakery. There's some suspicion she's angling to marry Italo, about which opinion is more divided than you might expect, but gradually, it becomes clear that Maria's assumed the role of maiden aunt, rather than wife-in-waiting. She'll maintain the position for the remainder of the family's stay at the camp.

XXX

Three years pass. Jacob's slow courtship of Lottie progresses to a long engagement, which leads to marriage right around the time the Reservoir's west basin starts being filled. The previous summer's been hot and dry, leaving the Esopus shrunken within its banks, and the water collects slowly in the great bowl—so much so there's fear that the Reservoir's been built too big, that it'll never be full. Those fears are put to rest the following fall, when a succession of storms pours rain into it and lifts the water level within sight of where it's supposed to be. Next spring—on June 19, 1914, to be exact—all the whistles in the camp will blow for a solid hour, announcing the completion of the majority of work on the Reservoir. Although it'll be another two years after that until the project is officially finished, the roar of the whistles echoing up the Esopus valley, off the surrounding mountains, overlapping itself to form layers of a sound, a geology of sound, serves notice to those working at the camp that the end is drawing nigh. Already, most of the crews who cleared the valley have been handed their walking papers. Some of the stoneworkers have been let go, too. What's next for them is a topic Rainer and Clara, Jacob and Lottie, have discussed, but after those whistles, there's an element of urgency mixed into their conversations.

Italo departs the camp first. Within six months of the whistles blowing, he's secured a position with a stonemason in Wiltwyck. The next year, Lottie and Jacob and their first child, Greta, will settle in Woodstock, so that Jacob can take up a job with a fellow who carves headstones. In order to continue their schooling, and to help with the baby, Lottie's sisters, Gretchen and Christina, accompany them. Rainer and Clara will remain at the camp the longest, as its streets empty, its houses become vacant, its bakery and general store close. At the end of 1916, when the Reservoir is formally pronounced done, Rainer and Clara will be among the only residents of the camp that's in the process of being taken down. Through the same talent for persuasion that brought him and his family to this place, Rainer succeeds in obtaining a position with the Water Authority that's been established to oversee the functioning and maintenance of the Reservoir and the tunnels that funnel its water to New York's thirsty taps. This is a time when the U.S. is on its way into the First World War, and you might not expect a fellow with a German accent to be hired to so sensitive a position. He convinces whoever needs it of his loyalty and his trustworthiness, and for the next decade, he travels up and down Ulster County, inspecting its portion of the Catskill Aqueduct—that's the tunnel that runs south out of the Reservoir. He and Clara relocate to Woodstock, to a modest house a couple of doors down from Lottie and Jacob, whose family has expanded to include a son, also Jacob, and another daughter, Clara. Christina, Rainer and Clara's youngest, has scandalized everyone by falling pregnant with the child of a much older man who has come north from Beacon to tend to his sick brother. After a hasty wedding, Christina and Tom head back down the Hudson to settle. Gretchen, the middle sister, attends the teachers' college in Huguenot, and takes a position teaching in Rhinebeck. She'll marry late, a railroad conductor with whom she develops a romance over the course of trips to Manhattan to visit the museums there.

Life goes on. That's the remarkable thing, isn't it? Not that everything the Schmidts and their companions had been through with the Fisherman wasn't incredible, but that the world could have continued as it always has, anyway, seems astonishing. Once or twice a year, usually when summer's at its height, Italo brings his family to visit. While Clara and Lottie fuss over how big the children have grown and listen to them report their latest activities, Rainer and Italo trade remarks about the weather and whatever news the headlines have been concerned with; while Jacob listens quietly, nodding every now and again to show he's paying attention. He's done quite well for himself, has Italo, buying out the stonemason who hired him, bringing on his son, Giovanni, to work with him. He has more business, he says, than he knows what to do with, but he's lucky to have such problems. Clara tells him he should find a nice woman, but Italo insists he doesn't have time for such things. Over the course of his visits, his hair whitens and thins, his skin takes on a gray pallor that Clara declares she does not care for. Italo poo-poos her worrying, but when word comes from Wiltwyck that he's suffered a heart attack and been hospitalized, her fears are borne out. Rainer and she set off for the hospital, but by the time they arrive, Italo's heart has failed, completely.

A year after his friend's death, Rainer will be retired from his job, forced to do so by the dramatic decline in his faculties that's been showing early symptoms for longer than he's wanted to admit. His short-term memory's crumbling. He loses the thread of a conversation mid-sentence. He forgets the name of the person he's talking to. He can't remember the date. Worse, he's started to slip from English to German unawares, then to become annoyed if whoever he's speaking with doesn't understand him. He resists accepting what's happening to him, which is the cause of several bitter arguments between him and Clara. In the end, his boss will deliver an ultimatum: either Rainer retires, or he'll be forced to fire him. Protesting the injustice of it all, Rainer opts to tender his resignation. Once he leaves his job, his condition falls off steeply, until he's little more than an oversized infant. There are moments, when she's spooning chicken soup past his quivering lips, that Clara will recall the pale light she saw washing over Rainer's features when he was engrossed in his books, trying to sort out the mess with the Fisherman. She'll remember the way it blurred her husband's face, and how she had to fight back the fear that clawed at her at the sight of him. Wiping his chin with a napkin, she'll think that it's as if that dead light sunk inside him, bleaching away whatever of him it fell on. When he's breathed his last, Clara, her eyes dry, will turn to Lottie and tell her that she lost her husband long before this. She lost him to light the color of the full moon, of the froth on top of a wave, of a burial shroud.

XXXI

Before his retirement and death, though, there's one more matter with which Rainer Schmidt concerns himself, and that's Dutchman's Creek. If you go back to older maps of the area, you'll find sections of streams and creeks that appear to follow some of the same route, but nothing substantial enough to count as a match. At first, the fishermen who come to try its waters assume it is one of those other streams, and that whatever map they've consulted is off, or their memories of the place mistaken. Over the course of a couple of years, those fellows talk to one another, compare notes, and gradually, it becomes clear to everyone that this in a new creek. Such things happen, of course: heavy flooding can carry away part of a stream's bank, open a fresh path for it; a rockslide can push its waters in another direction. This creek runs all the way to the Hudson, through banks steep and thickly forested. Not a few of the men who trade their impressions of it agree that the stream looks as if it's been there for a goodly number of years. It's as if the land has unfolded a little extra of itself. No one can remember noticing it, previously, but no one can recall not noticing it, either.

What brings Rainer to it is the notice the creek draws from the Water Authority. A few men have tried, but no one has been able to pinpoint the location of the stream's headwaters. As you trace it back, the creek appears to be headed directly towards the Reservoir. However, its upper reaches snake through dense woods that seem to confound anyone who ventures too far into them. A couple of fellows were lost for a day and a night amidst the evergreens, and one old man spent upwards of three days wandering the area, as the pines and spruce gave way to tall trees unlike any he'd seen. Through their trunks, he claims to have seen a distant body of water, what he thought was the Reservoir, except the water looked dark. Everyone who hears his story dismisses it as a hallucination brought on by combined exposure and lack of proper nourishment. Concerned about a possible leak, the higher-ups at the Water Authority have had the Reservoir inspected, from dam to weir to bed. Nothing has been found amiss.

This is when Rainer arrives. At first, he hadn't paid much attention to the talk about the new creek. You might imagine, he isn't much on fishing. As the talk of the stream has continued, though, his interest has been stirred. The more he's heard of it, the less Rainer has liked what he's hearing. It would be easy enough to dismiss the reports of enormous fish whose like no fisherman has seen—and which conveniently snap whatever line has them as they're on the verge of being landed—as the usual exaggerations of men who've used their trip to the woods to sneak a little moonshine. Had Rainer not been through the events at the camp, he might discount the other stories he hears as further evidence of that liquor's potency. A pair of boys playing hooky is gone much longer than they'd planned when they become lost trying to follow a pale figure they glimpse in the woods upstream. An old man returns to the same spot every day for two weeks, not to fish, but to listen to a voice he swears is that of his son, killed in the War. One member of a fishing party falls into the creek and would likely have drowned were his companions not excellent swimmers; the man insists he saw his brother, dead these many years from pneumonia, staring up at him from beneath the water's surface. When Clara and Lottie ask him what's happening, Rainer gives his usual answer—he isn't sure—but this time around, he doesn't wait for things to grow worse before he acts. He convinces whoever requires it that his position patrolling the aqueduct makes him perfectly suited for getting to the bottom of this matter, then tells Jacob he'll have need of him the following Sunday, after church.

It's a hot, humid afternoon when Jacob parks his car on one side of Tashtego Lane and sets off with his father-in-law in search of the stream. You can be sure, he's thinking about the last excursion he accompanied Rainer on. They don't have axes, don't have any tools, at all, which Jacob hopes is a good sign. They walk a few hundred yards across a meadow to a low ridge. Rainer and Jacob climb the ridge, then half-slide down its far side to the modest valley it forms with the ridge behind it. This second ridge is steeper, taller, an earth and stone wall, but it's heavily forested with evergreens the men use as handholds to help themselves up it. Just past the top of the hill, he looks down through the spruce and pine and sees a creek white and foaming below. Digging their heels into the soil, zigzagging from tree to tree, he and Rainer descend the hillside, until they're on the narrow shelf that borders this side of the stream. Maybe a dozen yards over the turbulent water, the other shore is a mirror of theirs, a slender strip of land at the foot of a ridge heavy with trees. On the left, the creek foams down an incline halfway to a waterfall; ahead and on the right, it runs level for ten or fifteen yards before plunging down another set of rapids. Jacob glances at Rainer, who's staring at the water's surface. Afraid that his father-in-law is having another of his spells—the name his wife and mother-in-law have given to his moments of blankness—Jacob touches Rainer's shoulder, whereupon the older man starts, shakes his head, and turns left. "This way," he says, heading upstream. Over his shoulder, he adds, "You remember from before. If you hear someone, do not listen to them. If you see someone, do not look at them." Jacob wants to ask how exactly he's supposed to avoid looking at someone he's seeing, but he understands the gist of Rainer's instruction, and hurries to keep up with him.

They don't travel far, for which Jacob is grateful. As the bank they're walking slants upwards, the mossy earth that covered it gives way to rock made slick by the water's spray. Although Jacob is aware of something in the creek's tumult, he's too busy concentrating on where to plant his next footstep to pay it much notice. (Later, he'll tell Lottie he had the impression the water was full of white bodies. "Like fish?" she'll ask. He'll shake his head.) But even as he leans forward to maintain his balance, all the while watching Rainer above him, pinwheeling his arms to keep from toppling backwards, Jacob hears a voice speaking to him.

His words a whisper in Jacob's ears, Angelo, the man he struck down with an axe, asks him what he's doing here. Doesn't he have a wife to kiss, children to embrace? Doesn't he live in a nice house, work at a good job? Why, then, is he here, in this place? Has he grown tired of his pleasant life? Does he want to know what Angelo knows? Would he like to raise his eyes to the sight of his companion's axe flashing towards him? Would he like to feel its edge bite deep into his flesh? Would he like to know the shock that stuns his brain, so that all he can do is stare at the wooden handle of the tool that has killed him, while the blood spills out of him? He could not say his prayers, Angelo continues, could not make a final Act of Contrition. He could only sit there as his thoughts spiraled down a black drain. Even after his heart had stopped beating, he did not leave that place. He remained, watching, as Jacob and the rest of their companions stood around his corpse. He saw Jacob excused of his murder. He witnessed their half-hearted attempt at a funeral, their flight before the black ocean's rising. He could not escape the water that rolled over him, that picked up his body and carried it far, far out, to the lightless depths where white demons sport amidst the coils of their great and terrible master. He was damned, Angelo says, *damned*, and he will be happy to share his dark eternity with Jacob: all he has to do is fling himself into the water to his right, and Angelo's new companions will bring Jacob to him, directly.

For Jacob Schmidt, one act has haunted him these last years, and that, of course, is Angelo's death. If it is a crime—and how, Jacob thinks, could it be anything but?—then it is as perfect a crime as any ever committed, since it happened in a place to which there would appear to be no chance of anyone ever gaining admission. Not to mention, Angelo's body must, as his voice insists, have been washed out to sea by the wave pushed up by the great beast's writhing. Even without any evidence of his act, however, Jacob has continued to carry the burden of it. For the longest time, afraid of the response it might provoke from her, he kept it a secret from Lottie. All through their courtship, the early years of their marriage, the births of their children, Jacob locked away the axe swing that claimed another man's life, his stutter a convenient excuse on the odd occasions the impulse to confess pricked him. Only when their oldest girl, Greta, was so sick with scarlet fever that the normally cheerful doctor had grown serious and quiet did Jacob reveal his past deed to his wife. Half out of his mind with worry, he'd convinced himself that his daughter was going to be taken from him as a punishment for the life he took, years before. At first, Lottie had no idea what Jacob was babbling on about; once she understood what he was saying, she said, "But my father did not condemn you?"

He didn't, Jacob admitted.

"Then that should be enough for you," Lottie said. "Now come help me with our daughter."

Greta survived her bought with scarlet fever, and while Jacob might have taken that as a sign that the powers-that-be weren't interested in collecting on his past misdeed, he has not. He's spent too much time brooding over it for him to be able to release it so easily. Angelo's voice, here, his litany of reproaches, makes perfect sense to Jacob. It wasn't his child whose life would be required: it's his. Jacob is of an age that still believes the taking of your own life is a guaranteed route to eternal damnation, but what else was he expecting? He steps towards the water.

In so doing, he collides with Rainer, who's come to a stop in front of him. Together, the men almost tumble into the raging stream, which suddenly strikes Jacob as a bad idea. He hauls himself and his father-in-law back from the edge. He's expecting a correction from Rainer, a "Watch where you're going!" but the man's eyes are full of tears. Rainer drags his sleeve across his face, and resumes scaling the incline. Jacob follows.

Already, they've reached the top of their climb. Here, the shelf runs level for at least fifty yards. Angelo's voice has returned, but it's delivered no more than a half-dozen words when, over his shoulder, Rainer says, "We don't speak of our life in the old country so much, do we? Sometimes, it seems as if it was a play in which I was cast, along with Clara and the girls. It happened—you could not say it was not real—but it had nothing to do with what our lives were to be. Or, not so much nothing as..." Unable to find the exact word, Rainer substitutes a shrug. "While I was in Heidelberg, at the University, I had a colleague named Wilhelm Vanderwort. He was a philologist, too. I would call him a friend, but that would not be accurate. We had great respect for one another, our work; our conversations were cordial. But we were too much in competition ever to be true friends. Our interest was the same: the languages that came before those we know, the tongues that lay beyond the beginning. Wilhelm was fond of saying that, once his work was finished, he would be able to tell what words Adam and Eve had spoken in the Garden. He had a habit of delivering such pronouncements, which went over well with his students but made his colleagues shake their heads. He was brilliant. With a difficult passage, he was capable of leaps of understanding that would light up the text in new and startling ways. What he was not so good at was the slower work, the careful

183

analysis that made his insights possible, and that built on them, afterwards. This was my strength.

"Our relation might have remained as it was—the tortoise and the hare, I thought of it—but, almost by accident, an old book came into my possession. Mostly, it was written in Middle French, in which I had little interest, but there were passages scattered throughout its pages in a language I had not seen before. The French portions claimed these were examples of exactly what I had been searching for, a tongue from prehistory. I dismissed the idea as ridiculous, but none of my research could find any other instance of these particular characters having been used. In and of itself, this proved nothing. They could have been a private code. But there were…" Rainer waves his hand, "things about these passages that caused me to doubt this. Anyway, the point is, I showed them to Wilhelm and asked for his assistance in translating them.

"At first, he believed I was playing a trick on him. I had to show him the book to prove I wasn't. He was equally certain the passages could not be what the book said they were, but he was intrigued by the challenge they offered. The book presented what it said were faithful translations of the first half of each selection, leaving the remainder for whoever was interested enough to complete. This gave us something to work with, a key—though a key that was missing some of its teeth, and in danger of snapping off in the lock. We treated the matter as a puzzle, half a joke. We talked about writing a paper on a hitherto-unknown instance of a secret medieval code."

To either side of Jacob and Rainer, the ridges that have dropped so starkly to the water's edge lean back. Ahead, the stream curves to the right. Rainer says, "Everything changed when I obtained another book, this one rarer than the one with which we were working. I leafed through it, and found myself looking at a fresh example of the language Wilhelm and I had been laboring over. It was as if I had been struck by lightning. I rushed out of the house to find Wilhelm in his office at the University and show it to him. It appeared we were onto something of genuine significance.

"How significant, we did not appreciate until we began our attempts to speak what had until now been confined to paper. The second book had provided us with a great many clues as to how this might be accomplished, along with cryptic warnings about the need for care in doing so. We dismissed these as rhetorical flourishes inserted to lend the text a more ominous character. We were wrong. The first word we tried to pronounce was 'dark.' It was among the most common of the words we'd encountered, and we felt confident we had its pronunciation settled. Although we scoffed at the second book's warnings, we waited until a Sunday when my family was safely asleep to attempt our experiment. We shut the door to my study, and uttered the word.

"The room was plunged into blackness. I did not understand what had happened; I thought something had gone wrong with the lamp. This did not explain why the hall light was not visible at the bottom of the study's door—or, for the matter, what had become of the city lights outside the window. The blackness was so complete, we might have been in a deep cave. I stumbled around, searching for the lamp, crashing into my desk and spilling books and papers onto the floor. A kind of panic was wrapping its hands around my throat; I was finding it difficult to breathe in this darkness.

"Then Wilhelm Vanderwort spoke a second word, and light, wonderful, rich, creamy light returned to the study. You will have guessed the word: it was 'light.' We had disagreed about the placement of the stresses in it, but it appeared Wilhelm's interpretation was correct. As soon as the study had become dark, he had apprehended what I had not, that the word that had passed our lips had done this. This was no language such as we had known, in which a word points in the direction of its object. Instead, this was a tongue which was woven into—into everything," Rainer sweeps his hands around him, "so that to name something was to call it forth.

"To you, who was part of the business with the Fisherman, this will not sound too strange. To us—well, you can imagine. This was more, much, much more, than a pair of university scholars had expected, ever. Our aspirations had been for a certain, limited fame within our community—to be one of those figures who excites the admiration of his juniors, and the respect and envy of his peers. Now…"

They've reached the place where the creek swings to the right. Rainer leaves the bank, heading for the rows of trees in front of them. He and Jacob walk in amongst their ranks a good fifteen, twenty yards, until they arrive at a low wall of the kind common in these parts, flat stones of assorted dimensions dug from the earth and layered together. Rainer turns and seats himself on it. Jacob remains standing. Rainer says, "Through the merchant who had provided the books for me, I made inquiries. Eventually, Wilhelm and I were put in touch with a small group of men who were familiar with the language we had begun translating, and more, besides. They were impressed with what we had achieved on our own, enough to accept us as… apprentices, you could say. There was a great deal to learn. There were other tongues, more ancient—and more powerful—still. There were histories of the peoples who had employed these languages, their beliefs, their customs, their rises and falls. There were maps of places that lie beside, below, the one we inhabit; there were accounts of their denizens.

"In our new passion, Wilhelm and I were as competitive as we had been in our previous one. Each of us did his best to show up the other. We spurred one another forward, faster, ever-faster, till we were standing in front of a large door set in the wall of a deep basement in one of Heidelberg's newer buildings. You would have recognized the fellow with the iron ring in his mouth: we saw his likeness on the door of the Fisherman's big house. One of our instructors took hold of the ring and pulled the door open. The basement was at least twenty feet underground, but when we looked through the doorway, we saw an alleyway. Wilhelm strode out of the basement into the alley as if it were the most natural thing. Trying to act as if I shared his calm, I crossed after him. We had come to…

"There are cities built along the shores of the black ocean. This was one of them. It was neither the largest nor the oldest of these places, but it was of sufficient size and age for our instructors' purposes. They had set us to a task—a kind of examination—to determine if Wilhelm and I were ready to proceed to the next stage in our learning. Our mission was simple: we were to make our way to the other side of the city, where we would find its necropolis. There, we were to locate a certain grave, and pluck from it a flower we would find growing in its soil. This was not as easy as you might suppose. Not only was the flower rare, it was regarded by the city's populace as the soul of the priest who was buried under it. To remove such a plant was considered a mix of heresy and murder. The streets were full of police, tall shapes dressed in black cloaks and wearing masks fashioned to resemble the curved beaks of birds of prey; they were armed with long, curved knives, which they would use without hesitation on any they caught engaged in a criminal activity such as ours. The geography of the city was strange, contradictory. Streets ended unexpectedly in blank walls, or climbed bridges which came to a stop high in the air; they arrived at circular courtyards from which a dozen alleyways branched out. We had to guide ourselves by the stars burning overhead. These were not arranged in the familiar constellations. Here, the images they drew had been given names such as the Rider, the Staff, and the Garland of Fruit.

"We succeeded. It was a difficult journey, which brought us frightfully near the figures in the bird-masks, but we found the plot of earth and the moon-colored flower rising from it in a slender arc. I removed it, Wilhelm concealed it in the folds of his jacket, and we navigated back to the alley whose end returned us to the basement in Heidelberg. We were exhausted, triumphant, and we passed what few hours remained of that night in celebration with our mentors. One of them had left with the flower, but the others were happy to share an assortment of very fine liquors with us. As dawn was breaking, we staggered off to our homes, shouting old songs, flushed with self-importance.

"By the afternoon of the next day, our triumph had turned to disaster. Wilhelm was on time for his scheduled lecture on Ancient Greek, but from the start, the students noticed something wrong with him. He did not speak with his usual gusto; instead, his voice was measured, even pained. He was well-known for moving around while he talked, pacing the front of the hall, gesturing dramatically with his hands. Today, he did not leave the lectern. A student said he appeared to be propping himself up on it. His face was pale, his eyes sunken, his hair a mess. Of course, all of that could have been attributed to the consequences of mixing considerable quantities of potent liquors. It never fails to astound students that their teachers may fall prey to the same lapses in judgment as they do, with the result that they might mistake a bad hangover for a terrible illness. But there was no confusing the black lines that had started to snake across Wilhelm's cheeks, his forehead, as if some hidden artist were tracing them. Nor could the darkening of his tongue, his teeth, escape the notice of the students seated nearest him. Not long into his remarks, Wilhelm began coughing, and it seemed to some of the closer students that, with each spasm of his lungs, the black lines spread over more of his face, until it resembled a porcelain mask whose surface was a network of cracks. His coughing continued, doubling him over. When he raised his head, there were little pieces of his cheeks, his forehead, missing, as if the porcelain mask was falling apart. Where the skin had been, there was no muscle, no bone, only blackness. Before the horrified eyes of almost one hundred students, Wilhelm Vanderwort collapsed in a shower of dust and darkness, leaving nothing of himself behind but his clothing and his shoes.

"This was what led to me being dismissed from the University. Questions were asked, my name came up, conversations were had, and in no time, I was readying my family to leave for America. I could have fought the move to oust me; I might have succeeded, too. I was well-liked, and had not divided my colleagues the way Wilhelm had. As it was, I did not argue my expulsion. It was, I felt, the least I deserved for what I had allowed to happen to Wilhelm." Rainer looks at Jacob. "I knew that, if the flower we had been sent for was not transported in the appropriate manner—wound about three times with a piece of cloth torn from the foot of a shroud— then the consequences for whoever was carrying it would be dire. I had come prepared for the task, but Wilhelm insisted he be the one to convey the object of our quest to our instructors. I asked him if he had brought the necessary materials. He laughed at me. 'Don't be such an old woman,' he said. I was halfway to passing him the length of cloth I had rolled up in my jacket pocket, but the sound of his laughter stayed my hand. I thought, *Fine. You can do this your way, if that is what you want. And let the blade that is to fall, fall on you.* Which it did. But I was cut by it, as well, which I suppose was just. In the aftermath of the scandal, our former instructors would have nothing to do with me. I tell myself that this was a good thing."

Rainer nods at the stream. "Here, though…Wilhelm tells me that I killed him. As surely as if I had poured poison into his coffee, I murdered him. Worse, he says, I did not have the courage to see my crime all the way through. Instead, I indulged my conscience, and threw away everything the two of us had worked so hard for. Now, he is dust, dust which remembers what it was to be a man and can do nothing with that knowledge. He curses me. He damns me as a coward and a fraud."

His tongue fighting him, Jacob asks his father-in-law where, exactly, they are.

Standing, Rainer says, "You are thinking, maybe, that this place is familiar?" He steps over the wall and walks ten feet to a young tree. He places his left hand against its trunk, his head bowed, and stands like that for a moment. Then he raises his head, reaches into the front pocket of his trousers, and withdraws a knife. It's a silver dinner knife, like the one Rainer employed against Helen, all those years ago; Jacob has an intuition that this is that same knife. In a series of quick strokes, Rainer slashes the tree. He must have sharpened the blade, Jacob thinks, because it opens deep grooves in the bark. When he's done, Rainer takes a step back to survey his work. Jacob looks past him to the tree, but he can make no sense of the marks struck in it—though they produce the strangest sensation of calm. His concentration loosens. It's difficult to recall what he and Rainer are doing here. He turns in the direction he came and is most of the way to the stream before he remembers his father-in-law. Cheeks flushed, he runs back to the wall and hurdles it. Careful to avert his eyes from the tree, he approaches Rainer, whose position is unchanged. He is gazing past the tree into the woods, as if he can discern something within them. Jacob risks a glance in that direction, but cannot make out anything other than row after row of trees. He hears Rainer murmuring a word that he does not recognize; it sounds like *"Thalassa, thalassa."* As Jacob draws up to him, Rainer turns, a grimace on his face, and sets off towards the car.

XXXII

The walk back is less eventful. While they're beside the stream, Angelo's voice resumes its accusations, but its volume is diminished, to the point Jacob could believe he's imagining it within the roar of the water, the way you might see a face within the grain of a piece of wood. Neither he nor Rainer speaks again until they've scaled the ridges that conceal the creek and are crossing the field to the car. There, Jacob asks Rainer if the problem has been solved.

"As much as it can be," Rainer says. "The mark on the tree will turn aside most who come near it. It is the best we can do, without a human sacrifice."

Jacob tells himself that his father-in-law is joking—although Rainer is not smiling.

XXXIII

At some point in the nineteen-twenties, a year or two after Jacob and Rainer's visit to it, the locals start referring to the new stream as *Deutschman's* Creek, which rapidly becomes Dutchman's Creek. Who originates the name, and why, is lost to history, but by the early thirties, the name and the stream have made their way onto maps of the area. Once she's heard the full story of the Fisherman from Jacob, Lottie will complain about the name. Ever the stickler for detail, she says that the Fisherman's Creek would be more accurate. Jacob doesn't argue with her, but he suggests that they take the name as a kind of memorial to her father. That's ridiculous, Lottie says, whoever named the stream could not have known anything about her father. Jacob can see, however, that the notion secretly pleases his wife. It helps her to recall her father as he was before the affliction that took him from her. Rather than the frail man who once was lost for almost a week, when he wandered away from his job into a work camp down in Orange County, she can picture him stepping into their undersized house after a day's labor with his fellow stonemasons, a handkerchief knotted around his neck, his shirt and trousers powdered with a fine dust. Jacob can almost share her vision, except that, in his imagining of it, Rainer's face is washed by white light.

There are moments, as the years slide by and their children grow, as Jacob's boss makes him a partner in the monument business, as the country plunges into the Great Depression, as another war with Germany looms, that neither Jacob nor Lottie can fully credit the events they were part of at the camp. All of it seems like a book they read, a movie they watched. After Jacob's death, from lung cancer, in late nineteen fifty-one, that sensation of unreality will assail Lottie more often. She'll have vivid dreams in which she's back in the house in Heidelberg, with the heavy oak table that has been in her mother's family for four generations, and the cabinet full of Dresden china, and the long lace curtains that her Aunt Gretchen made for her parents as a wedding present. When she wakes in her bed with the lumpy mattress and the fraying blankets, and looks at the plain dresser, its top crowded with pictures of her family, and the open closet, still hung with Jacob's clothes—though she keeps saying she'll sort through them and give what's in decent condition to charity—Lottie will be swept by the certainty that this is the dream. This life in which she left her home for a country whose language has never felt right on her tongue, where she once stood face to face with a woman who had been dead, where she married and bore children to a shy man from Austria who expressed himself more elegantly through the work of his hands than through his speech: it's all the invention, the yield of an adolescent imagination desperate for experience. If only she could find her way back to the blank space that borders dreaming and remain there long enough to navigate its gray emptiness, then the next time she opens her eyes, it will be to Clara calling her to come downstairs to kiss her father before he's off to the University.

She's never able to stay in that empty place, to slip out of it into her old existence. Instead, she'll rise from her bed and cross to the dresser. She'll slide out the top drawer, and search beneath the undergarments layered within it until her fingers touch the edge of a small box. It's the kind of reinforced cardboard box that a department store would use for a piece of jewelry. Lottie will lift it out and set it on top of the dresser. She'll open the lid and part the tissue paper inside it, exposing the piece of metal concealed by its folds.

It's a fishhook. It's a couple of inches long, no different from what you might tie to the end of your line. The metal is tarnished, crusted with a dark substance that Lottie would tell you is her late husband's blood. This is the hook that stuck into Jacob's cheek, right below his eye, when his axe severed the Fisherman's line and the power it contained burst outwards, spraying the hooks that had dangled from it in all directions. So stunned and exhausted from that adventure had Jacob been that he had walked to the bunkhouse and collapsed onto his bed with the hook lodged in his flesh. The next day, he awakened with his cheek swollen and painful. A bunkmate pulled the hook free, releasing a pocket of pus and blood and leaving Jacob with a small white scar. Jacob kept the hook folded in a handkerchief. Once Lottie learned of its existence, she asked for the hook, which Jacob presented to her in the jewelry box. She'll pinch it between her thumb and index finger and hold it up to the light. She'll do the same for the Reverend Mapple, near the end of her long life and at the end of the fantastic tale she's told him. He'll squint at the curved bit of metal in her fingers, its surface patterned with the blood of a man long dead, its barbed point still sharp.

PART 3:

ON THE SHORE OF THE BLACK OCEAN

IV

WORDS READ
BY TRAFFIC LIGHT

H is story done, Howard seemed relieved, as if that burden I'd sensed behind his words at the beginning of his tale had passed from him. I felt oddly disoriented, disconnected from the diner's chrome and glass, the way you do after you've finished a book or movie in which you've been absorbed and which hasn't loosened its hold on you. Dan and I could take what he'd told us or leave it, Howard said, but he'd recommend taking it, and maybe giving Onteora Lake, which was just up the road, a try. With that, he ambled back to the kitchen.

Outside the diner's windows, rain fell in a wall that gave me the momentary sensation we were at the bottom of the sea. I half-expected to see the shadow of some enormous fish glide past. I shook my head and reached for my wallet. Not until after Dan and I had paid our check, and run through the rain to my truck, and I had turned right out of the diner's parking lot onto 28, did I say, "What in the hell was all that?"

Dan shook his head. "Crazy."

"Crazy…" That was one word for it. I was annoyed, the way you are when you aren't sure if someone's had you on or not. I know: how could How-

197

ard have been doing anything else? Dead people standing up and walking around, black magic, monsters: it was the stuff of a scary movie, a fishing yarn gone feral. I was pretty sure that Dan and I had just had our legs pulled so hard, we'd be tilting to one side. Howard had said he'd wanted to be a writer; I had the strong suspicion he'd just related his first novel to us.

But...while I couldn't credit the stranger events he'd related, let alone the outright fantastic ones, not once during his story had Howard given me the impression he was lying. Which, I knew, was the hallmark of an accomplished liar. But there was something to his words, some undercurrent, that hinted at a modicum of truth to them, and that irritated me more than anything. He had seemed unhappy with the tale he'd related to us, as if he hadn't liked its details any more than he expected us to.

All the same, those details. If, as the saying goes, that's where the devil is, then half of hell seemed to be crowded into this story. I mean, magic symbols carved with kitchen knives? Ropes braided with fishing hooks? Axe blades dipped in a dead man's blood? The rain eased, the air lightening as the sun struggled to push through the clouds. Not to mention, that business with the painter fellow, Otto, cutting his throat after he saw the woman in black.

Despite myself, I stepped on the brake. What the hell was that I was remembering? Howard hadn't said anything about a painter, had he? Where was that coming from? I eased into the left-turn lane by the barbecue place. Trying to keep my voice light, I said, "You're sure you want to fish this place?"

"Are you serious?" Dan said.

I didn't answer; instead, I steered left onto 28A and headed west, towards the southern edge of the Reservoir. It was a route I'd taken plenty of times, first with Marie when we went for a Sunday drive, then by myself when I was searching for places to fish, then with Dan when I took him to some of those fishing spots. This morning, the road seemed more narrow, its curves harder to navigate my truck around. At every bend, water streamed across it, and the tires shimmied when they hit it. Their branches weighted with the rain, the trees that grew thick by the sides of the road reached down to us. One of the limbs dragged over the roof of the cab, and the metal shrieked.

Get a grip, I told myself. After all, Howard's wasn't the only tale I'd heard about what was supposed to lie beneath the Reservoir's waters. I believe the first must have concerned the towns that had been abandoned to make way for it. I encountered it when I was still at college, during what was likely my first visit to the place. A half-dozen of us had driven up in someone's station wagon to drink beers and gaze up at the stars. I'd been included because I had a guitar on which I could pick out some of the more popular songs on the radio. While I was taking a break from playing beside the modest fire we'd built, one of the girls who'd made the trip sat down next to me and asked if I knew about the Reservoir. I can't remember what I said, probably no. It had been built, the girl said, on the spot where a town had stood. The residents were evicted, and their home was flooded. Supposedly, the girl went on, if you rowed out on the water when the weather was calm, and your boat drifted over the town's location, and you looked down, you would see the top of the church steeple, rising out of the depths below.

To be honest, for a long time, I believed that story, even passed it along, myself, a few times, until another friend set me straight, years later. It's one of those tales I've noticed attaches to spots where water covers the site of human dwelling. There's something haunting about the image of those houses, those shops, those churches, submerged in darkness, schools of fish darting amongst them, the light a distant glow overhead. It's as if you're seeing how time works, or some such.

Now the road climbed, scaling the faces of the hills that overlooked the Reservoir's southern shore. To our right, the ground dropped, lowering the trees there half-, then all the way, down, leaving us looking out over green crowns poking through the low clouds drifting up the hillside. In the distance, the Reservoir was a reach of gray water framed by mist and mountain, a blank piece of paper available for anyone to write on. And if the story you put there featured a woman whose ruined body left a trail of water behind her as she staggered along in search of her children, and a language that could force you to see the other side of the veil screening this world from another, where the original greatest catch coiled beneath the surface of the ocean, then what?

"So," I said, the sound of my voice unexpectedly loud, "what did you make of old Howard's story?"

"I think if that shaggy-dog story had been any hairier," Dan said, "it would have been a carpet."

"All the same…"

"All the same what?"

I shrugged. "I don't know. It was strange, was all."

For an answer, Dan snorted.

The other tale I'd heard about this place concerned an actual ghostly encounter. Not long after my inaugural visit to it, a friend—who was more of an acquaintance—claimed that a guy he'd met down at Pete's had told him something insane. According to this random stranger, he had been driving home along the eastern end of the Reservoir the previous week when he'd noticed a girl, standing at the side of the road ahead. She was barefoot, wearing a long, white dress. The stranger had rolled up beside her and asked if she needed a ride. Without answering, the girl had opened the door and slid into the passenger's seat. She had directed the fellow down unfamiliar roads until they'd arrived at a gate set back a ways from the asphalt. Here, the girl had left the car, though not before kissing her driver's cheek with lips so cold they burned. The next day, when the curious stranger returned to the spot where he'd dropped the girl the previous night, he discovered that the gates through which she'd passed led to a cemetery. As my friendly acquaintance told it, what had leant the stranger's tale that tiny bit of extra credibility had been the spot on his right cheek where the girl's kiss had landed. The skin was raw, red, the outline of her lips still visible.

They call this second story The Phantom Hitchhiker, and you find versions of it all over the place—all around the world, I'd bet. That I heard a variation connected to the Reservoir was pure chance. It could as easily have been set any location with no effect to its integrity. Most of the ghost and strange stories I've heard are like this, local riffs on a more general theme. If you tried, I suppose you could find a meaning for them, a moral they embody. In the case of the Hitchhiker, I guess it would have to do with being leery of strangers, and there's probably a caution about desire in there, too, isn't there? With Howard's tale, I couldn't figure out what lesson to draw from it, what message it was trying to convey. What was I supposed to think about, say, the stone those workers had unearthed on the Dort House's property? Stone? I thought. Howard hadn't said anything about a stone. What was this? Only, I knew exactly what stone, the large, blue one in whose depths a worker had glimpsed a distant, fiery eye. My foot slacked on the gas.

To our left, one end of a driveway looped towards a sizable house whose fieldstone walls, tall windows, and jagged roofline appeared intended to suggest a fairy castle, a suggestion the no-less-sizable outbuildings gathered near it picked up and reinforced. At the top of the manicured lawn next to it, an Italianate villa brooded over a yard full of statuary. Beside me, Dan was silent, his thoughts his own. I kept on 28A as it descended the hillside, past a boxy church, a pair of semitrailers parked in an improvised lot, and houses whose pretensions skewed middle-class, until the road leveled. I veered left, onto Stone Church Way, away from the Reservoir, and took it till Ashokan Lane branched to the right. I was reasonably sure Howard had mentioned the Sheriff who saw to the Dort House's eventual destruction, but I was less certain whether he had described that official's look at the interior. Here, the houses tucked in amidst the trees were more modest than those we'd passed at the top of the hillside, raised ranches, cottages, the occasional farmhouse. The cars in their driveways were not the newest models; their bumper stickers proclaimed their pride in their honor students, their loyalties in the last couple of elections. A mile or so up the road, past a heavy stand of trees, a sign for Tashtego Way marked the opening to a narrow lane on the left. I turned onto it.

Trees grew at the very edge of the road. Their branches and in some cases trunks weighted with rain, they leaned towards one another, forming a tunnel of bark and leaf. Concerned I might clip one of them, I eased off the gas and steered towards the middle of the blacktop. Overhead, the rain clung to the branches and swelled into large drops that dangled and then dropped, striking the roof of the cab with a bang. Dutchman's Creek was supposed to be somewhere off this road, but as yet, I had not spotted any potential parking spots, only trees walling us in on either side. Briefly, I wondered if the Creek actually existed—if it might not be some kind of local legend—but the trees on the right fell away to reveal a stretch of marsh, a meadow along from it, a low ridge backing both. I braked to a crawl, rolling past the marsh until we came to the meadow. After about ten feet, I turned the wheel slightly, testing the soil with the right-hand tires. The truck had four-wheel drive, so I most likely could have driven straight into the tall grass with full confidence I'd be able to drive out again, but I hated to tear up a stretch of land like that if I didn't have to. Not to mention, if I was wrong, it would be an expensive proposition to have a tow-truck come all the way out here to extricate me from my error. The ground felt solid enough. I turned the wheel a little more, until the truck was completely in the meadow, with a good five-foot margin between my door and the road. I shifted into park, set the parking brake, and cut the engine.

As if my turning the key had summoned it, the rain fell with renewed force, washing away the view out the windows. Dan sighed and reached for his hat, but I caught his arm. "Let's wait a minute," I said. "It won't last for long like this."

"All right," he said.

"Anyway, it'll give me a chance to ask you something."

"Oh?" He raised an eyebrow.

"Yeah," I said. "Exactly how did you find out about this place?"

He had to have known what my question was going to be. After Howard's story, what else would I have wanted to know? Yet he jerked his head back, shifted in his seat, and said, "What? I told you, Alf Evers's book."

"Bullshit," I said, not unkindly.

"What do you—"

"I'm guessing if we had a copy of that book, we wouldn't find a single reference to Dutchman's Creek in it." I held up a hand to forestall his protest. "What is it you aren't telling me?"

"Jesus, Abe," Dan said. He grabbed his hat, jammed it on his head, and flung open his door with sufficient force to shake the truck. He stepped down into the rain, and reached behind the seat to where we'd stored our gear. I sat where I was while he removed his rod and tacklebox and the knapsack holding our food and drink. Once he had the knapsack shouldered, he glared at me, his face red, and said, "Well? Are you coming?"

There was no way I wasn't going with him. I opened my door as he slammed his and stormed off across the meadow. I fetched my gear, locked the truck, and set after him. The rain had not let up the way I'd predicted, and the grass and ground were soaked. Water streamed off the bill of my cap, and mud tugged at the boots I was glad I'd worn. By the time I was at the bottom of the ridge, which is to say, not much time, at all, the lower halves of my jeans were wet and heavy. My cap was saturated. The ridge was forested with decent-sized trees, which offered a modicum of shelter. I ducked in among them and continued on my way. It's funny: although the air was full of the sound of the rain thundering down, and, closer to home, my breathing as I pushed up the slope, I could hear a couple of birds in the branches somewhere nearby, chirping these snippets of song that cut through all the water. It was such a cheering sound, I thought, *I'll have to figure out what bird that is.*

The crest of the ridge didn't take that long to reach. To be honest, it was more a hump in the earth than a proper hill. From its top, I saw Dan starting down the other side, into a valley formed by the low hill we were on and the larger wall of earth and rock behind it. I don't mind a walk to a fishing spot, but I have to admit, as the years have piled on, I've come to like climbing to a location less and less. I feel it in my knees, my problems with which, I guess I inherited from my pa, who was plagued with knee trouble for almost as long as I could remember. I suppose I should have been grateful my knees had held out the length of time they had. Well, in for a penny, and all that; with a sigh, I started my descent.

Just beyond the foot of the first ridge, a ribbon of water crossed the valley. You would have been forgiven for calling it a puddle, except that it was flowing, trickling from left to right through the black, muddy ground. Something—some trick of the light, I judged, the effect of all the trees looming over it, the earth below it—made the water look black as ink. What light there was didn't skip on its surface; it seemed to float further down in it, as if the rivulet ran far deeper than I knew must be the case. I thought of Howard's black ocean, and the memory angered me. I was half-tempted to stomp my boot in it, to prove it was no more than the overflow from some nearby pond or stream, but the prospect of my foot touching that black water made my mouth go dry, my heart hammer. "Damn fool," I muttered, and hopped over it.

My progress up the second ridge was not as quick. The ground was steeper, its surface broken by stretches of rock washed slick by the rain. Caution was the order of the day. Above me, Dan was at the top of the hill. Should I slip, fall, and injure myself, I wasn't sure he'd hear me calling for help from the other side of it. Tacklebox and rod in one hand, the other free to catch hold of the nearest tree, I started up the ridge, leaning forward to help my balance. The soil was shallow, crisscrossed by exposed tree roots. I stepped carefully, using the roots as footholds. Patches of pale green lichen wrapped the tree trunks, flaking off onto my palms when I grabbed them. I know I was ruminating over Howard's story, but it had been pushed from the forefront of my thoughts by a vague unease that I attributed to Dan's behavior, his lying and his outburst. I'd witnessed his difficulties at work; I'd had a much closer view of them this past February, the night he'd come to dinner. I'd told myself that fishing was an oasis for him, a place of respite from the desert of his days. Now, pushing up this steep hill, I wondered if I'd been wrong, if the scorched ruin of his life had swept over his refuge, burying its sweet water under burning sand. I wasn't afraid of Dan, but I was concerned for him, and for me, chasing him through rows of Hemlock and Maple.

In front of me, a large birch had fallen across the hillside. I half-climbed over it, and saw the remains of a campfire and a pile of empty beer cans. The aftermath of a teenage party, no doubt. The mess grated on me, as such carelessness always did, but mixed in with that sourness was a faint taste of, not relief, exactly, but reassurance. The dented and crushed aluminum, the charred sticks, meant that someone else had been here, and not that long ago, either.

As I drew nearer to the top of the ridge, the Hemlocks grew closer together, and taller, which seemed a good thing, since from the sound of it, the rain was heavier than ever. Feeling somewhat like a mouse in a maze, I picked my way through the trunks, until the ground leveled and I was at the crest of the hill. Because of the trees, there wasn't much of a view in any direction, but in the distance across from me, I could make out the bulk of another ridge I prayed I wouldn't have to climb. The surface of this hill already sloped down, at a steeper angle than the one I'd just ascended, but the trees continued dense enough for me to use them and their roots to help my footing. *There had better be some Goddamned monster fish in this stream,* I thought as I placed my foot between a pair of roots. I was sweating, and the lightweight raincoat of which I was so proud had trapped the moisture within itself, giving me my own portable sauna.

For what felt like much longer than I'm sure it was, I mountain-goated it down the ridge. Not until I was almost at its foot, and the trees were spreading out, allowing me a better view of the torrent of water below me, did I realize that roar I'd been listening to wasn't the rain, but Dutchman's Creek. Swollen with the past week's downpour, the stream galloped over this stretch of rapids in a white rush. Something about the acoustics of the place—the closeness of the ridge on the other side of the creek—caught the water's noise and amplified it. To the eye, the stream was maybe thirty feet across, not as large as many of the spots I'd fished much further into the Catskills. To the ear, however, Dutchman's Creek was a river in flood.

At the base of the hill, earth gave way to bare rock, which shelved this side of the stream to left and right. A quick survey showed Dan off to the right, downstream. I sighed. I was straining to be patient with him. I had decided he must have had the name of the place from a woman, one with whom he'd had some measure of involvement. Their affair might have lasted no longer than a single night, but the loss of his family was recent enough for Dan to fear he'd betrayed them. Whatever comfort he'd sought, I didn't begrudge him. His wounds cut down to the bone—through the bone, to the marrow—and any relief you can find from that kind of pain, however temporary, you take. The trick is, enduring the guilt that grabs you in its broken teeth the minute that comfort ebbs. What came across as a snit, I reminded myself, was symptom of an affliction more profound, one with which I was only too well-acquainted. So although I was tempted to turn left, upstream, in search of solitude to cast my line, I opted to go right.

Even without the addition of seven days' worth of rain, the rapids I had emerged beside would have been serious business. For a good hundred yards, they descended in a series of drops so regular they might have been enormous steps. This entire portion of the stream was strewn with boulders, gray blocks whose edges the water appeared to have done little to soften. It was as if the side of a mountain had let go and come to rest here. There are fish that will brave such turbulent conditions, and under other, less extreme circumstances, I might have tried my luck for one. I caught a glimpse of a good-sized something sporting in the spray. My ambition, however, is tempered by my common sense, and while every fisherman understands that he's going to sacrifice his fair share of tackle to his passion, there's no point in throwing it away, which was what I'd be doing if I cast into this white roaring. Not to mention, between the rain and the spray, the shore was dangerously slick. I continued toward Dan.

When I caught up to him, he had his line in the water. He was standing at the opposite side of a wide pool into which the creek poured itself over a waterfall. Thirty yards across, the pool was a stone cup whose sides fell sharply into the water. Where the stream splashed into it, the pool churned and foamed, cloudy with sediment. Out towards the middle, the water cleared to the point of glass, and despite the raindrops puckering its surface, I picked out the shapes of several large-ish fish congregating there. Trout, I hoped, below whom the water darkened—the dirt and whatnot that had been flung over the waterfall billowing across the pool's bottom. That I could tell, Dan hadn't hooked anything, yet. He had positioned himself at the spot where the water exited the pool through a broad channel. His tacklebox was open on the rock next to him, its shelves up and extended, which I took as an indication he planned to stay here a little while. I wasn't in a hurry to make conversation with him; as long as I could see him, that was fine with me. About halfway round the pool's circumference, the edge dipped to a ledge that slanted into and under the water. I set down my gear at the top of the incline, bent to open my tacklebox, and in short order was raising my arm to cast.

God, but I love that first cast. You pinch the line to the rod, open the bail, lift the rod over your head, and snap your wrist, releasing the line as you do. The motion whips up the rod, taking the pink and green spinner-bait at the end of the line back and then out, out and out and out, trailing line like a jet speeding ahead of its contrail, climbing to the top of the parabola whose far end is going to put the lure right next to those fish. The reel feeds out more and more line, making a quick, whizzing sound as it spins; while the lure nears the apex of its flight and starts to slow, causing the line to bunch up right behind it. When the lure falls toward the water, it takes longer than it seems it should, so that for a moment, you wonder if it's already hit the surface and somehow you missed it, and you're almost to the point of searching for the spot where it went in when the spinner flashes and you look in time to see the water leap up with a plunk. You drop the bail to secure the line, counting, "One-Mississippi, two-Mississippi, three-Mississippi," trying to let that little assembly of wood and metal you call your watermelon spinner sink to the level of those fish, watching the line that had fallen slack on the water straighten and submerge, and then it's four-Mississippi and you start drawing in that line, and the day's fishing is well and truly underway.

I've tried to find something to compare the sensation to, but the closest I've ever been able to come is the moment after you've swept your fingers down the guitar strings and sounded the opening note of your first song. Or the second after the baseball has slipped your fingertips and is turning in the air as it steaks toward the catcher's open mitt. There's a similar feeling of having started something whose outcome you can't be one-hundred-percent sure of—sometimes, the percentage is significantly lower—but there isn't the same openness that accompanies the lure's trajectory. Sure, you think you know what's waiting for you under the water, but believe you me, you can never be sure what's going to take your hook.

Right away, the fish I had aimed at were interested in my lure, a couple of them breaking away from the group to dart after it. I wound the handle faster, trying to goad them into striking, but they held back until I had the lure in sight, the spinner winking as it sped through the water, when each of them shot off in a different direction. I didn't worry about them; I had the lure in and was lifting my arm for a second attempt at the spot where I could make out a number of fish maintaining their position. This time, I let the lure descend through the water for an extra –Mississippi before drawing it in. A new fish peeled away from the school after it. I decided not to speed up my retrieve, but kept winding the handle one-two one-two one-two. Below the fish, which appeared larger than either of the first pair by a couple of inches, the murk that hung in the water churned. I wound the line in, one-two one-two. The fish was at the lure—

—and was gone, chased away by the thing that rose from the murk beneath it, took the bait in its mouth, and rolled into a dive. I had an impression of a body thick as the trunk of a small tree, covered with scales pale as the moon. Had I not left the drag loose, the fish would have snapped my line like thread. As it was, the rod bowed with the pressure the thing applied to it. The fish wasn't swimming especially fast—the line spooled out of the reel at an almost leisurely pace—but it was going far. It sank deep into the murk, to what I estimated must be the bottom of the pool, before turning into a wide circle. I had no idea what had taken my lure. It certainly wasn't a trout, or a bass, or any of the panfish. From its size and its strength, I guessed it might be a carp, which was not a fish I'd anticipated running into here. But there are times you pull something out of the water for which there's no accounting, the only remnant of a story whose contours are a mystery. However it had come to inhabit this pool, a carp had the power to break my line with a toss of its head. If I wanted to land it, I was going to have to alter my usual strategy. I tested the handle, the rod dipping as the line tightened. "Easy," I murmured, half to myself, half to the fish. I could feel him down there in the dark, feel his weight and his muscle. I gave the handle another turn, stopping when the fish began to draw more line, doubling back into a wider circle. I guessed he was testing this thing that had jabbed into him. I waited to see whether he would maintain his present course, or take off in a new direction. Once he appeared content to continue swimming in a broad circle, I started turning the handle slowly, gradually shifting his sweep closer to me.

At some point during this long process, Dan noticed that I had something on the end of my line and that it wasn't behaving in the usual fashion. I can't say exactly how long his curiosity as to what, exactly, I was doing required to overcome his annoyance with my questioning him, but by the time I had the fish in near enough that I could see the murk churning as he plowed through it, Dan was standing at my right side. He said, "What've you got?"

"Don't know," I said. "Carp, maybe."

"Carp? Here?"

"Too big for a trout or bass."

"Maybe it's a pike."

"Could be," I said. "Doesn't act like one."

"Doesn't act much like a carp, either," Dan said.

"No argument there."

Because Dan was next to me, when the fish swam up out of the murk into view, I had his reaction to gauge mine against, his "What the hell?" to reassure me that he'd witnessed what I had. How I didn't drop the rod, or jerk it up and snap the line, I can't say. For one thing, the fish was huge, easily four feet from nose to tail. Too big, I would have said, to have survived in a spot this size for very long—unless it went much, much deeper than it seemed. For another thing, what I glimpsed of its head was unlike anything I'd encountered in any of the places I'd cast my line. Rounded, its large, dark eyes set forward, its mouth jammed with teeth like steak knives, the front end of the thing resembled what you'd expect to run across in the depths of the ocean.

"Guess it isn't a carp, after all," I said.

"What..." Dan's voice trailed off.

"I don't know." The fish was slowing, the tension on the line slacking. I turned the handle faster, tightening the line, ready for the fish to change course. If he didn't, if he completed another circuit of the pool, his next pass would bring him close enough for me to attempt bringing him in. Although one part of my mind had picked up Dan's "What the hell?" and was chanting it like a mantra, and another section of my mind was working at answering how an apparent denizen of the lower deep could have found its way into a small body of water in upstate New York, enough of my brain remained available to calculate the best trajectory for guiding the fish onto the spit of rock supporting me. The fish was swinging in my direction, rising in the water as he came. His dorsal fin, a fan of pale flesh stretched between spines the length of my forearm, broke into the air like the back of a dragon. I said, "Dan."

"Yeah."

"I'm going to see if I can't steer this fellow right up onto this ledge in front of me. You see what I'm talking about?"

"Sure, but—"

"Once I get him on the rock, I'm going to hand the rod to you and do my best to manhandle him out of the water."

"But—"

"Just be ready to take the rod from me."

The more I said, the better I felt, the more confident. It was as if, by speaking my plan, I was setting it up to happen. The fish was slowing, the spines on his back listing as he swam nearer. I resisted the urge to wind the handle as fast as I could. He might be done, or he might be readying for a dive. He was close, now, so close I could see his face in all its hideous glory. Dan leaned in to me, his hands out for the rod. "Almost there," I said, "almost there." The front half of the fish slid over the rock shelf. There was barely enough line for me to reel in, but I drew him up the shelf, to where the water shallowed. Once his tail was over the rock, I passed the rod to Dan and took a step towards the fish. As I did, he raised his head and neck partway out of the pool, as if readying to fling himself off the rock. His eyes, I saw, were empty pits. While I was debating whether to grab the line or tackle him, the fish settled back under the water and was still.

I splashed into the pool and plunged my hands into it, well back of the fish's weird head and its sharp teeth. His gills were barely moving. I gripped the forward gill on either side of him and backed up. Ready for a fight, I moved fast, hauling his bulk most of the way out of the water before releasing my hold and falling on my ass. I had been expecting the edges of his gills to be sharp, and was prepared to chance the injury to my hands to secure such a catch, but the flaps of skin were rubbery, almost soft. When it thumped onto the rock, tremors shivering its bulk, its entire body gave the impression that it was less solid than gelid. Strange, yes, but no more so than this creature being in this pool in the first place. I could feel the grin splitting my mouth. I was in a position the envy of everyone who's ever spent any time working the rod and reel: I had my fantastic story, and I had the proof of it. Who knew what this would mean for me? My picture in the paper, an honored spot on Howard's wall, at least. I turned to Dan, who had not relaxed his hold on the rod. "It's okay," I said, pushing myself to my feet, "we got him." I held out my hand, and Dan returned the rod. "Thanks," I said. "Couldn't have done it without you, buddy."

"Abe," Dan said.

"Definitely not a carp," I said. "Definitely, positively." I was trying to figure out the best means for transporting my catch over the hills to my truck. Maybe if I took off my raincoat, we could fashion a sling out of it that we could hoist on a pair of branches. It would require some work, but—

"Abe," Dan said.

"What?"

"I—that isn't a fish."

"Come again?" I glanced at Dan. His eyes big, he was staring past me at the fish. "That isn't," he said. "Look at it, Abe. *Look at it.*"

"Okay," I said, "okay." I did, and what Dan had seen slipped into focus for me. "Jesus!" I shouted, jumping back and colliding with him. "What the hell?"

The fish's face, as I've said, was rounded, its eyes a pair of large, forward-facing sockets. No doubt, its resemblance to a human skull had factored into my initial shock at its appearance. What I'd been too concerned with bringing the thing in to realize was that the face wasn't shaped like a skull, it was shaped around a skull. Imagine a good-sized fish, something like a salmon, whose head has been cut away. In its place, someone has set a human skull, stretching the fish's skin over the bone to hold it there. Finally, whoever has performed this bizarre transplant has given his new creation a mouth, a slit at the bottom of its face whose bloodless gums are jammed with fangs like a drawer of knives. Behind its gills, a sizable pair of pectoral fins splayed on the rock, while a smaller set of ventral fins spread out nearer the tail, whose top lobe drooped to the left. The sight of it hurt my eyes to behold. I wanted to turn my head; the breakfast boiled at the back of my mouth. Maybe there was a natural explanation for what I dragged out of the pool, but if there was, I didn't want anything to do with the nature that could fashion such a creature. At the same time, I could not stop looking at the fish, which blew out air through its forest of teeth in a tired grunt.

"It was in my grandfather's fishing journal," Dan said.

I had no response—had no notion what he was talking about.

"He was a fisherman, too," Dan said. His voice shook with the strain of the sight before us. "He and my dad used to go fishing on weekends. Sometimes, they took me. Not too often, but sometimes. He kept a record of the places he'd fished. It was just a ruled notebook, the kind of thing you get for school. He was pretty thorough. For each spot, he recorded the date he went, the hours he spent there, the weather, the condition of the water, the lures he used, and the fish he caught. Once in a while, he'd add a comment underneath the data: 'Good luck above dam,' or, 'Hooked huge catfish near 32 bridge but lost him.' When he returned to a site, he updated the entry in different-colored ink. I never knew about his journal. He wasn't exactly what you'd called a forthcoming man. It wouldn't have mattered much if I had been aware of it. I liked to fish, but I wasn't interested in that kind of exhaustive note-taking.

"Then, this past February, my cousin, Martine, came to visit with her family. I think I told you about that. Right at the last possible minute, as they're loading the car for the trip back to Cincinnati, she reaches into her suitcase and comes out with Grandpa's journal. 'Here,' she says. I had no idea what she was handing me. She'd had the book bound in leather, with 'Fishing Journal' embossed on the cover in gold lettering. I thought it was a blank book, and she was going to tell me to write my feelings in it. She teaches high school English, and we'd talked about that. Well, she'd talked about it, as what she called a 'therapeutic exercise.'

"But no, it was our grandfather's record of his fishing trips. Her mother had come into possession of it after Grandpa's death, and she gave it to Martine. I couldn't figure out what Aunt Eileen would have wanted with the notebook. From what I understood, she'd always been focused on religion, to the point she'd flirted with converting to Catholicism, so she could become a nun. No one had mentioned her being interested in fishing.

She wasn't, Martine said. Her mother hated fishing. She was jealous of it, of the time and attention Grandpa gave to it, and of him sharing it with my father. I had no idea; no one else did, either. I'm surprised she didn't burn the journal, you know, take revenge that way. When Martine's older son, Robin, was born, her mother passed the journal to her, for the baby. Robin wasn't interested in fishing, though; neither was his younger sister. My cousin left the journal in her dresser drawer, said she'd practically forgotten it. Then, after," his voice hitched, "everything happened with Sophie and the kids, and you and I started fishing together, Martine remembered our grandfather's notebook. She dug it out from underneath the socks and underwear and decided it would be of more use to me than it had been to anyone in her family. She found a place to give the journal a nice binding, and here it was. 'I hope you'll find something in these pages that will be of help to you,' she said.

"It was a while before I looked inside the notebook. To be honest, Abe, I wasn't sure I wanted to keep fishing with you. No reflection on you: I wasn't sure I wanted to continue fishing, period. You probably noticed, things with me got a little worse this winter. I know I kind of fell apart that night you had me over for dinner. As long as we were fishing, I was—I wasn't good, not by any stretch of the imagination, but I was able to go from one day to the next. After the season ended, and I put away my rod and tacklebox in the spare room, everything became harder. It didn't happen overnight. There were still the holidays and visits from family to distract me. But more and more, it seemed to me I was caught, trapped in a whirlpool that had swept me in the morning that truck—that truck…"

Dan shook his head fiercely, tearing his gaze from the thing in front of us. Focusing on me, instead, he said, "A maelstrom: that's what they call an especially big and bad whirlpool, the kind of funnel in the ocean that could draw down a ship. I was in a maelstrom, spun around and around a cone of black water, my wife and my children somewhere in there with me, their screams and cries impossible to pinpoint. The longer it had hold of me, the harder it was to believe that there had been anything else, any standing beside the Svartkil talking about work and waiting for a bite. All of those trips, those days sitting on the bank of this stream or that, were a dream, a delusion I'd foisted on myself to escape that relentless spin. Do you know—where the accident happened, they put a light, there."

THE FISHERMAN

"Yes," I said.

"Most mornings, I drive down there. We're talking three, four a.m., when it still feels like nighttime. I have trouble sleeping very long. I pull off the road, turn off the car, and sit staring at that light."

"I know," I said.

"You do?"

"You told me," I said, "the night you came over for dinner."

"I did?"

"After a lot of wine."

"Oh." For a moment, the thread of Dan's narrative appeared to have slipped through his fingers. "Huh," he said. "Okay. So. I watch the traffic light and think about things. I probably said what kind of things, didn't I?"

"Yeah."

"Night after night—or morning after morning—it's the same. The light cycles through its commands and the maelstrom drags me deeper. I'm aware how bad conditions at work are, and I understand that I'm inviting management to add my head to the pile of those they've hacked off, already, but I can't muster enough concern to lead to any action. I watch the green replaced by yellow, yellow by red, and…"

"Yeah."

"Then, one morning, I glance at the passenger's seat and there's Grandpa's fishing journal. I can't remember putting it there—can't remember why I would have put it there—but that's all right. I go through a lot of my day on autopilot, I've noticed. Maybe I thought it was something else. Doesn't matter. My curiosity's been pricked. I pick up the book and start turning the pages. They're stiff with the dried ink. As I go, I recognize some of the names he's written. The Esopus. The Rondout. The Svartkil. I pause at some of the entries, trace my finger over the words as I try to decipher the old man's handwriting. He caught whatever would take his hook, but it seems he preferred catfish. Caught an enormous channel cat right where the Rondout empties into the Hudson. Reading his notes, re-creating the days he'd had—it's comforting, in a strange kind of way. I look at the pages for places I haven't been. I see an entry for Dutchman's Creek."

I don't mind saying, I was feeling a tad story'd-out. First Howard's extravaganza, and now Dan's more restrained example, and in the meantime, a human skull wrapped in translucent skin was grinning at me over a mouth

213

of fangs. "So that's how you found out about this place," I said. "Great. Now—"

"'Saw Eva,'" Dan said. "That's why we're here. Underneath all the usual information, he'd written those two words. Eva was his wife—my grandmother. She died in 1945, on New Year's Day. A stroke, I think. My dad was only seven at the time, and was never able to find out exactly what had happened. Anyway, the point is, the entry Grandpa made for Dutchman's Creek was dated July 1953. My grandmother had been dead eight and a half years, which means she couldn't have accompanied him on the trip.

"I know." Dan held up his hand, palm outward, a cop halting the protest about to leave my mouth. "I flipped to the first page of the book and checked the date. He'd started this log in May of 1948. This wasn't an earlier entry that had been misdated. I checked the other pages in the journal, every last one of them. There were no other references to seeing my grandmother. It wasn't some kind of code for a good day of fishing. It was—I didn't know what it was. Saw Eva."

"Did he ever go back to Dutchman's Creek?" I said.

"No. At least, not that he recorded in the notebook. He continued fishing for a long time after that. I wondered why he hadn't returned. I mean, this was the place where he'd seen the woman he'd lost, and suddenly at that. How could he have gone anyplace else? Unless—unless whatever he'd seen, whatever glimpse of her he'd had, had been enough. We talk about that, don't we? 'Oh, if only I had a chance to say all the things I should've to her.' 'If only I could have one last hour with her, or half an hour, or ten minutes.' What if he'd said what he'd wanted to say? What if he'd had that hour? Would that have been enough?

"And yes, I realize how this sounds. From the start, I knew what it sounded like, a grieving husband and father, trapped in denial, unable to transition out of it. I couldn't ask my grandfather about the entry: he died in '75. I went to visit my dad in his nursing home, but he's half-senile. From what I could tell, he wasn't along for the trip to Dutchman's Creek; nor had Grandpa spoken to him about it. Mom's been gone since '88. I called my brother and sister, my aunts and uncles, my cousins, but none of them could remember Grandpa mentioning Dutchman's Creek, much less, encountering Grandma, there.

"Of course I checked the map. I had to find out if the place was even real. Took me a couple of tries, but once I could put my finger on it, follow its course to the Hudson, somehow, that made Grandpa's words seem that much more convincing, you know?"

The nutty thing was, I did. At least, I could recognize the train of wishful thinking Dan had boarded. I said, "That was when you decided we had to come here."

"You're always looking for new fishing spots," Dan said. "Tell me you aren't."

"Fishing spots," I said, "not…" I waved my hand at the weird fish, the murky pool I'd drawn it from, "this."

"Saw Eva, Abe, saw Eva." All the strain had long since left Dan's voice, as the beast on the rock went from frightening monster to sign that his hopes for Dutchman's Creek had been justified. "He saw her. My grandfather saw my grandmother, his wife, who had been dead for years. I—morning after morning, I sat in my car at that light with the fishing journal propped against the wheel, open to that entry, to those words. When the light turned the page red, the letters were darker, almost blurred at the edges. When it clunked over to green, the words were lighter, harder to see. Only when the light switched to yellow did the words return to normal. Saw Eva. What were the chances, right? That I could see Sophie, Jason, Jonas. That I could speak to them, tell them—everything. Tell Sophie she was the best thing that had ever happened to me, that I wouldn't have gotten nearly as far in life as I had without her, that I was sorry I'd pushed off as much of caring for the boys onto her as I had. Tell the boys how much better they had made my life—our life—apologize for not having been more patient with them when they were still so small. Tell them I loved them, I loved them, I loved them, and that being without them was killing me. Saw Eva—why not, Saw Sophie? Saw Jonas? Saw Jason? What about you? Wouldn't you like to be able to say, Saw Marie?"

"You can leave Marie out of this," I said. The sound of her name snapped whatever hold the fish had on me. I turned my head away from it, and pushed myself up onto legs that had gone to sleep from sitting too long. Wincing, I said, "I have no idea what in the hell this thing is. But it's a fish. This is a stream. That's all."

If I was anticipating an argument from Dan, he disabused me of that expectation right away. Nodding at the fish, he said, "I figure this must have originated upstream. Where I was fishing, the water flows into a wide bed that's too shallow for something this size to have swum up it." He retreated a step. "I guess it's back the way we came. Are you with me?"

"Dan," I said.

Without another word, he set off upstream, walking at a brisk pace.

"Dan!" I called after him. He did not acknowledge me. "Goddamnit." For a moment, I was caught between conflicting priorities. Whatever my doubts about his present mental state—in fact, because of those reservations—I was not about to let my friend go wandering away on some insane quest. At the same time, I had pulled a fish from this pool that was unlike any that had been fished in this area—in every area, I was willing to bet. The thing appeared motionless, but there was at least a chance of it convulsing itself into the water. Were it to remain on the ledge, a passing predator or predators might be drawn by its smell and make a meal of it. I realize how cold-blooded this must sound. How could I have debated my choice at all, right? Chalk part of it up to anger. Dan's account of the actual source of his information about the Creek—not to mention, his motivation for bringing us here—had kindled the annoyance I'd felt since his outburst at the truck into genuine ire. Along with that emotion had come another, unease, shading into outright fear. Not so much for Dan's sanity: I was concerned about it, yes, but I thought I understood what had happened to his mind. What made my palms sweat and my heart quicken was the fish lying on the stone in front of me, the skull embedded in its flesh. Was the skull even human? The eye-sockets looked more pronounced than they should have, the brown sloped back at too sharp an angle. I had told Dan this creature was a fish, because it had to be, there was no way for it to be anything other than a fish. Except, I didn't quite believe my assertion. The thing was impossible, yet here it was. If so fantastic a creature could take my lure, then maybe what Dan's grandfather had written in his journal wasn't so out of the question, after all. Which meant that the story Howard had told us might not have been complete bullshit, after all.

"Goddamnit," I said again. Apparently, Dan's and Howard's lunacy was catching. I turned and knelt beside my tacklebox. At the bottom of it, underneath packets of rubber worms and loose bobbers, was a knife I'd picked up at a yard sale a few years ago. It looked like your average wooden ruler, a foot long, blond wood, but there was a seam at the six-inch mark.

Grip the ruler to either side of that and tug, and a six-inch filleting blade slid out of inches six through twelve. I was thinking that I would draw a little more line out of my reel, then use the knife to cut it. I could secure the extra line to a rock, and if there was any mercy in heaven, once I returned from fetching Dan, the fish would still be here.

As I was standing, something caught at the top of my vision. At the edge of the treeline, thirty feet away, a slender white figure rested its right hand on the trunk of a hemlock. Naked, her hair and skin soaking, a young woman regarded me from eyes as golden as any fish's. I want to say it took a moment for her face to register, but that isn't true. Immediately, I knew her, as if I'd only just now watched her chest rise and fall for the last time.

It was Marie.

V

THERE FISSURE

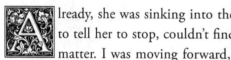lready, she was sinking into the woods. I couldn't find the words to tell her to stop, couldn't find the voice to utter them. It didn't matter. I was moving forward, propelled by legs still half-asleep. Arms out, mouth moving dumbly, steps stumbling, I staggered after her like a kid playing Frankenstein. My heart—I could not feel my heart, nor the emotion gripping it. What I felt was too big—it was as if it were outside me, a current that had swept me up and was rushing me along. Everything around me, the rock, the trees, the Creek, the rain, seemed to be part of that feeling, of that motion. The only thing separate from it was her, Marie, whose golden eyes did not blink as her bare feet took her deeper into the forest. Her skin was pale, pale as the flesh of a lily, but it was as unblemished as it had been the first time she had dropped her robe in front of me in a hotel room in Burlington. She might have stepped to this moment directly from that one, before the scars on her chest, the bruises on her arms, before her scalp bared, her cheeks dulled, before her body shrank to her bones as the cancer consumed her. All that was different were her eyes, whose metallic hue seemed in keeping with the strangeness of seeing her, here.

You may have read or watched reports of folks who thought a loved one was dead, killed in an accident or catastrophe, and subsequently had that news contradicted when the supposedly deceased opened the front door. You can appreciate how those people must have felt. Here they were, trying to adjust to their loved one's having been wrenched from the category of the living and thrust into that of the dead. Of course the mind resists such a dramatic change, so in addition to the joy that leapt in them at the sight of their loved one, a small voice inside them must have whispered, "I knew it." No matter that your wife is lying without breathing on the hospital bed before you, that the nurses have switched off all the machines that were monitoring her and disconnected the wires that allowed them to, you can't accept it. You may understand it, but you can't admit the fact into yourself. That surrender has to be negotiated over time. Once it has been accomplished, however, you can imagine how upsetting—how deeply, fundamentally traumatic—it would be to find yourself confronted by the person you had relinquished to death.

My strides were more confident, hers, not as quick. I might have guessed she wanted me to catch her, but I couldn't read anything in those eyes. At last, she stopped, her back to a large maple. I was so focused on her face that I almost crashed into her. Closer to her than I had intended, I halted, the momentum of my pursuit carrying speech past my lips. "Marie," I said, the name somewhere between a question and a statement. "Marie."

"Abe," she said in the voice I'd resigned myself to hearing only on our wedding video's tinny soundtrack. Not like this, the rich, slightly throaty tone that rose up into whatever she was saying, filling it with her warmth and intelligence. At the sound of it, my vision swam with tears.

I wiped my eyes, swallowed. "How?"

For a reply, she lifted her right hand to my face and pressed her fingers to my lips. Her fingertips were cool, her skin charged with the briny smell of the sea, but her touch was as solid, as real, as ever it had been. I caught her hand in both of mine. She raised her other hand to my cheek.

A sob I hadn't been aware was forming burst from me. A second, and a third, followed it, each eruption of sound a convulsion that doubled me over, squeezing tears from my eyes. Marie's hand in mine, I dropped to my knees, sobs shaking me. She sank beside me, her free hand touching my face, my ear, pushing back my cap to slide her fingers into my damp hair. "Shhh," she said, "shhhh." My tears pattered on the dead leaves underneath me. Interspersed with my sobs, a low, keening moan escaped my lips. To be sure, I had wept over Marie, before this. I had cried at her bedside. I had cried at her graveside. I had cried liquor-flavored tears many a night thereafter. The river of tears that rolls through all those old sad songs had poured down my cheeks. But what had me now was of a different order of magnitude entirely. This was no river; it was an ocean forcing its way through a canal. I brought Marie's hand to my mouth and kissed it over and over again. Her left hand shoved my cap off and stroked my hair. She leaned in to me. The briny tang of her skin filled my nostrils.

She pressed her lips to my forehead. Then to my eyebrows. Then to my eyelids. When she reached the bridge of my nose, she started to make the soft noises, little sighs and groans, which in another life had signaled her growing arousal. She slipped her hand out of mine and used it to lift my chin so that my lips could meet hers. Her mouth was as cool as the rest of her, but she kissed me the way she always had, a press that softened into a caress. She took my head in her hands as she extended the kiss. I was not done sobbing, but the sobs lessened as I responded to her. The moan that was issuing from me was changing tone, sorrow giving way to desire. Marie's hands were moving down my neck, to the collar of my shirt, to the zipper of my raincoat, which she pinched and lowered. My hands were clasped in front of me, as if I were praying, but when her fingers started unbuttoning my shirt, I released them and reached for her breasts. They were full in my hands, the nipples raised at my touch, and she gasped into my mouth as I cupped them. Her hands moved faster, tugging my shirt out of my jeans, slipping up under my t-shirt and sliding over my chest. I was fever-hot with the want of her, and her cool skin was a balm on mine. Her hands were at my belt; mine were on her hips.

I have desired women before: Marie, yes, and the handful who preceded her, and the few who followed her. I've known the hand-shaking eagerness of the young, and the dry-mouthed anticipation of the more experienced. There was a time I broke the speed limit and blew through at least two stop-signs in response to a suggestive phone call Marie made. There was another time I emerged from what had seemed a particularly vivid dream of us making love to discover Marie moving on top of me. The emotion that filled me now, though—it was as if the grief that had been pouring through me had ignited, sparked furnace hot. There was desire present in it, but it was fueled by the grief, which gave my appetite a searing urgency. As Marie dragged my fly down, I pushed her over onto her back. Leaves rustled; twigs cracked. I could not read the expression in her eyes, but her hands guided me into her. She was as cool inside as she was outside, but I was plenty hot for the both of us. "Oh, Abe," she said. I tried to reply, but couldn't, all my attention taken by what was happening between us. Her legs raised, clasped my hips. I pressed against her. She gasped and turned her head to the right, closing her golden eyes. I kissed the corner of her mouth. She murmured the sweet obscenities that had first shocked and then aroused me. I groaned. Her head tilted back. We moved faster. She pushed her hands through my hair. We moved slower. She flung her arms out to either side of her. We moved faster again. She cried out a long series of cries, and I shouted as the torrent that had been rising within me found release.

Head swimming, I eased myself off Marie and onto my back. Once upon a time, I would have cracked a joke—at the very least, said, "I love you." But nothing I could think of seemed appropriate—adequate. Truth to tell, there wasn't a whole lot of organized activity happening between my ears. The conflagration roaring through me had blown out, extinguished by the finish to Marie's and my lovemaking, leaving me empty, scoured and scorched by its ferocity. Aware of her beside me, I gazed up at the trees pointing to the clouds overhead, blinking at the rain that made it through the lattice of branches. Mother-of-pearl, the clouds struck me as blindingly beautiful. My mind a pleasant blank, I turned to Marie.

What was sharing the forest floor with me had the same gold eyes, but the rest of its face might have leapt out of a nightmare. Its nose was flat, the nostrils a pair of slits over a broad mouth whose lower jaw jutted forward, exposing the row of daggered teeth lining it. Its hair was stringy, a mane of tendrils. The hand it rested on my chest was webbed, each thick finger capped by a heavy claw. Its mouth opened, and gave forth a sigh of post-coital contentment.

More than anything else, that exhalation sent me scrambling away, crab-crawling as fast as my arms and legs would move me. Had my pants not been bunched around my ankles, I might have gotten further; as it was, my legs caught on one another and set me down on my ass, hard. I grabbed for my belt, simultaneously trying to raise myself to my feet, but the thing that had taken Marie's place—the thing that had been Marie—was up and approaching me, its webbed hands out in front of it. "Abe," it said.

Despite myself, I said, "Marie?"

The thing's features shimmered, as if I were seeing them through a layer of water across which a succession of ripples passed. They settled, and I was looking at Marie. "Abe," she said, and stepped toward me.

"You stay right there!" I backpedaled, yanking up my jeans as I went. My heel caught a root, dumping me on my ass, yet again. When I stood this time, I had found the filleting knife where I'd slipped it into the pocket of my raincoat and had it out and unsheathed; although, to be honest, I'd never appreciated quite how small it was. Not to mention, I had no idea how to use it outside of cleaning a fish.

"Abe," Marie—I didn't know how else to think of her—said.

"What are you?" I said.

She didn't answer.

"What are you!" The knife trembled in my grip.

"A reflection," Marie said.

"Of what?"

She smiled, faintly.

I didn't understand. I said, "You are not my wife."

She didn't answer that, either.

"Where are we? What is this place?"

"Dutchman's Creek."

"That's—what about the fish?" I said. "The one I caught over there," I flung my arm in the general direction of the pool.

"What about it?"

"What is it?"

"A nymph," Marie said.

"I don't—what do you mean?"

"You'll have to come upstream to find out."

Upstream reminded me of Dan, who had vanished from my mind the instant I'd recognized Marie. "Sonofabitch," I said. If I had encountered Marie—or this thing passing for Marie—did that mean he'd found what he was searching for? Or that he thought he'd found it? "I came here with a friend," I said.

"Yes," Marie said. "Dan. Your fishing buddy."

"I think—he wanted to go upstream. He was hoping he'd find—"

"His family, Sophie and their boys."

"Did he?"

"Would you like me to take you to him?"

I could not conceive of any way in which accompanying Marie to wherever she had in mind could be a good idea. But what else was there for me to do? I swallowed. "I guess you'd better."

"It's this way." She turned away from me and set off through the woods on a course roughly parallel to that of the stream. Keeping my knife in hand, I followed her, stooping to pick up my cap where it had fallen. I figured we'd be climbing and traveling the ridge I'd crossed to find the Creek; for the moment, though, our path ran more or less level. I used my free hand to stuff my t-shirt inside my jeans, but couldn't button my shirt one-handed. I solved the problem by clenching the knife between my teeth long enough for me to button and tuck my shirt. Ridiculous as it sounds, I was worried about Dan taking one look at me and knowing I'd had sex with whatever Marie was. It was a way, I suppose, for me to keep from dwelling on our act in the leaves. I could not believe this shape picking its way through the branches and twigs strewn on the ground was not my wife. She lifted her leg, her foot pointing down like a ballerina's, and I saw her stepping into the bath. The cheeks of her ass rolled up and down, and I was propping myself up on one elbow, watching her cross the bedroom to the dresser. What I had glimpsed of her other face had been as real as what was in front of me—or no more unreal, if that makes any sense—and if I pictured that Marie moaning underneath me, her mouth opening and closing like a bass gasping in the air, I had to fight the urge to run in the direction of the Creek with all due haste. But looking at the curve of her spine brought to mind all the times I'd pressed my thumbs into the muscles to either side of it, massaging away the day's tension. Maybe it was the afterglow, or maybe, when you got right down to brass tacks, I wasn't that much different from Dan, desperate for any chance to recover what I'd lost, no matter what I had to look past to do so.

Ahead of me, Marie stopped. I slowed, drawing up to her but maintaining what I hoped was a safe distance. In front of us, a road ran across the forest floor. Composed of rounded stones sunk into the earth beside one another, it reminded me of the cobblestoned streets workmen in Wiltwyck occasionally uncovered when they were repairing a city street. These stones, though, were much larger, a yard across, and had been worn flat. I'm not much of a geologist: they might have been marble, or they might have been another, whitish rock. Stalks of grass sprouted from the spaces between the stones, while the ground to either side of the road, which was clear of leaves, had a red tint I hadn't encountered in these parts. This could have been an old country road, bypassed by newer and better routes and forgotten, but it didn't feel like that. It seemed ancient, as if it had been supporting the footsteps of men and women for as long as they'd been around. Which was impossible for this area, I knew, where the Native peoples had not favored this type of construction, and where the European settlers who had succeeded them and who would have laid such a path had been present for only the last few centuries.

My impression of the pathway's age, however, was buttressed by the pedestal situated on the other side of the road about twenty yards to the left. A simple column, four feet high or thereabouts, supported a statue carved in that idealized way that reminds you of classical Greece or Rome. More or less life-sized, the sculpture was of a woman wearing a plain, sleeveless dress that reached to her feet. The woman was pregnant, enormously so, on-the-verge-of-delivering-her-baby big. She cradled her belly in her hands, the way that expectant mothers sometimes do. She was also headless, her neck a smooth stump. From where I was standing, I couldn't tell if the statue's headlessness was intentional, or an act of vandalism. What appeared to be red paint, long faded to brown, had been splashed around the sculpture's neck, but that could as easily have been dirt from beside the road someone had smeared on it.

"The Mother," Marie said.

"What?"

"The statue you're staring at. It's of the Mother."

"Who's that?"

"A very old goddess."

"Oh. What about this?" I pointed my knife at the road.

"That takes you to a city."

"A city?"

"A city by the sea," she said. "I don't think you'd care to visit it."

"By the sea?"

"It's different here."

"What does that mean?"

"You'll see," she said, and crossed the road. I went after her, but I continued to glance at the statue of the deity Marie had named the Mother, until the trees obscured my view of it.

Across the road, the forest floor was less crowded with dead leaves and fallen branches. Around me, the trees, mainly evergreens, seemed ranked in straight lines. I supposed we might be passing through a tree farm of some sort, or could be, it was a patch where the trees happened to grow like this. The rain was no longer falling—hadn't been for some time, now that I thought of it. I wasn't sure exactly how long, but since before we'd arrived at the road, anyway.

One of the trees Marie was walking to the left of caught my eye. It was unlike any of the local trees I'd come to recognize over the course of years spent wandering through them on the way to the day's fishing spot. If anything, it resembled a young child's image of a tree, a straight trunk crowned with a large ball of leaves. But, to carry the comparison a tad further, it was as if the kid who'd committed this tree to paper had used oil paint, while the rest of the kids in the daycare stuck to whatever used crayons they'd been given. The tree was so vivid you might have believed it wasn't an actual, living thing but a sculpture cast in metal and lit from within. Had I not had a view of other, similar trees standing beyond it, I would have been tempted to such a view. The rough bark that wrapped the trunk held what light there was and shone a dull bronze; the leaves clustered above it seemed to pass different shades of green back and forth amongst themselves. As I approached the tree, a citrus smell, like oranges on the turn, saturated the air. The individual leaves were shaped like spearheads, their edges serrated. I held up my hand to touch one of them, and hesitated at the prospect of those jagged edges. When I lowered my arm, Marie, who had stopped a slight distance ahead to watch me, said, "That was the right decision. If you aren't careful, the leaves will slice to the bone."

"Right." The prospect of more of these trees in front of us was not reassuring.

I found, though, that while the Vivid Trees—as I thought of them—gradually supplanted the assortment of evergreens, maples, and birch that had surrounded us on the other side of the strange road, they didn't appear to grow especially close together, allowing us a reasonable amount of room to pass safely among them. Nor did they hinder the progress of the person I saw walking through them in our direction. The moment's hope I had it was Dan, searching for me, died as I saw the man striding towards us wearing a large, baggy coat that hung most of the way down his legs. It was dark, from wear more than its tailor's design. The fellow's chest was crisscrossed by the straps of an assortment of bags and sacks he was carrying, all of which bounced against him with each step. He was wearing a hat that resembled a nightcap someone had forgotten to finish. He was younger than I was, but older than Dan, the stringy beard on his jaw a failed effort he hadn't given up on. His eyes were brown and big, and they grew bigger still at the sight of Marie naked before him. He called out a greeting I couldn't distinguish, raising his right hand in what I took for a friendly wave. I figured him for a fellow-traveler, lost in wherever-the-hell-this-was.

Marie had halted when the man came into view. As he neared, she seemed to go out of focus, the ripple I'd witnessed previously sweeping over her. When the stranger was within ten or fifteen feet of her, the distortion blew away and she was transformed. Taller by a good six inches, her hair darker, curled, her pale form was covered by the most horrendous wounds. Great gashes peeled back the skin and meat of her arms, her ribs, her legs, left flesh hanging in ribbons and flaps. Deeper punctures opened her back. A ragged gash ran most of the way round her neck. Those places her skin had remained uncut, it was heavily bruised. A sound swelled from her torn throat, a scream that was as much fury as agony. My knees shook with it—with all of it.

His expression slackened by astonishment, the traveler stuttered a brace of words I couldn't hear for the screaming. In answer, Marie shrieked at him in a language I didn't recognize; though I didn't have to understand it to feel the venom coursing through it. Whatever she said, the fellow flinched as if she'd slapped him full across the face. Her outburst continued, and as it did, she appeared to gain in height, her hair to rise off her shoulders, her feet to lift from the ground. The man had removed his cap and was twisting it in his hands, tears streaking his face, attempting a reply, but Marie would have none of it. She spat a series of phrases at him, the exclamation points at the end of each practically visible. At last, the fellow could take it no more, and fled from her, sprinting to his right, packs flapping, in the direction Marie had said the city by the sea lay. She flung a scattering of invectives after him.

The furious ruin she'd become turned in my direction. I was standing with my knife held out in front of me like an undersized sword, a look of stunned horror weighting my face. Marie's features were charged with a violence that, for a moment, I feared she would direct at me. Then she shimmered, settling to the ground, and resolved into herself, again.

"Marie?" I said.

"Yes," she said, considering my knife as if noticing it for the first time.

"What—what was all that?"

"An image."

"Of what?"

"Something that happened a long time ago."

"Do you know who that man was?"

"Yes," she said, "I will."

"I don't know what you mean."

"It isn't important. He needed to go someplace. I helped him." Apparently satisfied with her answer, she resumed her course. I was quaking-in-my-boots-afraid to keep after her, but I was absolutely terrified to walk away from her. Allowing an extra ten feet between us—which I guessed wouldn't be much help if she resumed this aspect—I pursued her.

My mind wasn't processing the events of the last couple of hours in any appreciable way. It was more taking each of them in and storing it for further review. I suppose this was because the morning had already been so fluid, one outrageous occurrence yielding to the next, even more outrageous one. Some underlying awareness of that quality allowed me not to surrender entirely to the extremes of emotion that buffeted me. I'd be lying, though, committing a sin of omission, if I didn't admit the role that watching Marie's calves move played in my decision to keep walking through the citrus-scented woods.

The trees had started to draw in closer together, not enough to hinder our passage, but sufficient for me to pay them extra attention. In front of us and to the left, they gathered in a small grove. Through the gaps among their trunks, I glimpsed what I took for other trees, their trunks white and smooth. As we approached the grove, I heard the wind picking up and falling off again; though the leaves on the trees beside us were undisturbed. Now I saw that the white trees were in fact stone columns, arranged in a circle, joined at the tops by their support of a domed roof, one part of which had fallen in. Temple or monument, the structure gave the same impression of incredible age as the road we'd crossed. I was tempted to detour to it, but decided it would be better to locate Dan first.

Beyond the temple and its grove, the smell of citrus was interrupted by another, the stench of meat a day into spoiling, accented by the copper reek of blood. The sound of the wind gusting was drowned out by the heavy buzz of flies. In a small clearing, we found the source of smell and sound: the carcass of a huge animal, its legs splayed out to either side of it, its head gone, cut from the thick neck that had spilled a lake of blood onto the forest floor. Fat, black and green flies half the length of my thumb roamed the beast's back, its flanks, sat at the shore of blood and sipped from it. From the sheer size of its remains, I assumed the animal must be an elephant, albeit one whose coat was a rich, red-gold. Its legs, however, ended in hooves, each one large as a man's chest. I had paused to survey the remains; Marie had stopped and was waiting for me. I said, "What is this?"

"One of the Oxen of the Sun," she said.

"I never knew cattle could grow so big."

"These are special—sacred, you could say."

"Not too sacred, if someone did this to it. Do you have any idea what happened?"

"It was taken," she said, "for bait."

"Bait? For what?"

She uttered a word I didn't recognize; it sounded like "Apep." I said, "I don't know what that is."

"Not what—who."

"Okay. I don't know who that is."

"Come this way," Marie said. "We're almost there."

Away from the carcass of the great cattle, the odor of decay receded, the ebb and flow of the wind returned. Except, I understood that I hadn't been listening to air, I'd been hearing water, the rush of the surf rolling itself up a beach. Marie and I had arrived at the edge of the woods we'd been crossing. The Vivid Trees ended in a line so straight it might have been planted there. Beyond them, an expanse of reddish ground rose into a low hill that Marie was already climbing. She continued over the top, and down the far slope. I stopped at the crest.

An ocean sprawled before me, its corrugated surface black as ink. Long, foaming waves tumbled and splashed onto a rocky beach. Distances are tricky to estimate over water, but at least two hundred yards offshore, a spur of gray rock slanted up from the water and ran parallel to the beach on my right, forming a kind of bay. Marie headed in this direction, picking her way across the stones that cluttered the beach. Larger waves burst against the stone wall, tossing spray high into a sky that was empty of the gulls you would have expected to see hanging in it, crying to one another. Nor did there appear to be any of the detritus you usually encounter on a beach, no clumps of dried seaweed hopping with sandfleas, no driftwood scrubbed and bleached into abstract sculpture, no fragments of crab left by sloppy gulls. Although the waves continued to collapse onto the shore, there were none of the tidal pools higher up that might have indicated the water had been any closer. There wasn't much of a sea smell, the briny stink of the ocean and its contents. A fine mist shone on the rocks closer to the water; otherwise, the scene was curiously static, as if I was surveying a vista that had not changed in millennia.

Already, Marie had moved uncomfortably far down the beach. I descended the hill. Stones clattered under my boots. To my left, the surf curled onto the beach with a hissing rumble, while further away, the ocean struck the rock wall with irregular booms. To my right, up the rise, the Vivid Trees maintained formation. A mile or so along the shore, the rock barrier swept in towards the shore, lifting into a cluster of large, jagged rocks. There was activity down there, a lot of it. Figures moved to and fro on the beach and, it appeared, in and out of the ocean—but I was too far removed to distinguish their actions.

I assumed Dan would be waiting for me, ahead. How he had found his way here, I couldn't guess; though after what had befallen me, I supposed I shouldn't have been too surprised at it. It seemed reasonable to imagine he'd encountered Sophie and his children, just as I'd met Marie. What it all meant was beyond me, which I knew was not a good thing, but which I hoped to delay reckoning with for as long as possible.

When we were still halfway there, I saw that the multitude of forms on the beach were the same fish-belly pale as Marie. I had no doubt the eyes of every last one of them would be gold. I was less certain of their features, and of what my reaction would be to a school of the creatures I'd glimpsed in Marie's place. Their activity was focused on the heap of sharp stones that marked this end of the rock wall; as we closed to a quarter mile, I made out long ropes spanning the distance from stones to beach. There were dozens of thick ropes, each one attached to a different spot on what I saw was a much more substantial formation than I had appreciated, each one gripped by anywhere from five to ten of the white figures, at points ranging from far up the beach's slope to well into the water. The ropes creaked with a sound like a big house in a bad storm. The forms holding them grunted and gasped with their effort.

That I could see, only one of the ropes was not held by ten or twenty hands. This rope ran from a horizontal crack in the formation near the water's edge to a sizable boulder on shore, which the rope wrapped around three or four times. It was to this spot that Marie headed. Doing my best not to look directly at any of the pale shapes amongst whom I now was passing, I followed. Although having the knife in my hand lent me the illusion of security, I wasn't sure if the things would take it as a provocation, so I slid my hand into the pocket of my raincoat and kept it there.

The boulder that was our destination was as large as a small house, a stone cube whose edges had been rounded by wind and time. We angled towards the water to reach the side of the rock that faced the ocean. In between watching my steps, I studied the pile of stone to which our goal was tethered. Separated from the beach by a narrow, churning strip of water, the formation was several hundred yards long, its steep sides half that in height. Its top was capped by huge splinters and shards of rock, the apparent remains of even larger stones that had been snapped by some vast cataclysm. The entire surface of the structure was covered in fissures and cracks. Some of the ropes the white creatures held were anchored in these gaps with what looked to be oversized hooks dug into the openings; while other ropes lassoed the ragged rocks on the formation's crest. I could not guess what enterprise the multitude of ropes was being employed toward; their arrangement was too haphazard for any kind of construction I could envision. I almost would have believed the mass of pale figures was engaged in tearing down the splintered endpoint, but their method of doing so was, to put it mildly, impractical.

For some time, in the midst of the other sounds of sea and strain surrounding me, I'd been conscious of another noise, a metallic jingle that seemed to come from all over the place. Only when we were at the large boulder did I understand what I was hearing: the sound of the hundreds, of the thousands, of fishhooks woven into and dangling from the rope that encircled the stone, swinging into one another as the rope shifted. There were hooks, I saw, strung along all the ropes.

You can be sure, throughout the journey Marie had taken me on, Howard's story had not been far from my thoughts. How could it have been anywhere else, right? But the sight of all those curved bits of metal, some wound tightly into the rope's fibers, others tied to those fibers by their eyes, a few of sufficient size to be hung on the rope properly—more than the Vivid Trees, or the black ocean, more than Marie, even, this was the detail that made me think, *Oh my God. I believe old Howard was telling the truth. Or close enough.* As Marie led me around to what I thought of as the front of the boulder, the man who was bound to it came into view, and any doubts that might have remained were swept away by the sight of the rope that crossed him from right hip to left shoulder, secured to him by the fishhooks that dug through the leather apron and worn robes to his flesh. The rope circled the stone behind him a few times, then ran out across the black waves to the end of the barrier.

The strangest thing was, I recognized this man. I'd met him in the woods on the way here, speaking a language I didn't understand, until Marie chased him off. What had been a matter of an hour, less, for me, had been much, much longer for him. At a glance, you might have mistaken him for my age, a tad older, but subject him to closer inspection, and the number of years piled on him was apparent. This fellow had seen enough time pass that he should have crumbled to dust several times over. His skin was more like parchment paper, and his face was speckled with some kind of barnacle. All the color had been washed from his eyes. They flicked toward me, and a spark of recognition flared in them. He didn't speak, though; he left that to Dan.

Dan was sitting cross-legged at the man's feet, his back to him and me. To his right, a slender naked woman, her skin pale as pearl, sat leaning against him. To his left, a pair of toddler boys, their bare bodies equally white, crawled in and out of his lap. His hat and raincoat were gone, his hair tousled, his clothes rumpled, as if he'd slept in them. When he turned to me, the stubble shadowing his face, way later than five o'clock, reinforced my impression that he'd already spent some time in this place. "Abe," he said. "I was wondering if you'd make it."

"Here I am."

231

Marie lowered herself to the ground next to the woman beside Dan—to Sophie. Dan eased himself from under Sophie, helped the boy who was crawling off him the rest of the way down, and stood, the wince as he did testament to how long he must have been holding that position. He smiled at Sophie. "This is my wife, Sophie." His hand swept over the boys. "And these young men are Jason and Jonas." The three of them swiveled their heads to regard me with flat, gold eyes.

"Dan," I said, "what is all this?"

"Isn't it obvious? It's what your friend was telling us about, at the diner. He got some of the details wrong, but as far as the big picture goes, he was pretty much on target."

"Big—I don't know what that means." I inclined my head to the man bound to the rock. "Is this the Fisherman?"

Dan nodded. "He doesn't say much. All of his energy is focused on…" He pointed to the end of the barrier and its web of ropes.

"Which is what, exactly?"

"I guess you could call it the great-grandfather of all fishing stories."

"The…" My voice died in my mouth. I must have noticed it during the walk to this spot, observed the odd striations in the stone of which the barrier was composed, even made the comparison to the scales of a titanic reptile. I must have seen the way the end of the barrier curved out and around from the main body the way the head of a snake flares from its neck. Maybe I'd likened the broken rocks ornamenting its crest to the ridges and horns that decorate the skulls of some serpents; maybe I'd judged the crack in which the Fisherman's rope was lodged to be in the approximate location of an eye, were this headland an actual head. Whatever I'd imagined, I'd done so because this was what you did when you saw something new, especially something large: you found the patterns in it, saw the profiles of giants in the outlines of mountains, found dragons rearing in the clouds overhead. It was a game your mind played with unfamiliar terrain, not an act of recognition, for God's sake. Of course it explained what all the ropes were for, identified the task towards which all the pale things were bent, but it was ridiculous, it was impossible, you could not have a creature that size, it violated I didn't know how many laws of nature.

The beach, Dan, the thing in the water, lost focus, receded from me. I felt Dan's hand on my arm, heard him saying, "Abe? Are you okay? Abe?"

I stepped away from him. "Fine," I said thickly. "I'm fine."

"It's a lot to take in," he said.

"Dan," I said. "Where do I—"

"Don't worry about it," Dan said. "It's fine. Everything is fine. I was right."

"Right?"

"Look at them," Dan said, gesturing at Sophie and the twins. "I was right. I was more than right—I was—look at them, Abe. There they are."

"Dan—"

"That's Marie beside them, isn't it?"

"That's—"

"You see: I was right."

I stared at my feet, forcing myself to breathe deeply. "Just tell me what happened to you."

"There isn't much to tell. I followed the creek upstream. Not that far— maybe a quarter-mile along—it swings to the right. Sophie was waiting for me there. I couldn't believe it. I mean, it was what I'd wanted, but I was sure I was hallucinating. You must have had the same reaction to meeting Marie."

"Close enough."

"Once I realized it was Sophie…" Dan blushed. "I—I let her know how happy I was to see her. Afterwards, she led me into the woods. I think I saw the tree Howard mentioned in his story, the one the guy marked. There's a crack running through the middle of it, looks as if lightning struck it. Sophie brought me here, where I met Jonas and Jason, met my boys."

"Did you cross the road?" I said. "What about the temple?"

Dan shook his head. "One minute, we were surrounded by trees, the next, we were at the beach."

"With the Fisherman."

"He lost his wife, too—his family," Dan said. "In front of him—in his house—he watched Hungarian soldiers butcher his wife and children, beat and hack them to death with clubs and swords, axes. The soldiers stabbed him first, when they broke down the door, so there was nothing he could do to stop them. He listened to his wife begging for their children's lives; he heard his children screaming as they were murdered. He saw their bodies split open, their blood, their…insides, their organs spilled on the floor. Everything that was good in his life was ripped from him. If he could have, he would have died there, with them, in the house whose walls had been painted with their blood. But he survived, and afterwards, once he had finished burying his family, he set off to find the means to get them back, to reclaim them from the axes and swords that had cut them from him.

"And the thing is, Abe, he did it. He learned how to retrieve them."

"I take it that has something to do with what he's got on the hook—hooks, I guess."

"He broke through the mask," Dan said. "It's like, what surrounds you is only a cover for what really is. This guy went through the cover—he punched a hole in the mask and came out here."

"It's not what I would have expected," I said.

"This place—you have to understand, it's like a metaphor that's real, a myth that's true."

"That sounds a little over my head."

"It doesn't matter. The point is, here, conditions are more…flexible than they are where we live. If you can master certain forces, you can accomplish," Dan waved his hands, "anything."

"That's a lot of information for an hour or two," I said.

"An hour?" Dan's eyes narrowed. "Abe, I've been here for days."

"Days?"

"It's kind of hard to be sure with the way the light is in this place, but I must've been here for three days, minimum."

"Three…" After everything I'd been part of, already, there was no sense in protesting. "Are you planning on returning to—"

"To what? The place where everything is a reminder of what I've lost?"

"Your home," I said.

"How is that my home?" Dan said. He strode to Sophie and his boys, who stood and gathered about him. "Where my family is—that's where my home is." He uttered the words with such conviction, I could almost take the sight of this tall man with his wild red hair and his wrinkled clothing, embraced by a wife and sons whose eyes shone gold and whose white skin appeared damp, as the portrait of happy family.

"And the Fisherman, there, is okay with you staying?"

"He's in rough shape," Dan said. He nodded at the man. "He exhausted himself regaining control of Apophis. It's pretty amazing, when you think of it. He caught *that*." He pointed towards what I still didn't want to think of as a vast head. "He had it pretty much secured when the guys from the camp showed up and started cutting lines. It's taken him decades to repair the damage they did. He isn't done, yet. I can help him."

"No offense," I said, "but I don't see how. You aren't talking about bringing in anything we've ever fished for. Hell, I don't know if you can call this fishing; I don't know what the name for it is."

"He needs strength," Dan said. "I can give that to him."

"How?"

Dan's eyes flicked away from me. "There are ways."

I thought about the grieving husband in Howard's tale, vomiting black water full of wriggling things like eyeballs with tails. I said, "He gets your strength. You get—"

"My family."

It felt odd, almost rude, to do so with the three of them hanging onto him, but I said, "Are you sure this is your family?"

"What do you mean?" Dan said, the tone of his voice one of indignation, but the expression that flitted across his face one of surprise, as if I'd given voice to a doubt he'd harbored in secret. "Are you saying they look different—changed?" he went on. "Isn't that what we've always been told happens to you after you die? You gain a new form?"

"I'm not sure this is what the religious folks had in mind."

"They didn't predict any of this, did they?"

He had a point there; though I had the suspicion I was listening to the arguments Dan had used to convince himself that what he'd found was what he'd been searching for, all along. "I don't suppose they did," I said.

"Has Marie acted the way you remember her acting?"

"She has."

"Then what more do you need?"

The more I needed was not to have seen that other, inhuman face staring back at me when I turned toward her; it was not having witnessed Marie's transfiguration into the savaged figure who had screamed at the younger version of the man bound to the boulder. I was on the verge of saying so, but something in the expressions of Sophie and the boys, a kind of attentiveness, chased the nerve from me. I settled for, "I don't know."

"It's hard," Dan said, "I understand. But you know, you could help."

"Oh?"

Dan disengaged himself from his family and approached me. "You could have Marie back, all the time. You could make up for those lost years."

"I could." I considered her, still sitting with her back to me, facing the black ocean and its monstrous resident. "How, exactly, could I do that?"

"Like I said, the Fisherman is weak."

"And he could use my strength."

"Yes."

I thought about it; I'd be lying if I said I didn't. Whatever this Marie was, she wasn't my Marie, just as I was certain this Sophie and twins weren't Dan's Sophie and twins. Maybe that didn't matter; maybe it would be enough to stay with this echo of my dead wife as the Fisherman siphoned the vitality from me. Might be, I wouldn't notice myself any weaker, too caught up in the illusion I'd surrendered to. At another moment in my life, when my grief was as proximate as Dan's, I wouldn't have debated the offer at all.

Now, though, I shook my head and said, "No, Dan, I'm afraid not."

"What?" Dan said. "Why not?"

"I have…appreciated my visit with Marie. But it's time for it to be done."

"You can't be serious. It's your wife: she can be yours, again."

"I understand what's on offer."

"Then how can you turn it down?"

"It's—I think I prefer to meet up with her in my own time."

"But—"

"You want to stay here. I get it."

"You could help him," Dan said.

"He'll have to make do without me."

"You would be helping me."

"I thought you already had everything you wanted."

"It's the Fisherman," Dan said. "What I'm giving him may not be enough. He might have to conserve his energy. If he does, I could lose Sophie and the boys. I can't do that, Abe, not again. The first time almost killed me. A second would be too much. If you joined with us—"

I glanced at the Fisherman, held fast beside us. With his skin bleached and worn by brine, his scraggle of a beard a-crawl with something like sand lice, his robes grown part of his body through the hooks that had driven them into him, he looked almost a natural formation, himself. His white eyes stared at the colossal form to which he was connected with such intensity, it was no trouble believing that all his being was bent to his struggle with it. It was hard to credit him having spoken to Dan, at all, even drops of information dripped out over a course of days. Easier to imagine him absorbed by the black water smashing against the flanks of the beast he'd snared.

Those pale eyes swung a second, longer glance in my direction, bringing with them the weight of the Fisherman's full attention. Most everyone, I suppose, has felt the gaze of someone whose burden of experience renders their regard a tangible thing. What poured from the Fisherman's eyes drove me back a step, would have forced me to my knees had he not returned it to the scene before him. It was threaded with currents of emotion so powerful they were visible. There was rage, a short man in a dirty tunic and pants gripping his sword two-handed and swinging it down onto the back of a tall woman with long brown hair as she bent over the bodies of her children. There was pain, that same woman and children lying mutilated in wide pools of blood. There was hope, a suggestive passage in what might have been Greek, beneath a woodcut of a fanciful sea-serpent, sporting amidst stylized waves. There was determination, a knock on yet another door to ask yet another old man or woman if they were in possession of certain books. The emotions flowed into a current whose name I couldn't give; if pressed, I would have said something like want, a gap or crack through the very core of the man. It was what had sustained this man when he had been dragged into the black ocean by one of the ropes he had employed in catching what he'd once glimpsed in a book. It had allowed him to struggle against the great beast, to reach through this underplace to a place that lay deeper still, and to draw on what he found there until he could begin to bring the monster that had broken free of his control once more under his sway. It had permitted him to rope himself to this rock as ballast to hold the beast. Sudden and overwhelming, the impression swept over me that the figure I was seeing was only part of the Fisherman, and a fairly small one, at that. The greater portion of him, I understood, was out of view, a giant with the marble skin and blank eyes of a classical sculpture. The apprehension was terrifying, made more so by the other emotions that impressed themselves on me: an amusement bitter as lemon, and a malice keen as the edge of a razor.

Someone was talking—Dan, continuing to plead his case. Without another word to him, I turned and started back the way that had brought me here. I managed half a dozen steps before Dan caught my shoulder and spun me around. His face was scarlet, the scar descending its right side bone white. He was shouting, spittle flying from his lips. "What the fuck, Abe? What the fuck? You're going to leave? You're going to abandon me? What about Sophie? What about Jonas and Jason? Are you thinking of us? Are you thinking of Marie? What about Marie, Abe? What about her?" Behind him, Marie maintained her vigil of the beast.

"Dan," I said. "Stop. It's too much. He's—"

"He's what?" Dan punctuated his question with a shove from his big hands that had the force of his long legs behind it. It sent me stumbling over the smooth, rounded stones. My foot slipped, and my balance went. I twisted as I fell, trying to catch myself, but all that accomplished was to bring me down on my right side. My arm, my ribs, my hip smashed into the waiting rocks; the pain forced the air from my lungs. Through some miracle, my head escaped colliding with a stone, and when I saw Dan bending towards me, my first thought was, *He's helping me*. But he wasn't close enough to offer me a hand, and he straightened almost immediately. Not until I saw the large, bluish rock his fingers stretched around did I understand what he was doing. "I don't want to do this," he said, "I really don't. It's—if he has your strength, then he won't have to take them away from me. I—if there were any other way, Abe. Honestly. I don't want to do this."

"Then don't," I managed, already aware that my words hadn't registered, because Dan was raising the stone, his body tensing as he made ready to lunge into a blow. That the man I counted my closest friend was about to inflict grievous harm on me, if not kill me outright, was the most monstrous thing I had encountered yet this strange, awful day. A wave of nausea rolled over me. Even as I watched him shift his grip, moving his fingers to one end of his improvised weapon in order to better control it, I half-expected him to pause, lower and allow the rock to fall from his hand, and shake the sense back into his head. Only when Dan was moving forward, swinging the stone towards me, his eyes wide, his lips pressed tightly together, did a surge of adrenaline send me rolling out of his way. His attack missed, the rock cracking on the one that had been under my head and flying from his grasp. My feet tangled with his, sweeping him to the ground but preventing me from rising. Instead, I kicked furiously, pushing away from where he lay stunned. This entire time, I had not forgotten the knife in my pocket, and as I struggled to my feet, I had it out and in hand.

"A knife?" From the tone of Dan's voice, you would have thought I was the one threatening him. He tried to raise himself on his arms, but he must have injured the left one. It gave out on him, and he barely saved himself from falling on his face. He looked up at me. "It doesn't matter."

I wasn't sure what he meant. My heart was pounding, hammering against my chest as if I'd finished a short, fast race. To my left, a stone shifted. A glance in that direction showed one of the boys—I couldn't tell them apart—toddling towards me. His brother was clambering in my direction from the right; Sophie was waiting a dozen feet behind me. I was about to call out to Dan, mock him for dragging his wife and babies into the dirty deed he was attempting, but something about whichever twin was on my left stilled my tongue. His chubby face, more baby than little boy, was wavering, the mouth stretching wider, splitting his cheeks most of the way to his ears, the blanched gums sprouting rows of serrated fangs that would not have been out of place in the mouth of a shark. His brother's face had undergone a similar transformation, as had Sophie's.

Dan had found his way to his feet, though he was rubbing that left arm. He had to have seen the change in Sophie and the boys, but nothing about him acknowledged it. Wincing, he stooped and scooped up a new, reddish rock with his right hand. Rising, he said, "It's a shame, Abe. I always thought Sophie and you would have gotten along with one another, appreciated each other's company."

I licked my lips, which had gone dry. Attempting to keep my eyes on all four figures surrounding me, I said, "This isn't your wife, Dan. You have to know that."

"Shut up," Dan said and, before I could offer a rejoinder, charged.

The last fight worth the name I had been in had occurred the better part of three decades ago. Dan was younger, at a guess stronger, and he was fighting for what he'd convinced himself was his family. He'd learned a little from his first pass at me: he faked a swing at my head with the stone, then whipped his left hand at me in a roundhouse that might have been smoother if he hadn't injured that arm. It clouted my ear with less force than he intended, leaving me able to jerk my head out of the path of his rock. I slashed the knife right to left across him, felt it drag on his shirt. He hissed, and swept the stone at me in an uppercut that hit me high in the chest. I grunted, and slashed left to right, feeling the knife catch on his skin.

Hugging his left arm to the vents I'd cut in his shirt, Dan stumbled back.

My chest was heaving, my temples pounding. "Dan," I said, "please." The tip of my knife wavered in front of me, Dan's blood scarlet on more of the blade than I'd anticipated.

Crouched forward, his own breath coming in pants, Dan said, "You cut me. You son of a bitch."

This did not seem the appropriate moment to point out that I had done so in response to his effort to crush my skull with the rock he continued to hold. To either side of me, the twins had drawn closer, their pudgy fingers ending in hooked claws. At my back, Sophie was also nearer, similarly changed. I'd cut Dan deeper than I'd intended. Where it pressed against him, his shirt sleeve was wet with blood. Without releasing his grip on the stone, he lowered himself to sitting. "Ow," he said. "You son of a bitch. You cut me."

"Sorry," I said; although I wasn't, not exactly. A mix of joy and revulsion swirled in my gut: joy that I'd survived Dan's assault; revulsion at the blood soaking his sleeve. Was there any way to find him some kind of medical care in this place?

Dan didn't answer me. Blood was dripping from his shirt cuff onto the rocks underneath him. The twins, their toes webbed and clawed, were less than a yard from me. I wasn't as concerned with turning the knife on them or Sophie, not with their appearances so changed, but I wasn't sure it would do me any good. Yes, they seemed solid, as much as Marie had earlier, in the forest, but the ease with which their forms shifted made me doubt the efficacy of any weapon I could muster against them. When the boys paused their flanking maneuver, I assumed it was to judge the best moment to strike. I didn't think I could evade the two of them. I was hoping to hop out of the range of one and deal with his brother; though their wide mouths, crammed with fangs, troubled me far more than had Dan's stones. Not to mention, as long as I was occupied with one of them, their mother would have the opportunity to move on me from behind.

It was the twin to my right who started towards Dan first. His brother looked at me quizzically, and turned after him. Dan raised his head to them. His skin was white, his eyes glazed—shock I guessed, at the wound I'd dealt him. He grinned sickly at the monsters working their way in his direction. "My boys," he said. "Come to your papa." The closer the things drew to him, the more their pale forms shimmered, until by the time they were standing beside Dan, they had resumed the appearance of toddlers, with the exception of their mouths, which retained their shark grins. Beneath Dan, the rocks were slick and red. With a broad tongue the color of liver, the boy on Dan's right licked his lips. His mouth opened, as if in a yawn, and kept opening, wider and wider, his notched teeth ringing a gullet studded with clusters of additional fangs. His attention returned to the blood trickling from him, Dan didn't notice the boy's head pivoting in his direction, the better to deliver a massive bite to his shoulder. To his left, the other twin was spreading his jaws, readying his strike. I went to speak, to call out a warning to him, but Sophie shoved me aside and strode past me. Her mouth was likewise open, the full set of her teeth on display.

What must Dan have thought, watching the creature he had called his late wife's name advance towards him, the lower portion of her face a stark refutation of the identity he'd tried to confer on her? Something was happening to Sophie, to the boys, another change rippling over them. Their flesh blackened as if burned, cracking and crumbling, showing charred muscle in some places, burnt bone in others. The odor of charcoaled meat filled the air. An expression of unutterable sadness dragged Dan's features down. As if to ward off what Sophie had become, he held up his right hand, and the boy to his right snapped his jaws shut on Dan's shoulder. At almost the same moment, the boy on Dan's left clamped onto his chest. Dan's head jerked up, his eyes starting, his arms flying out to either side of him, his back rigid, as if he'd been struck by lightning. His mouth worked to release some sound, a scream or a curse, but Sophie swallowed it in the terrible kiss she lowered on him. As her jaws closed around his face, what sounded like a frantic humming rose from deep in his chest; while his legs spasmed underneath him, as if he were trying to stand. The trio that had him in their teeth kept him in place. Without surrendering her hold on him, Sophie pressed Dan's arms down.

His family's attack on him could not have lasted more than a couple of seconds, yet it seemed as if I had been standing watching the three of them savage Dan for hours. So much useless, bloody metal, the knife hung in my hand. Somewhere in the recesses of my brain, a voice was shouting at me to do something; it hadn't been that long; though hurt, Dan might be savable; even if he weren't, no one deserved to die like this, devoured alive. My eyes focused on the knife and shifted to Sophie. Her spine was visible at a couple of points through her burned flesh. If I stabbed the knife icepick-fashion on the back of her neck, that might be sufficient to cause her to release Dan. I switched my grip on the handle.

Whichever boy had bitten into Dan's shoulder pulled his mouth from it and leveled his metallic gaze at me. His face was a patchwork of cinder and ash, his lips and chin splashed scarlet, his teeth hung with shreds of meat. Dan shuddered; his right arm lifted, the hand cupped, and swept in to his chest, as if beckoning me to approach. The boy stared at me with eyes in whose depthless shine I saw all the intelligence of a trout, or pike.

Before I fully understood what I was doing, I bolted. As fast as my feet could pick a path across the stones, I fled that place, ran from Dan and the family he had literally imagined for himself, from Marie looking out across the waves, from the Fisherman engaged in his titanic contest, from the unimaginable creature with which he contested, from the black ocean roaring to the horizon. I made no attempt to retrace the route that had brought me here; instead, I headed straight for the Vivid Trees lining the top of the beach. Loose rocks rattled and snapped as my boots landed on them. I slipped and slid from side to side like someone trying ice skates for the first time. Point down, the knife was in my hand. Stones skipped and rolled away, kicked free by my boots. Beyond the clatter of my passage, I could hear nothing except the breath rushing in and out of my mouth and the waves foaming on the shore. Sophie and the twins—Marie, her bloodlust aroused—any of the pale creatures stationing the beach could be pacing me, waiting for the misstep that would allow them to share Dan's fate with me.

At the head of the beach, calves and thighs burning from my sprint up the sandy margin, I stopped, bent over, chest heaving. A survey of the path I'd run showed no one following me, no one close, at all. Where Dan had been were several smaller shapes, islands in the crimson pool surrounding them. I could distinguish the forms of Sophie and the twins next to the carnage; although their features were difficult to pick out in any detail. Only their eyes were clearly visible, flashing across the distance, and that because they were watching me. All of the white things were. To a one, they had turned in my direction. Dozens, scores of gold eyes regarded me. In the midst of the heaving ocean beyond them, a tremor passed along the great beast held there. The earth rumbled under my feet. The tremor concentrated at the fissure above the waves in which the end of the Fisherman's line was embedded. The split trembled, and widened, top and bottom retracting to reveal a gold expanse whose center was bisected by a black ellipse. An eye the size of a stadium cast its gaze out over the scene in front of it.

If the Fisherman's regard had buffeted me like a strong wind, this creature's attention howled over me with hurricane force. There was no emotion in it. What streamed from the enormous eye was either so deep below or so high above any discrete sentiment as to be unrecognizable as such. There was only absence, a void as big and grand as everything. It wasn't white, or black; it wasn't anything. Perfect in its nothingness, its nullity, it had been contravened, somehow, sundered, confined to the form before me. Imprisoned, but not separated, it was the black ocean, and the pale creatures grasping the lines that held it, and the Fisherman tied to his rock, and me. To understand this, to appreciate it, might be the beginning of a kind of wisdom.

It was not a wisdom I had any desire for. The great beast's awareness saturating the very air, I ran into the woods. The trees grew more closely together, here, their leaf-crowns closer to the ground, the outermost branches weaving around one another. My arms brushed an especially low-hanging limb, and what felt like a dozen razor blades parted the sleeves of my raincoat and shirt, and the skin they covered, in as many places. I sucked in my breath, stumbling as the pain flared up my arm, but although the fingers of my other hand came away bloody from their exploration of my injuries, I did not slow my flight. Tiny white cracks had begun to open in my surroundings, the trees, the leaves, the ground, all of it, as if I were running through a very old painting whose surface had dried out. I struggled not to glance down, afraid I would see myself fracturing, too.

Horror so pure it arrested any thought more elaborate than *Run*, filled me. For that reason, though I saw the ground ahead fall away, heard the sound of moving water, I continued forward without pause, until I had raced the top of the bank and was half-sliding, half-falling down it into the galloping stream below.

Warm water embraced me, tumbling me end over end. I seemed to pass a long time submerged in depths shot through with black currents. Dark shapes darted around me. I kicked my legs, pulled my arms, attempting to right myself. White cracks split the water. I pulled my arms and kicked my legs. All at once, the stream caught hold of me and whisked me forward. Lungs at the point of bursting, I pushed for the surface and broke through. Spitting out brackish water, I inhaled lungfuls of air. Already, my boots had filled with water and were dragging me back under. I slid my legs against one another and forced the right boot off. The other held tight, until I ducked my head beneath the waves so I could grab the boot and twist it off.

Feet unencumbered, it was easier for me to keep my head above water, which was good, because the stream slid into heavy rapids. Gray boulders rose amidst the churning foam, signposting the underwater labyrinth through which the stream was racing. A low slab of stone loomed in my path; I breast-stroked around it, skimming the tops of a cluster of rocks that smacked my knees and shins. The current took me between the halves of a massive, split boulder, and dumped me over a short waterfall onto a pile of stones close enough to the water's surface for it to offer no cushion. Something cracked in my chest. I grasped at the stones below me, but they were too slippery, the current too strong. A rock like the finger of a giant thrust out of the water ahead of me. I threw my arm over my head. The impact shocked through me. The stream rolled me off the stone and spun me into a wide pool. Below me, clouds of sediment billowed in the water's depths. I was finding it difficult to keep above them: my clothes were waterlogged, and my body seemed to consist of more bruises, breaks, and cuts than it did muscles to propel me to the edge of this quieter patch. To be sure, I was exhausted, but the image of that great eye unlocking, of Dan's fate on the beach, offered sufficient incentive for me to force my limbs into an approximation of the dog-paddle.

I didn't see the figure that swam up out of the murk below, wasn't aware of anything until the hand seized my ankle and yanked me under. In the time it took me to realize what had happened, I was dragged to the edge of the churning sediment. I knew it must be one of the pale creatures, possibly Sophie, finishing what had begun on the beach. My knife was long gone, lost at some point during my flight. I kicked at the thing with my free foot, but even panicked, I had little strength left me. Releasing my leg, the creature caught my belt and hauled me down until we were floating face-to-face.

Her hair fluttering in the current, Marie regarded me with her shining eyes. My surprise was succeeded by resignation. *Of course,* I thought. *Sophie takes care of Dan, and Marie sees to me.* I could almost appreciate the symmetry. I hoped that she would simply keep me here until I had no choice but to inhale the stream; after the initial unpleasantness, I had heard, drowning was supposed to be a peaceful way to die—unlike being torn apart by mouths jammed with fangs. Marie caught my shoulders, and pushed me deeper, down into the sediment cloud.

Immediately, I lost sight of her, of everything but the murk tumbling about me. Bubbles leaked from my lips. Whatever acceptance I'd imagined I'd felt departed, swept aside by a desire to escape that had me twisting in Marie's grasp, striking her arms with my fists. All at once, her hands were gone, and I swam for the surface with my lungs searing, my arms and legs full of lead. I emerged near a shore fronted by trees I recognized, hemlock and birch, maple. Screaming with the effort, I paddled until the water grew shallow. I crawled out of the water onto dry land, where I collapsed, coughing up the water that had found its way into my lungs. Spent, shivering, I surrendered to the blackness that rose around me in a tide.

VI

HUNDRED-YEAR FLOOD

A pair of high school kids, who claimed they were out on a hike, but who I suspect were searching for a secluded spot to experiment with illicit substances of one form or another, found me washed up on the south shore of Dutchman's Creek, almost to the Hudson. My clothes were shredded, my body scraped, battered, and cut, and I was running a fever high enough to induce hallucinations, which was what the doctors, nurses, and police detectives who attended me made of my more fantastical claims. The doctors and nurses were present because I was in Wiltwyck Hospital, being treated for the infection that was causing my temperature to spike and was proving stubbornly resistant to a range of increasingly powerful antibiotics. The detectives drifted in and out of my room because, in my delirium, I ranted about Dan's death. There was little trouble tracing my movements: the cops checked with Howard, who verified that I'd been in for breakfast with another fellow, tall, with red hair and a scar all the way up the right-hand side of his face. The two of us had been bound for Dutchman's Creek, Howard said, though he'd advised against it. (I don't know for sure, but I doubt he shared Lottie Schmidt's long, strange tale with them.) After a brief search, the detectives came across my tacklebox on the stone ledge where I'd caught what Marie had

246

called a nymph; of course, the fish and my rod were nowhere to be found. Downstream a ways, the police located Dan's gear, which apparently had been washed there by the flooded creek. Of Dan himself, there was no trace, and this, together with the wounds on my arm, which seemed to have been inflicted with a knife or similar weapon, raised their suspicions as to what, exactly, had transpired during our fishing trip.

I didn't help matters any by ranting about Dan's attempt to club me with a rock so he could feed my essence to a centuries-old magician, or his death at the teeth of his dead wife and children. It sounded mad, yes, but combined with Dan's apparent disappearance and the cuts on me, the scenario I was narrating seemed as if it might be describing the substance, if not the exact details, of an actual event. I was under suspicion; though what friends and co-workers the detectives interviewed spoke well of me; nor did Dan's friends or family voice any reservations about our fishing trips. Had the remains of Dan's body turned up, I'm not certain what effect they would have had on the cops. I want to say they would have exonerated me beyond a shadow of a doubt, but the same evidence can lead to diametrically opposed conclusions, depending on who's reviewing it. Of Dan, however, there remained no sign, despite a widening of the search area to include the stretch of the Hudson south of where Dutchman's Creek empties into it. In the end, Dan would be declared officially missing, and a few of his cousins from up around Phoenicia would drive down to see to the disposition of his goods, the selling of his and Sophie's house.

The police, though, did not let go of questioning me that easily. I suppose it is fortunate for them that I was stuck in a hospital bed, taking one step forward, two back in my contest with an infection whose diagnosis changed every few days. I could have requested a lawyer, and had I been in more of my right mind at the outset, I might have. By the time this occurred to me, the detectives had pretty much lost interest in me as anything other than the fellow victim of a fishing mishap that had almost certainly claimed my buddy's life. At some point when my sickness was still causing me to see Dan, Sophie, and the twins silhouetted on the curtain that hung around my bed, I realized that neither of the men who continued to ask me what had happened the morning Dan and I went fishing would—or could—believe what I was telling them. In my fever, it was an insight I resisted, but eventually, I began crafting a story that sounded like something they would, and could, accept. I sometimes wondered if they were aware of my ploy, but if so, they let slip no sign of it. Maybe they were grateful for what I was doing, fashioning them a story that would account for most of the details they had to reckon with.

Much of my narrative of that morning, I left unchanged. As my pa used to say, If you have to concoct a lie, be sure to mix in as much of the truth as you can. I told the police about picking up Dan at his place in the pre-dawn hours, about stopping off at Herman's Diner for breakfast, about the story Howard recounted to us after we informed him of our destination. Of course I didn't believe Howard's tale, I said, but it seemed to work to powerful effect on Dan, so that by the time we were at Dutchman's Creek and fishing, he admitted that his reason for selecting this spot was what he took to be a hint from his grandfather's fishing journal that he might meet his dead wife and children here. Didn't I think this was, well, crazy? one of the cops asked. Yes, I said, but we were already at the creek. All I could do was try to reason with Dan, and when that failed and he set off to find his family upstream, follow him. The creek was in flood, the shore slippery; a couple of times, I almost fell in. Dan refused to wait for me. I lost my balance one time too many, and went into the stream. Right away, I struck my head on a rock, and that was about as far as my memories went. Frankly, I was surprised to be among the living. Did I have any guess as to what might've happened to Dan? the detectives asked. I did not. I had fallen into Dutchman's Creek, but I had a few years on Dan. All I could say was, the last I'd seen of him, he was walking upstream.

Useful though it might be, neither detective appeared especially happy with my version of events; whether because they sensed me holding back, or because their occupation had made them suspicious of everyone, I couldn't say. How did I explain the cuts on my arm? they wanted to know. I didn't, I said. I was in the water with all kinds of debris. Who knew what I'd run into? They asked what had happened to my fishing rod. I said I wished I knew. That rod had done well by me; the detectives would not have believed some of the fish I'd hooked on it. I supposed it had been carried away by the creek, or maybe by a fellow fisherman with an eye for value and flexible morals. The two of them did their best to determine how I'd felt about Dan, which was to say, whether I'd had the urge to murder him, but I could answer without any dissembling that Dan had been about the best friend I'd had, and the prospect of not seeing him again filled me with grief.

And for a long time after that, I did mourn Dan. My bruises and cuts healed, the rib I'd cracked knit, and my immune system got the upper hand on the infection long enough for me to be discharged, finally, from the hospital. While I was recuperating at home, my manager stopped over to visit me; though his purpose had more to do with business than solicitude. Technically, I was already supposed to have decided if I wanted to take early retirement and the one-time payout being offered to incentivize it, or if I preferred to stay with the company and risk being laid off. Because of my accident, my boss had convinced his boss and those above him to grant me an extension. He never came out and said so, but there was no doubt in my mind that, were I not to choose to exit my job under my own steam, I would be shoved out the door. It's funny: with all I'd been through, you would expect that this would have appeared, in comparison, of little consequence. Yet I was furious, so much so that I stood from the kitchen table, asked the young fellow to excuse me, and walked out into my front yard.

I'll say this to my manager's credit, he let me go. My head abuzz, I stalked around the bungalow Marie and I had intended for a starter home. I don't suppose my sentiments were any different from those of the thousands of others who'd been in this spot before me. *This isn't right. I've given years— decades—of my life to this business. I've done my part to make if the success it has been for so long. I've been genuinely proud of it, to count myself among its employees. Hell, I wouldn't have met my wife without it. This isn't fair.*

All of which was true, as far as it went, and none of which made the least bit of difference. I flirted with telling my boss I'd take my chances, only I knew there'd be no chance involved. Nor was there any point to remaining outside. Before I could second-guess myself, I returned inside, thanked my manager for his patience, and told him I'd decided to take the buyout. He seemed relieved.

Like that, I was without my job, without my closest friend, and without the activity that had organized the most recent part of my life, and that I had anticipated structuring my retirement around. Gone fishin', right? I tried to return to it, the following year, after a winter spent watching too much TV and eyeing the liquor cabinet. I outfitted myself with good gear, not quite the top of the line, but not too far removed from it. The first day of trout season, I pulled out of my driveway with the moon tucking itself under the horizon, headed for a stream on the other side of Frenchman's Mountain where my luck had held more often than not. I was the first one at what I thought of as my spot; although a group of other, younger guys in a jeep with Pennsylvania plates parked behind me five minutes later. We exchanged nods as they walked past me sitting in the cab, sipping coffee from my travel mug, and we acknowledged one another again in the mid-afternoon, as they made their way back to their vehicle. I was in the driver's seat, still, from which I'd moved only to relieve my bladder. During the sixty seconds I'd spent outside my truck, I had listened to the water splashing on the other side of a line of maples, and had thought that it would be very easy for me to stroll down to it for a look. Then I'd climbed into the cab and locked the door. The light was draining from the sky before I admitted defeat and started the engine.

My next attempts were no more successful. The drive to and from whatever point on the map I'd selected presented no difficulty. To a certain extent, neither did sitting beside whatever stream or river I'd chosen. Any effort I made to approach the water for purposes of fishing sent me straight to the truck, do not pass go, do not collect two hundred dollars. There was no particular emotion associated with it, no upwelling of panic, or terror; my body simply refused to entertain, much less obey, my brain's commands.

The panic and terror were reserved for my dreams, which would replay and remix the images and actions of that Saturday for years to come. My lost fishing rod in my hands, I reeled in the large fish Marie had called a nymph; only, when I hauled it out of the water this time, its front end encased not a skull, but Dan's head, his eyes gone, his mouth open in a bloody scream. A traffic light hanging amidst the trees overhead, Marie's feet rose from the forest floor, her skin peeling off in ribbons and streamers, her hair streaming around her head like water grass. His face rigid with anger, Dan lifted a rock that through some trick of perspective was also the boulder to which the Fisherman was tied and brought it crashing down on my head. The vast eye of the Fisherman's catch opened, and black water spilled from the great crack of its pupil in a flood. If I slept during the day, in the sunlight, I found the dreams weren't quite as bad, so I spent much of each night channel surfing and paging through whatever books I'd checked out of the library, trying to keep myself awake until the eastern sky began to forecast the sun's arrival.

When I wasn't trapped in terrifying dreams of him, I grieved for Dan; though my grief, as you might expect, was a somewhat complicated affair. I fancied I understood the desperation that had led Dan to Dutchman's Creek, and the Fisherman, and whatever the exact deal he'd struck with that being. I knew first-hand the exhilaration of finding your dearly departed—or a nearly perfect approximation—waiting for you, and I could appreciate what a motivation Sophie and the boys must have been for Dan. As bad a state as I'd witnessed him in at work—and as he'd confessed himself to be, circling his maelstrom—he must have felt as if he'd been thrown a life-preserver, pulled back from ruin by the very figures whose deaths had spun him towards it.

The problem was, there must have been a moment when Dan had seen Sophie and the boys for what they were, had glimpsed their true faces, if only for a second. He must have realized that, even if these creatures were what remained of his wife and children, they had been changed, transformed by their passage out of this life into something else, something fundamentally different from him. He must have known that he was buying into a scenario that was, on some level, a lie, and he had been willing to sacrifice the reality of friendship, however mundane, in favor of that lie. I reckon I shouldn't sound as surprised as I'm sure I do; the world's full of folks who've done the same, if not in as dramatic a fashion. It's just, you think all those hours sitting beside one another, watching the water of this stream or that slide by, waiting for a fish to take our bait, making small talk and occasionally bigger talk—you think all of that would count for something, that the fact of it would weigh against the fantasy that tempted him.

But I guess it didn't. Not enough, anyway. I missed Dan's company, and the memory of his end filled me with horror, but no matter how kind or generous my recollections of Dan Drescher were, a certain bitterness flavored them. To be honest, the week Dan's cousins were around to dispose of his house and possessions, I was nervous they might request a visit with me, which I didn't see how I could refuse, but which I couldn't imagine how I could go through with—at least, in a way that didn't leave them confused and angry. Fortunately, the phone never rang.

The years that unwound after this, I spent trying to occupy myself. Earlier in my life, if you'd asked me how I envisioned spending my retirement, my answer would have centered on Marie, the children I projected us having. Maybe we would drop in on them at their colleges, or tour some distant country, like India, or do one of those stereotypically old-people things, like board a cruise to Alaska. Later, after she was gone, I would have pictured post-employment taken up by fishing, with Dan, once he started to accompany me. Absent Marie, Dan, and fishing, I cast about for things to do. I visited family, met former co-workers from IBM out for a beer and a burger. I saw a lot of Frank Block when his wife left him for their dentist, but those meals were more therapy sessions for him than actual conversations, and they tapered off pretty soon after he took up with one of his neighbors. I did what I could to renew my interest in live music, driving into Huguenot or up to Woodstock to listen to whoever was playing the local clubs. Most of what I heard was earnest, if unexciting, but every now and again, a singer would lean into the mic, draw her fingers down the strings of her guitar, open her mouth, and I would lean forward in my chair, attentive. I hadn't anticipated my retirement consisting of this much empty time to fill; though I chalked that up to my having entered it at least a decade ahead of schedule, and in pretty good health, too.

As for everything I'd seen, heard, touched—everything I'd learned, or thought I'd learned—on that last fishing trip: most of the time, I didn't dwell on it. It was there, the great mass of it was always there, wherever I was, whatever I was doing, but short of returning to Dutchman's Creek to see if I could find my way back to the black ocean, there wasn't much for me to do about it. On and off, I did a little bit of digging around, opening the family Bible, rereading portions of *Genesis* and *Job*, checking books on comparative mythology out of the library, but none of it added up to anything resembling sense. When the internet became widely available, I put it to work interpreting my experience, but the only site that looked as if it might be of use crashed each time I consulted it. The problem was, my desire to know did not exceed my desire to allow sleeping dogs to enjoy their dreams. Could be, if there had been any hope of such information serving a practical purpose, such as easing my nightmares, my sentiments might have been different. But it was hard to conceive how the things I'd witnessed could have been salved by anything I might learn about them, so in the end, I let my investigations, such as they were, stop.

Something similar, a kind of parallel process, returned me to fishing. About three years ago, now, a young family moved into the house next to mine. Father, mother, and two girls, one fifteen, the other ten and every bit the outdoorswoman. Within a day or two of their arrival, I saw the younger girl, Sadie, striking out across her backyard, a fishing rod in one hand, a tacklebox in the other. A quarter-mile or so in back of both our properties, there's a small stream that descends from Frenchman's Mountain and winds its way to the Svartkil. I guessed this was Sadie's destination, and while I wasn't sure how wise it was for a child her age to go tramping off into the woods on her won, I was more sure how it would appear were her older male neighbor to run after her. I had a pair of binoculars Marie had used for bird watching in its case in the hall closet; I dug them out and used them to keep a discrete eye on Sadie for the couple of hours she spent at the stream.

Later that night, I made sure to be out wheeling my garbage can to the end of the driveway when Sadie's dad, Oliver, was setting out his trash. I'd already introduced myself to the family, offered what assistance was mine to give should they require it. I called hello to Oliver, asked him how he and his family were settling in. Pretty well, he answered, which gave me the opening I needed to remark that I thought I'd noted one of his daughters with her fishing rod out. He laughed and said I must've seen Sadie, on her way to check the stream behind the house. Oh, I said, did he fish, too? Not as much as he used to, Oliver said, but Sadie more than made up for him. His younger girl was obsessed with fishing. Is that so? I said. I used to do a little fishing, myself, from time to time. If he or his daughter had any questions as to what they might catch where, I'd be happy to share what I knew. Oliver thanked me, but with a reserve that suggested maybe I'd overplayed my hand.

The next day, however, there was a knock on my front door, and when I opened it, I found Sadie and her mom, Rhona, standing there. Rhona was carrying a plate layered with freshly baked chocolate-chip cookies. She was so sorry to bother me, she said, but Sadie's dad had told her I knew about fishing this area, and ever since, his daughter had been insisting she had to come over here and talk to me. Rhona would have called, only their phone hadn't been turned on yet, and anyway, they didn't have my number. She was hoping she could offer me a bribe of cookies to answer a couple of her daughter's questions.

Plus, you want to check out the old man who lives on his own next door, I thought but did not say. I took no umbrage at Rhona's prudence, which struck me as entirely reasonable. Apologizing for the messiness of my house, which wasn't that untidy, I held the door wide and invited them in. Sadie's dad hadn't been kidding about her passion for fishing. For the next hour and change, she alternated detailed questions as to what varieties of fish I'd hooked in the local waters with accounts of her exploits with the rod and reel in their previous home, in Missouri. Rhona let her daughter ramble on until we'd cleared about half the cookies from the plate, when she announced that it was time for her and Sadie to go, they still had a lot of unpacking to do. Sadie protested, but I told her to mind her ma. I wasn't going anywhere; we could talk some more later on, once she and her family were properly settled.

As far as these things go, it was a pleasant visit. I was surprised by how much I enjoyed our conversation. Trading stories with Sadie about what we'd caught, and how, and where, it was as if I'd found my way back to the part of my life that had been closed off since that distant Saturday—to speaking about it, anyway. I don't know if this'll sound odd, but it was almost like what happened to me after Marie died. For the longest time, talking about her—thinking about her—was an exercise in agony, because I couldn't separate my wife from the fact of her death. Then, gradually, that stopped being the case. My memory relaxed its grip on Marie's death; although it felt more as if her dying loosened its hold on me. The myriad of experiences that had composed our time together became available as more than prompts to grief. Her mouth still full of a generous bite of her mother's cookie, Sadie asked me what kind of catfish swam the waters around here. She intended to catch a catfish in every state in the union, if she could, and since she was living in New York, now, she supposed she should start finding out about its catfish population. Well, I said, the trout was my fish, but I'd pulled my fair share of bullhead and even one or two channel cats out of the Rondout and the Svartkil—and that was that; I was off; I had raced across ice I wasn't sure would take my weight and it had held.

If I was caught off guard at how easy it had been for me to return to talking about fishing, I was astonished at how simple it proved for me to take it up, again. I didn't see Sadie or either of her parents the next day, or the one after that, or the one after that, which was Friday. I wasn't expecting to see any of them, not specifically, but I guess I was waiting to find out what result, if any, our visit would have. Having spoken about fishing once, I found I wanted to do so a second time. When the doorbell rang on Saturday morning, I'll confess, my pulse gave a jump at the prospect of another chat with Sadie and Rhona.

Instead, I opened the door to Oliver, dressed in his weekend jeans and sweatshirt. He was sorry to bother me at such an earlier hour, he said, but he had promised Sadie he would take her fishing, this morning, and she had asked if they could extend an invitation for me to join them. He'd already warned her I would probably have plans, so there was no problem about me refusing their last-minute request.

I'm pretty sure he was startled by how quickly I said, "Sure—I'd be happy to come along with you." I know I was, startled but also kind of giddy. The gear I'd bought for my previous try at fishing was in the guest room closet, aside from a little dust as ready to use as it had been seven years earlier. My weekend clothes weren't any different from those I wore during the week, jeans, a flannel shirt, and work boots. All I needed was a hat, to replace the Yankees cap that had been another casualty of my last trip. After I'd retired, Frank Block and a couple of the other fellows I'd worked with had chipped in to buy me a nice cowboy hat, on account, they said, of how much I loved country music. It was a ridiculous thing, white as toothpaste, that might've sat on John Wayne's head in one of his early westerns. There was nothing else to hand, though, so I grabbed it. Oliver did his best not to laugh at the sight of it, but Sadie declared it cool.

That first trip, I suggested we drive over to the same spot on the Svartkil I'd wound up at when I started fishing. My reasons were more practical than sentimental. That stretch of the river is just downstream from Huguenot's waste-treatment plant, which in my experience had drawn the catfish on which Sadie had set her sights. I warned her to watch for the trees whose limbs stretched over the water, but she'd noted them and succeeded in staying mostly clear of them, unlike her father, who sacrificed three hooks and a good length of line to the branches above him. I gave most of my attention to helping him work his line from the trees, and to keeping an eye on Sadie, who, as we were preparing to pack up, caught a decent-sized bullhead that I netted for her, almost sliding into the brown water in my haste. I wasn't overeager to pick up my rod, but there were a couple of times Sadie and Oliver were occupied watching their lines, and I felt conspicuous standing around watching them. While I was aware of the length of years that had passed since I'd last cast a lure, the rod was comfortable in my hand. Before I could overthink it, I snapped my wrist; though I kept my cast short, to where the water wasn't too deep. Nothing so much as looked at my lure, but that was all right.

Like that, I was back fishing. For the next couple of years, whenever Sadie and Oliver went out in search of fish, they took me with them. Mostly, this was on the weekends, for two or three hours at a time, which was never enough for Sadie. I spent as much of these trips chatting with Oliver as I did with my line in. Oddly enough, he was an IBM'er, and we passed a few hours comparing the company as it was with the company as it had become. I did what I could to broaden their musical horizons, playing Hank Sr. and Johnny Cash for them, but their tastes remained sadly limited. After a couple of seconds, Sadie announced that she had no interest in hillbilly music. Oliver said that his dad used to listen to these guys. When I joined him and Sadie fishing, I let my casts fall close to shore. On more than one occasion, Sadie reproached me for this. "You should cast farther," she said. "That's where the big fish are."

"If I catch all the big ones," I said, "there won't be any left for you."

The snort she gave showed her opinion of that likelihood.

Around us, the twentieth century emptied into the twenty-first, one millennium flowing into another. I'd kept abreast of the news. On the international front, the actors kept replaying the bloody melodrama of genocide, from Bosnia to Rwanda to Kosovo. At home, the dot.com bubble was backdrop for the mad fury of the Oklahoma City bombing and the farce of the Monica Lewinsky affair. I waited up to watch 1999 tick over into 2000, reasonably confident in Oliver's reassurances concerning the Y2K threat. Eleven months later, the debacle of the 2000 presidential election took over the news, and I found myself reflecting that the aughts were off with more of a whimper than a bang.

The following fall, that changed, the new decade showing its true face in fire and ruin with the destruction of the Twin Towers, the attack on the

Pentagon, the crashing of Flight 93. Sadie was twelve, old enough that shielding her from the horrors of that morning was impossible. Her mom taught ninth-grade history at Huguenot High, so I figured she'd have a handle on how to explain the geopolitics that underlay the attacks. The why of it was a bit trickier. Sadie asked me about it the next Saturday, when we walked to the stream behind our houses. Her mom, Sadie told me, said that the terrorists believed they were doing God's work and would earn themselves a place in heaven. Her dad said they were evil, hateful. From what she could tell, they had to be insane. How about me? she said. What did I think?

I didn't know, I said. I wasn't sure I understood enough of all that was involved to speak with any kind of authority about it. But from what I knew at the moment, the best I could tell was, if the men responsible for this carnage intended it for some greater purpose, then their means had hopelessly defiled their ends.

I half-expected Sadie to ask what that meant, but she did not.

The years that followed the attacks, which seemed to echo and amplify their violence, were marked by changes in the weather. The very atmosphere seemed more turbulent, prone to storms that dumped record-setting amounts of rain on us on a regular basis, swelling our neighborhood stream up and over its banks. Could be, the rough weather was part of a larger cycle. If that was the case, then we'd entered the next phase of it, because every few months, it felt like, the local streams and rivers flooded. The Svartkil spread over the fields to the west of Huguenot, forming a great lake which required anyone on its opposite shore who needed to drive to Huguenot to take a considerable detour, turning what should have been a ten- or fifteen-minute trip into an hour-plus trek. My house was situated high enough above the flood plain for me not to be too nervous about the water rolling over it. The principle threat to me came from my little stream, which upon occasion burbled across the field separating it from my place and surrounded me with a good six inches of water. This was how I discovered that my basement had been only partially water-sealed. Fortunately, there wasn't much of value down there, and Oliver had a wet-vac he loaned me. Sadie suggested I should have left the water in the basement and stocked it with fish. I feigned exasperation with her, but the image of that water remaining under my floorboards made my palms sweat.

What the meteorologists would designate a hundred-year flood occurred three years after my return to fishing. It was mid-October, that point when the warmth that summer lent to autumn is nearing its end. The husk of what had swelled to a Category 4 hurricane as it roared through the Caribbean, but which had worn itself down to a tropical storm as it trudged north through the Carolinas and Virginia, limped into the sky, bringing with it a day and a half of torrential rain and gusting winds that cleaned what leaves remained on the trees from their branches.

Sadie and her family were out of town, driving through the Midwest on a tour of prospective colleges for her older sister. I had assured Oliver and Rhona I'd keep an eye on their place for the eight days they were away, which, since they owned no pets save a goldfish whose tank Sadie had transferred to my kitchen counter, was an easy promise to keep. I collected their mail, and was on hand in case any packages required signing for. (None did.) In the hours prior to the storm's arrival, I toured their yard, picking up anything that seemed prone to blowing or floating away and carrying it into their garage. I'd already done the same for my place, but after I was finished with theirs, I gave it one last circuit before retiring inside.

I was reasonably well-prepared for what I assumed would be the inevitable loss of power the storm would cause. I had candles in candle-holders stationed in the kitchen, living room, bathroom, and bedroom, with a box of matches set beside each candle. My cupboards were stocked with plenty of non-perishable foodstuffs. There was a stack of library books next to the living room couch and another beside the bed. My transistor radio was running on fresh batteries and I had several unopened packages in reserve. There was nothing to do but wait.

To my surprise, I didn't lose power at all during the storm. From late Wednesday, throughout the night, until Thursday afternoon, waves of gray clouds, bulled across the sky by the wind, emptied their cargo of rain. The Svartkil climbed its margins and sprawled across the farmland west of Huguenot, submerging the portion of 299 that traversed it, as well as the southern reach of Springvale Road. Water swirled around the farm stand on 299, lifting the pumpkins waiting to be bought for jack-o-lanterns and floating them off in the direction of Wiltwyck. Trees that had been swept into the Svartkil upstream jammed under and then against the bridge out of Huguenot. Closer to home, the stream behind my house spread into a vast shallow lake from which my house and those of my neighbors rose like blocky islands. Between my place and Sadie's family's, the water ran a foot deep, except for a dip on my side of their driveway that plunged me to my thighs when I waded over to check their house for flooding. The water was muddy, flowing against and around our houses, spinning the leaves and branches riding its surface off in wide whirlpools. Every so often, an object I hadn't seen before—a white plastic barrel, a red and gold dragon-kite wrapped around a log, the carcass of a deer, legs stiff and turning up to show its belly bloated and white—floated in front of the living room window, and I watched as it bobbed along, heading east to where the lake that had emerged behind my house slid down a long incline to join the Svartkil. Had Sadie been present, she would have been at my door, her rod and tacklebox in hand, ready to cast off my back porch and see what our luck and the storm brought us. I left my rod undisturbed, preferring the classic western marathon on TCM. I watched John Wayne and Jimmy Stewart and Gary Cooper deal justice in an arid land, and did what I could to steer my thoughts from what might be swimming the waters outside.

I have to admit, once the rain tapered off, and the wind fell away, and the sun appeared, and my lights were still on, my TV still broadcasting, I sighed with relief. Yes, it would be a good two or three days until the water started to recede; in fact, the chances were, it would rise higher, first, as the flooding upstream pushed its way here. But there was nowhere I had to be, and as long as I had electricity, I could ride out my temporary isolation in comfort.

Which, needless to say, was the exact moment the lights flickered, dimmed, brightened, and went out entirely. I sighed again. At least there was sufficient daylight left for me to make my way through the house, lighting candles. And at least I had my transistor radio, and the college station was playing its bluegrass show. It was the retreating sun, I told myself, that made the water encircling the house appear dark, in places, black.

As a distraction, I started to prepare dinner. At the back door, the portable propane stove I'd purchased for an Adirondack fishing trip that had never happened leaned against the wall. I carried it out onto the porch and opened it on the picnic table. The evening air was tropical. I screwed in the new gas canister I'd picked up the day before yesterday, turned the valves, pressed the starter button, and was rewarded with a puff of blue flame around the burner ring. Leaving the back door open but the screen door closed, I returned inside for the frying pan, the can of cooking spray, and the eggs I planned to scramble. The frying pan was on the stove where I'd left it. I picked it up and set it on the kitchen table. I unsealed the refrigerator long enough to snatch a quartet of eggs from the door and hurried it shut. The eggs I set in the pan. A little cheese would go nicely melted on top of the scrambled eggs, so I reopened the refrigerator door and grabbed a couple of slices of American. The screen door slapped in its frame; the wind, I guessed, shoving it. The cheese slices joined the eggs. All I needed was the cooking spray, but it was not in its usual place, next to the olive oil and the canola oil. The candles glowing on the table rendered the interior of the kitchen almost fuzzy, like in a Rembrandt painting. There was a group of cylinders gathered on the countertop on the other side of the table, cans of spray paint I'd set there in preparation for a touch-up job on the porch I hadn't found my way to, yet. I crossed the room, and there was the cooking spray, ranked among them. I had no idea what it was doing there.

A half-second, less, before I heard him speak, I registered the presence filling the archway that led to the back door. When he said, "Abe," I knew it was Dan.

Or something that looked an awful lot like my old friend. Tall, sharp-featured, hair red and curly, he even bore the scar that lined the right side of Dan's face, descending his neck to halfway down his chest. But his naked skin was a corpse-pale to which the candlelight added no warmth, and his eyes glittered flat and gold as any fish's. On some floor of my brain, I suppose I must have been anticipating this, dreading it, yet the shock of seeing Dan standing at the entrance to my kitchen like this fell over like a wall of freezing water. Clutching the cooking spray to my chest as if it were some kind of relic, I said, "Dan?"

"The one and only," he said with a pleasantness that was halfway to snarling.

"What are you doing here?"

"You didn't think I'd forget about my old fishing buddy, did you? My old pal," he said, bringing teeth that suddenly appeared sharp as a barracuda's together on the last l.

"Dan," I said.

"Oh, don't worry, Abe: there's no hard feelings," he said. "At first, there were. There were a *lot* of hard feelings. I have to tell you. You can't go through what I did and not emerge from it feeling a tad ornery. You were there for part of it; you can understand. If I could have come to you then…"

"But that's all in the past, isn't it? I am what I've become, and you—you've gone back to fishing, haven't you? With that family next door, that cute little girl. Not much chance of her trying to sacrifice you to an undying wizard, is there?"

"What is it you want?" I said. "Why are you here, now?"

"I've been close to you before," Dan said, "you have no idea. But you're right: this is different. The storm that's just passed has widened the crack that leads to this place. With the situation this fluid—sorry—I couldn't resist paying you a visit."

"If I'd known you were coming—"

"You'd have baked a cake?"

"I was going to say, I'd have baited a hook."

Dan's brows lowered, his mouth rippling, filling with curved fangs that retreated a moment later. "You did this to me," he said when his mouth was clear. "What I am is the work of your hand."

Unexpected, a wave of pity threatened to swamp me. I swallowed it. "What you are is the result of your own actions," I said. "Now get out."

"It's not that easy," Dan said. "I've come a long way to see you, Abe, an unbelievably long way. You can't ask me to turn away the second after I arrive."

"I don't believe the rules of hospitality apply to monsters," I said.

"Abe," Dan said, his face shimmering, another, inhuman one coming into view, "you're starting to hurt my feelings."

"Dan," I said, "go."

Whatever words he was trying to pronounce, he was having difficulty forcing through the fangs jutting from his mouth. His speech had become guttural, a harsh, grating noise that rasped against my ears. My vision wavered, and for an instant, something threatened to come into view, a huge shape that was somehow in the same place as Dan. He stepped into the kitchen, raising a hand whose fingertips had sprouted claws. I held the can of cooking spray out from me and depressed the button on its top. A narrow cone of pressurized oil hissed across the room at him. On its way, it touched the tops of the candles on the table and blossomed into a tongue of fire. Yellow and orange flame wreathed Dan's torso and head. Shrieking, he stumbled backwards, while I emptied the rest of my improvised flame-thrower at him. Light and heat filled the kitchen. I threw my arm up to shield my face, feeling around the counter with my free hand for something else to spray through the candles at him.

I needn't have bothered. Arms flailing, Dan ran from the house, out the screen door, and onto the porch, from which he vaulted into the surrounding water. Although I would have sworn it could not have been any more than one or two feet deep, the water swallowed him whole, sending up a great, hissing column of foul-smelling smoke where he'd entered. I'd followed close on his heels, a can of spray paint I hoped was flammable in my hand. When he did not resurface, I set it down on the porch and, suddenly dizzy to the point of fainting, slumped against the outside of the house. For what could have been a long time, I remained there, my heart galloping, my head full of white noise.

After my pulse had settled to a trot, I pushed myself to standing. The burner on the portable stove was still on. Absurdly, I was starving, but I crossed the porch and turned the gas off. I paused, surveying the flat reach of dark water behind my house for further signs of Dan. There were none I could see.

Which did not mean the water was empty. On the contrary, as my eyes adjusted to the early evening, I saw that the water was full of objects, crowded with shapes whose details my vision was on the verge of deciphering, until it did, and what I recognized had me in the house, the back door closed and me locking it. For the rest of the night, I stayed in the upstairs bedroom with the door locked and the bed and dresser pushed against it. I didn't sleep. The next morning, when the Sheriff's deputies pulled up in their boat to offer me the choice of rescue, I leapt onboard with tears in my eyes, which I let them attribute to my age. What I saw out there in the water set me to wrestling with this story, with the strange, knotted length of it. I'm not sure what else is left for me to do with it, except tell you what I saw in the water.

People—rows and rows of people floated there, most of them submerged to their shoulders, a few to their chins, fewer still to their eyes. I couldn't guess their number, because they extended into the deeper dark. Their skin was damp, white, their hair lank, their eyes gleaming gold. It didn't take me long to pick out Marie in the midst of them, not as close as I would have supposed. Her face was blank, as were those of the children to either side of her. A girl and a boy, their features in that in-between stage when childhood is beginning to make way for adolescence. Their mouths were open; I glimpsed rows of serrated teeth. Their eyes were vacant of any intelligence. They had, I fancied, my mother's nose.

THE END

ACKNOWLEDGMENTS

When I started writing the story that would become this book, my wife was pregnant with our son. He's now twelve-going-on-thirteen. Needless to say, that's a long time from start to finish. A lot has happened during that time, a lot has changed, but the love and support of my wife, Fiona, has remained a constant. More than that: as the years slid by, she was the one who said, every now and again, "You have to get back to *The Fisherman*." This book wouldn't be here without her. Thanks, love, for everything.

That twelve-going-on-thirteen-year-old has blossomed into quite the fisherman, himself, these last few years, pretty much on his own. (I basically sit nearby with a book and try to make comments that don't sound too ignorant.) David Langan's technical advice helped a great deal in making the fishing-related portions of this narrative more accurate, while his love and all-around awesomeness made the rest of my life better.

My older son, Nick, and my daughter-in-law, Mary, and their trio of astounding kids, my brilliant grandchildren, Inara, Asher, and Penelope the Bean, have brought and continue to bring more joy into my life than I probably deserve.

It's becoming a critical commonplace to say that we're currently experiencing a resurgence in the field of dark/horror/weird/whatever fiction. I happen to think this is true, but what matters more to me is the friendship so many of my fellow writers have offered me. Laird Barron and Paul Tremblay have been the other brothers I never knew I had, even as their work has made me grit my teeth and tell myself to do better. Sarah Langan, Brett Cox, and Michael Cisco are pretty good, too.

These last few years, I've continued to benefit from the kindness of writers whose work inspired my own. Both Peter Straub and Jeffrey Ford have been unfailingly generous in their support and example. While I am at it, let me raise a glass to the memory of the late, great Lucius Shepard, whose encouragement, praise, and fiction I continue to treasure.

My indefatigable agent, Ginger Clark, has been a champion of this book since I sent her its first three chapters a long, long time ago. Every now and again, Ginger would send an e-mail encouraging me to finish the novel, and when at last I did, there was nobody happier. I'm grateful for her continuing faith in me and my work.

As was the case with my previous novel, *House of Windows*, *The Fisherman* took a while to find a home. The genre publishers said it was too literary, the literary publishers, too genre. Thanks to Ross Lockhart and Word Horde for responding so immediately and enthusiastically to the book.

While this is a work of fiction, its composition was aided by details found in Bob Steuding's *The Last of the Hand Made Dams: The Story of the Ashokan Reservoir* (1989) and the 2002 documentary, *Deep Water: The True Story of the Ashokan Reservoir*, by Tobe Carey, Bobbie Dupree, and Artie Traum. Alf Evers' *The Catskills: From Wilderness to Woodstock* (1972) is a treasure-trove of information about the Catskill region.

And a final, heartfelt thank you to you, the reader, for the gifts of your time and attention. You make this writing life I have possible, and I'm grateful for it.

TITLES AVAILABLE FROM WORD HORDE

ABOUT THE AUTHOR

John Langan is the author of a previous novel, *House of Windows* (Night Shade, 2009), and three collections of stories: *Sefira and Other Betrayals* (Hippocampus, 2016), *The Wide, Carnivorous Sky and Other Monstrous Geographies* (Hippocampus, 2013), and *Mr. Gaunt and Other Uneasy Encounters* (Prime, 2008). With Paul Tremblay, he co-edited *Creatures: Thirty Years of Monsters* (Prime, 2011). One of the co-founders of the Shirley Jackson Awards, he served as a juror for their first three years. He lives in New York's Hudson Valley with his wife, younger son, and a houseful of animals.

CPSIA information can be obtained
at www.ICGtesting.com
Printed in the USA
BVHW031355271020
591929BV00001B/61